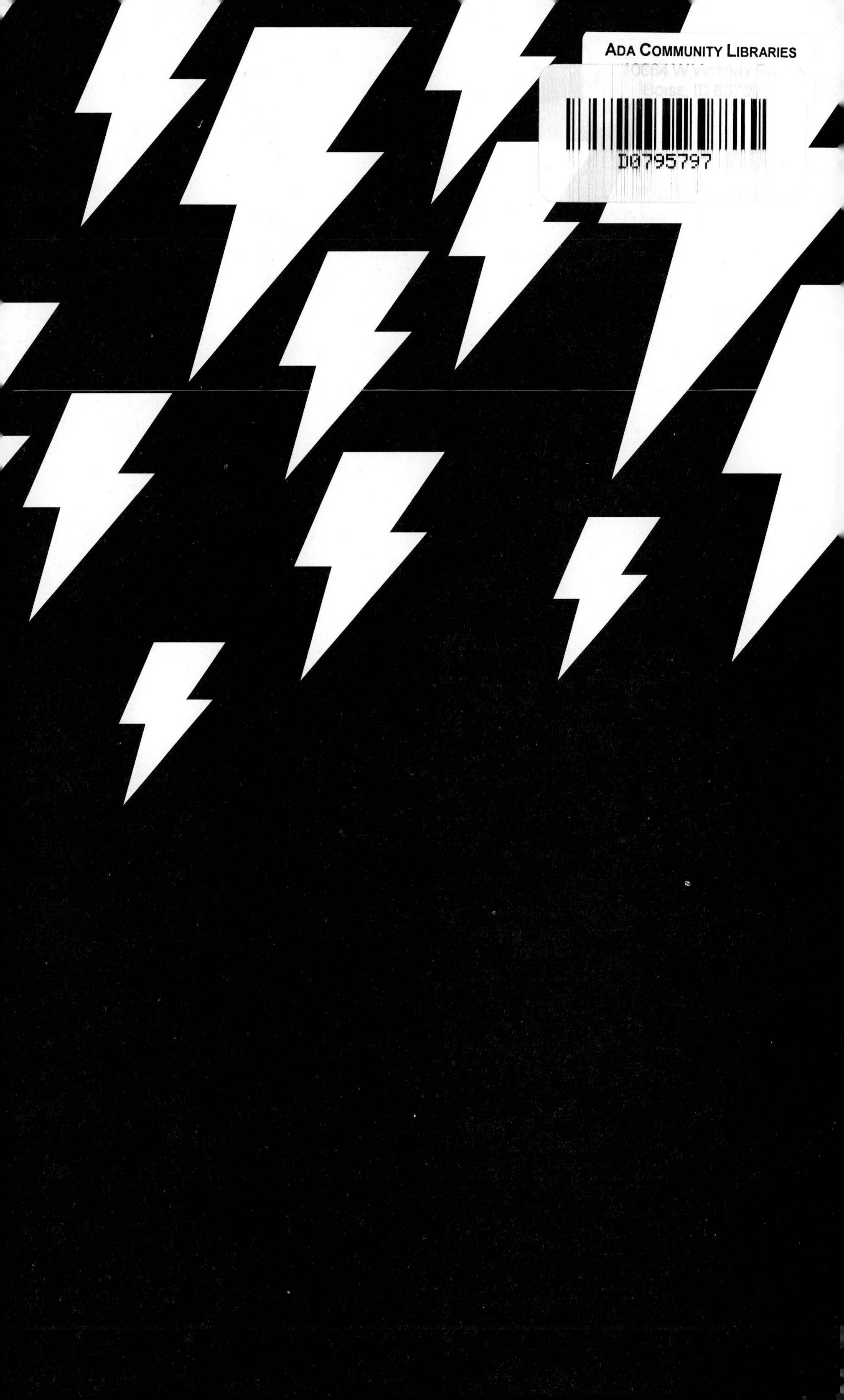

Dedicated to Maria, who made everything perfect,
and Nash, who made it even better.

THANK YOU

Paul Bradshaw, Eric Stephenson & all at Image! Justin "Moritat" Norman, Casey Silver, Dan Veesenmeyer, Butcher Billy, Melch, David Bowie, Darwyn Cooke, Prince, Stan, Jack and Steve, Alix & Thomas Enright, Paul Dickman, Michael Clare, Phil & Annie Bradford, Robert Simonds, Don Rose, Arthur Mann, Bill Hein and all my Rykodisc people, Steve Kiwus, Rick Hutchins, Jeff Whalen, Steve Coulter, the Pino Brothers, Jimmy Palmiotti, Rev. Dave Johnston, Jesse Hamm, Coop, Chris Samnee, Matthew Southworth, Nick Bertozzi, and most of all, my wonderful family.

Special thanks to all who supported this comic
in a tough climate for new ideas.

May all your guitars be forever loud!

GUNNING FOR HITS
MUSIC THRILLER

VOLUME ONE: SLADE

Created and written
by Jeff Rougvie

Art by Moritat

Colors and letters
by Casey Silver

SUPERMEGABOT HEADQUARTERS

IMAGE COMICS, INC. • **Robert Kirkman:** Chief Operating Officer • **Erik Larsen:** Chief Financial Officer • **Todd McFarlane:** President • **Marc Silvestri:** Chief Executive Officer • **Jim Valentino:** Vice President • **Eric Stephenson:** Publisher / Chief Creative Officer • **Jeff Boison:** Director of Publishing Planning & Book Trade Sales • **Chris Ross:** Director of Digital Sales • **Jeff Stang:** Director of Direct Market Sales • **Kat Salazar:** Director of PR & Marketing • **Drew Gill:** Art Director • **Heather Doornink:** Production Director • **Nicole Lapalme:** Controller • **IMAGECOMICS.COM**

Thanks for picking up GUNNING FOR HITS. You are clearly an intelligent and attractive person. Here are a few things I'd like you to know before you start reading:

First, music and comics have always been a weird mix, so we thought a lot about how to depict music. We landed on this pretty simple visual solution:

Good music = (lightning bolts)

Bad music = (cardiogram)

We didn't bother with an ordinary music symbol, because why celebrate mediocrity? I'd rather listen to bad music than "okay" music any day of the week.

Second, GUNNING FOR HITS isn't just this book, it's a multimedia experience, because why wouldn't it be? We have a Spotify playlist (GUNNING FOR HITS SOUNDTRACK) and a Twitter account that publishes excerpts from Martin Mill's journals, @MartinMillsHits. The latter will help you piece together Martin's life story. We also have the usual Facebook and Instagram pages, and a website (gunningforhits.com) that has more info about all of these things, because why wouldn't we?

Third, the premise for this book bloomed in 1989, when I first started working with David Bowie. More on that in the back of the book, and I'll warn you with peace and love not to jump ahead to that part because there are spoilers.

Fourth, even though the story of Martin Mills felt like a very real thing to me for the next few decades, it took the Very Miserable Year of Our Lord, 2016 to get me moving on it.

It wasn't just Bowie's death that prompted me to take action; it was also Prince, Darwyn Cooke and finally, Muhammad Ali. Don't let anyone tell you 2016 wasn't a brutal year. It sucked even before the election.

All these ass-kickings finally compelled me to write the long-simmering arc of Martin's story in this book. I'm not sure what took hold of me, but when I started typing, in addition to this story, I wrote his entire biography — from cradle to grave.

This includes his high-school years, the Iran-Iraq war, his life outside the law, his entrée into the music business, the tragedy that made him a sociopath, and his many attempts to redeem himself. It all resides in 12 three-ring binders that form a complicated tale, encompassing big questions about morality, corporate culture, the unstated attack on artists, politics, remorse, why we're awful to each other when we need each other, love, and death – lots and lots of death.

It'll make a swell TV series, but that's not why I did it.

Fifth, music is the best. It binds us together, ignoring our differences. The Internet was supposed to unite us, and it's great for lots of things — calling each other out on our bullshit, for instance. It's not great for music.

As I write this, complex but poorly functioning algorithms are deciding what music we should hear – this is wrong.

Thousands go to Coachella every year to share selfies with their squads, but ignore the music – this is wrong.

The way we interact with music has changed dramatically in the last 20 years. Change is fine, but when it minimizes art, it minimizes connection, and that's problematic.

So share some music you love with your friends, talk about it, then repeat. Cool? Now let's kill some people for the love of a good song!

Yours Thru' Sport,

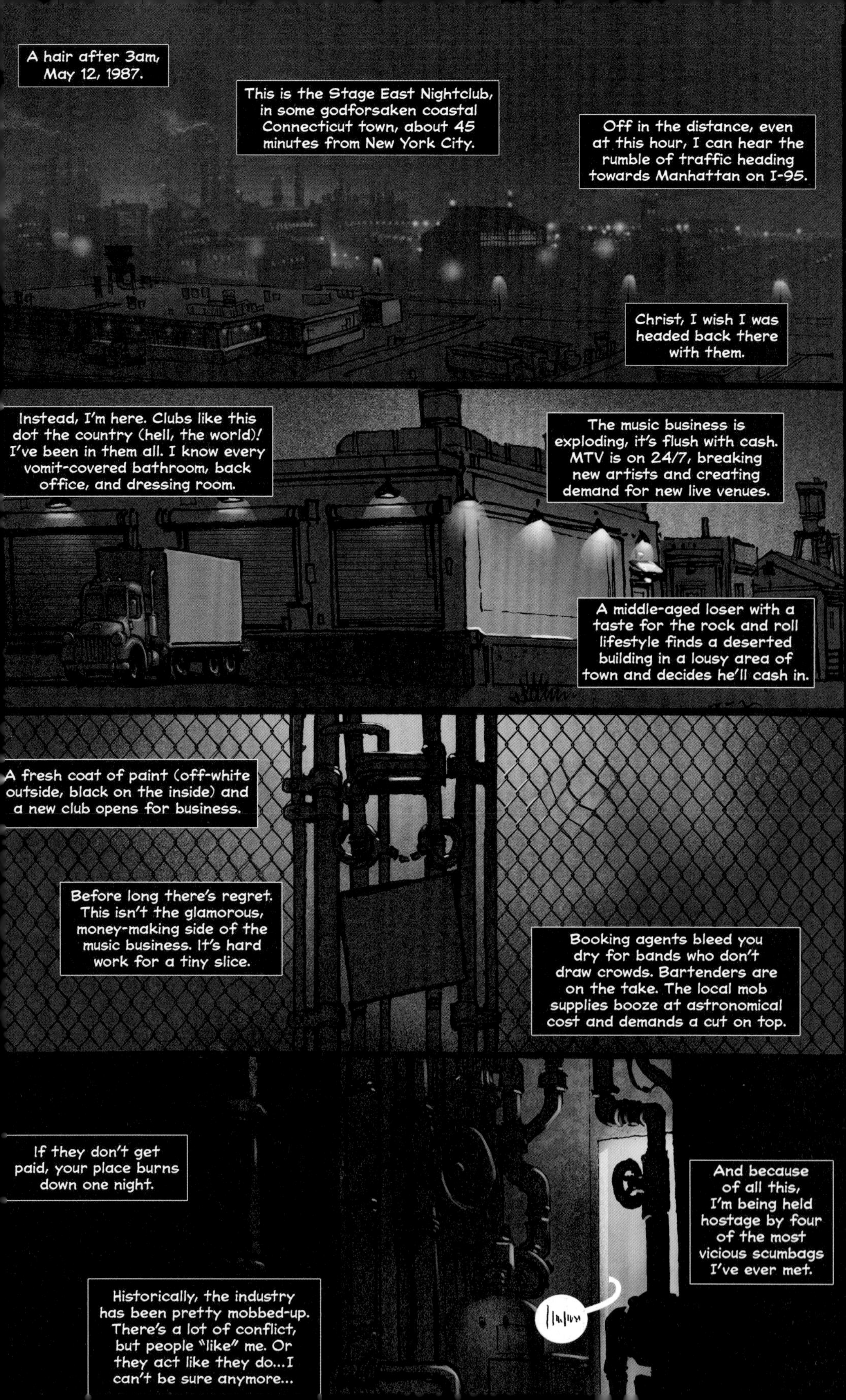
A hair after 3am, May 12, 1987.
This is the Stage East Nightclub, in some godforsaken coastal Connecticut town, about 45 minutes from New York City.
Off in the distance, even at this hour, I can hear the rumble of traffic heading towards Manhattan on I-95.
Christ, I wish I was headed back there with them.
Instead, I'm here. Clubs like this dot the country (hell, the world)! I've been in them all. I know every vomit-covered bathroom, back office, and dressing room.
The music business is exploding, it's flush with cash. MTV is on 24/7, breaking new artists and creating demand for new live venues.
A middle-aged loser with a taste for the rock and roll lifestyle finds a deserted building in a lousy area of town and decides he'll cash in.
A fresh coat of paint (off-white outside, black on the inside) and a new club opens for business.
Before long there's regret. This isn't the glamorous, money-making side of the music business. It's hard work for a tiny slice.
Booking agents bleed you dry for bands who don't draw crowds. Bartenders are on the take. The local mob supplies booze at astronomical cost and demands a cut on top.
If they don't get paid, your place burns down one night.
Historically, the industry has been pretty mobbed-up. There's a lot of conflict, but people "like" me. Or they act like they do...I can't be sure anymore...
And because of all this, I'm being held hostage by four of the most vicious scumbags I've ever met.

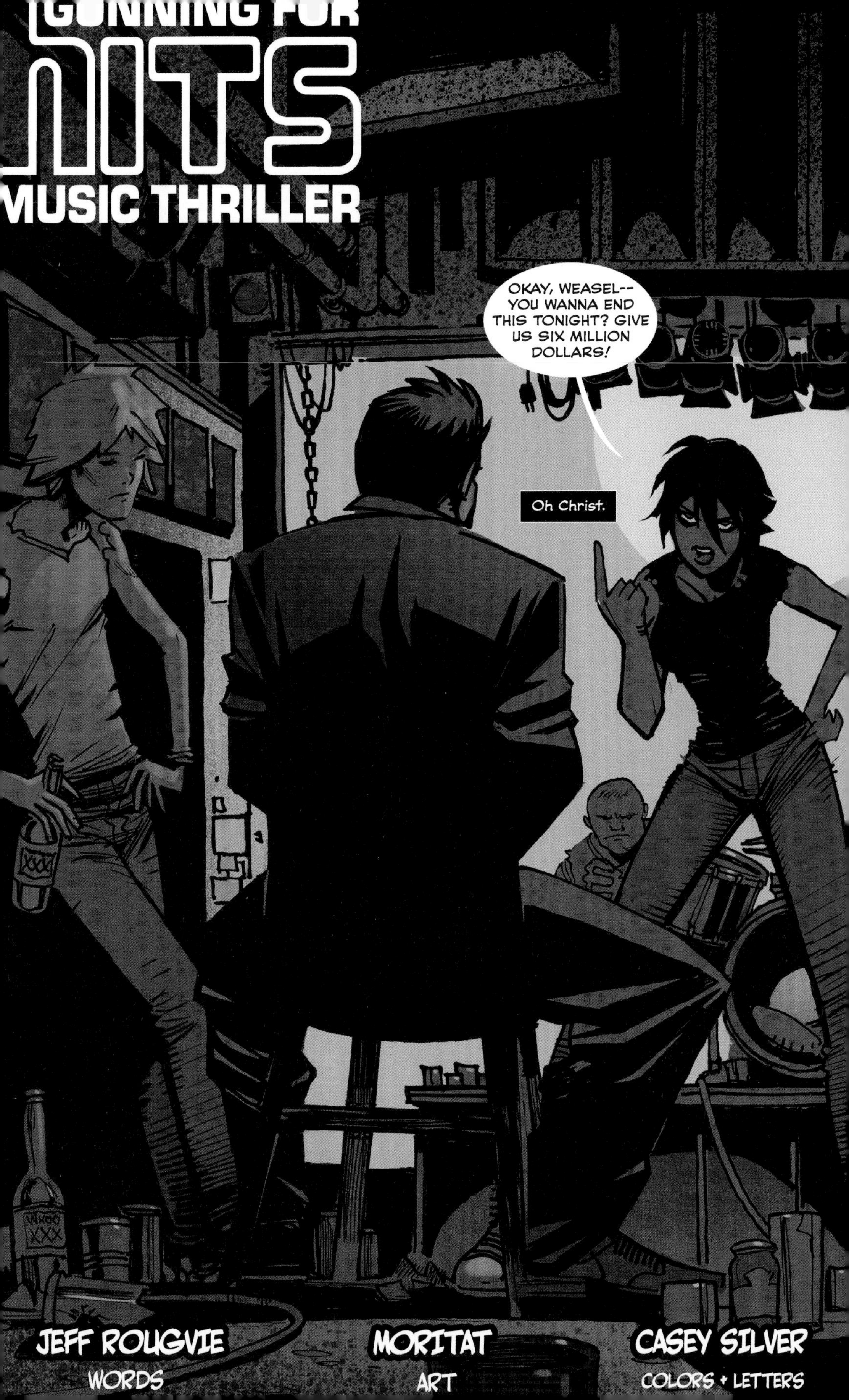
GUNNING FOR
HITS
MUSIC THRILLER
OKAY, WEASEL-- YOU WANNA END THIS TONIGHT? GIVE US SIX MILLION DOLLARS!
Oh Christ.
JEFF ROUGVIE
WORDS
MORITAT
ART
CASEY SILVER
COLORS + LETTERS

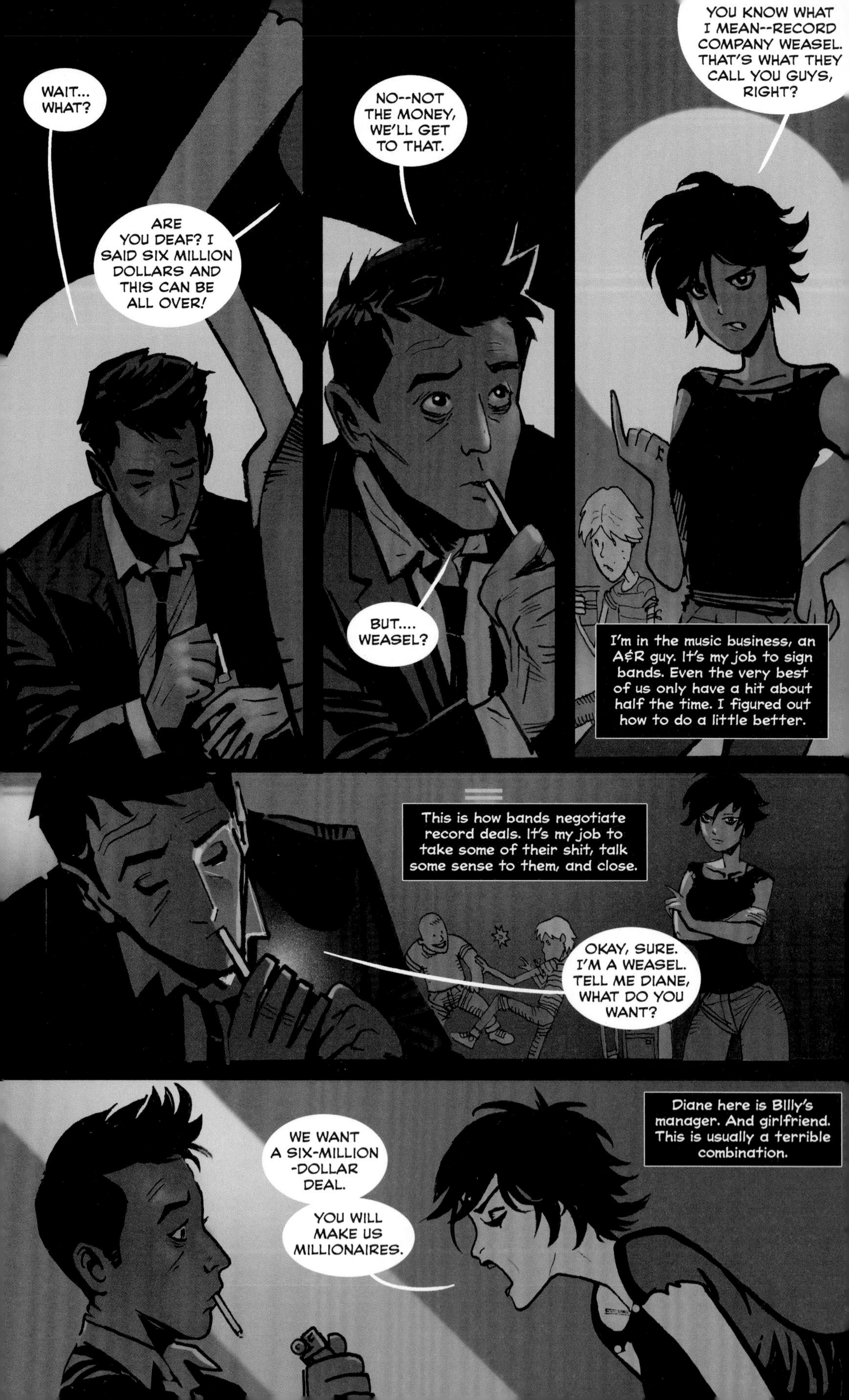
WAIT... WHAT?
ARE YOU DEAF? I SAID SIX MILLION DOLLARS AND THIS CAN BE ALL OVER!
NO--NOT THE MONEY, WE'LL GET TO THAT.
BUT.... WEASEL?
YOU KNOW WHAT I MEAN--RECORD COMPANY WEASEL. THAT'S WHAT THEY CALL YOU GUYS, RIGHT?
I'm in the music business, an A&R guy. It's my job to sign bands. Even the very best of us only have a hit about half the time. I figured out how to do a little better.
This is how bands negotiate record deals. It's my job to take some of their shit, talk some sense to them, and close.
OKAY, SURE. I'M A WEASEL. TELL ME DIANE, WHAT DO YOU WANT?
WE WANT A SIX-MILLION -DOLLAR DEAL.
YOU WILL MAKE US MILLIONAIRES.
Diane here is Billy's manager. And girlfriend. This is usually a terrible combination.

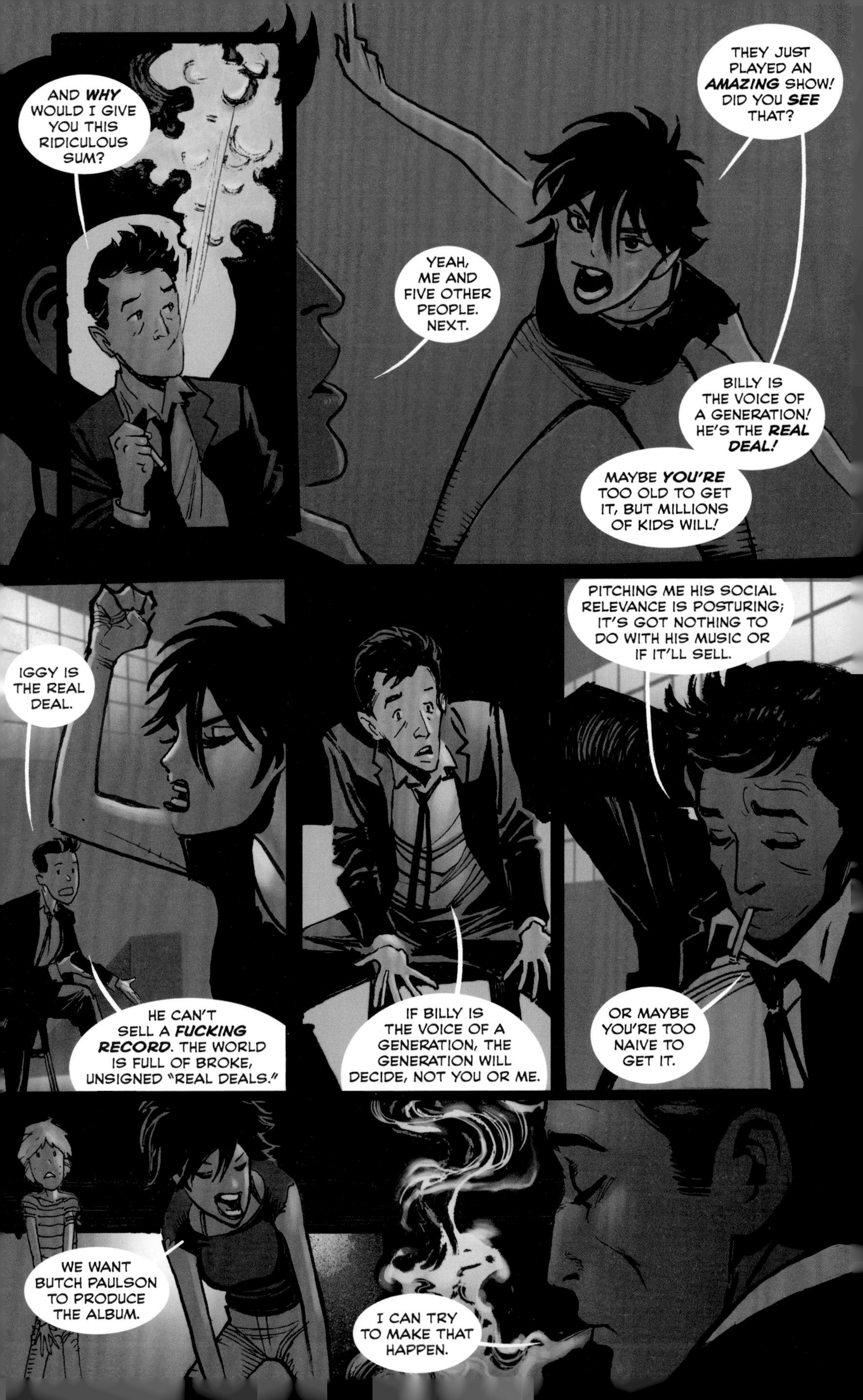
AND WHY WOULD I GIVE YOU THIS RIDICULOUS SUM?
THEY JUST PLAYED AN AMAZING SHOW! DID YOU SEE THAT?
YEAH, ME AND FIVE OTHER PEOPLE. NEXT.
BILLY IS THE VOICE OF A GENERATION! HE'S THE REAL DEAL!
MAYBE YOU'RE TOO OLD TO GET IT, BUT MILLIONS OF KIDS WILL!
IGGY IS THE REAL DEAL.
HE CAN'T SELL A FUCKING RECORD. THE WORLD IS FULL OF BROKE, UNSIGNED "REAL DEALS."
IF BILLY IS THE VOICE OF A GENERATION, THE GENERATION WILL DECIDE, NOT YOU OR ME.
PITCHING ME HIS SOCIAL RELEVANCE IS POSTURING; IT'S GOT NOTHING TO DO WITH HIS MUSIC OR IF IT'LL SELL.
OR MAYBE YOU'RE TOO NAIVE TO GET IT.
WE WANT BUTCH PAULSON TO PRODUCE THE ALBUM.
I CAN TRY TO MAKE THAT HAPPEN.

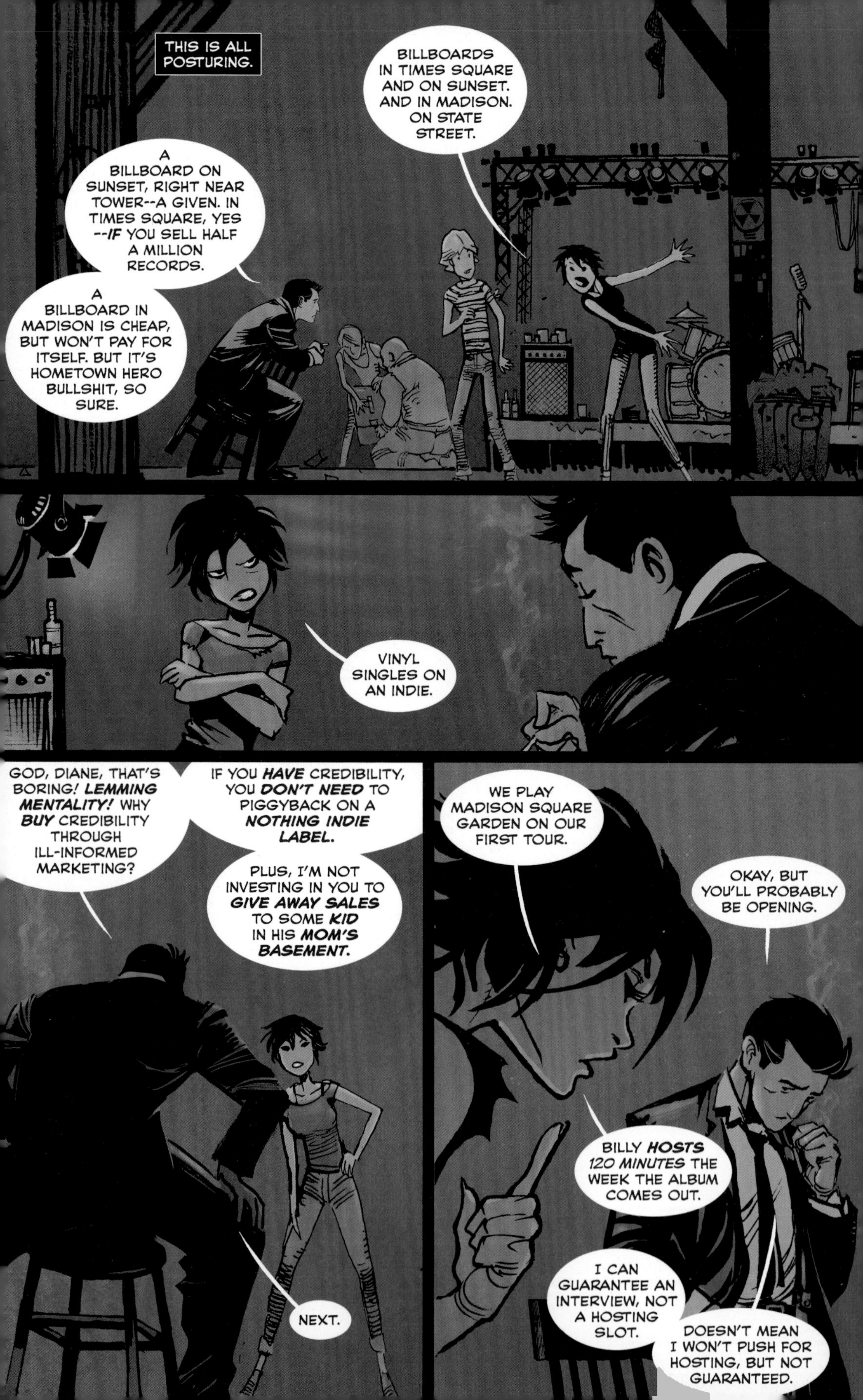
THIS IS ALL POSTURING.
A BILLBOARD ON SUNSET, RIGHT NEAR TOWER--A GIVEN. IN TIMES SQUARE, YES --IF YOU SELL HALF A MILLION RECORDS.
A BILLBOARD IN MADISON IS CHEAP, BUT WON'T PAY FOR ITSELF. BUT IT'S HOMETOWN HERO BULLSHIT, SO SURE.
BILLBOARDS IN TIMES SQUARE AND ON SUNSET. AND IN MADISON. ON STATE STREET.
VINYL SINGLES ON AN INDIE.
GOD, DIANE, THAT'S BORING! LEMMING MENTALITY! WHY BUY CREDIBILITY THROUGH ILL-INFORMED MARKETING?
IF YOU HAVE CREDIBILITY, YOU DON'T NEED TO PIGGYBACK ON A NOTHING INDIE LABEL.
PLUS, I'M NOT INVESTING IN YOU TO GIVE AWAY SALES TO SOME KID IN HIS MOM'S BASEMENT.
NEXT.
WE PLAY MADISON SQUARE GARDEN ON OUR FIRST TOUR.
OKAY, BUT YOU'LL PROBABLY BE OPENING.
BILLY HOSTS 120 MINUTES THE WEEK THE ALBUM COMES OUT.
I CAN GUARANTEE AN INTERVIEW, NOT A HOSTING SLOT.
DOESN'T MEAN I WON'T PUSH FOR HOSTING, BUT NOT GUARANTEED.

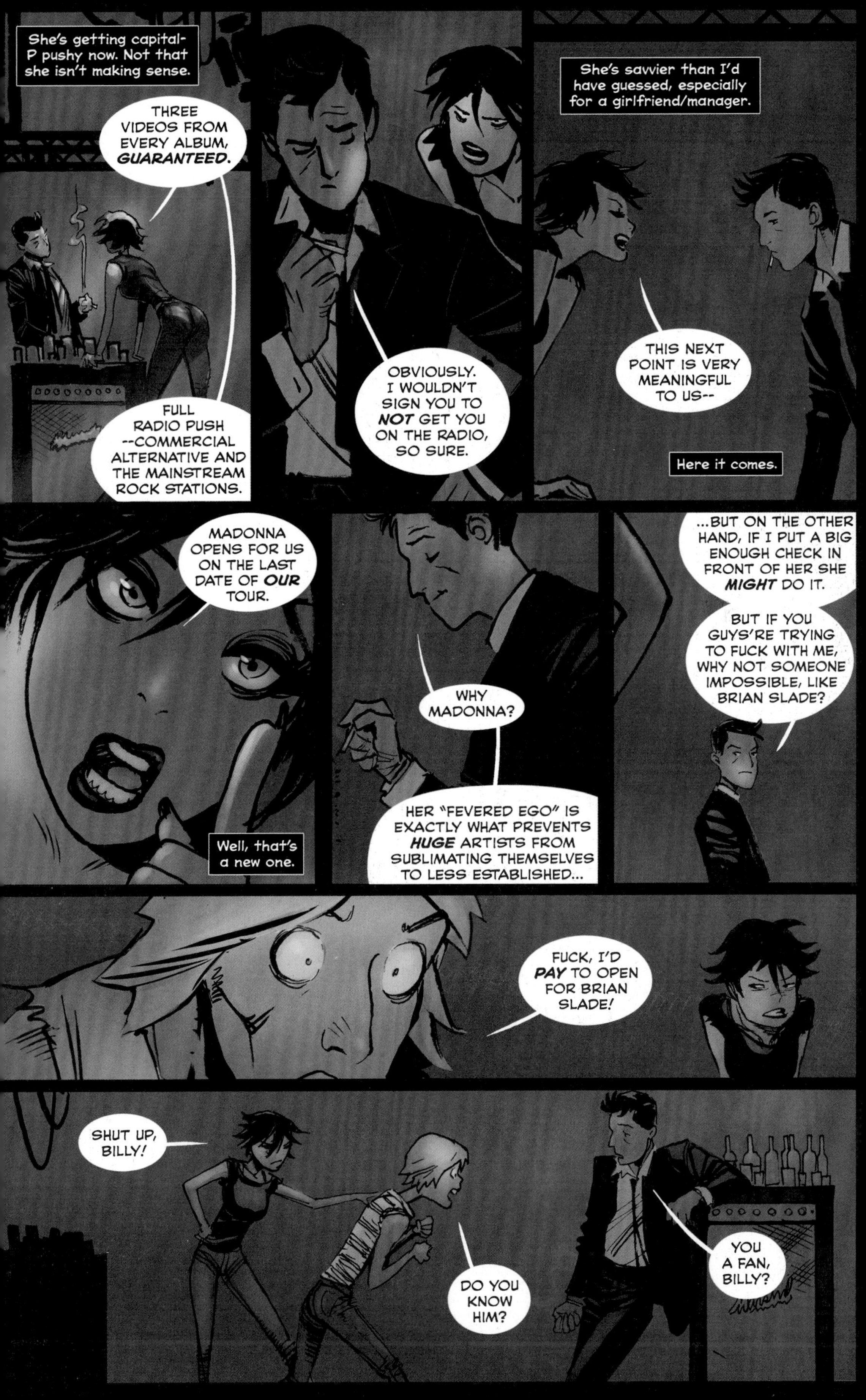
She's getting capital-P pushy now. Not that she isn't making sense.
THREE VIDEOS FROM EVERY ALBUM, GUARANTEED.
FULL RADIO PUSH --COMMERCIAL ALTERNATIVE AND THE MAINSTREAM ROCK STATIONS.
OBVIOUSLY. I WOULDN'T SIGN YOU TO NOT GET YOU ON THE RADIO, SO SURE.
She's savvier than I'd have guessed, especially for a girlfriend/manager.
THIS NEXT POINT IS VERY MEANINGFUL TO US--
Here it comes.
MADONNA OPENS FOR US ON THE LAST DATE OF OUR TOUR.
Well, that's a new one.
WHY MADONNA?
HER "FEVERED EGO" IS EXACTLY WHAT PREVENTS HUGE ARTISTS FROM SUBLIMATING THEMSELVES TO LESS ESTABLISHED...
...BUT ON THE OTHER HAND, IF I PUT A BIG ENOUGH CHECK IN FRONT OF HER SHE MIGHT DO IT.
BUT IF YOU GUYS'RE TRYING TO FUCK WITH ME, WHY NOT SOMEONE IMPOSSIBLE, LIKE BRIAN SLADE?
FUCK, I'D PAY TO OPEN FOR BRIAN SLADE!
SHUT UP, BILLY!
DO YOU KNOW HIM?
YOU A FAN, BILLY?

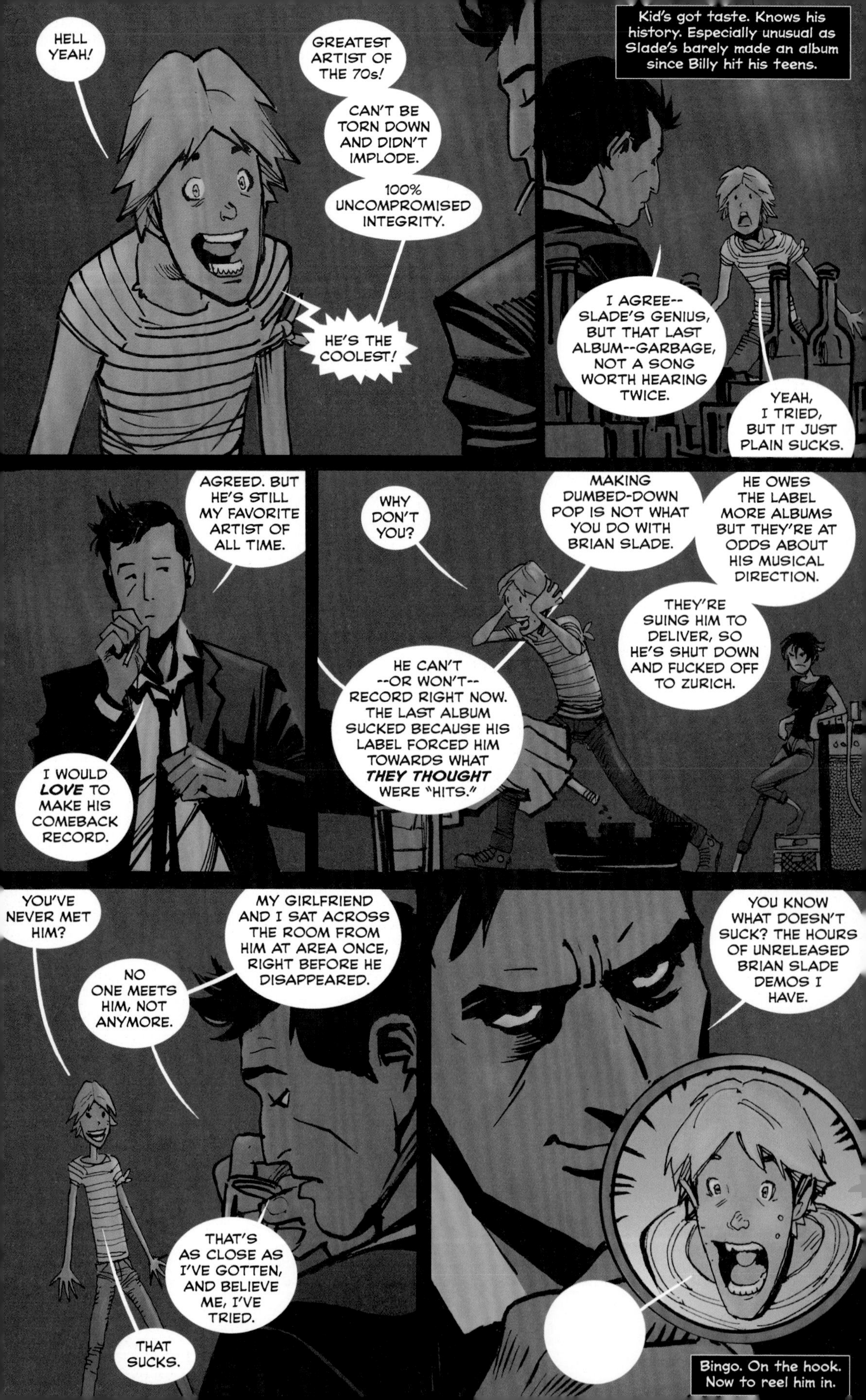
HELL YEAH!
GREATEST ARTIST OF THE 70s!
CAN'T BE TORN DOWN AND DIDN'T IMPLODE.
100% UNCOMPROMISED INTEGRITY.
HE'S THE COOLEST!
Kid's got taste. Knows his history. Especially unusual as Slade's barely made an album since Billy hit his teens.
I AGREE-- SLADE'S GENIUS, BUT THAT LAST ALBUM--GARBAGE, NOT A SONG WORTH HEARING TWICE.
YEAH, I TRIED, BUT IT JUST PLAIN SUCKS.
AGREED. BUT HE'S STILL MY FAVORITE ARTIST OF ALL TIME.
I WOULD LOVE TO MAKE HIS COMEBACK RECORD.
WHY DON'T YOU?
HE CAN'T --OR WON'T-- RECORD RIGHT NOW. THE LAST ALBUM SUCKED BECAUSE HIS LABEL FORCED HIM TOWARDS WHAT THEY THOUGHT WERE "HITS."
MAKING DUMBED-DOWN POP IS NOT WHAT YOU DO WITH BRIAN SLADE.
HE OWES THE LABEL MORE ALBUMS BUT THEY'RE AT ODDS ABOUT HIS MUSICAL DIRECTION.
THEY'RE SUING HIM TO DELIVER, SO HE'S SHUT DOWN AND FUCKED OFF TO ZURICH.
YOU'VE NEVER MET HIM?
NO ONE MEETS HIM, NOT ANYMORE.
MY GIRLFRIEND AND I SAT ACROSS THE ROOM FROM HIM AT AREA ONCE, RIGHT BEFORE HE DISAPPEARED.
THAT'S AS CLOSE AS I'VE GOTTEN, AND BELIEVE ME, I'VE TRIED.
THAT SUCKS.
YOU KNOW WHAT DOESN'T SUCK? THE HOURS OF UNRELEASED BRIAN SLADE DEMOS I HAVE.
Bingo. On the hook. Now to reel him in.

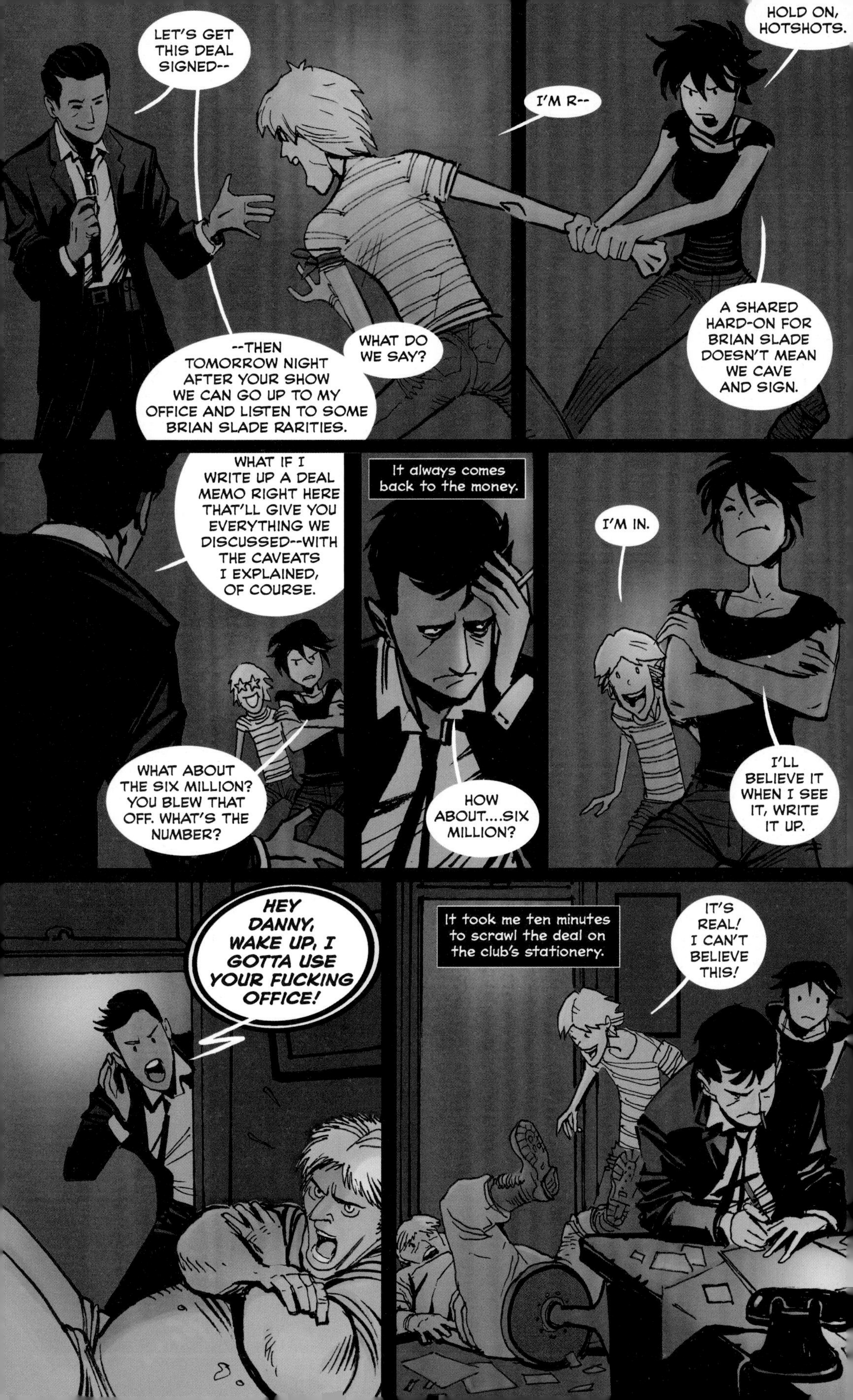
LET'S GET THIS DEAL SIGNED--
--THEN TOMORROW NIGHT AFTER YOUR SHOW WE CAN GO UP TO MY OFFICE AND LISTEN TO SOME BRIAN SLADE RARITIES.
WHAT DO WE SAY?
I'M R--
HOLD ON, HOTSHOTS.
A SHARED HARD-ON FOR BRIAN SLADE DOESN'T MEAN WE CAVE AND SIGN.
WHAT IF I WRITE UP A DEAL MEMO RIGHT HERE THAT'LL GIVE YOU EVERYTHING WE DISCUSSED--WITH THE CAVEATS I EXPLAINED, OF COURSE.
WHAT ABOUT THE SIX MILLION? YOU BLEW THAT OFF. WHAT'S THE NUMBER?
It always comes back to the money.
HOW ABOUT....SIX MILLION?
I'M IN.
I'LL BELIEVE IT WHEN I SEE IT, WRITE IT UP.
HEY DANNY, WAKE UP, I GOTTA USE YOUR FUCKING OFFICE!
It took me ten minutes to scrawl the deal on the club's stationery.
IT'S REAL! I CAN'T BELIEVE THIS!

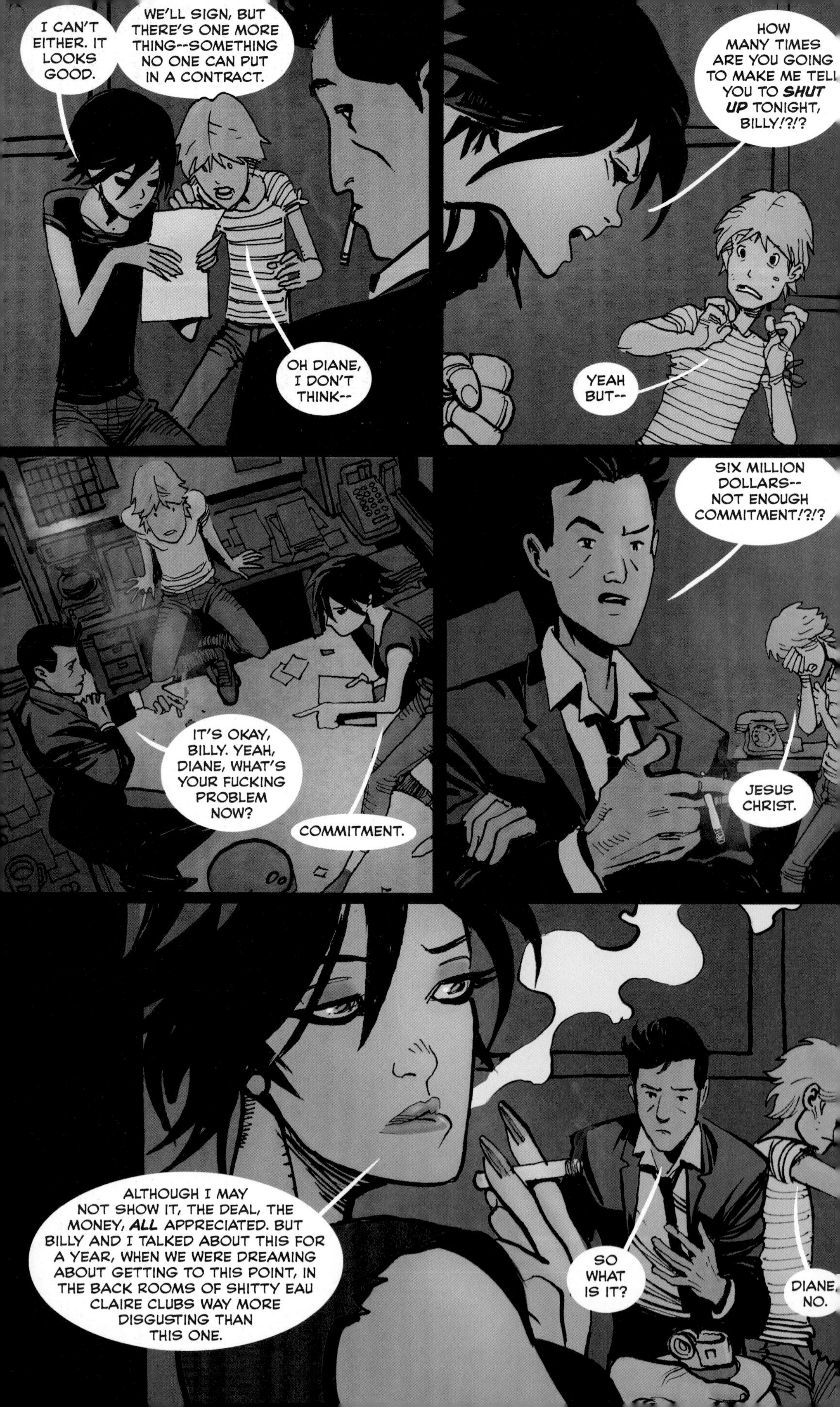

I CAN'T EITHER. IT LOOKS GOOD.
WE'LL SIGN, BUT THERE'S ONE MORE THING--SOMETHING NO ONE CAN PUT IN A CONTRACT.
OH DIANE, I DON'T THINK--
HOW MANY TIMES ARE YOU GOING TO MAKE ME TELL YOU TO **SHUT UP** TONIGHT, BILLY!?!?
YEAH BUT--
IT'S OKAY, BILLY. YEAH, DIANE, WHAT'S YOUR FUCKING PROBLEM NOW?
COMMITMENT.
SIX MILLION DOLLARS-- NOT ENOUGH COMMITMENT!?!?
JESUS CHRIST.
ALTHOUGH I MAY NOT SHOW IT, THE DEAL, THE MONEY, **ALL** APPRECIATED. BUT BILLY AND I TALKED ABOUT THIS FOR A YEAR, WHEN WE WERE DREAMING ABOUT GETTING TO THIS POINT, IN THE BACK ROOMS OF SHITTY EAU CLAIRE CLUBS WAY MORE DISGUSTING THAN THIS ONE.
SO WHAT IS IT?
DIANE, NO.

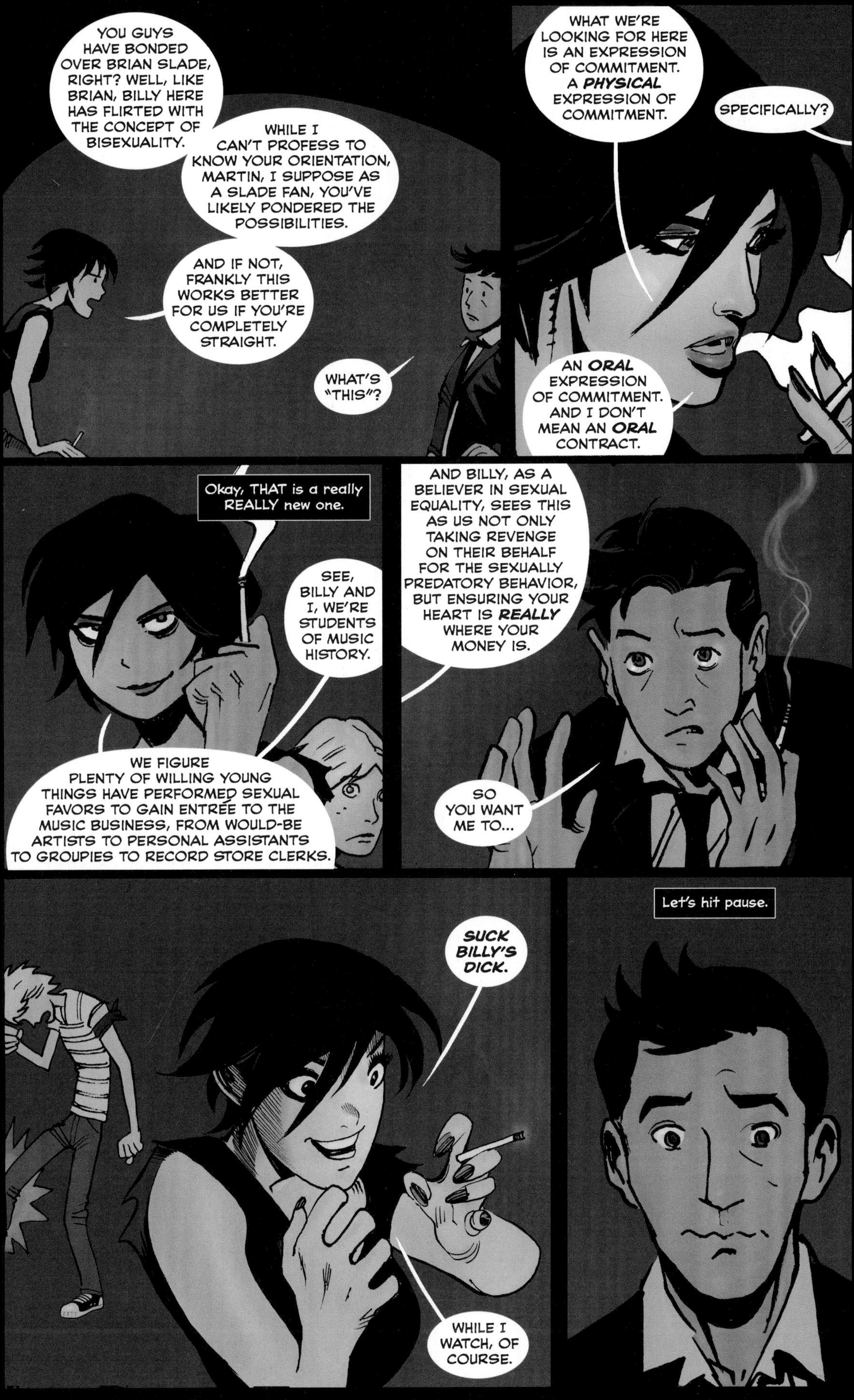
YOU GUYS HAVE BONDED OVER BRIAN SLADE, RIGHT? WELL, LIKE BRIAN, BILLY HERE HAS FLIRTED WITH THE CONCEPT OF BISEXUALITY.
WHILE I CAN'T PROFESS TO KNOW YOUR ORIENTATION, MARTIN, I SUPPOSE AS A SLADE FAN, YOU'VE LIKELY PONDERED THE POSSIBILITIES.
AND IF NOT, FRANKLY THIS WORKS BETTER FOR US IF YOU'RE COMPLETELY STRAIGHT.
WHAT'S "THIS"?
WHAT WE'RE LOOKING FOR HERE IS AN EXPRESSION OF COMMITMENT. A ***PHYSICAL*** EXPRESSION OF COMMITMENT.
SPECIFICALLY?
AN ***ORAL*** EXPRESSION OF COMMITMENT. AND I DON'T MEAN AN ***ORAL*** CONTRACT.
Okay, THAT is a really REALLY new one.
SEE, BILLY AND I, WE'RE STUDENTS OF MUSIC HISTORY.
WE FIGURE PLENTY OF WILLING YOUNG THINGS HAVE PERFORMED SEXUAL FAVORS TO GAIN ENTRÉE TO THE MUSIC BUSINESS, FROM WOULD-BE ARTISTS TO PERSONAL ASSISTANTS TO GROUPIES TO RECORD STORE CLERKS.
AND BILLY, AS A BELIEVER IN SEXUAL EQUALITY, SEES THIS AS US NOT ONLY TAKING REVENGE ON THEIR BEHALF FOR THE SEXUALLY PREDATORY BEHAVIOR, BUT ENSURING YOUR HEART IS ***REALLY*** WHERE YOUR MONEY IS.
SO YOU WANT ME TO...
SUCK BILLY'S DICK.
WHILE I WATCH, OF COURSE.
Let's hit pause.

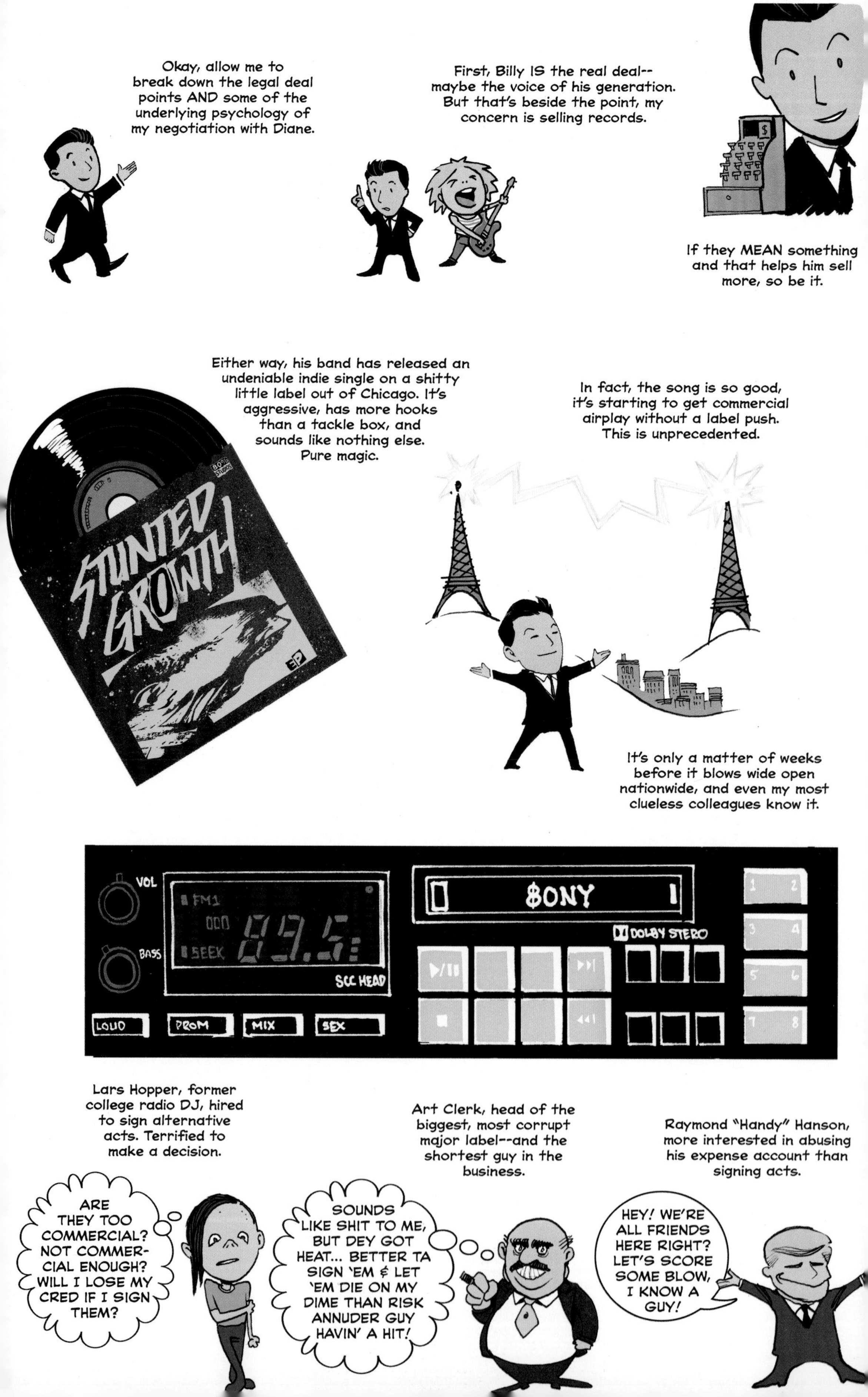
Okay, allow me to break down the legal deal points AND some of the underlying psychology of my negotiation with Diane.
First, Billy IS the real deal--maybe the voice of his generation. But that's beside the point, my concern is selling records.
$
If they MEAN something and that helps him sell more, so be it.
Either way, his band has released an undeniable indie single on a shitty little label out of Chicago. It's aggressive, has more hooks than a tackle box, and sounds like nothing else. Pure magic.
STUNTED GROWTH
EP
In fact, the song is so good, it's starting to get commercial airplay without a label push. This is unprecedented.
It's only a matter of weeks before it blows wide open nationwide, and even my most clueless colleagues know it.
VOL
BASS
FM1
SEEK
89.5
SCC HEAD
$ONY
DOLBY STEREO
LOUD
PROM
MIX
SEX
Lars Hopper, former college radio DJ, hired to sign alternative acts. Terrified to make a decision.
ARE THEY TOO COMMERCIAL? NOT COMMERCIAL ENOUGH? WILL I LOSE MY CRED IF I SIGN THEM?
Art Clerk, head of the biggest, most corrupt major label--and the shortest guy in the business.
SOUNDS LIKE SHIT TO ME, BUT DEY GOT HEAT... BETTER TA SIGN 'EM & LET 'EM DIE ON MY DIME THAN RISK ANNUDER GUY HAVIN' A HIT!
Raymond "Handy" Hanson, more interested in abusing his expense account than signing acts.
HEY! WE'RE ALL FRIENDS HERE RIGHT? LET'S SCORE SOME BLOW, I KNOW A GUY!

Second, I arranged this off the map, unpromoted gig by paying my sleepy pal the club owner an outrageous amount of money to book them.

This was their first gig outside their hometown of Madison, Wisconsin since the single took off.

NOWHERE!

NYC

LA

And it was amazing. They have no idea how great they are, especially Billy.

Tonight they played at least THREE more songs with the same potential of the first single, most acts have one or two truly great songs--

--the kind that make the hair on the back of your neck stand up and do that magic only a perfect song can--

--ripping through your brain and blasting endorphins into your bloodstream.

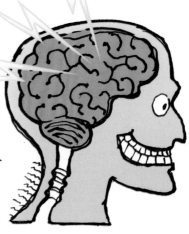

This kid has at least four--already.

If I can make the right record with him, this thing could sell MILLIONS of copies.

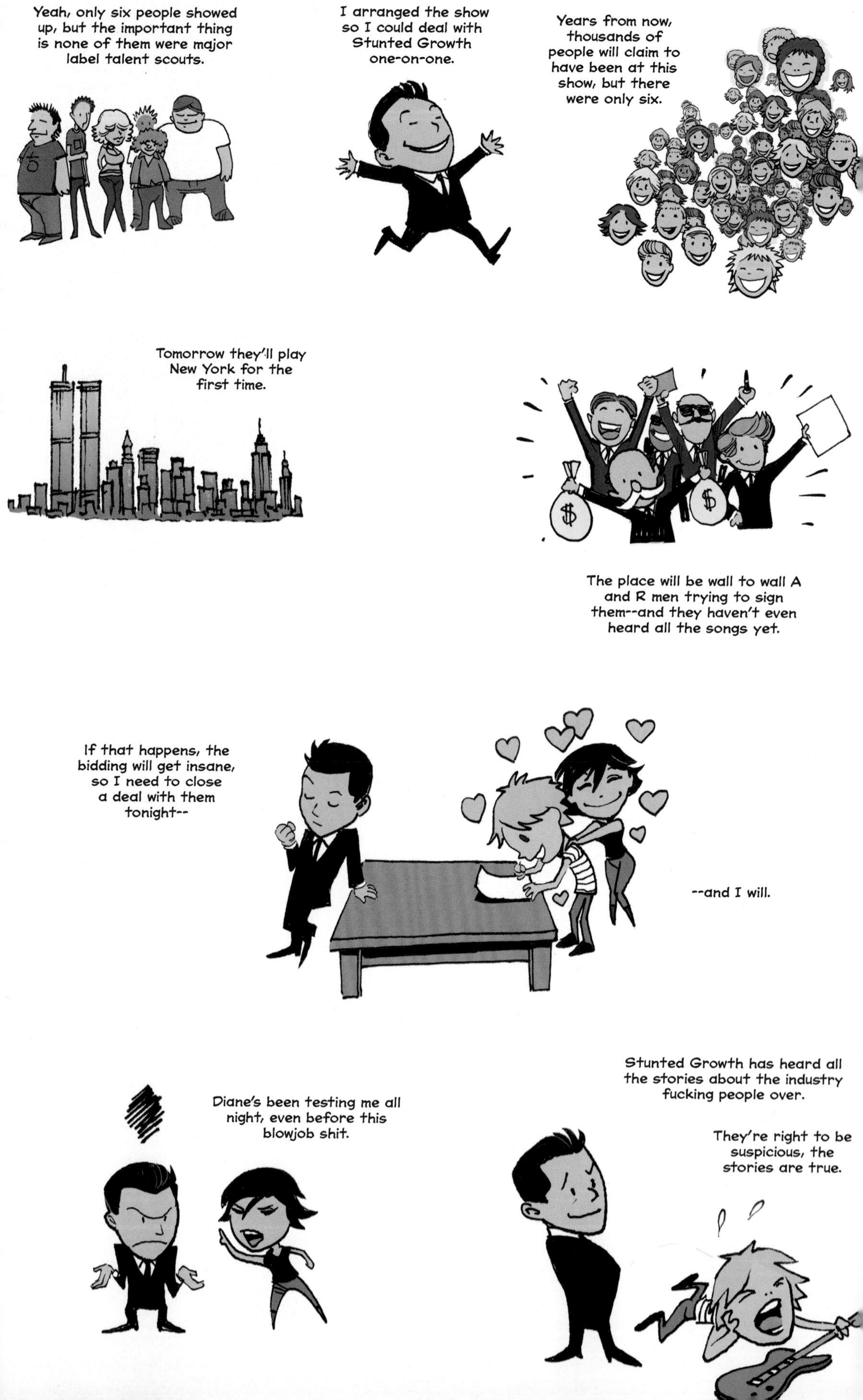
Yeah, only six people showed up, but the important thing is none of them were major label talent scouts.
I arranged the show so I could deal with Stunted Growth one-on-one.
Years from now, thousands of people will claim to have been at this show, but there were only six.
Tomorrow they'll play New York for the first time.
The place will be wall to wall A and R men trying to sign them--and they haven't even heard all the songs yet.
If that happens, the bidding will get insane, so I need to close a deal with them tonight--
--and I will.
Diane's been testing me all night, even before this blowjob shit.
Stunted Growth has heard all the stories about the industry fucking people over.
They're right to be suspicious, the stories are true.

They want to see how bad I want them; if I can I hang with their bad-boy bullshit. They want to see me yawn because it's nearly daybreak and I'm ten years older than them.

They are kids feeling out their first taste of power. They want to push back on the man. I play this game, because they want to play this game.

Stunted Growth wants to be huge, they all do. They don't really know why. I do.

Their parents didn't love them enough or their friends made fun of them or worse. They're damaged and seeking approval.

I don't enjoy this part of the job, but when I sign them my approval becomes their everything. It's the worst.

PAPA!

As for Diane's demands, I've given her nearly everything she asked for, but not exactly the way she imagines it. Here's how it works, demand by demand:

Multimillion-dollar contract: this is the easiest to accommodate--the business is bursting with money. This comes from exposure of new artists on MTV and re-releases of 60s and 70s classic rock on a shiny new format, the CD. This little disc sells for nearly three times the other, rapidly dying, formats. "Resuscitating the collateral," Melch calls it.

Selling old shit to yuppies is what I call it.

Obviously we don't just hand over six million dollars to fucking teenagers--they'd vanish, pissing it away on drugs, ugly mansions and gold-plated jeeps with earth-shattering sound systems.

We get to the guaranteed six-million-dollar contract by building in options that we may or may not ever pick up. The fewer we pick up, the less the bands make, but they can tell their pals back home they signed a contract worth six million dollars.

SIX MILLION!

OOH! AAH!

Record labels, with record-setting annual income, are signing acts like crazy--even if the acts only break even or lose money. Even better, all record contracts are loans. We call them advances, but really they're loans to artists. They pay back the loan from their cut of future sales.

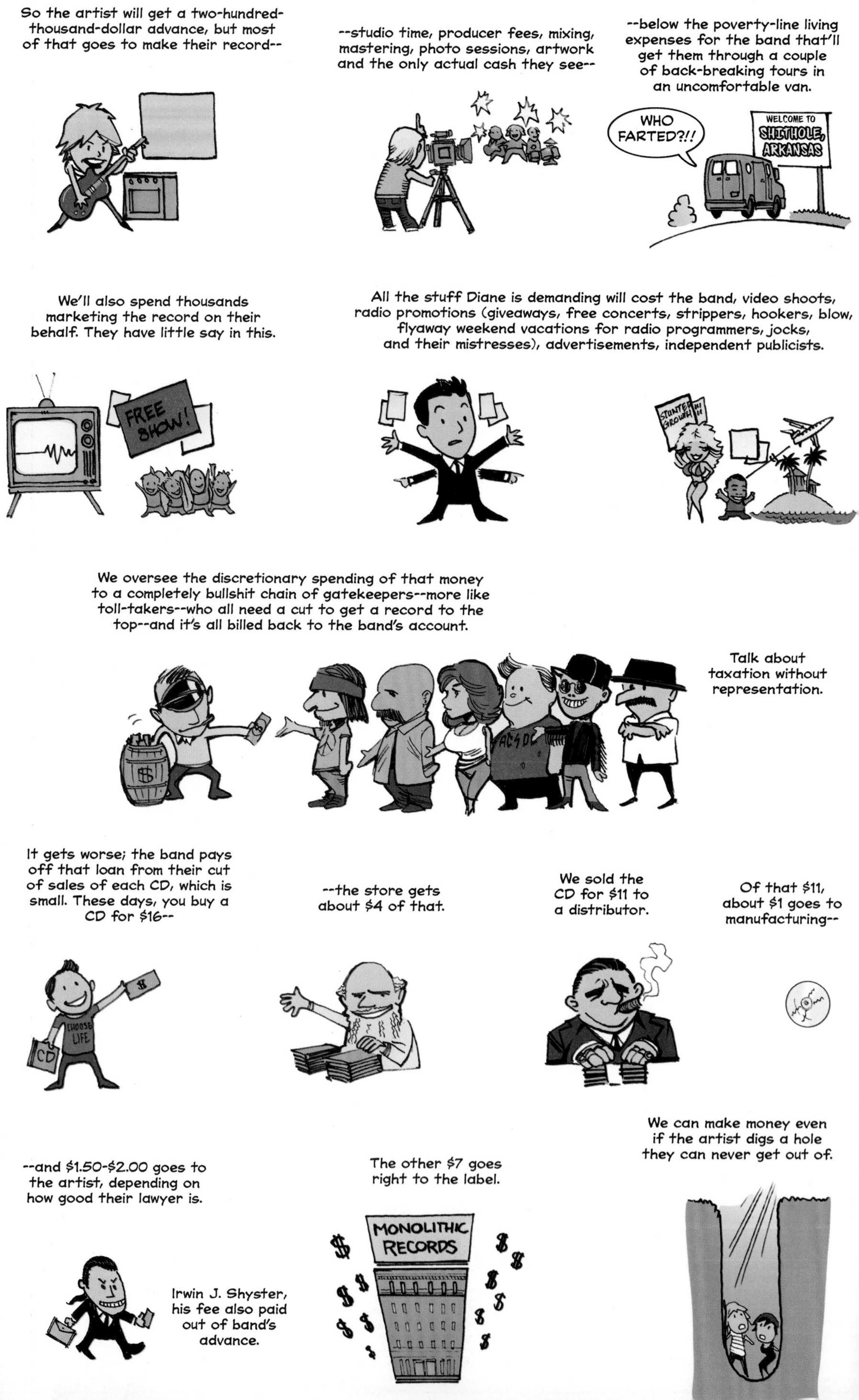
So the artist will get a two-hundred-thousand-dollar advance, but most of that goes to make their record--
--studio time, producer fees, mixing, mastering, photo sessions, artwork and the only actual cash they see--
--below the poverty-line living expenses for the band that'll get them through a couple of back-breaking tours in an uncomfortable van.
WHO FARTED?!!
WELCOME TO SHITHOLE, ARKANSAS
We'll also spend thousands marketing the record on their behalf. They have little say in this.
FREE SHOW!
All the stuff Diane is demanding will cost the band, video shoots, radio promotions (giveaways, free concerts, strippers, hookers, blow, flyaway weekend vacations for radio programmers, jocks, and their mistresses), advertisements, independent publicists.
We oversee the discretionary spending of that money to a completely bullshit chain of gatekeepers--more like toll-takers--who all need a cut to get a record to the top--and it's all billed back to the band's account.
Talk about taxation without representation.
It gets worse; the band pays off that loan from their cut of sales of each CD, which is small. These days, you buy a CD for $16--
CHOOSE LIFE
CD
--the store gets about $4 of that.
We sold the CD for $11 to a distributor.
Of that $11, about $1 goes to manufacturing--
--and $1.50-$2.00 goes to the artist, depending on how good their lawyer is.
Irwin J. Shyster, his fee also paid out of band's advance.
The other $7 goes right to the label.
MONOLITHIC RECORDS
We can make money even if the artist digs a hole they can never get out of.

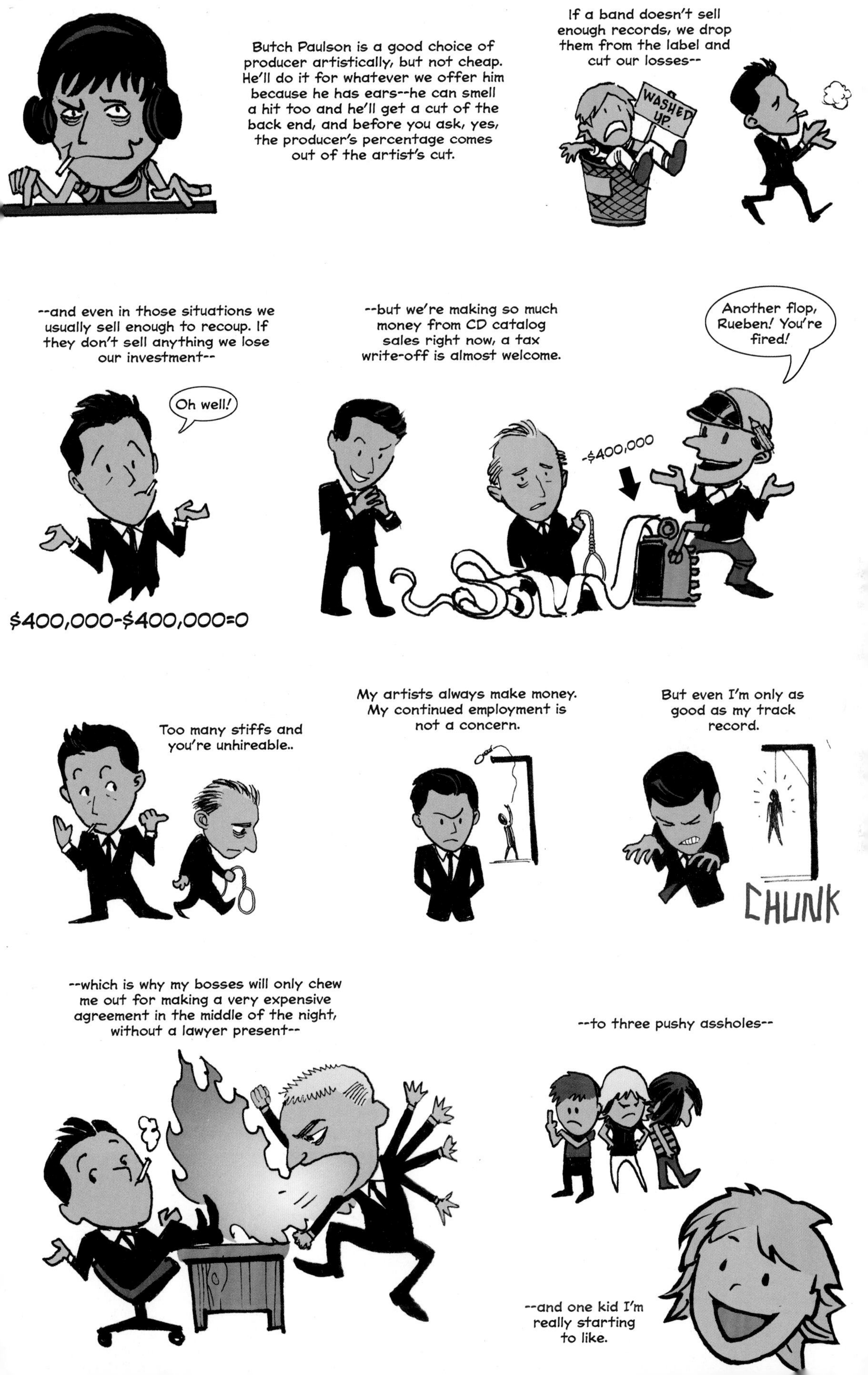
Butch Paulson is a good choice of producer artistically, but not cheap. He'll do it for whatever we offer him because he has ears--he can smell a hit too and he'll get a cut of the back end, and before you ask, yes, the producer's percentage comes out of the artist's cut.
If a band doesn't sell enough records, we drop them from the label and cut our losses--
WASHED UP.
--and even in those situations we usually sell enough to recoup. If they don't sell anything we lose our investment--
Oh well!
$400,000-$400,000=0
--but we're making so much money from CD catalog sales right now, a tax write-off is almost welcome.
Another flop, Rueben! You're fired!
-$400,000
Too many stiffs and you're unhireable..
My artists always make money. My continued employment is not a concern.
But even I'm only as good as my track record.
CHUNK
--which is why my bosses will only chew me out for making a very expensive agreement in the middle of the night, without a lawyer present--
--to three pushy assholes--
--and one kid I'm really starting to like.

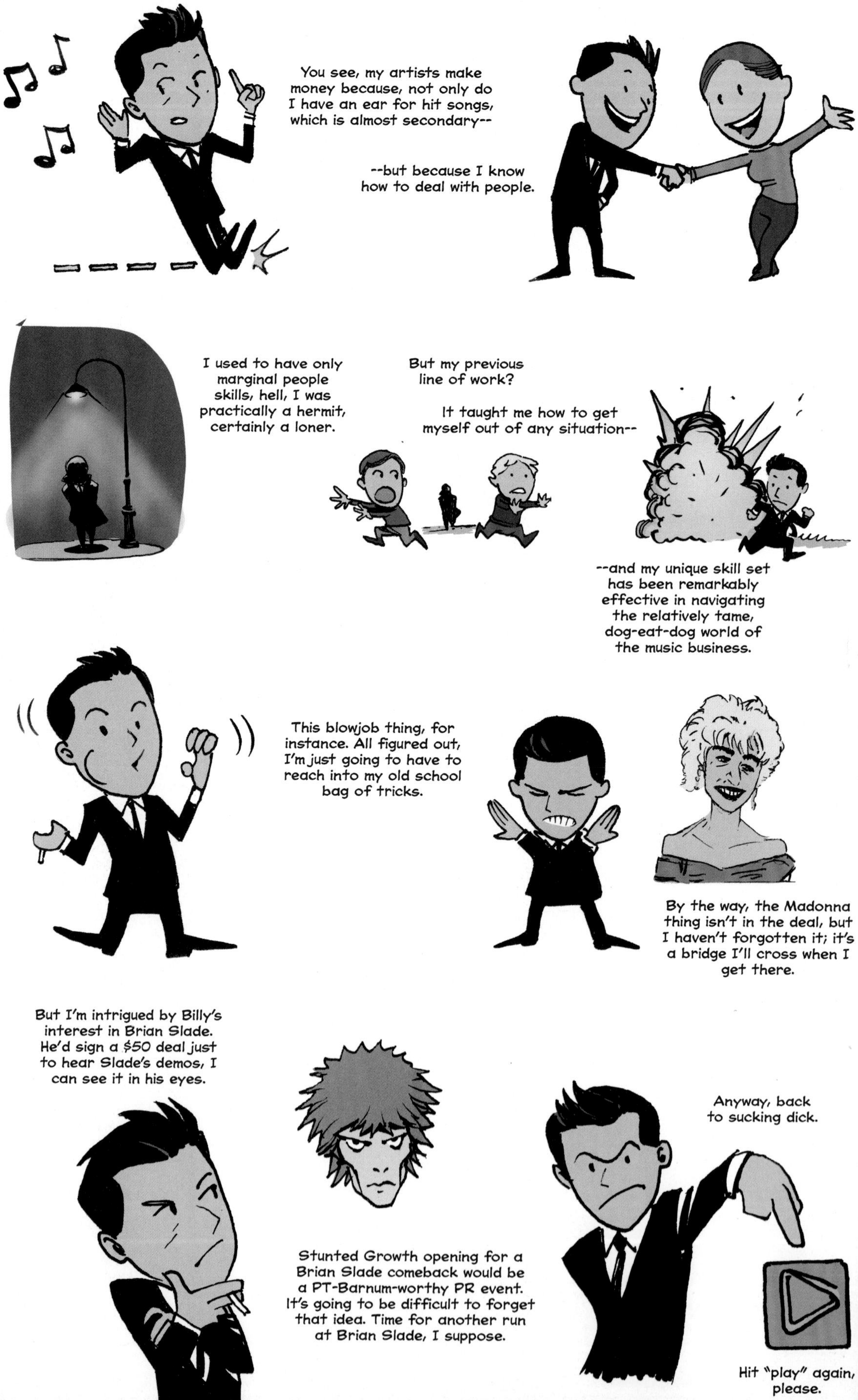
You see, my artists make money because, not only do I have an ear for hit songs, which is almost secondary--
--but because I know how to deal with people.
I used to have only marginal people skills, hell, I was practically a hermit, certainly a loner.
But my previous line of work?
It taught me how to get myself out of any situation--
--and my unique skill set has been remarkably effective in navigating the relatively tame, dog-eat-dog world of the music business.
This blowjob thing, for instance. All figured out, I'm just going to have to reach into my old school bag of tricks.
By the way, the Madonna thing isn't in the deal, but I haven't forgotten it; it's a bridge I'll cross when I get there.
But I'm intrigued by Billy's interest in Brian Slade. He'd sign a $50 deal just to hear Slade's demos, I can see it in his eyes.
Stunted Growth opening for a Brian Slade comeback would be a PT-Barnum-worthy PR event. It's going to be difficult to forget that idea. Time for another run at Brian Slade, I suppose.
Anyway, back to sucking dick.
Hit "play" again, please.

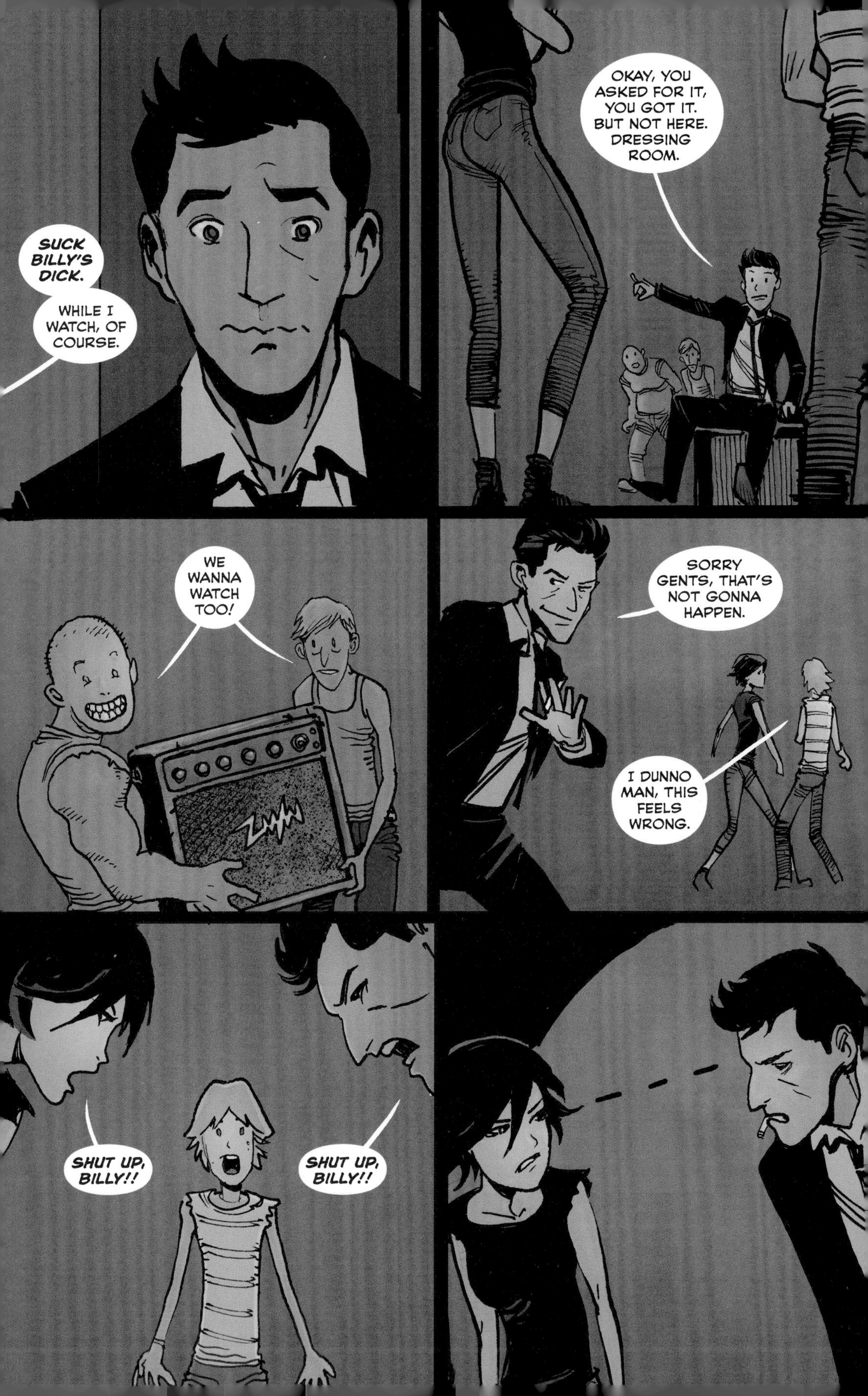
SUCK BILLY'S DICK.
WHILE I WATCH, OF COURSE.
OKAY, YOU ASKED FOR IT, YOU GOT IT. BUT NOT HERE. DRESSING ROOM.
WE WANNA WATCH TOO!
SORRY GENTS, THAT'S NOT GONNA HAPPEN.
I DUNNO MAN, THIS FEELS WRONG.
SHUT UP, BILLY!!
SHUT UP, BILLY!!

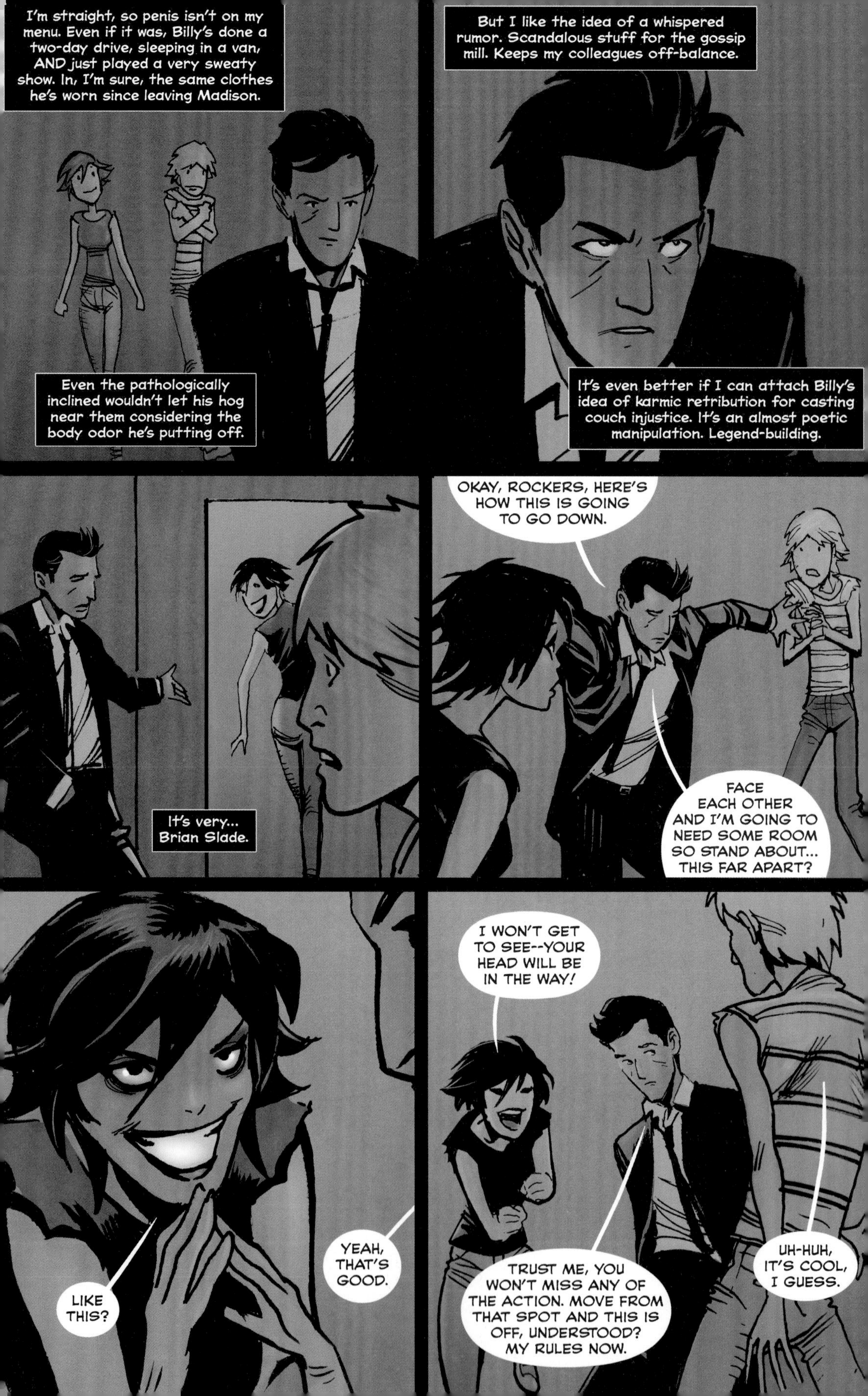
I'm straight, so penis isn't on my menu. Even if it was, Billy's done a two-day drive, sleeping in a van, AND just played a very sweaty show. In, I'm sure, the same clothes he's worn since leaving Madison.
Even the pathologically inclined wouldn't let his hog near them considering the body odor he's putting off.
But I like the idea of a whispered rumor. Scandalous stuff for the gossip mill. Keeps my colleagues off-balance.
It's even better if I can attach Billy's idea of karmic retribution for casting couch injustice. It's an almost poetic manipulation. Legend-building.
It's very... Brian Slade.
OKAY, ROCKERS, HERE'S HOW THIS IS GOING TO GO DOWN.
FACE EACH OTHER AND I'M GOING TO NEED SOME ROOM SO STAND ABOUT... THIS FAR APART?
LIKE THIS?
YEAH, THAT'S GOOD.
I WON'T GET TO SEE--YOUR HEAD WILL BE IN THE WAY!
TRUST ME, YOU WON'T MISS ANY OF THE ACTION. MOVE FROM THAT SPOT AND THIS IS OFF, UNDERSTOOD? MY RULES NOW.
UH-HUH, IT'S COOL, I GUESS.

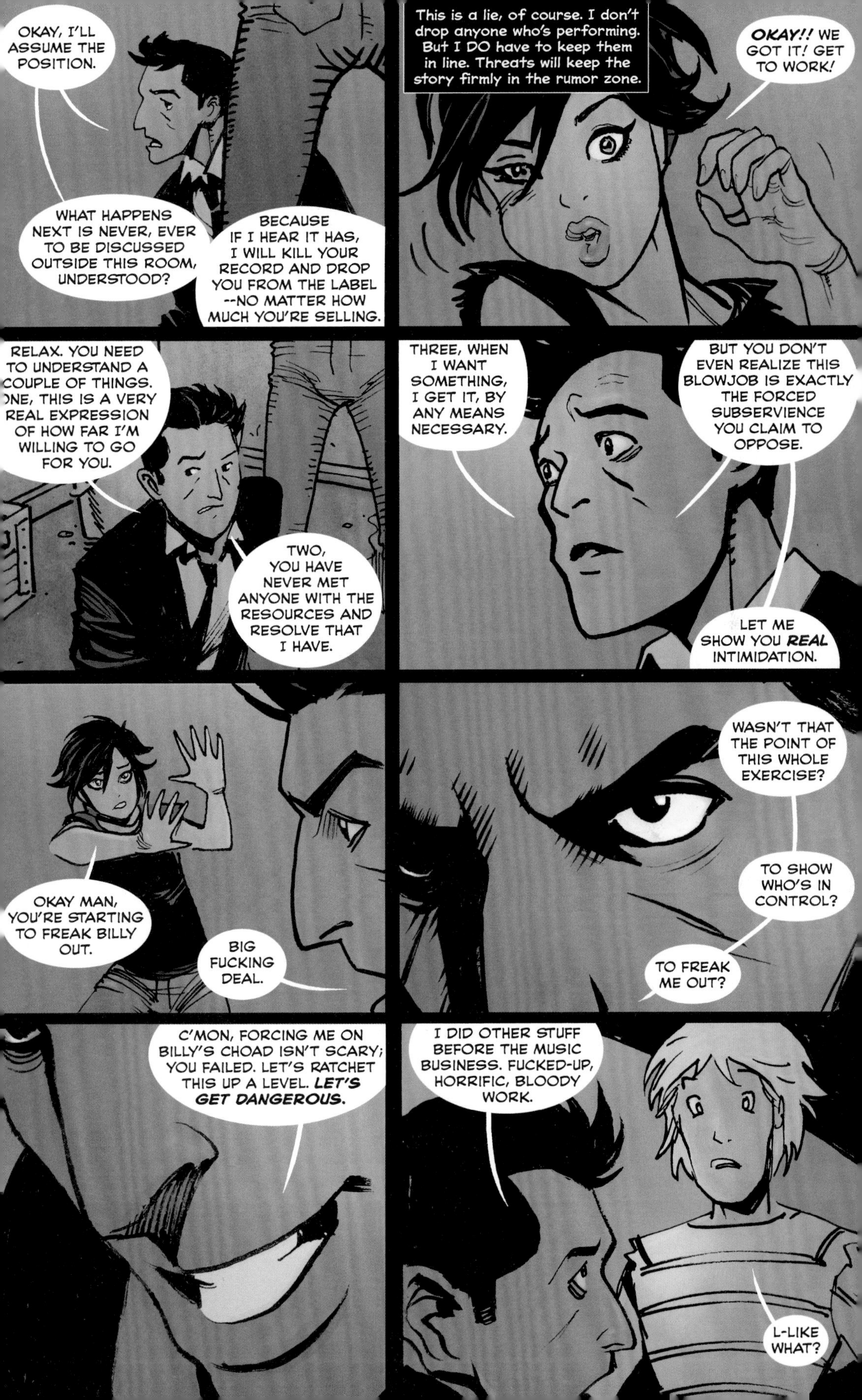
OKAY, I'LL ASSUME THE POSITION.
WHAT HAPPENS NEXT IS NEVER, EVER TO BE DISCUSSED OUTSIDE THIS ROOM, UNDERSTOOD?
BECAUSE IF I HEAR IT HAS, I WILL KILL YOUR RECORD AND DROP YOU FROM THE LABEL --NO MATTER HOW MUCH YOU'RE SELLING.
This is a lie, of course. I don't drop anyone who's performing. But I DO have to keep them in line. Threats will keep the story firmly in the rumor zone.
OKAY!! WE GOT IT! GET TO WORK!
RELAX. YOU NEED TO UNDERSTAND A COUPLE OF THINGS. ONE, THIS IS A VERY REAL EXPRESSION OF HOW FAR I'M WILLING TO GO FOR YOU.
TWO, YOU HAVE NEVER MET ANYONE WITH THE RESOURCES AND RESOLVE THAT I HAVE.
THREE, WHEN I WANT SOMETHING, I GET IT, BY ANY MEANS NECESSARY.
BUT YOU DON'T EVEN REALIZE THIS BLOWJOB IS EXACTLY THE FORCED SUBSERVIENCE YOU CLAIM TO OPPOSE.
LET ME SHOW YOU ***REAL*** INTIMIDATION.
OKAY MAN, YOU'RE STARTING TO FREAK BILLY OUT.
BIG FUCKING DEAL.
WASN'T THAT THE POINT OF THIS WHOLE EXERCISE?
TO SHOW WHO'S IN CONTROL?
TO FREAK ME OUT?
C'MON, FORCING ME ON BILLY'S CHOAD ISN'T SCARY; YOU FAILED. LET'S RATCHET THIS UP A LEVEL. ***LET'S GET DANGEROUS.***
I DID OTHER STUFF BEFORE THE MUSIC BUSINESS. FUCKED-UP, HORRIFIC, BLOODY WORK.
L-LIKE WHAT?

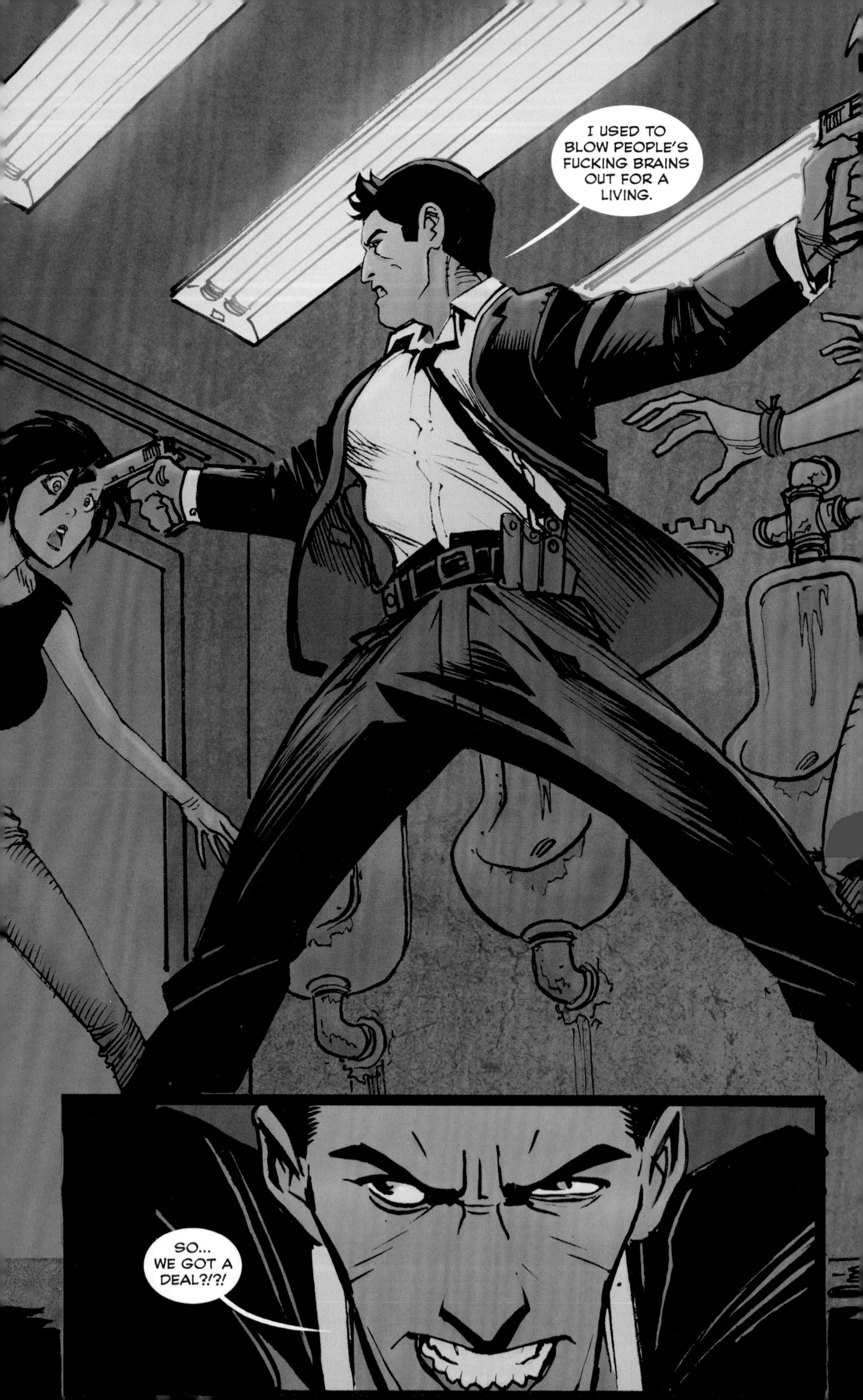
I USED TO BLOW PEOPLE'S FUCKING BRAINS OUT FOR A LIVING.
SO... WE GOT A DEAL?!?!

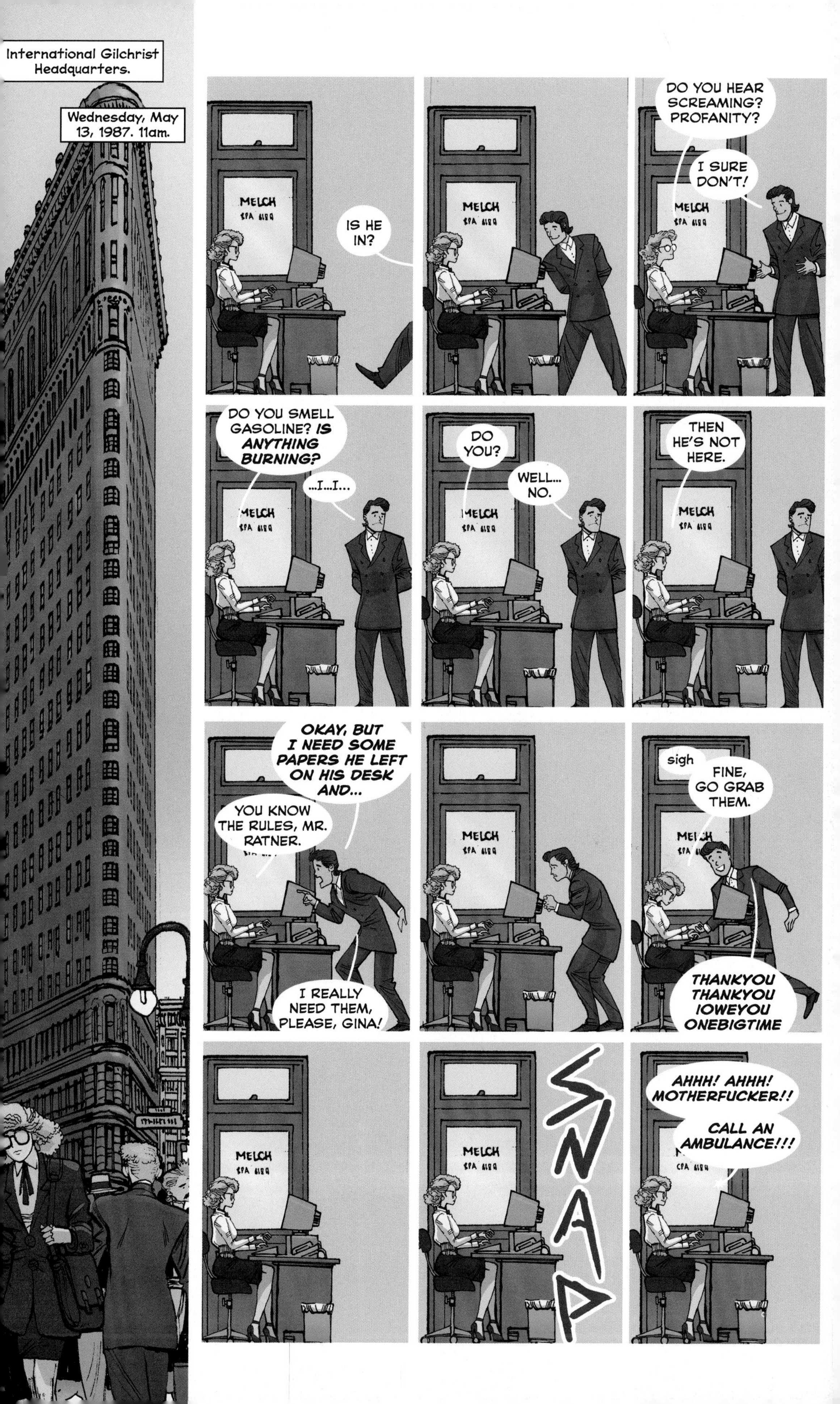

International Gilchrist Headquarters.
Wednesday, May 13, 1987. 11am.
MELCH
IS HE IN?
DO YOU HEAR SCREAMING? PROFANITY?
I SURE DON'T!
DO YOU SMELL GASOLINE? IS ANYTHING BURNING?
...I...I...
DO YOU?
WELL... NO.
THEN HE'S NOT HERE.
OKAY, BUT I NEED SOME PAPERS HE LEFT ON HIS DESK AND...
YOU KNOW THE RULES, MR. RATNER.
I REALLY NEED THEM, PLEASE, GINA!
sigh
FINE, GO GRAB THEM.
THANKYOU THANKYOU IOWEYOU ONEBIGTIME
SNAP
AHHH! AHHH! MOTHERFUCKER!!
CALL AN AMBULANCE!!!

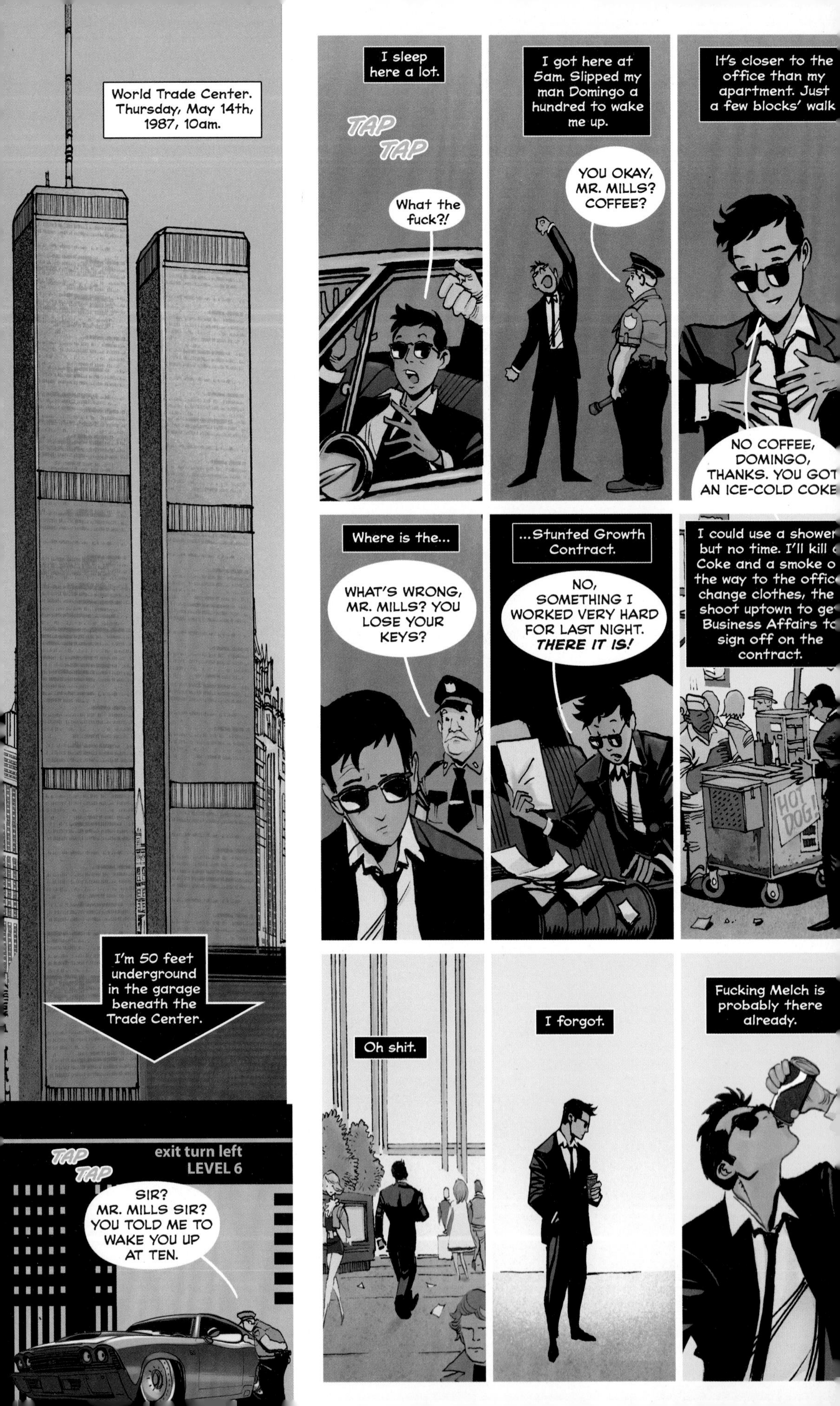
World Trade Center. Thursday, May 14th, 1987, 10am.
I'm 50 feet underground in the garage beneath the Trade Center.
TAP TAP
exit turn left
LEVEL 6
SIR? MR. MILLS SIR? YOU TOLD ME TO WAKE YOU UP AT TEN.
I sleep here a lot.
TAP TAP
What the fuck?!
I got here at 5am. Slipped my man Domingo a hundred to wake me up.
YOU OKAY, MR. MILLS? COFFEE?
It's closer to the office than my apartment. Just a few blocks' walk
NO COFFEE, DOMINGO, THANKS. YOU GOT AN ICE-COLD COKE
Where is the...
WHAT'S WRONG, MR. MILLS? YOU LOSE YOUR KEYS?
...Stunted Growth Contract.
NO, SOMETHING I WORKED VERY HARD FOR LAST NIGHT. *THERE IT IS!*
I could use a shower but no time. I'll kill Coke and a smoke o the way to the offic change clothes, the shoot uptown to ge Business Affairs to sign off on the contract.
HOT DOG!
Oh shit.
I forgot.
Fucking Melch is probably there already.

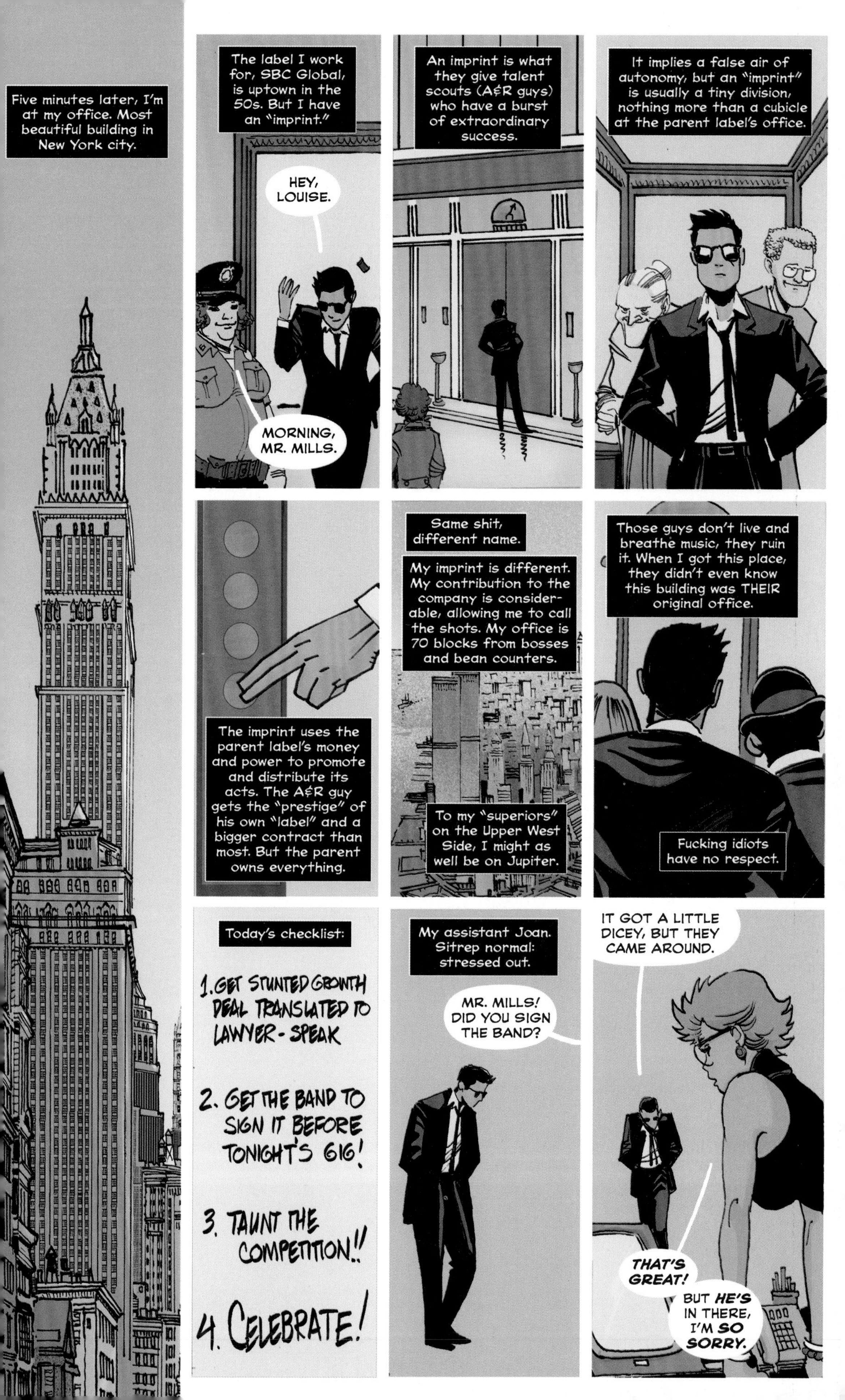

Five minutes later, I'm at my office. Most beautiful building in New York city.
The label I work for, SBC Global, is uptown in the 50s. But I have an "imprint."
HEY, LOUISE.
MORNING, MR. MILLS.
An imprint is what they give talent scouts (A&R guys) who have a burst of extraordinary success.
It implies a false air of autonomy, but an "imprint" is usually a tiny division, nothing more than a cubicle at the parent label's office.
The imprint uses the parent label's money and power to promote and distribute its acts. The A&R guy gets the "prestige" of his own "label" and a bigger contract than most. But the parent owns everything.
Same shit, different name.
My imprint is different. My contribution to the company is considerable, allowing me to call the shots. My office is 70 blocks from bosses and bean counters.
To my "superiors" on the Upper West Side, I might as well be on Jupiter.
Those guys don't live and breathe music, they ruin it. When I got this place, they didn't even know this building was THEIR original office.
Fucking idiots have no respect.
Today's checklist:
1. GET STUNTED GROWTH DEAL TRANSLATED TO LAWYER-SPEAK
2. GET THE BAND TO SIGN IT BEFORE TONIGHT'S GIG!
3. TAUNT THE COMPETITION!!
4. CELEBRATE!
My assistant Joan. Sitrep normal: stressed out.
MR. MILLS! DID YOU SIGN THE BAND?
IT GOT A LITTLE DICEY, BUT THEY CAME AROUND.
THAT'S GREAT!
BUT HE'S IN THERE, I'M SO SORRY.

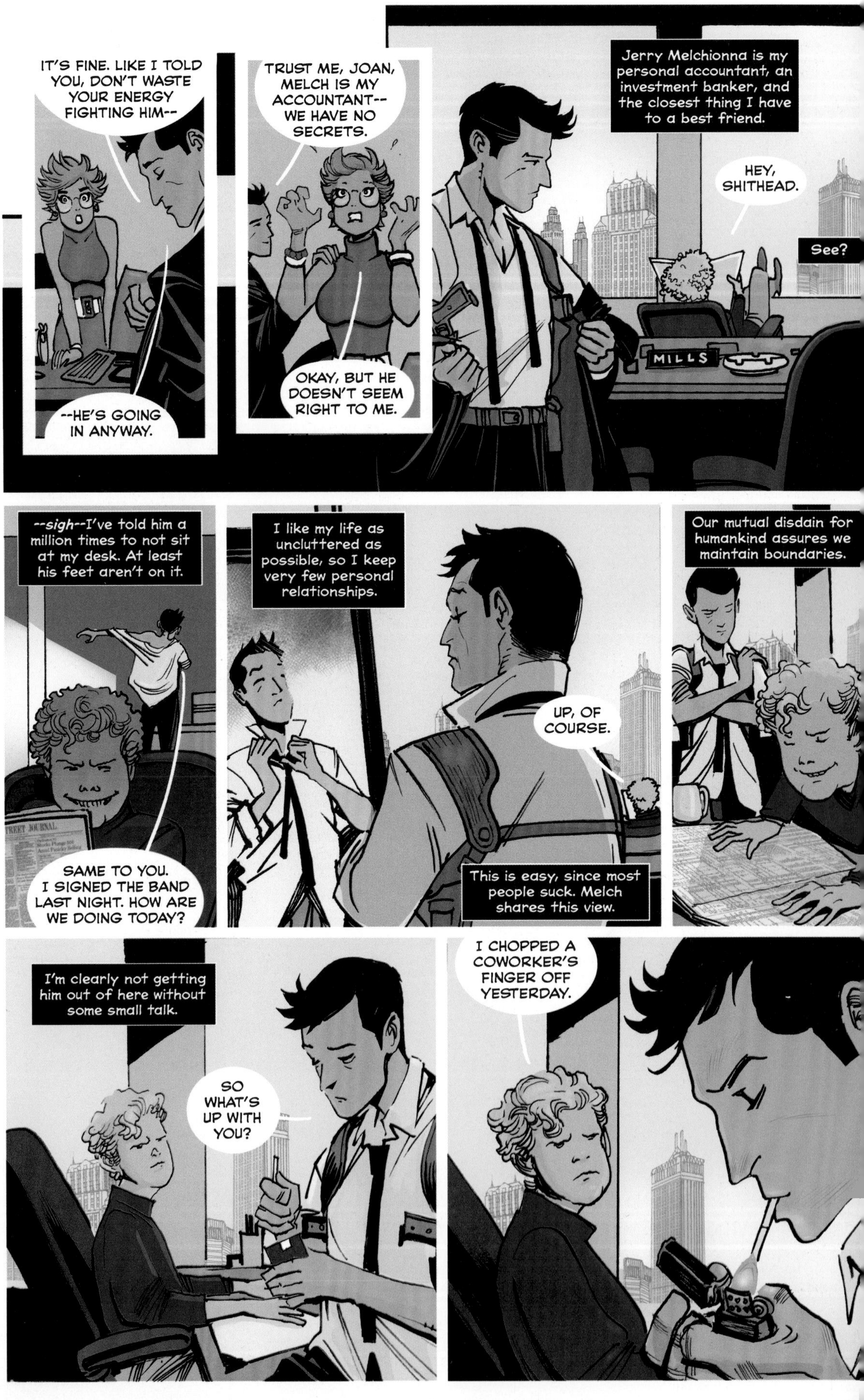
IT'S FINE. LIKE I TOLD YOU, DON'T WASTE YOUR ENERGY FIGHTING HIM--
--HE'S GOING IN ANYWAY.
TRUST ME, JOAN, MELCH IS MY ACCOUNTANT-- WE HAVE NO SECRETS.
OKAY, BUT HE DOESN'T SEEM RIGHT TO ME.
Jerry Melchionna is my personal accountant, an investment banker, and the closest thing I have to a best friend.
HEY, SHITHEAD.
See?
MILLS
--sigh--I've told him a million times to not sit at my desk. At least his feet aren't on it.
SAME TO YOU. I SIGNED THE BAND LAST NIGHT. HOW ARE WE DOING TODAY?
I like my life as uncluttered as possible, so I keep very few personal relationships.
UP, OF COURSE.
This is easy, since most people suck. Melch shares this view.
Our mutual disdain for humankind assures we maintain boundaries.
I'm clearly not getting him out of here without some small talk.
SO WHAT'S UP WITH YOU?
I CHOPPED A COWORKER'S FINGER OFF YESTERDAY.

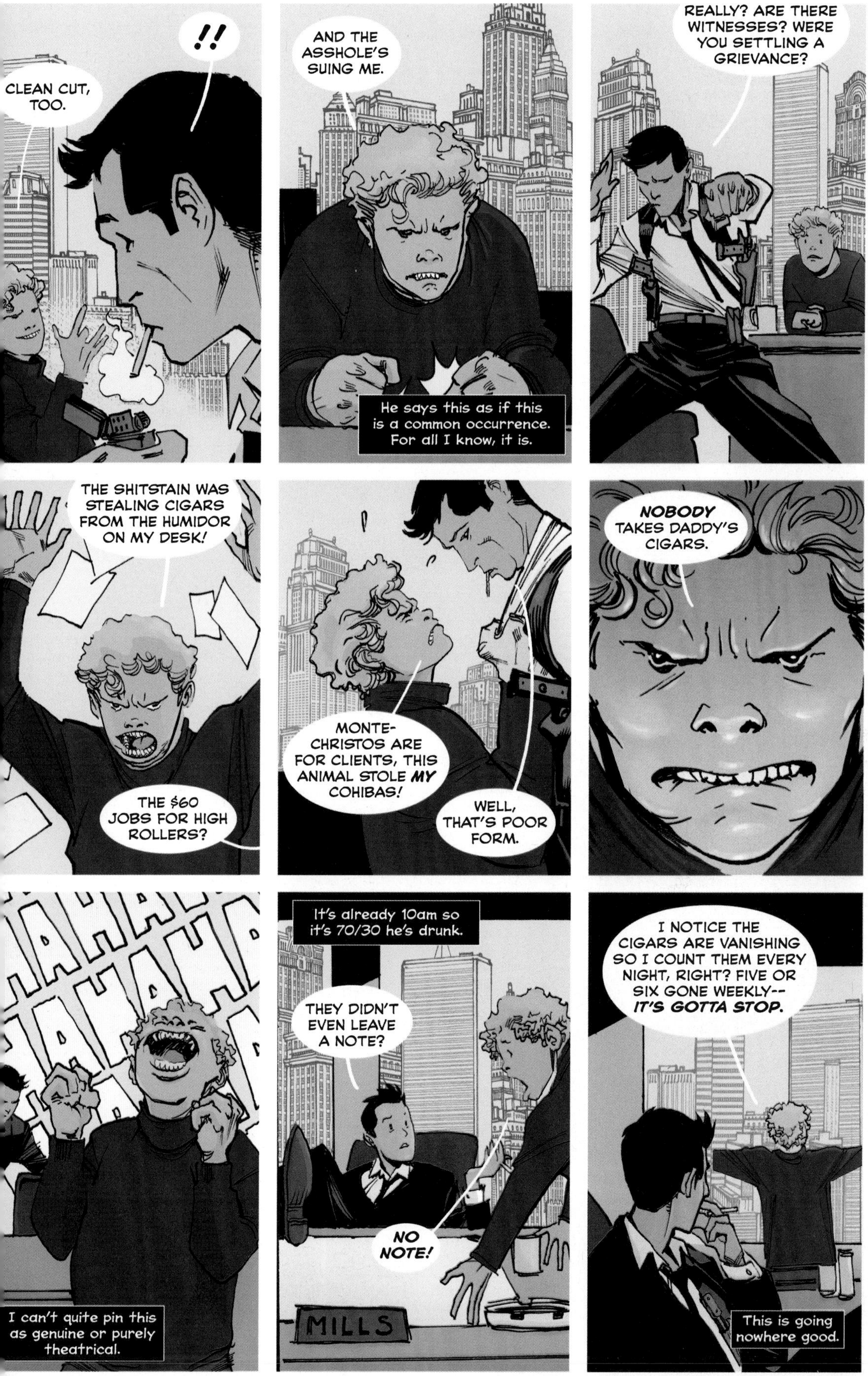
CLEAN CUT, TOO.
!!
AND THE ASSHOLE'S SUING ME.
He says this as if this is a common occurrence. For all I know, it is.
REALLY? ARE THERE WITNESSES? WERE YOU SETTLING A GRIEVANCE?
THE SHITSTAIN WAS STEALING CIGARS FROM THE HUMIDOR ON MY DESK!
THE $60 JOBS FOR HIGH ROLLERS?
MONTE-CHRISTOS ARE FOR CLIENTS, THIS ANIMAL STOLE MY COHIBAS!
WELL, THAT'S POOR FORM.
NOBODY TAKES DADDY'S CIGARS.
HAHAHAHAHAHA
I can't quite pin this as genuine or purely theatrical.
It's already 10am so it's 70/30 he's drunk.
THEY DIDN'T EVEN LEAVE A NOTE?
NO NOTE!
MILLS
I NOTICE THE CIGARS ARE VANISHING SO I COUNT THEM EVERY NIGHT, RIGHT? FIVE OR SIX GONE WEEKLY-- IT'S GOTTA STOP.
This is going nowhere good.

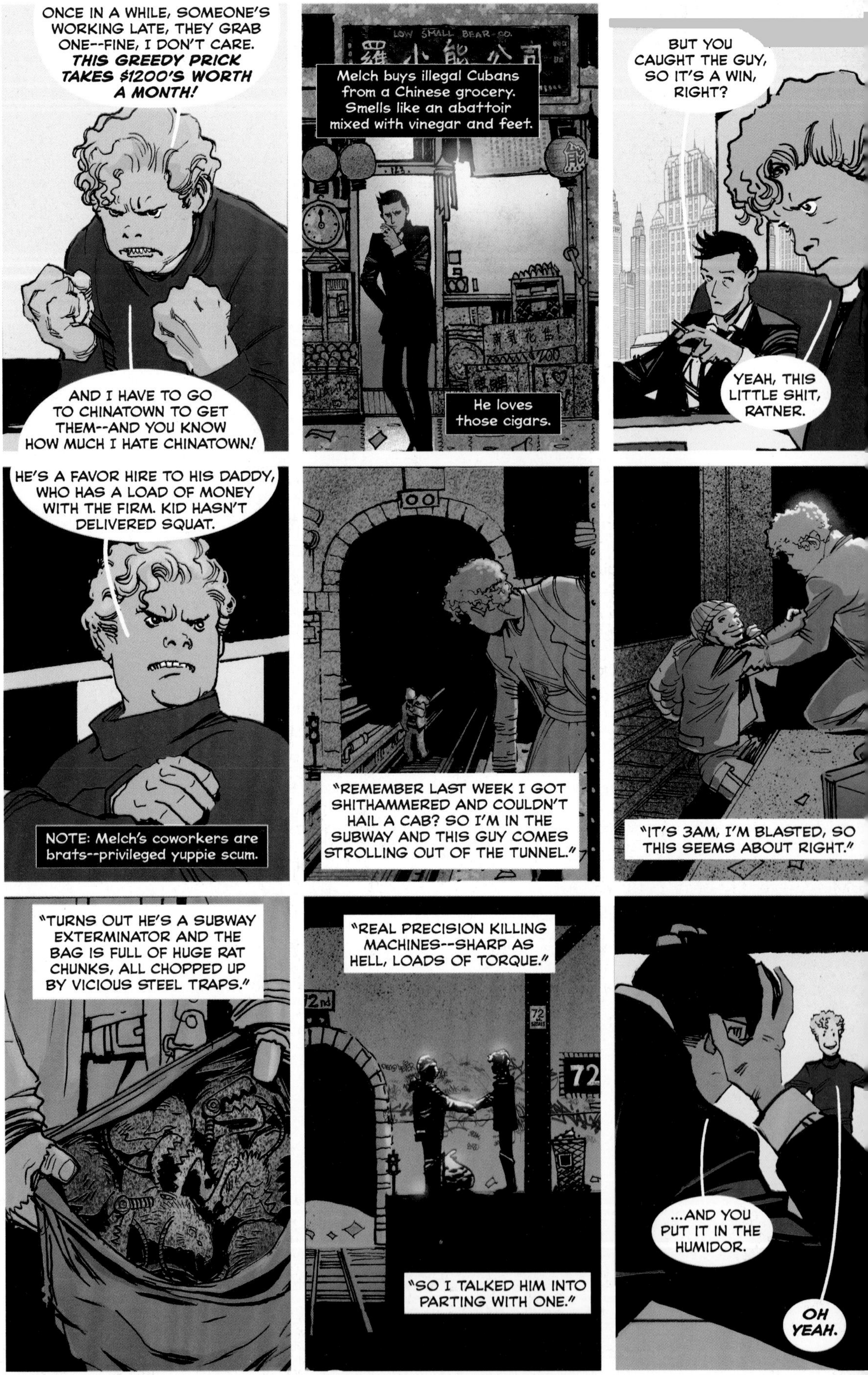
ONCE IN A WHILE, SOMEONE'S WORKING LATE, THEY GRAB ONE--FINE, I DON'T CARE. ***THIS GREEDY PRICK TAKES $1200'S WORTH A MONTH!***
AND I HAVE TO GO TO CHINATOWN TO GET THEM--AND YOU KNOW HOW MUCH I HATE CHINATOWN!
LOW SMALL BEAR CO.
羅小熊公司
Melch buys illegal Cubans from a Chinese grocery. Smells like an abattoir mixed with vinegar and feet.
He loves those cigars.
BUT YOU CAUGHT THE GUY, SO IT'S A WIN, RIGHT?
YEAH, THIS LITTLE SHIT, RATNER.
HE'S A FAVOR HIRE TO HIS DADDY, WHO HAS A LOAD OF MONEY WITH THE FIRM. KID HASN'T DELIVERED SQUAT.
NOTE: Melch's coworkers are brats--privileged yuppie scum.
"REMEMBER LAST WEEK I GOT SHITHAMMERED AND COULDN'T HAIL A CAB? SO I'M IN THE SUBWAY AND THIS GUY COMES STROLLING OUT OF THE TUNNEL."
"IT'S 3AM, I'M BLASTED, SO THIS SEEMS ABOUT RIGHT."
"TURNS OUT HE'S A SUBWAY EXTERMINATOR AND THE BAG IS FULL OF HUGE RAT CHUNKS, ALL CHOPPED UP BY VICIOUS STEEL TRAPS."
"REAL PRECISION KILLING MACHINES--SHARP AS HELL, LOADS OF TORQUE."
72nd
72
"SO I TALKED HIM INTO PARTING WITH ONE."
...AND YOU PUT IT IN THE HUMIDOR.
OH YEAH.

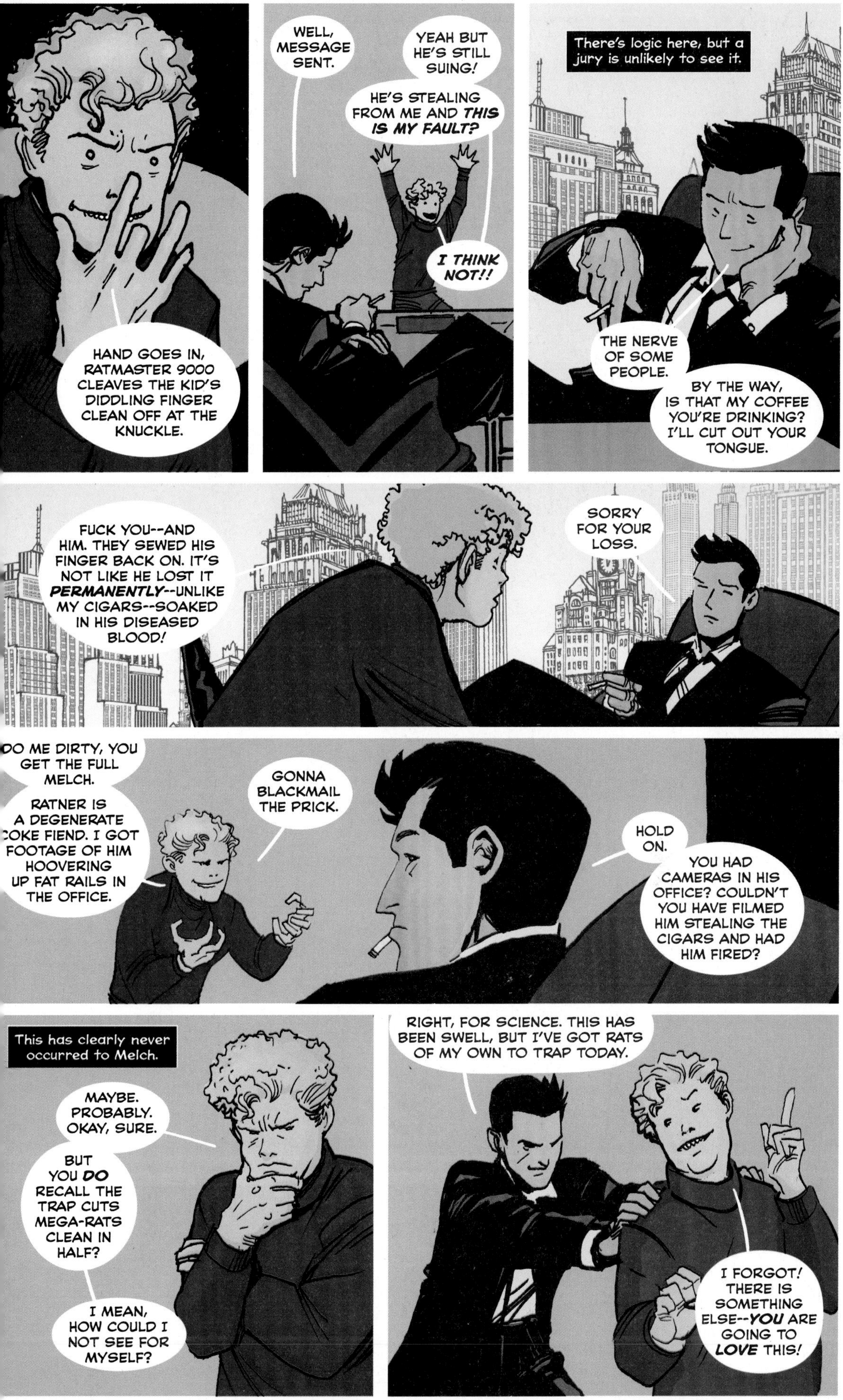
HAND GOES IN, RATMASTER 9000 CLEAVES THE KID'S DIDDLING FINGER CLEAN OFF AT THE KNUCKLE.
WELL, MESSAGE SENT.
YEAH BUT HE'S STILL SUING!
HE'S STEALING FROM ME AND THIS IS MY FAULT?
I THINK NOT!!
There's logic here, but a jury is unlikely to see it.
THE NERVE OF SOME PEOPLE.
BY THE WAY, IS THAT MY COFFEE YOU'RE DRINKING? I'LL CUT OUT YOUR TONGUE.
FUCK YOU--AND HIM. THEY SEWED HIS FINGER BACK ON. IT'S NOT LIKE HE LOST IT PERMANENTLY--UNLIKE MY CIGARS--SOAKED IN HIS DISEASED BLOOD!
SORRY FOR YOUR LOSS.
DO ME DIRTY, YOU GET THE FULL MELCH.
RATNER IS A DEGENERATE COKE FIEND. I GOT FOOTAGE OF HIM HOOVERING UP FAT RAILS IN THE OFFICE.
GONNA BLACKMAIL THE PRICK.
HOLD ON.
YOU HAD CAMERAS IN HIS OFFICE? COULDN'T YOU HAVE FILMED HIM STEALING THE CIGARS AND HAD HIM FIRED?
This has clearly never occurred to Melch.
MAYBE. PROBABLY. OKAY, SURE.
BUT YOU DO RECALL THE TRAP CUTS MEGA-RATS CLEAN IN HALF?
I MEAN, HOW COULD I NOT SEE FOR MYSELF?
RIGHT, FOR SCIENCE. THIS HAS BEEN SWELL, BUT I'VE GOT RATS OF MY OWN TO TRAP TODAY.
I FORGOT! THERE IS SOMETHING ELSE--YOU ARE GOING TO LOVE THIS!

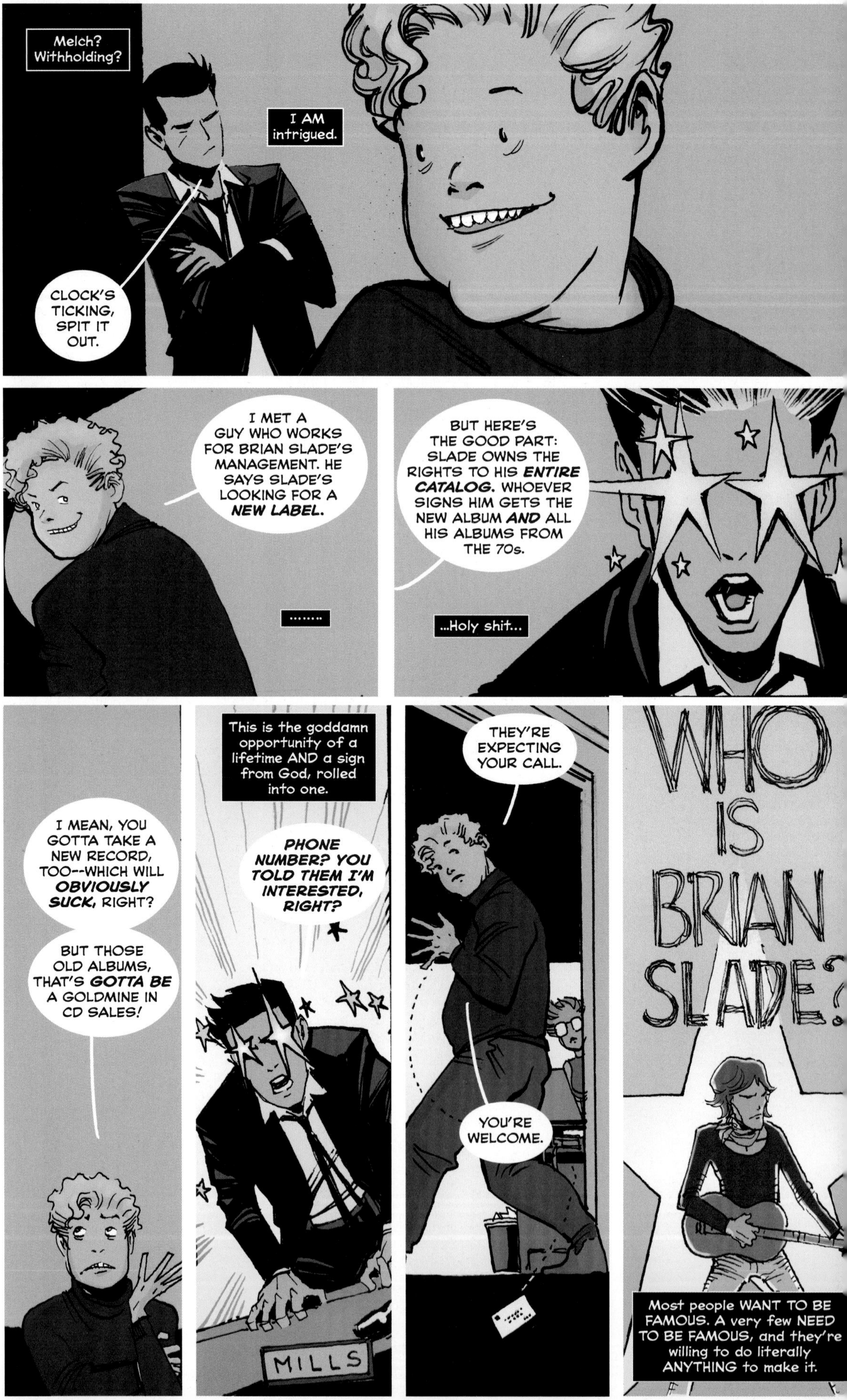
Melch? Withholding?
I AM intrigued.
CLOCK'S TICKING, SPIT IT OUT.
I MET A GUY WHO WORKS FOR BRIAN SLADE'S MANAGEMENT. HE SAYS SLADE'S LOOKING FOR A NEW LABEL.
....
BUT HERE'S THE GOOD PART: SLADE OWNS THE RIGHTS TO HIS ENTIRE CATALOG. WHOEVER SIGNS HIM GETS THE NEW ALBUM AND ALL HIS ALBUMS FROM THE 70s.
...Holy shit...
I MEAN, YOU GOTTA TAKE A NEW RECORD, TOO--WHICH WILL OBVIOUSLY SUCK, RIGHT?
BUT THOSE OLD ALBUMS, THAT'S GOTTA BE A GOLDMINE IN CD SALES!
This is the goddamn opportunity of a lifetime AND a sign from God, rolled into one.
PHONE NUMBER? YOU TOLD THEM I'M INTERESTED, RIGHT?
MILLS
THEY'RE EXPECTING YOUR CALL.
YOU'RE WELCOME.
WHO IS BRIAN SLADE?
Most people WANT TO BE FAMOUS. A very few NEED TO BE FAMOUS, and they're willing to do literally ANYTHING to make it.

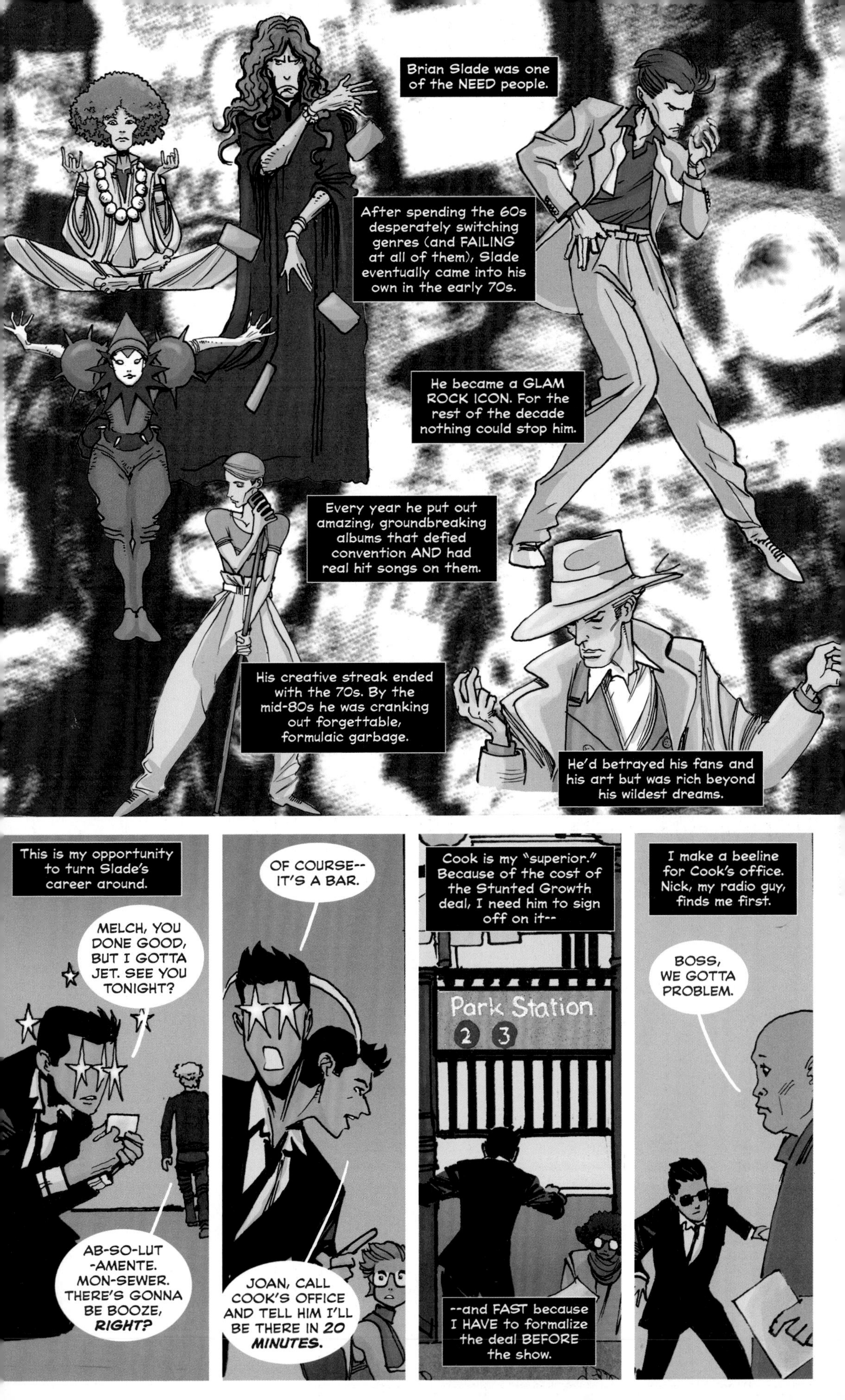
Brian Slade was one of the NEED people.
After spending the 60s desperately switching genres (and FAILING at all of them), Slade eventually came into his own in the early 70s.
He became a GLAM ROCK ICON. For the rest of the decade nothing could stop him.
Every year he put out amazing, groundbreaking albums that defied convention AND had real hit songs on them.
His creative streak ended with the 70s. By the mid-80s he was cranking out forgettable, formulaic garbage.
He'd betrayed his fans and his art but was rich beyond his wildest dreams.
This is my opportunity to turn Slade's career around.
MELCH, YOU DONE GOOD, BUT I GOTTA JET. SEE YOU TONIGHT?
AB-SO-LUT -AMENTE. MON-SEWER. THERE'S GONNA BE BOOZE, ***RIGHT?***
OF COURSE-- IT'S A BAR.
JOAN, CALL COOK'S OFFICE AND TELL HIM I'LL BE THERE IN ***20 MINUTES.***
Cook is my "superior." Because of the cost of the Stunted Growth deal, I need him to sign off on it--
Park Station
2 3
--and FAST because I HAVE to formalize the deal BEFORE the show.
I make a beeline for Cook's office. Nick, my radio guy, finds me first.
BOSS, WE GOTTA PROBLEM.

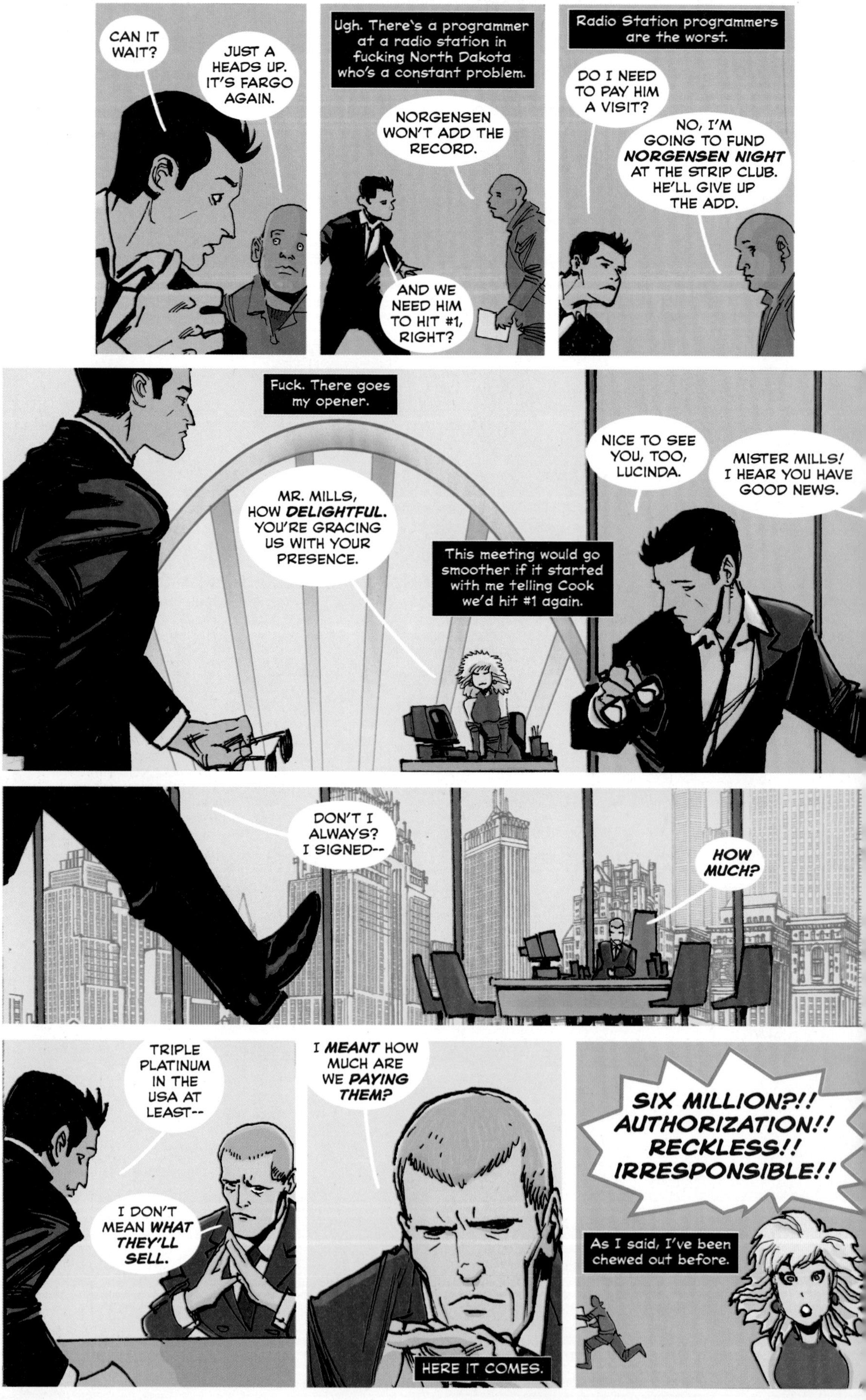
CAN IT WAIT?
JUST A HEADS UP. IT'S FARGO AGAIN.
Ugh. There's a programmer at a radio station in fucking North Dakota who's a constant problem.
NORGENSEN WON'T ADD THE RECORD.
AND WE NEED HIM TO HIT #1, RIGHT?
Radio Station programmers are the worst.
DO I NEED TO PAY HIM A VISIT?
NO, I'M GOING TO FUND NORGENSEN NIGHT AT THE STRIP CLUB. HE'LL GIVE UP THE ADD.
Fuck. There goes my opener.
MR. MILLS, HOW DELIGHTFUL. YOU'RE GRACING US WITH YOUR PRESENCE.
This meeting would go smoother if it started with me telling Cook we'd hit #1 again.
NICE TO SEE YOU, TOO, LUCINDA.
MISTER MILLS! I HEAR YOU HAVE GOOD NEWS.
DON'T I ALWAYS? I SIGNED--
HOW MUCH?
TRIPLE PLATINUM IN THE USA AT LEAST--
I DON'T MEAN WHAT THEY'LL SELL.
I MEANT HOW MUCH ARE WE PAYING THEM?
HERE IT COMES.
SIX MILLION?!! AUTHORIZATION!! RECKLESS!! IRRESPONSIBLE!!
As I said, I've been chewed out before.

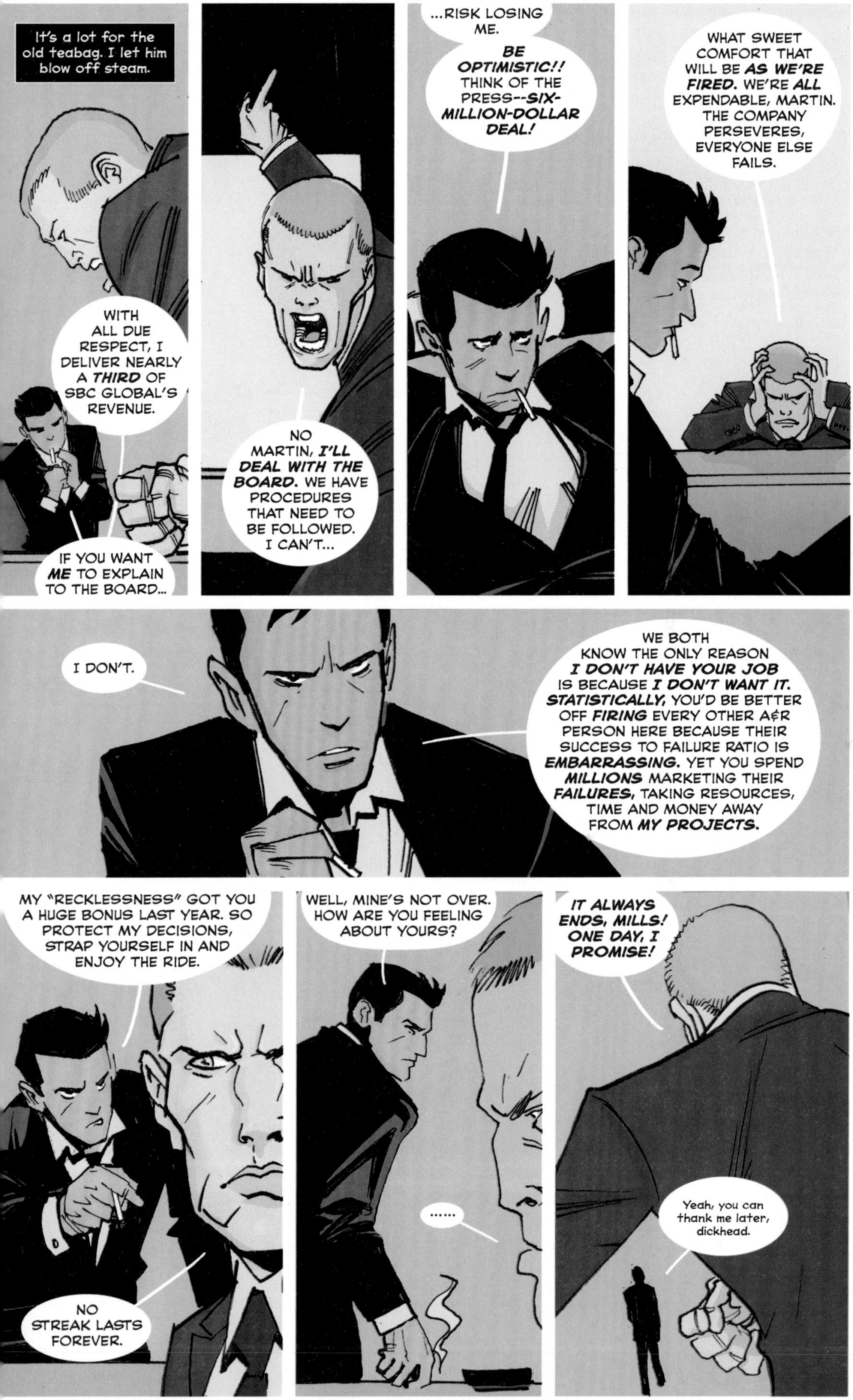
It's a lot for the old teabag. I let him blow off steam.
WITH ALL DUE RESPECT, I DELIVER NEARLY A *THIRD* OF SBC GLOBAL'S REVENUE.
IF YOU WANT *ME* TO EXPLAIN TO THE BOARD...
NO MARTIN, *I'LL DEAL WITH THE BOARD.* WE HAVE PROCEDURES THAT NEED TO BE FOLLOWED. I CAN'T...
...RISK LOSING ME.
BE OPTIMISTIC!! THINK OF THE PRESS--*SIX-MILLION-DOLLAR DEAL!*
WHAT SWEET COMFORT THAT WILL BE *AS WE'RE FIRED.* WE'RE *ALL* EXPENDABLE, MARTIN. THE COMPANY PERSEVERES, EVERYONE ELSE FAILS.
I DON'T.
WE BOTH KNOW THE ONLY REASON *I DON'T HAVE YOUR JOB* IS BECAUSE *I DON'T WANT IT. STATISTICALLY,* YOU'D BE BETTER OFF *FIRING* EVERY OTHER A&R PERSON HERE BECAUSE THEIR SUCCESS TO FAILURE RATIO IS *EMBARRASSING.* YET YOU SPEND *MILLIONS* MARKETING THEIR *FAILURES,* TAKING RESOURCES, TIME AND MONEY AWAY FROM *MY PROJECTS.*
MY "RECKLESSNESS" GOT YOU A HUGE BONUS LAST YEAR. SO PROTECT MY DECISIONS, STRAP YOURSELF IN AND ENJOY THE RIDE.
NO STREAK LASTS FOREVER.
WELL, MINE'S NOT OVER. HOW ARE YOU FEELING ABOUT YOURS?
......
IT ALWAYS ENDS, MILLS! ONE DAY, I PROMISE!
Yeah, you can thank me later, dickhead.

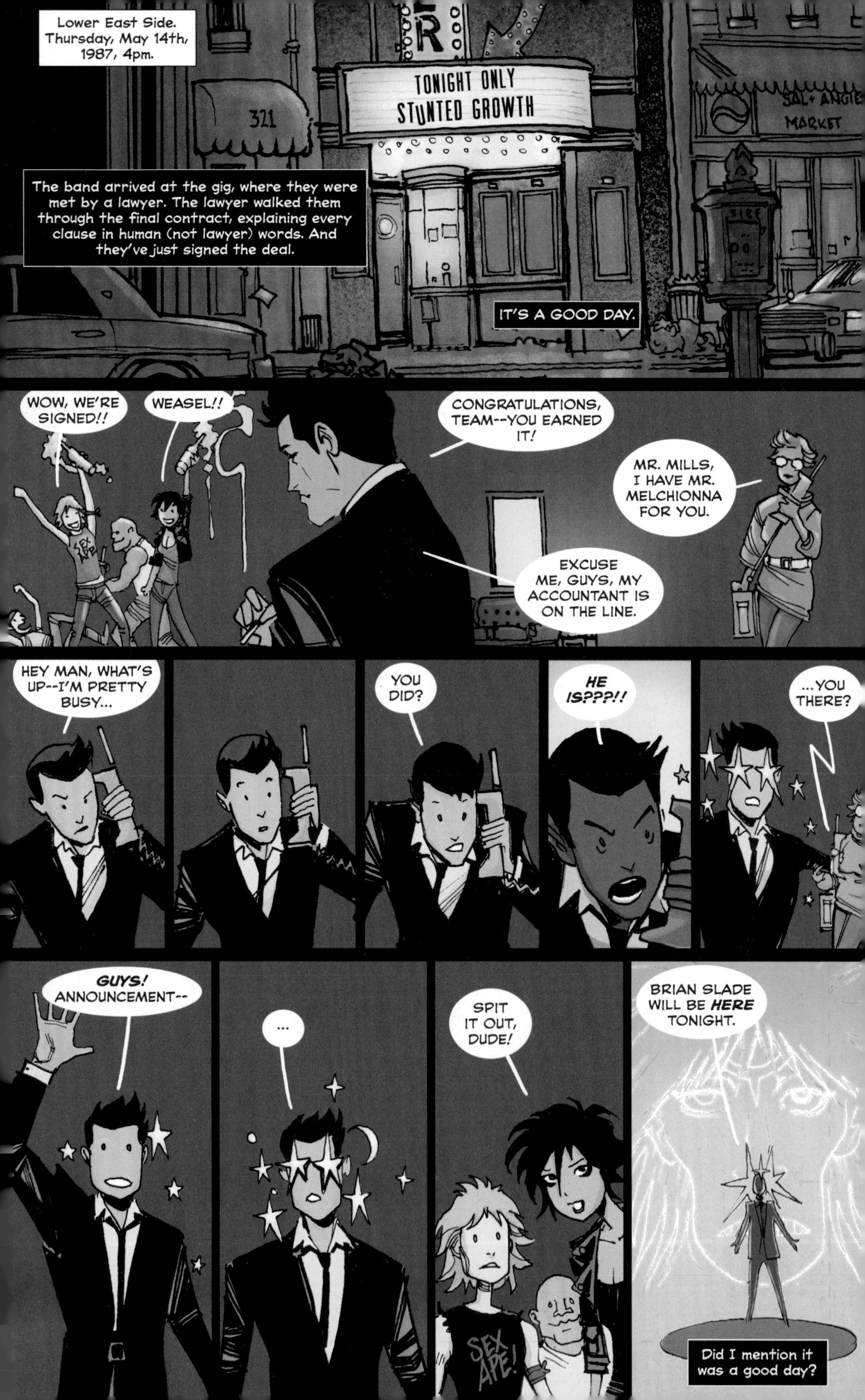

Lower East Side. Thursday, May 14th, 1987, 4pm.
TONIGHT ONLY STUNTED GROWTH
321
SAL + ANGIE MARKET
The band arrived at the gig, where they were met by a lawyer. The lawyer walked them through the final contract, explaining every clause in human (not lawyer) words. And they've just signed the deal.
IT'S A GOOD DAY.
WOW, WE'RE SIGNED!!
WEASEL!!
CONGRATULATIONS, TEAM--YOU EARNED IT!
MR. MILLS, I HAVE MR. MELCHIONNA FOR YOU.
EXCUSE ME, GUYS, MY ACCOUNTANT IS ON THE LINE.
SEX APE
HEY MAN, WHAT'S UP--I'M PRETTY BUSY...
YOU DID?
HE IS???!!
...YOU THERE?
GUYS! ANNOUNCEMENT--
...
SPIT IT OUT, DUDE!
SEX APE!
BRIAN SLADE WILL BE HERE TONIGHT.
Did I mention it was a good day?

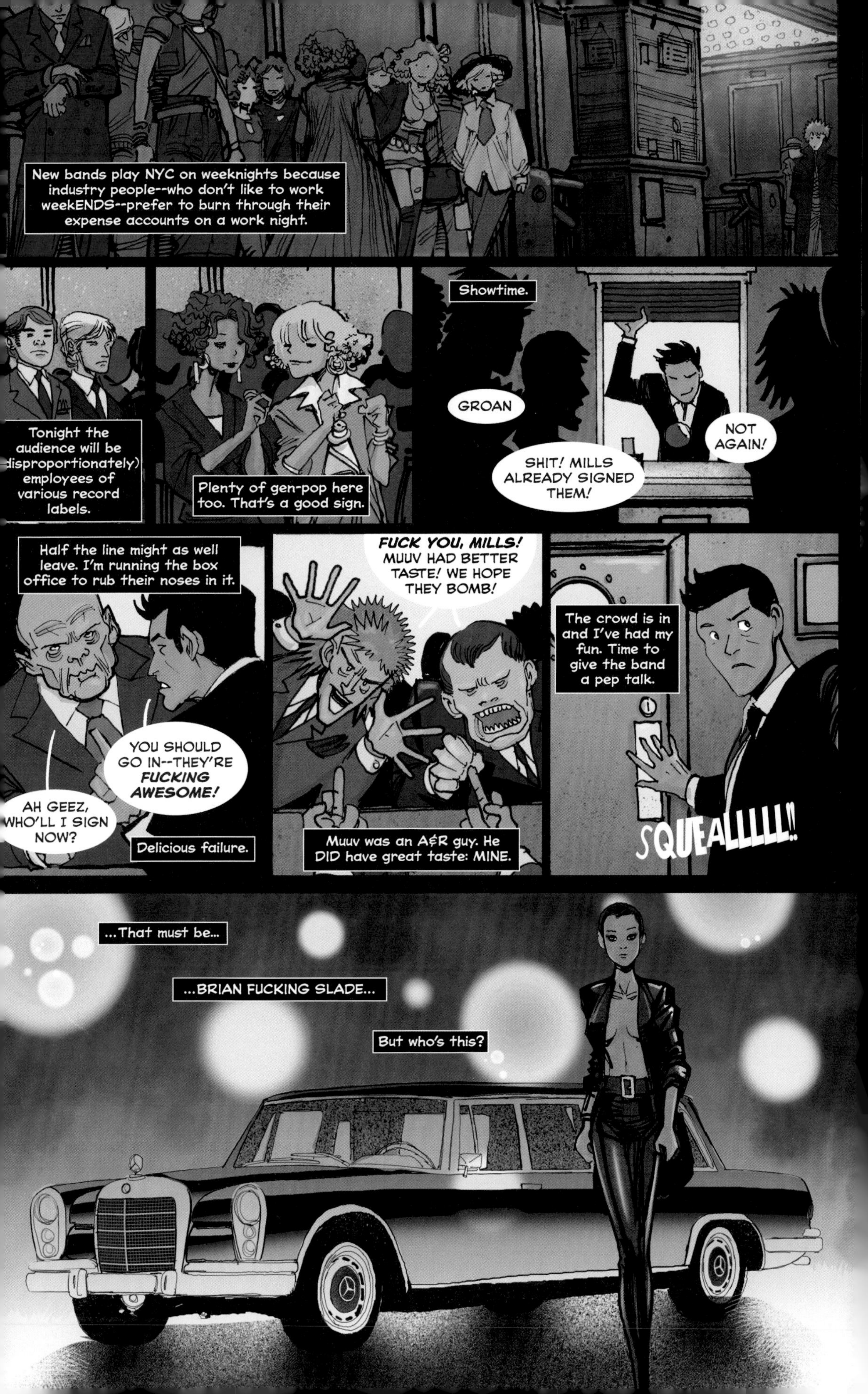
New bands play NYC on weeknights because industry people--who don't like to work weekENDS--prefer to burn through their expense accounts on a work night.
Tonight the audience will be (disproportionately) employees of various record labels.
Plenty of gen-pop here too. That's a good sign.
Showtime.
GROAN
SHIT! MILLS ALREADY SIGNED THEM!
NOT AGAIN!
Half the line might as well leave. I'm running the box office to rub their noses in it.
YOU SHOULD GO IN--THEY'RE FUCKING AWESOME!
AH GEEZ, WHO'LL I SIGN NOW?
Delicious failure.
FUCK YOU, MILLS! MUUV HAD BETTER TASTE! WE HOPE THEY BOMB!
Muuv was an A&R guy. He DID have great taste: MINE.
The crowd is in and I've had my fun. Time to give the band a pep talk.
SQUEALLLLL!!
...That must be...
...BRIAN FUCKING SLADE...
But who's this?

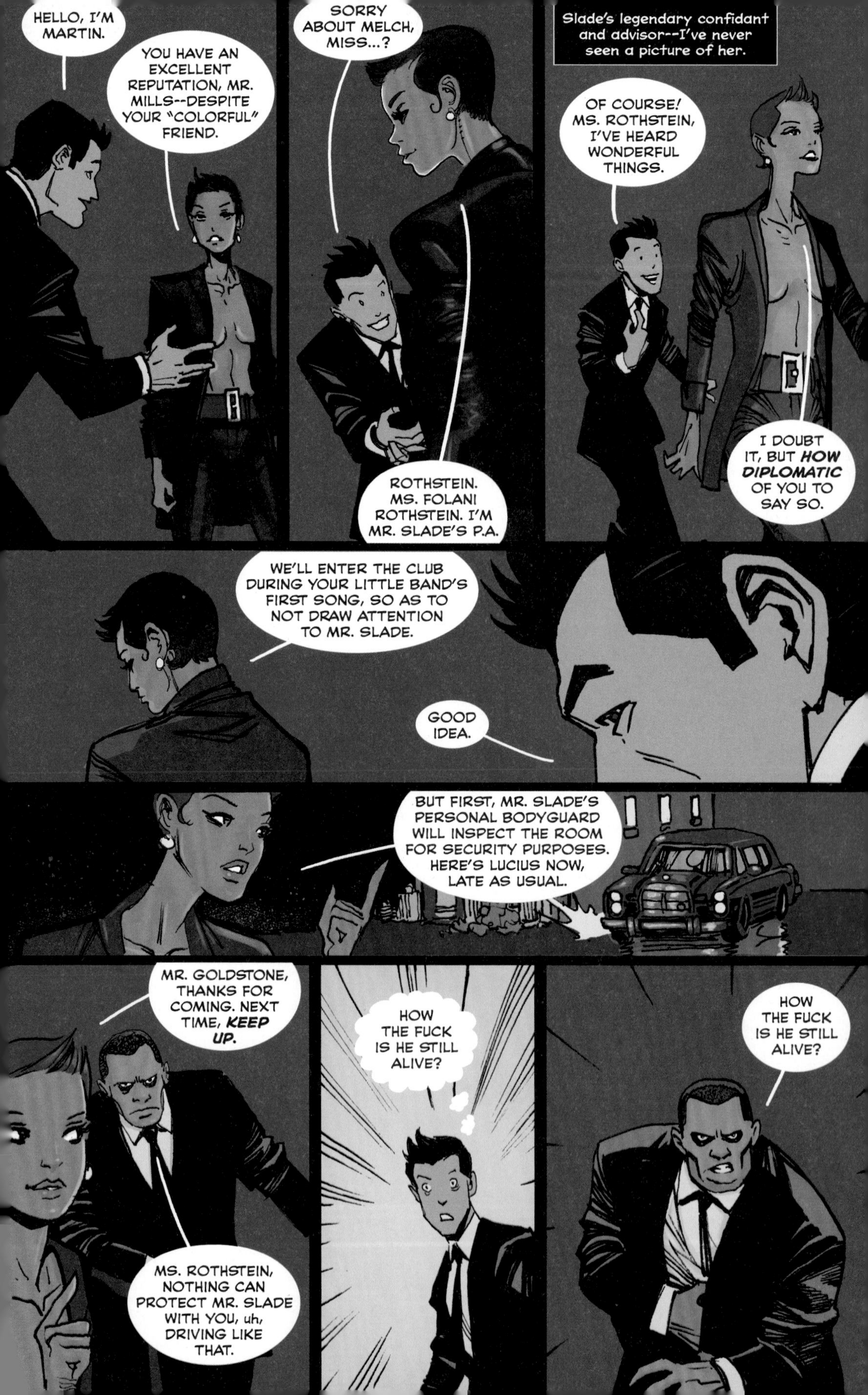

HELLO, I'M MARTIN.
YOU HAVE AN EXCELLENT REPUTATION, MR. MILLS--DESPITE YOUR "COLORFUL" FRIEND.
SORRY ABOUT MELCH, MISS...?
ROTHSTEIN. MS. FOLANI ROTHSTEIN. I'M MR. SLADE'S P.A.
Slade's legendary confidant and advisor--I've never seen a picture of her.
OF COURSE! MS. ROTHSTEIN, I'VE HEARD WONDERFUL THINGS.
I DOUBT IT, BUT HOW DIPLOMATIC OF YOU TO SAY SO.
WE'LL ENTER THE CLUB DURING YOUR LITTLE BAND'S FIRST SONG, SO AS TO NOT DRAW ATTENTION TO MR. SLADE.
GOOD IDEA.
BUT FIRST, MR. SLADE'S PERSONAL BODYGUARD WILL INSPECT THE ROOM FOR SECURITY PURPOSES. HERE'S LUCIUS NOW, LATE AS USUAL.
MR. GOLDSTONE, THANKS FOR COMING. NEXT TIME, KEEP UP.
MS. ROTHSTEIN, NOTHING CAN PROTECT MR. SLADE WITH YOU, uh, DRIVING LIKE THAT.
HOW THE FUCK IS HE STILL ALIVE?
HOW THE FUCK IS HE STILL ALIVE?

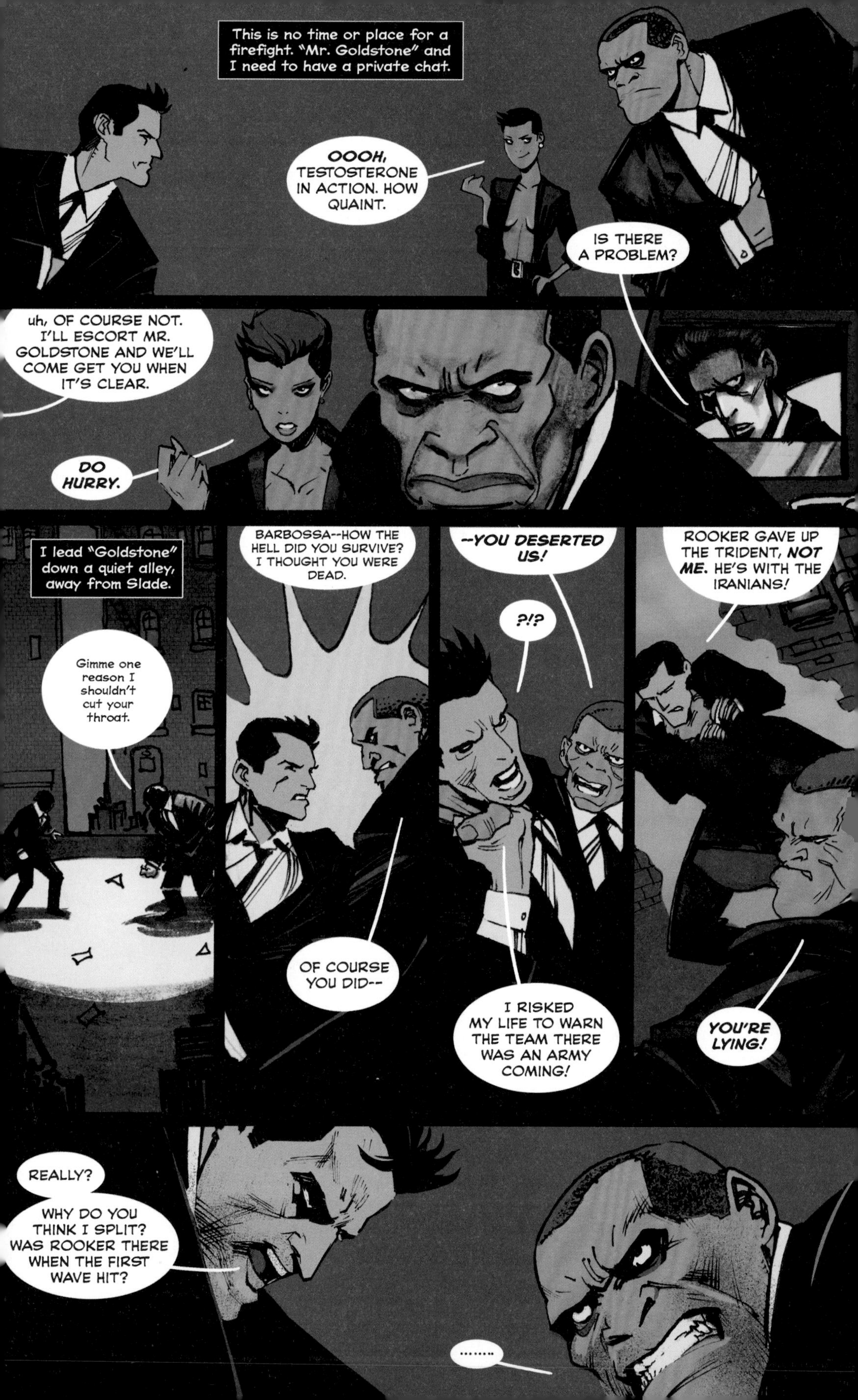
This is no time or place for a firefight. "Mr. Goldstone" and I need to have a private chat.
OOOH, TESTOSTERONE IN ACTION. HOW QUAINT.
IS THERE A PROBLEM?
uh, OF COURSE NOT. I'LL ESCORT MR. GOLDSTONE AND WE'LL COME GET YOU WHEN IT'S CLEAR.
DO HURRY.
I lead "Goldstone" down a quiet alley, away from Slade.
Gimme one reason I shouldn't cut your throat.
BARBOSSA--HOW THE HELL DID YOU SURVIVE? I THOUGHT YOU WERE DEAD.
OF COURSE YOU DID--
--YOU DESERTED US!
?!?
I RISKED MY LIFE TO WARN THE TEAM THERE WAS AN ARMY COMING!
ROOKER GAVE UP THE TRIDENT, NOT ME. HE'S WITH THE IRANIANS!
YOU'RE LYING!
REALLY?
WHY DO YOU THINK I SPLIT? WAS ROOKER THERE WHEN THE FIRST WAVE HIT?
....

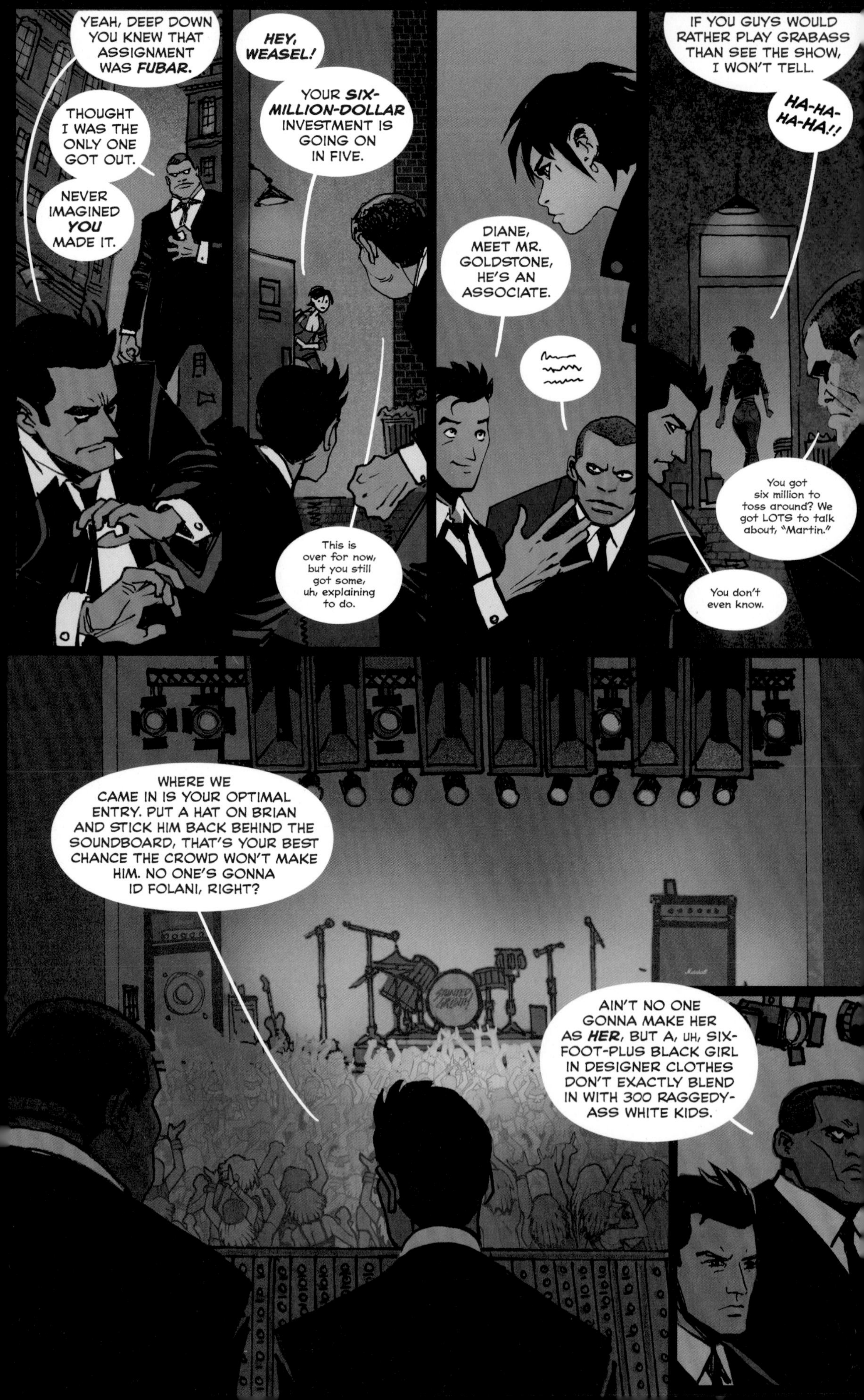
YEAH, DEEP DOWN YOU KNEW THAT ASSIGNMENT WAS FUBAR.
THOUGHT I WAS THE ONLY ONE GOT OUT.
NEVER IMAGINED YOU MADE IT.
HEY, WEASEL!
YOUR SIX-MILLION-DOLLAR INVESTMENT IS GOING ON IN FIVE.
This is over for now, but you still got some, uh, explaining to do.
DIANE, MEET MR. GOLDSTONE, HE'S AN ASSOCIATE.
IF YOU GUYS WOULD RATHER PLAY GRABASS THAN SEE THE SHOW, I WON'T TELL.
HA-HA-HA-HA!!
You got six million to toss around? We got LOTS to talk about, "Martin."
You don't even know.
WHERE WE CAME IN IS YOUR OPTIMAL ENTRY. PUT A HAT ON BRIAN AND STICK HIM BACK BEHIND THE SOUNDBOARD, THAT'S YOUR BEST CHANCE THE CROWD WON'T MAKE HIM. NO ONE'S GONNA ID FOLANI, RIGHT?
AIN'T NO ONE GONNA MAKE HER AS HER, BUT A, UH, SIX-FOOT-PLUS BLACK GIRL IN DESIGNER CLOTHES DON'T EXACTLY BLEND IN WITH 300 RAGGEDY-ASS WHITE KIDS.

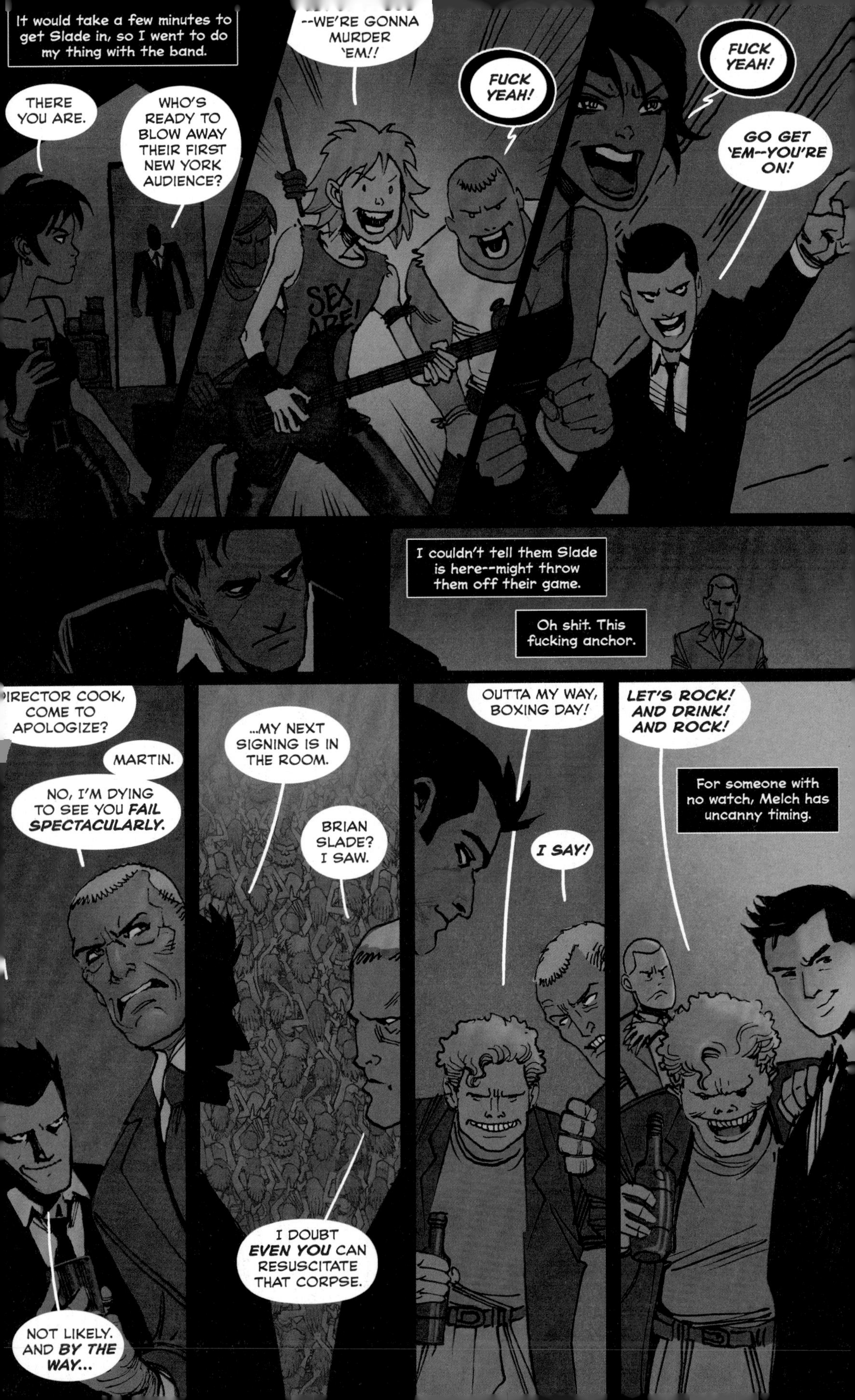
It would take a few minutes to get Slade in, so I went to do my thing with the band.
THERE YOU ARE.
WHO'S READY TO BLOW AWAY THEIR FIRST NEW YORK AUDIENCE?
--WE'RE GONNA MURDER 'EM!!
FUCK YEAH!
FUCK YEAH!
GO GET 'EM--YOU'RE ON!
I couldn't tell them Slade is here--might throw them off their game.
Oh shit. This fucking anchor.
IRECTOR COOK, COME TO APOLOGIZE?
MARTIN.
NO, I'M DYING TO SEE YOU FAIL SPECTACULARLY.
NOT LIKELY. AND BY THE WAY...
...MY NEXT SIGNING IS IN THE ROOM.
BRIAN SLADE? I SAW.
I DOUBT EVEN YOU CAN RESUSCITATE THAT CORPSE.
OUTTA MY WAY, BOXING DAY!
I SAY!
LET'S ROCK! AND DRINK! AND ROCK!
For someone with no watch, Melch has uncanny timing.

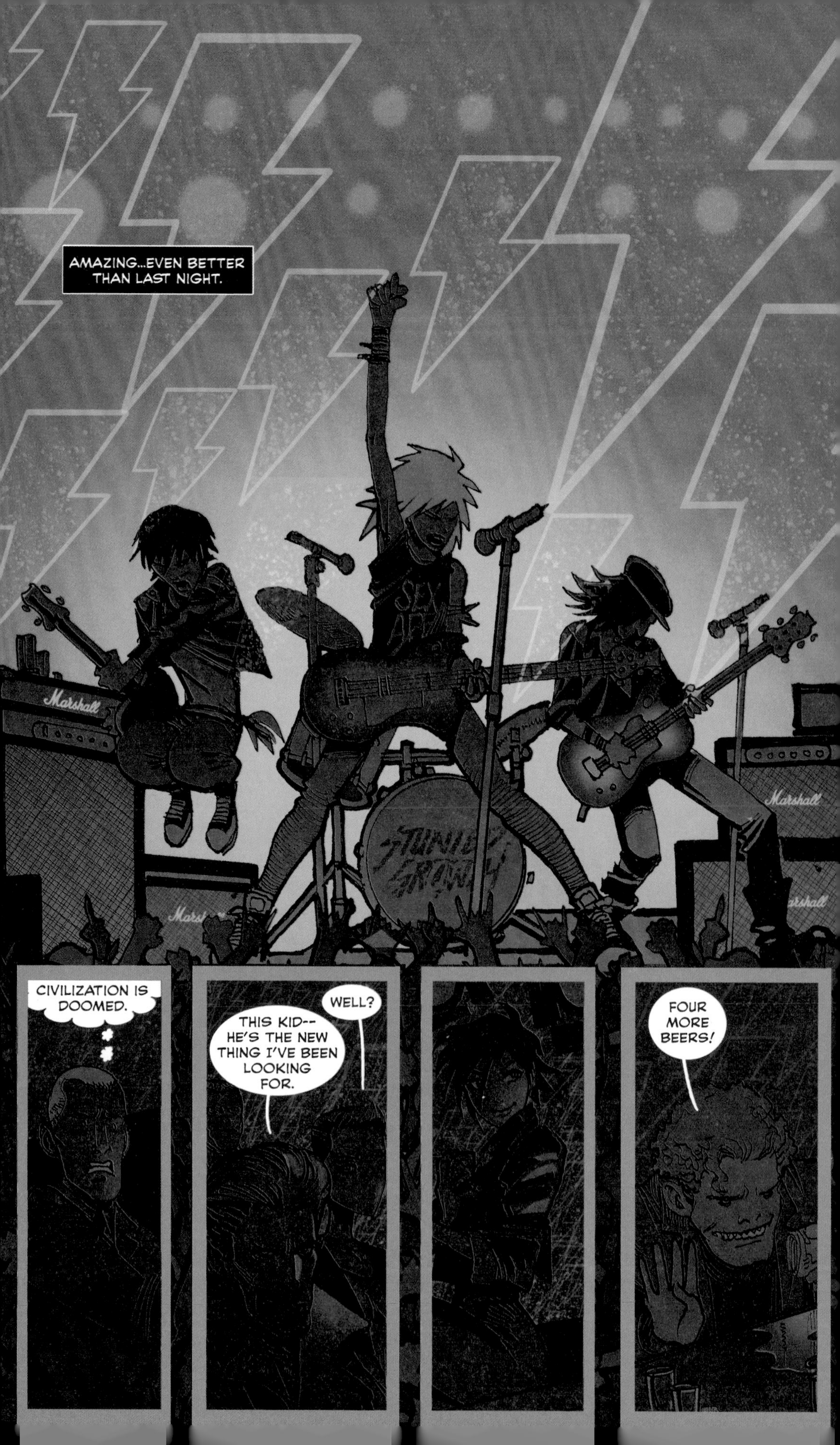

AMAZING...EVEN BETTER THAN LAST NIGHT.
CIVILIZATION IS DOOMED.
WELL?
THIS KID-- HE'S THE NEW THING I'VE BEEN LOOKING FOR.
FOUR MORE BEERS!

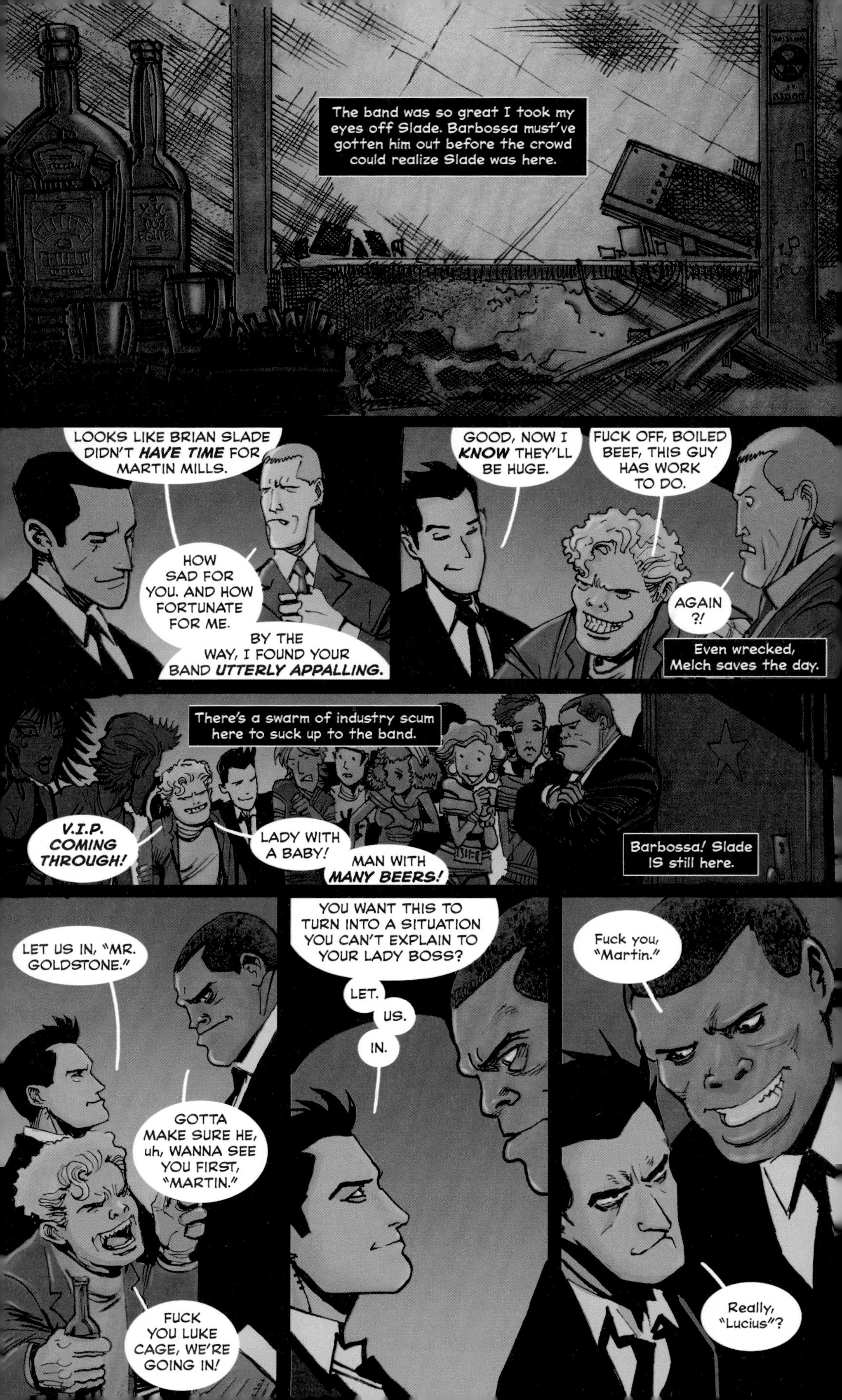

The band was so great I took my eyes off Slade. Barbossa must've gotten him out before the crowd could realize Slade was here.
LOOKS LIKE BRIAN SLADE DIDN'T HAVE TIME FOR MARTIN MILLS.
HOW SAD FOR YOU. AND HOW FORTUNATE FOR ME.
BY THE WAY, I FOUND YOUR BAND UTTERLY APPALLING.
GOOD, NOW I KNOW THEY'LL BE HUGE.
FUCK OFF, BOILED BEEF, THIS GUY HAS WORK TO DO.
AGAIN ?!
Even wrecked, Melch saves the day.
There's a swarm of industry scum here to suck up to the band.
V.I.P. COMING THROUGH!
LADY WITH A BABY!
MAN WITH MANY BEERS!
Barbossa! Slade IS still here.
LET US IN, "MR. GOLDSTONE."
GOTTA MAKE SURE HE, uh, WANNA SEE YOU FIRST, "MARTIN."
FUCK YOU LUKE CAGE, WE'RE GOING IN!
YOU WANT THIS TO TURN INTO A SITUATION YOU CAN'T EXPLAIN TO YOUR LADY BOSS?
LET.
US.
IN.
Fuck you, "Martin."
Really, "Lucius"?

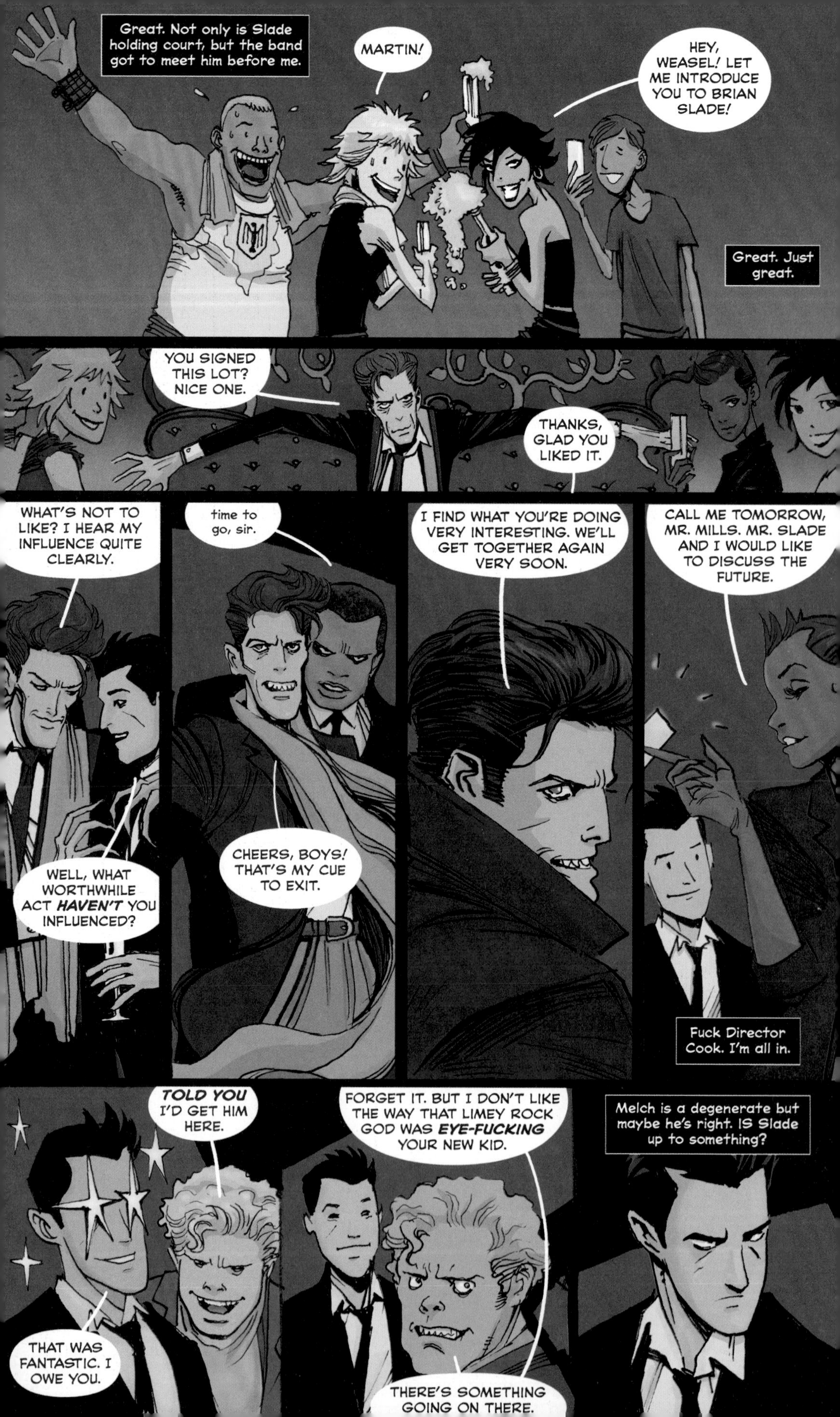

Great. Not only is Slade holding court, but the band got to meet him before me.
MARTIN!
HEY, WEASEL! LET ME INTRODUCE YOU TO BRIAN SLADE!
Great. Just great.
YOU SIGNED THIS LOT? NICE ONE.
THANKS, GLAD YOU LIKED IT.
WHAT'S NOT TO LIKE? I HEAR MY INFLUENCE QUITE CLEARLY.
WELL, WHAT WORTHWHILE ACT ***HAVEN'T*** YOU INFLUENCED?
time to go, sir.
CHEERS, BOYS! THAT'S MY CUE TO EXIT.
I FIND WHAT YOU'RE DOING VERY INTERESTING. WE'LL GET TOGETHER AGAIN VERY SOON.
CALL ME TOMORROW, MR. MILLS. MR. SLADE AND I WOULD LIKE TO DISCUSS THE FUTURE.
Fuck Director Cook. I'm all in.
THAT WAS FANTASTIC. I OWE YOU.
TOLD YOU I'D GET HIM HERE.
FORGET IT. BUT I DON'T LIKE THE WAY THAT LIMEY ROCK GOD WAS ***EYE-FUCKING*** YOUR NEW KID.
THERE'S SOMETHING GOING ON THERE.
Melch is a degenerate but maybe he's right. IS Slade up to something?

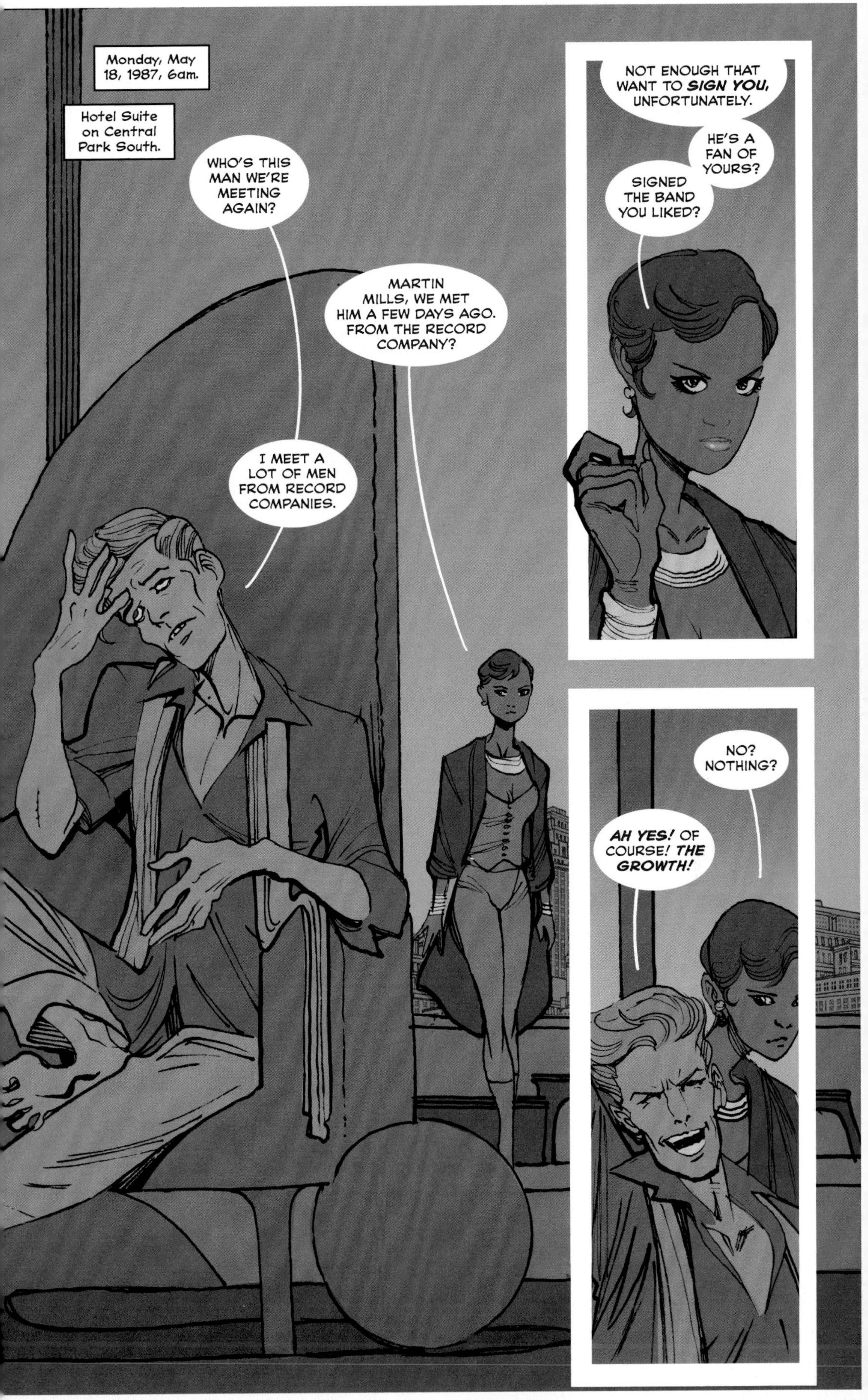
Monday, May 18, 1987, 6am.
Hotel Suite on Central Park South.
WHO'S THIS MAN WE'RE MEETING AGAIN?
MARTIN MILLS, WE MET HIM A FEW DAYS AGO. FROM THE RECORD COMPANY?
I MEET A LOT OF MEN FROM RECORD COMPANIES.
NOT ENOUGH THAT WANT TO *SIGN YOU,* UNFORTUNATELY.
HE'S A FAN OF YOURS?
SIGNED THE BAND YOU LIKED?
NO? NOTHING?
AH YES! OF COURSE! *THE GROWTH!*

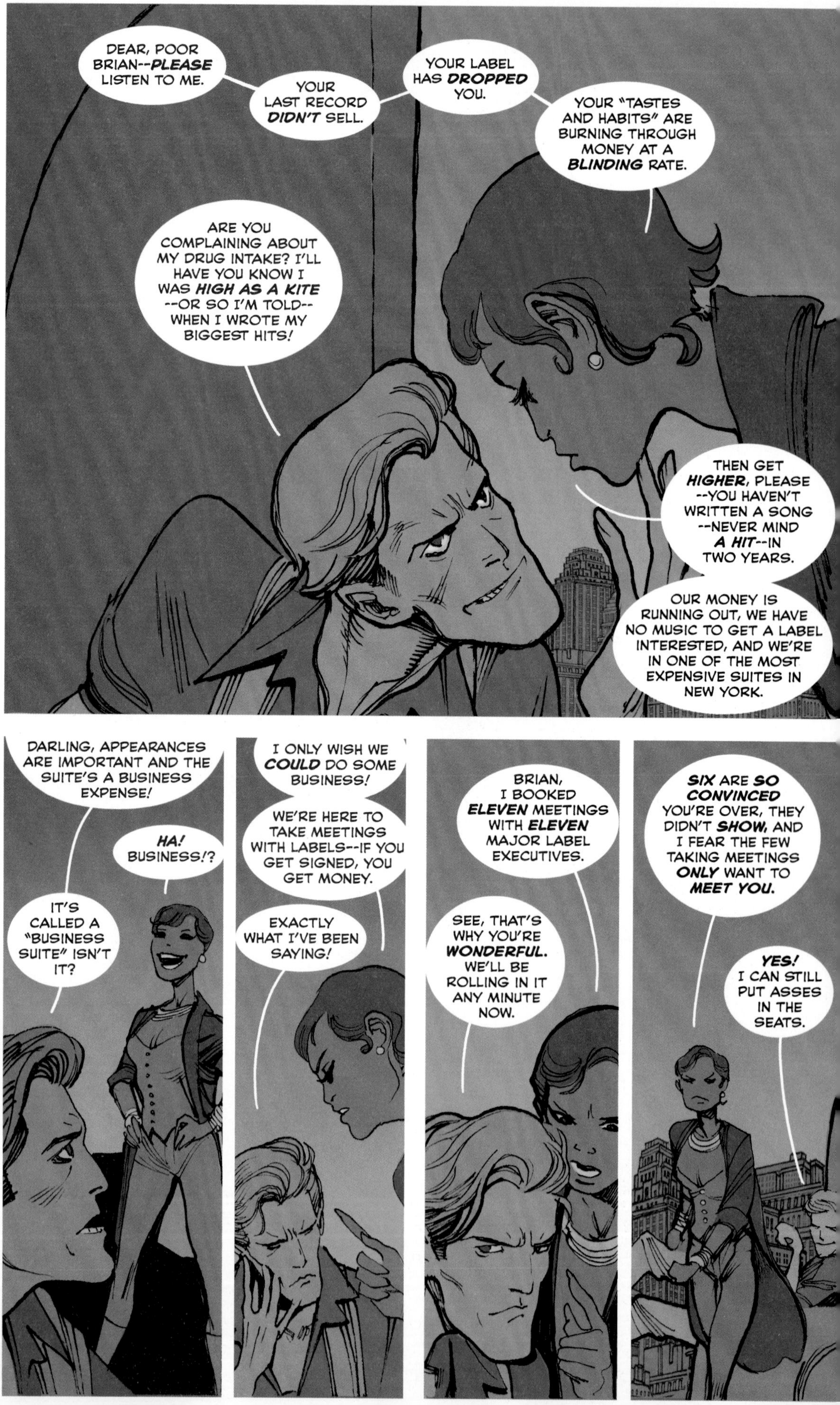
DEAR, POOR BRIAN--PLEASE LISTEN TO ME.
YOUR LAST RECORD DIDN'T SELL.
YOUR LABEL HAS DROPPED YOU.
YOUR "TASTES AND HABITS" ARE BURNING THROUGH MONEY AT A BLINDING RATE.
ARE YOU COMPLAINING ABOUT MY DRUG INTAKE? I'LL HAVE YOU KNOW I WAS HIGH AS A KITE --OR SO I'M TOLD-- WHEN I WROTE MY BIGGEST HITS!
THEN GET HIGHER, PLEASE --YOU HAVEN'T WRITTEN A SONG --NEVER MIND A HIT--IN TWO YEARS.
OUR MONEY IS RUNNING OUT, WE HAVE NO MUSIC TO GET A LABEL INTERESTED, AND WE'RE IN ONE OF THE MOST EXPENSIVE SUITES IN NEW YORK.
DARLING, APPEARANCES ARE IMPORTANT AND THE SUITE'S A BUSINESS EXPENSE!
HA! BUSINESS!?
IT'S CALLED A "BUSINESS SUITE" ISN'T IT?
I ONLY WISH WE COULD DO SOME BUSINESS!
WE'RE HERE TO TAKE MEETINGS WITH LABELS--IF YOU GET SIGNED, YOU GET MONEY.
EXACTLY WHAT I'VE BEEN SAYING!
BRIAN, I BOOKED ELEVEN MEETINGS WITH ELEVEN MAJOR LABEL EXECUTIVES.
SEE, THAT'S WHY YOU'RE WONDERFUL. WE'LL BE ROLLING IN IT ANY MINUTE NOW.
SIX ARE SO CONVINCED YOU'RE OVER, THEY DIDN'T SHOW, AND I FEAR THE FEW TAKING MEETINGS ONLY WANT TO MEET YOU.
YES! I CAN STILL PUT ASSES IN THE SEATS.

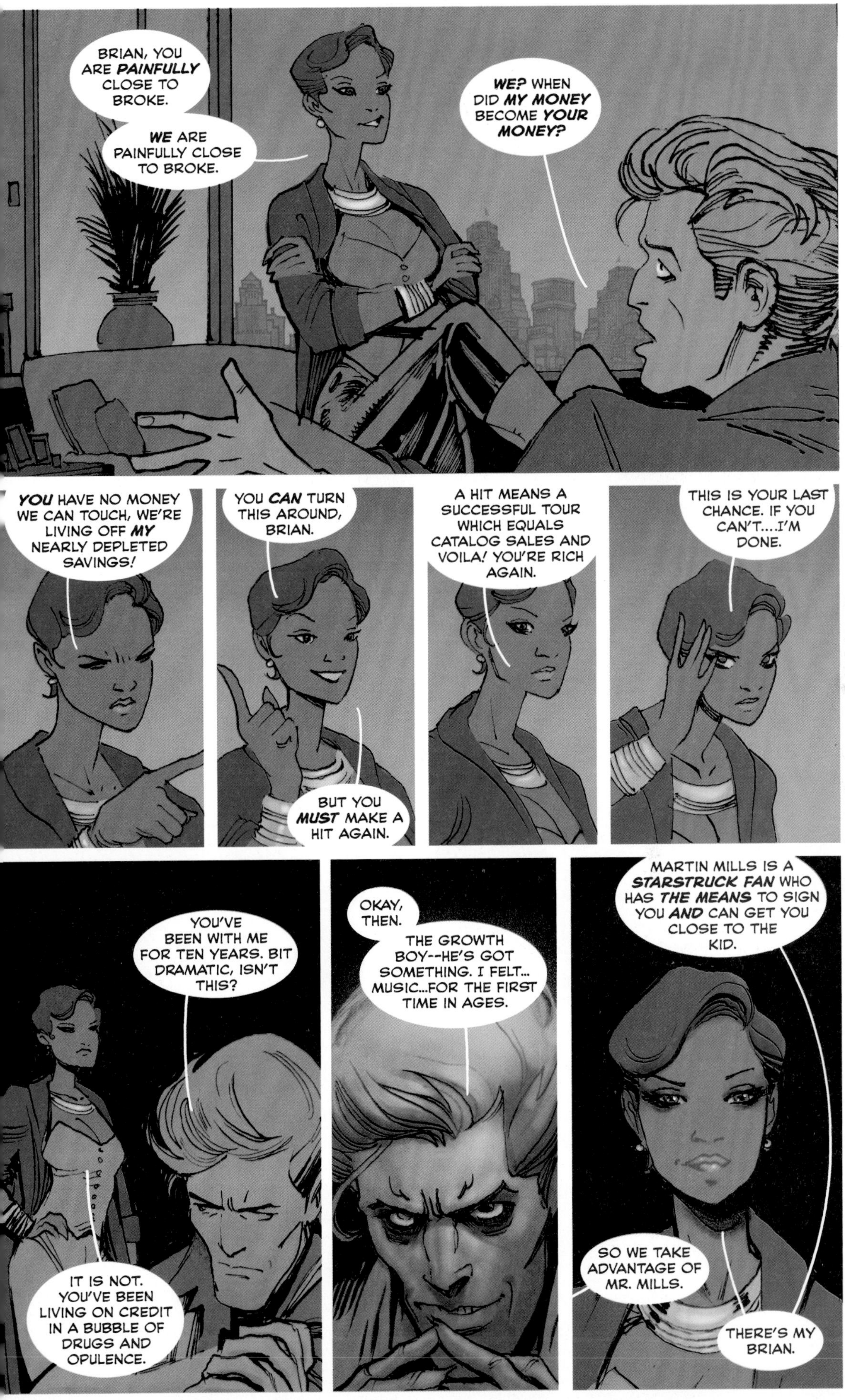
BRIAN, YOU ARE PAINFULLY CLOSE TO BROKE.
WE ARE PAINFULLY CLOSE TO BROKE.
WE? WHEN DID MY MONEY BECOME YOUR MONEY?
YOU HAVE NO MONEY WE CAN TOUCH, WE'RE LIVING OFF MY NEARLY DEPLETED SAVINGS!
YOU CAN TURN THIS AROUND, BRIAN.
BUT YOU MUST MAKE A HIT AGAIN.
A HIT MEANS A SUCCESSFUL TOUR WHICH EQUALS CATALOG SALES AND VOILA! YOU'RE RICH AGAIN.
THIS IS YOUR LAST CHANCE. IF YOU CAN'T....I'M DONE.
YOU'VE BEEN WITH ME FOR TEN YEARS. BIT DRAMATIC, ISN'T THIS?
IT IS NOT. YOU'VE BEEN LIVING ON CREDIT IN A BUBBLE OF DRUGS AND OPULENCE.
OKAY, THEN.
THE GROWTH BOY--HE'S GOT SOMETHING. I FELT... MUSIC...FOR THE FIRST TIME IN AGES.
MARTIN MILLS IS A STARSTRUCK FAN WHO HAS THE MEANS TO SIGN YOU AND CAN GET YOU CLOSE TO THE KID.
SO WE TAKE ADVANTAGE OF MR. MILLS.
THERE'S MY BRIAN.

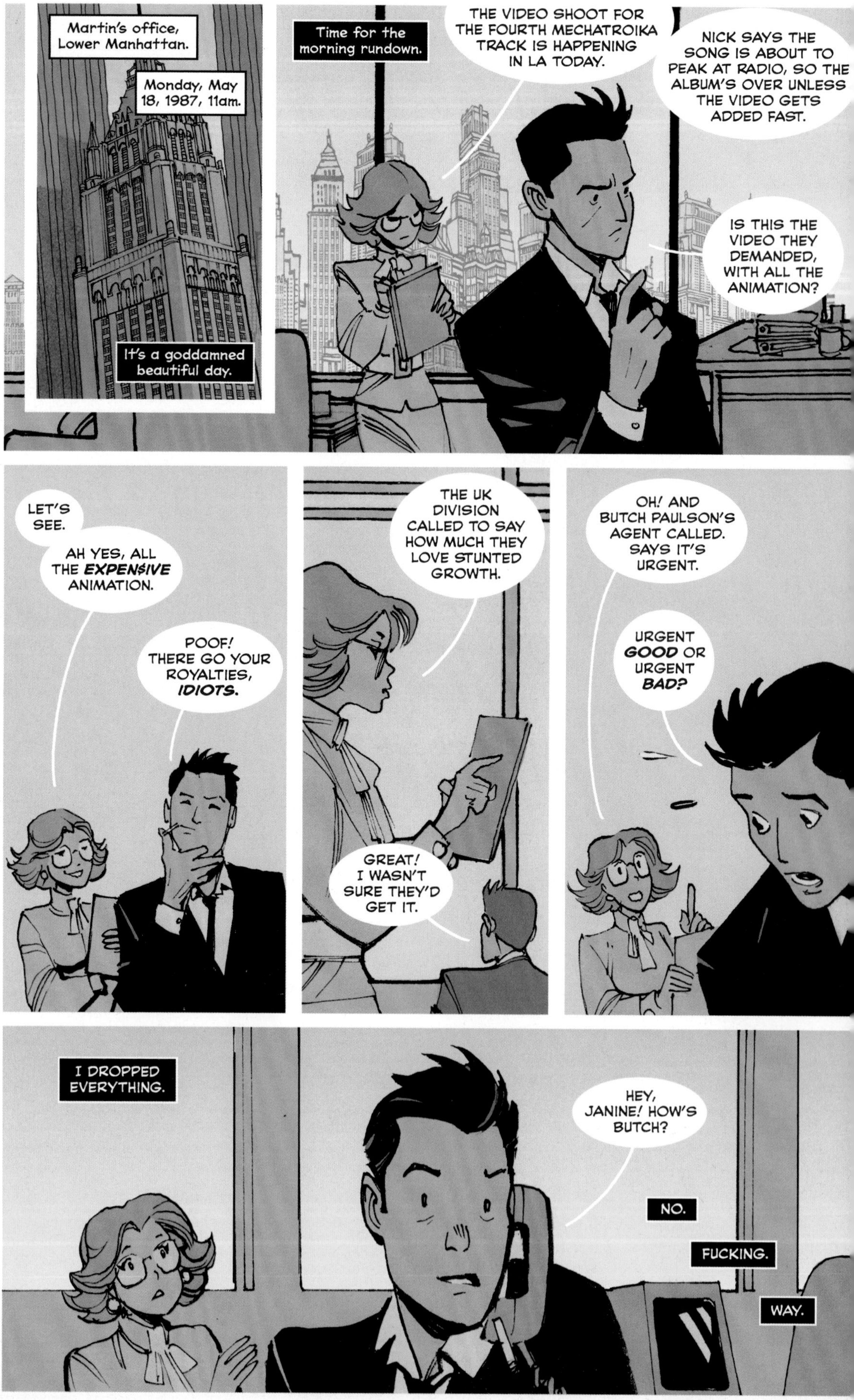
Martin's office, Lower Manhattan.
Monday, May 18, 1987, 11am.
It's a goddamned beautiful day.
Time for the morning rundown.
THE VIDEO SHOOT FOR THE FOURTH MECHATROIKA TRACK IS HAPPENING IN LA TODAY.
NICK SAYS THE SONG IS ABOUT TO PEAK AT RADIO, SO THE ALBUM'S OVER UNLESS THE VIDEO GETS ADDED FAST.
IS THIS THE VIDEO THEY DEMANDED, WITH ALL THE ANIMATION?
LET'S SEE.
AH YES, ALL THE *EXPEN$IVE* ANIMATION.
POOF! THERE GO YOUR ROYALTIES, *IDIOTS.*
THE UK DIVISION CALLED TO SAY HOW MUCH THEY LOVE STUNTED GROWTH.
GREAT! I WASN'T SURE THEY'D GET IT.
OH! AND BUTCH PAULSON'S AGENT CALLED. SAYS IT'S URGENT.
URGENT *GOOD* OR URGENT *BAD?*
I DROPPED EVERYTHING.
HEY, JANINE! HOW'S BUTCH?
NO.
FUCKING.
WAY.

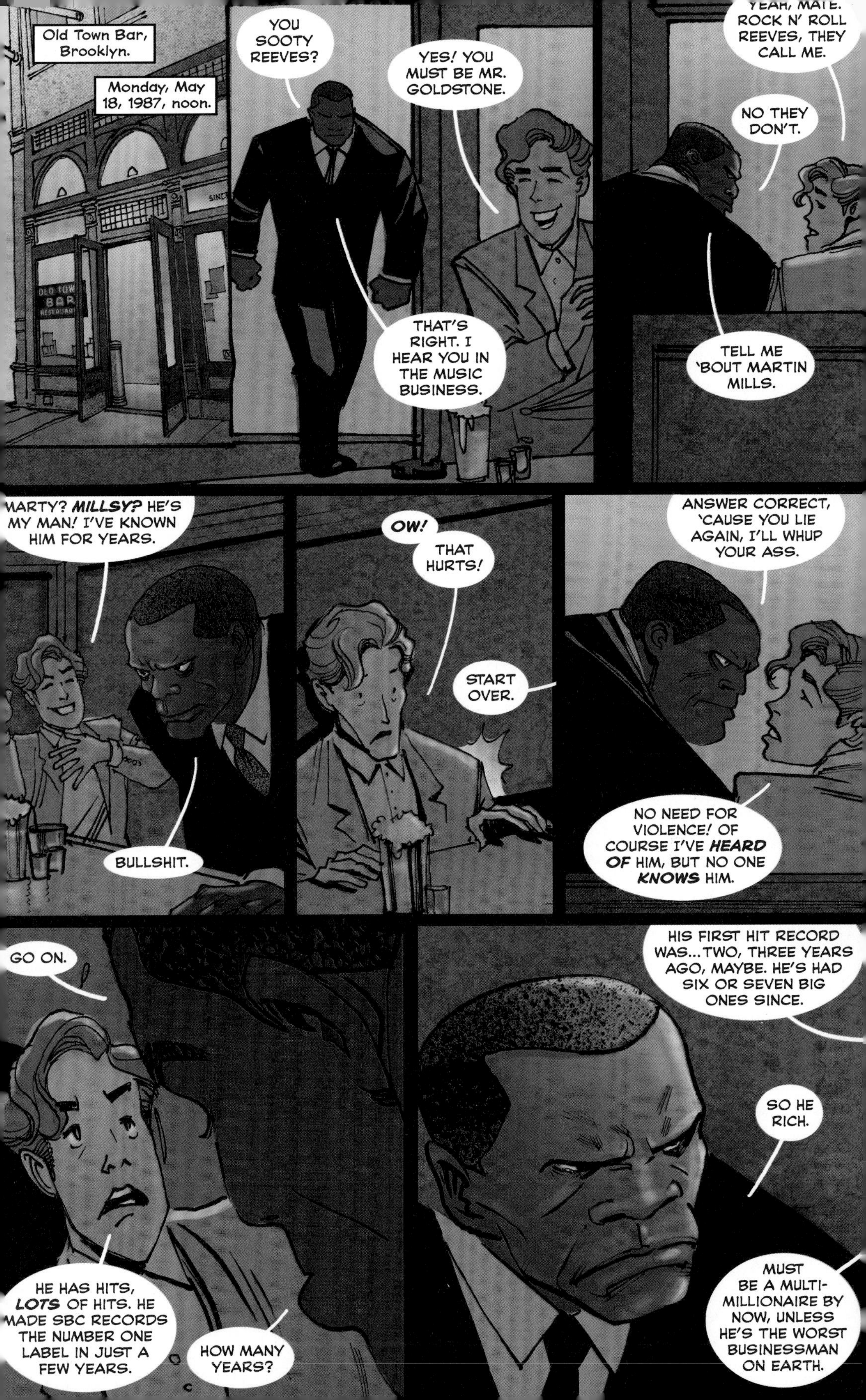
Old Town Bar, Brooklyn.
Monday, May 18, 1987, noon.
OLD TOWN BAR RESTAURANT
YOU SOOTY REEVES?
YES! YOU MUST BE MR. GOLDSTONE.
THAT'S RIGHT. I HEAR YOU IN THE MUSIC BUSINESS.
YEAH, MATE. ROCK N' ROLL REEVES, THEY CALL ME.
NO THEY DON'T.
TELL ME 'BOUT MARTIN MILLS.
MARTY? MILLSY? HE'S MY MAN! I'VE KNOWN HIM FOR YEARS.
BULLSHIT.
OW!
THAT HURTS!
START OVER.
ANSWER CORRECT, 'CAUSE YOU LIE AGAIN, I'LL WHUP YOUR ASS.
NO NEED FOR VIOLENCE! OF COURSE I'VE HEARD OF HIM, BUT NO ONE KNOWS HIM.
GO ON.
HE HAS HITS, LOTS OF HITS. HE MADE SBC RECORDS THE NUMBER ONE LABEL IN JUST A FEW YEARS.
HOW MANY YEARS?
HIS FIRST HIT RECORD WAS...TWO, THREE YEARS AGO, MAYBE. HE'S HAD SIX OR SEVEN BIG ONES SINCE.
SO HE RICH.
MUST BE A MULTI-MILLIONAIRE BY NOW, UNLESS HE'S THE WORST BUSINESSMAN ON EARTH.

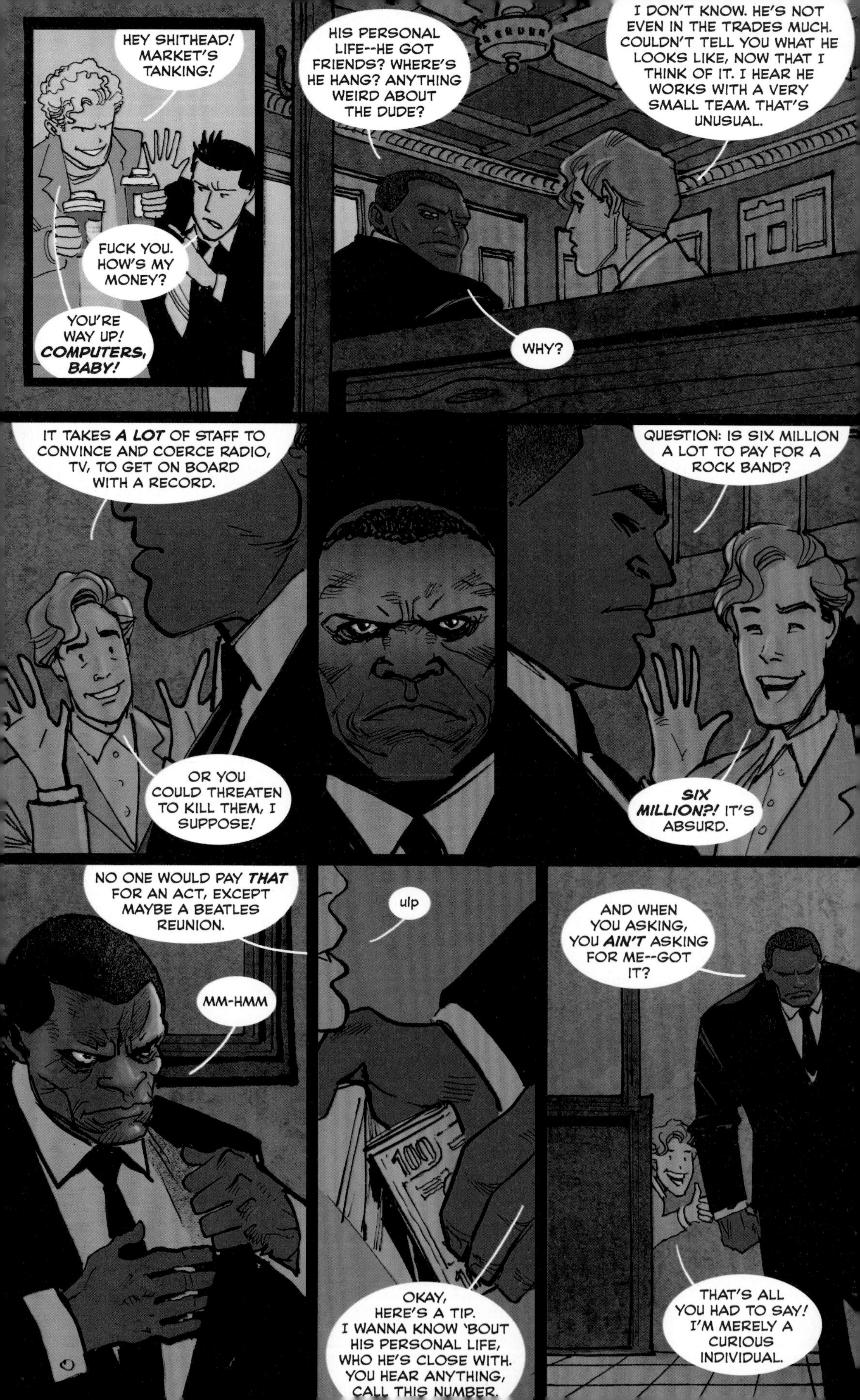
HEY SHITHEAD! MARKET'S TANKING!
FUCK YOU. HOW'S MY MONEY?
YOU'RE WAY UP! COMPUTERS, BABY!
HIS PERSONAL LIFE--HE GOT FRIENDS? WHERE'S HE HANG? ANYTHING WEIRD ABOUT THE DUDE?
I DON'T KNOW. HE'S NOT EVEN IN THE TRADES MUCH. COULDN'T TELL YOU WHAT HE LOOKS LIKE, NOW THAT I THINK OF IT. I HEAR HE WORKS WITH A VERY SMALL TEAM. THAT'S UNUSUAL.
WHY?
IT TAKES A LOT OF STAFF TO CONVINCE AND COERCE RADIO, TV, TO GET ON BOARD WITH A RECORD.
OR YOU COULD THREATEN TO KILL THEM, I SUPPOSE!
QUESTION: IS SIX MILLION A LOT TO PAY FOR A ROCK BAND?
SIX MILLION?! IT'S ABSURD.
NO ONE WOULD PAY THAT FOR AN ACT, EXCEPT MAYBE A BEATLES REUNION.
MM-HMM
ulp
OKAY, HERE'S A TIP. I WANNA KNOW 'BOUT HIS PERSONAL LIFE, WHO HE'S CLOSE WITH. YOU HEAR ANYTHING, CALL THIS NUMBER.
AND WHEN YOU ASKING, YOU AIN'T ASKING FOR ME--GOT IT?
THAT'S ALL YOU HAD TO SAY! I'M MERELY A CURIOUS INDIVIDUAL.

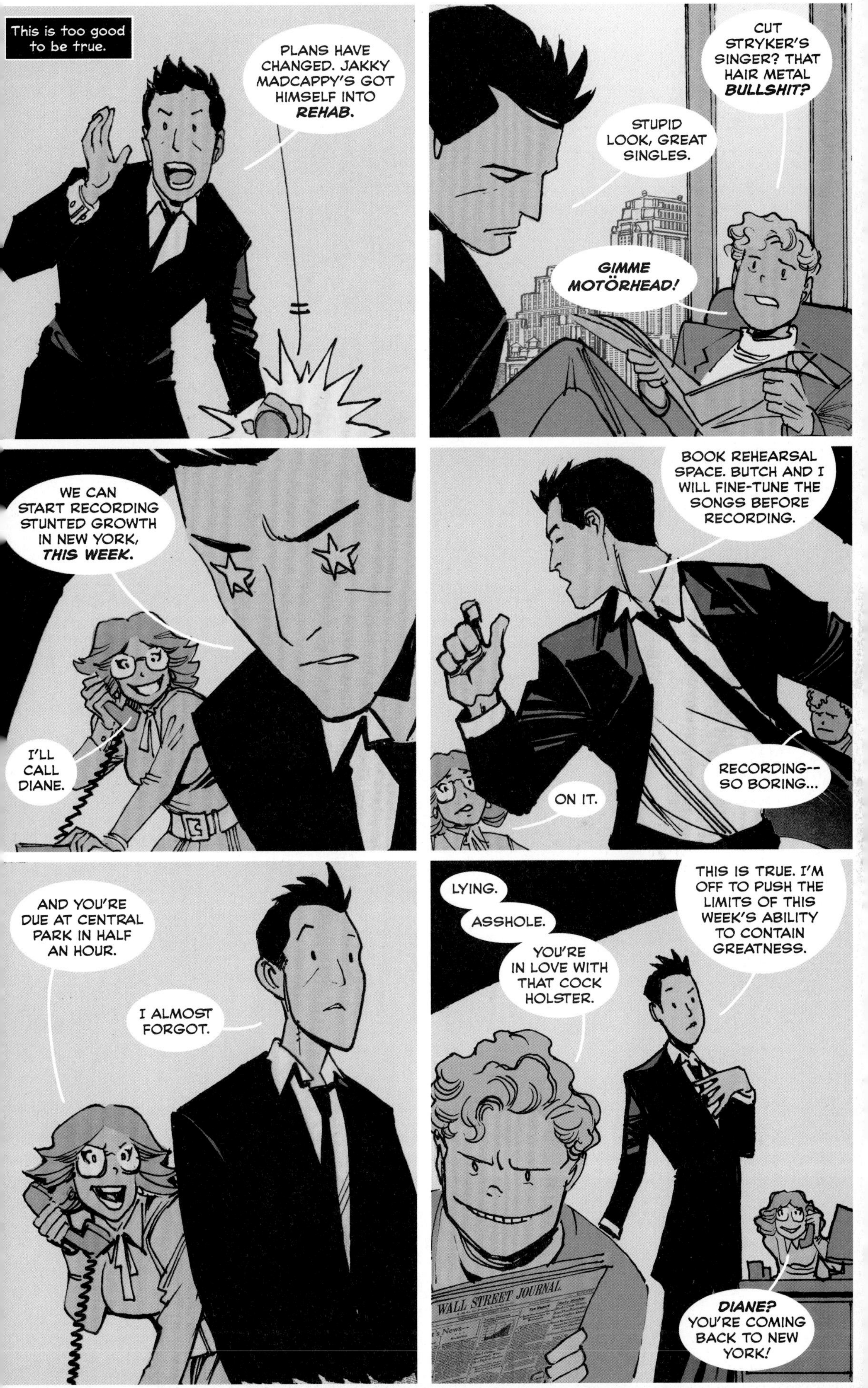
This is too good to be true.
PLANS HAVE CHANGED. JAKKY MADCAPPY'S GOT HIMSELF INTO ***REHAB.***
CUT STRYKER'S SINGER? THAT HAIR METAL ***BULLSHIT?***
STUPID LOOK, GREAT SINGLES.
GIMME MOTÖRHEAD!
WE CAN START RECORDING STUNTED GROWTH IN NEW YORK, ***THIS WEEK.***
I'LL CALL DIANE.
BOOK REHEARSAL SPACE. BUTCH AND I WILL FINE-TUNE THE SONGS BEFORE RECORDING.
RECORDING-- SO BORING...
ON IT.
AND YOU'RE DUE AT CENTRAL PARK IN HALF AN HOUR.
I ALMOST FORGOT.
LYING.
ASSHOLE.
YOU'RE IN LOVE WITH THAT COCK HOLSTER.
THIS IS TRUE. I'M OFF TO PUSH THE LIMITS OF THIS WEEK'S ABILITY TO CONTAIN GREATNESS.
WALL STREET JOURNAL
DIANE? YOU'RE COMING BACK TO NEW YORK!

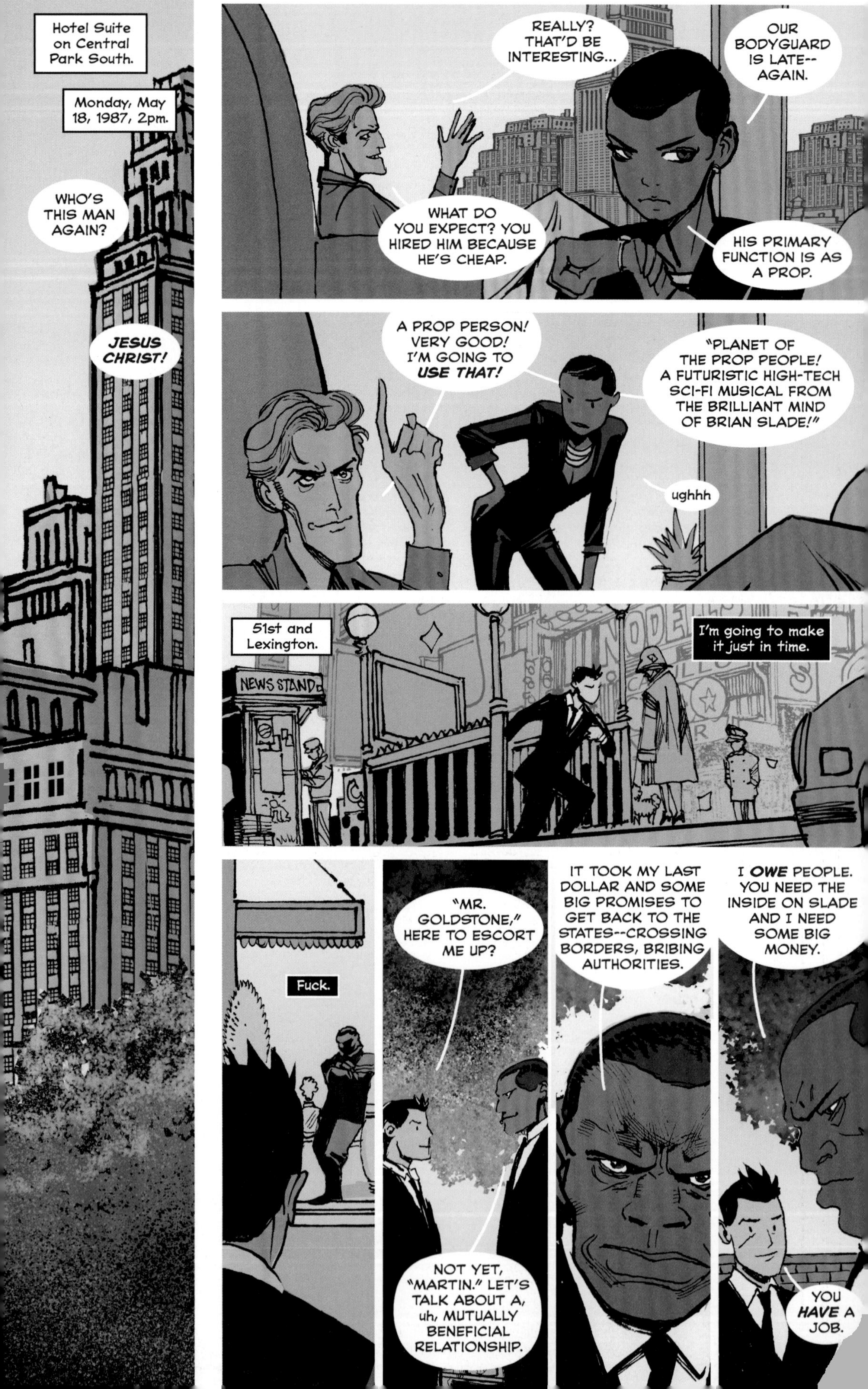

Hotel Suite on Central Park South.
Monday, May 18, 1987, 2pm.
WHO'S THIS MAN AGAIN?
JESUS CHRIST!
REALLY? THAT'D BE INTERESTING...
OUR BODYGUARD IS LATE-- AGAIN.
WHAT DO YOU EXPECT? YOU HIRED HIM BECAUSE HE'S CHEAP.
HIS PRIMARY FUNCTION IS AS A PROP.
A PROP PERSON! VERY GOOD! I'M GOING TO USE THAT!
"PLANET OF THE PROP PEOPLE! A FUTURISTIC HIGH-TECH SCI-FI MUSICAL FROM THE BRILLIANT MIND OF BRIAN SLADE!"
ughhh
51st and Lexington.
I'm going to make it just in time.
NEWS STAND
Fuck.
"MR. GOLDSTONE," HERE TO ESCORT ME UP?
NOT YET, "MARTIN." LET'S TALK ABOUT A, uh, MUTUALLY BENEFICIAL RELATIONSHIP.
IT TOOK MY LAST DOLLAR AND SOME BIG PROMISES TO GET BACK TO THE STATES--CROSSING BORDERS, BRIBING AUTHORITIES.
I OWE PEOPLE. YOU NEED THE INSIDE ON SLADE AND I NEED SOME BIG MONEY.
YOU HAVE A JOB.

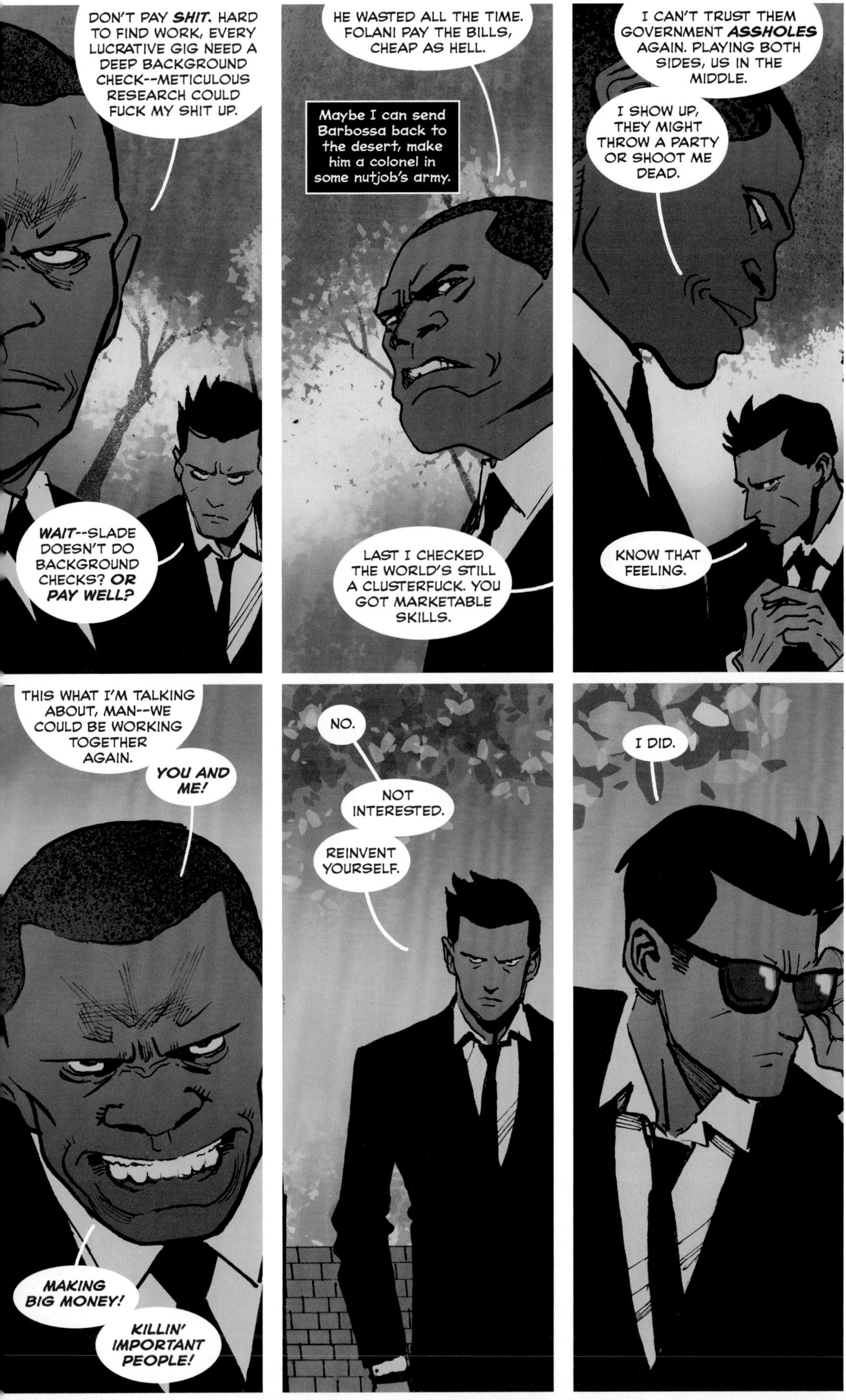

DON'T PAY SHIT. HARD TO FIND WORK, EVERY LUCRATIVE GIG NEED A DEEP BACKGROUND CHECK--METICULOUS RESEARCH COULD FUCK MY SHIT UP.
WAIT--SLADE DOESN'T DO BACKGROUND CHECKS? OR PAY WELL?
HE WASTED ALL THE TIME. FOLANI PAY THE BILLS, CHEAP AS HELL.
Maybe I can send Barbossa back to the desert, make him a colonel in some nutjob's army.
LAST I CHECKED THE WORLD'S STILL A CLUSTERFUCK. YOU GOT MARKETABLE SKILLS.
I CAN'T TRUST THEM GOVERNMENT ASSHOLES AGAIN. PLAYING BOTH SIDES, US IN THE MIDDLE.
I SHOW UP, THEY MIGHT THROW A PARTY OR SHOOT ME DEAD.
KNOW THAT FEELING.
THIS WHAT I'M TALKING ABOUT, MAN--WE COULD BE WORKING TOGETHER AGAIN.
YOU AND ME!
MAKING BIG MONEY!
KILLIN' IMPORTANT PEOPLE!
NO.
NOT INTERESTED.
REINVENT YOURSELF.
I DID.

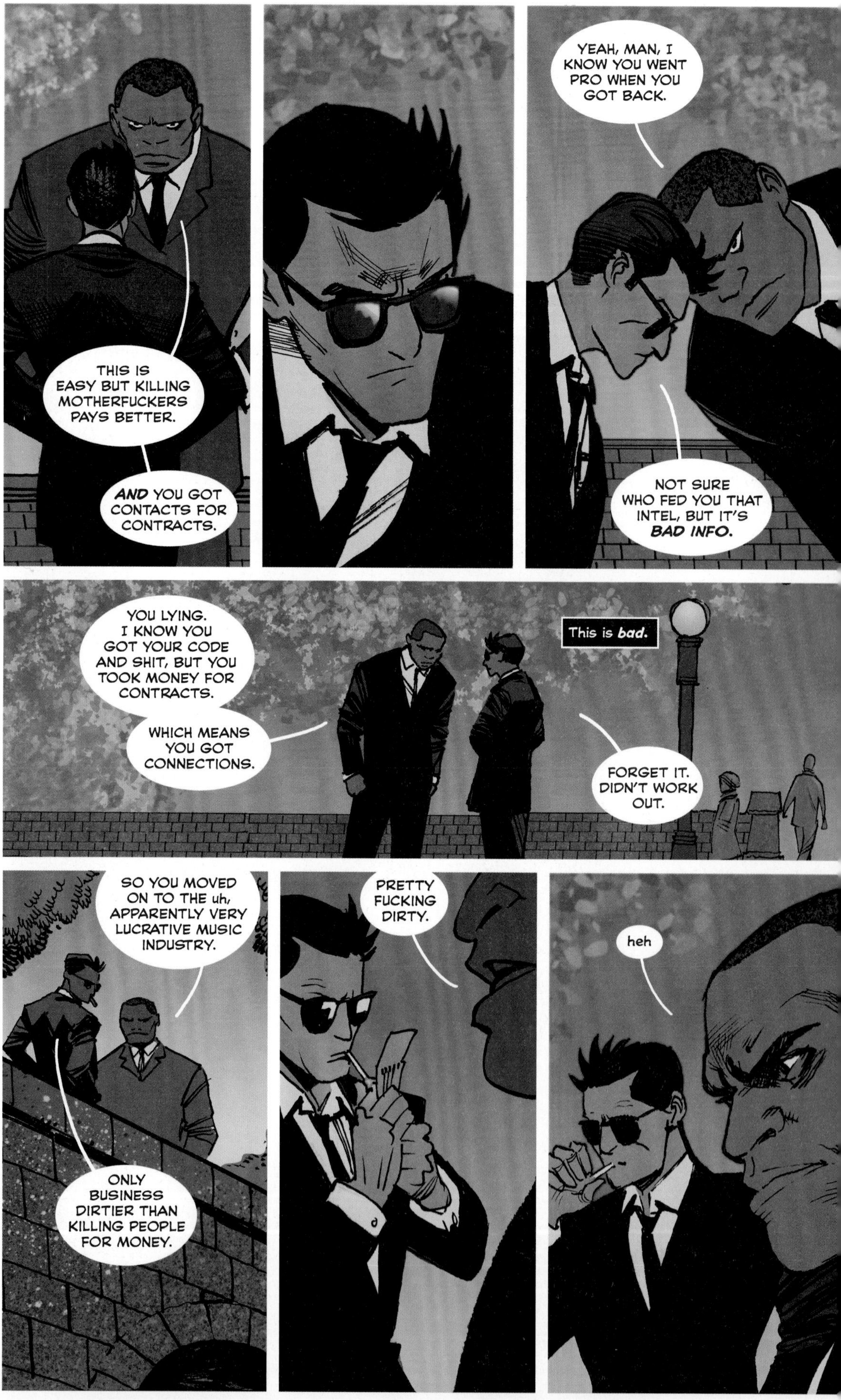
THIS IS EASY BUT KILLING MOTHERFUCKERS PAYS BETTER.
AND YOU GOT CONTACTS FOR CONTRACTS.
YEAH, MAN, I KNOW YOU WENT PRO WHEN YOU GOT BACK.
NOT SURE WHO FED YOU THAT INTEL, BUT IT'S **BAD INFO.**
YOU LYING. I KNOW YOU GOT YOUR CODE AND SHIT, BUT YOU TOOK MONEY FOR CONTRACTS.
WHICH MEANS YOU GOT CONNECTIONS.
This is **bad.**
FORGET IT. DIDN'T WORK OUT.
SO YOU MOVED ON TO THE uh, APPARENTLY VERY LUCRATIVE MUSIC INDUSTRY.
ONLY BUSINESS DIRTIER THAN KILLING PEOPLE FOR MONEY.
PRETTY FUCKING DIRTY.
heh

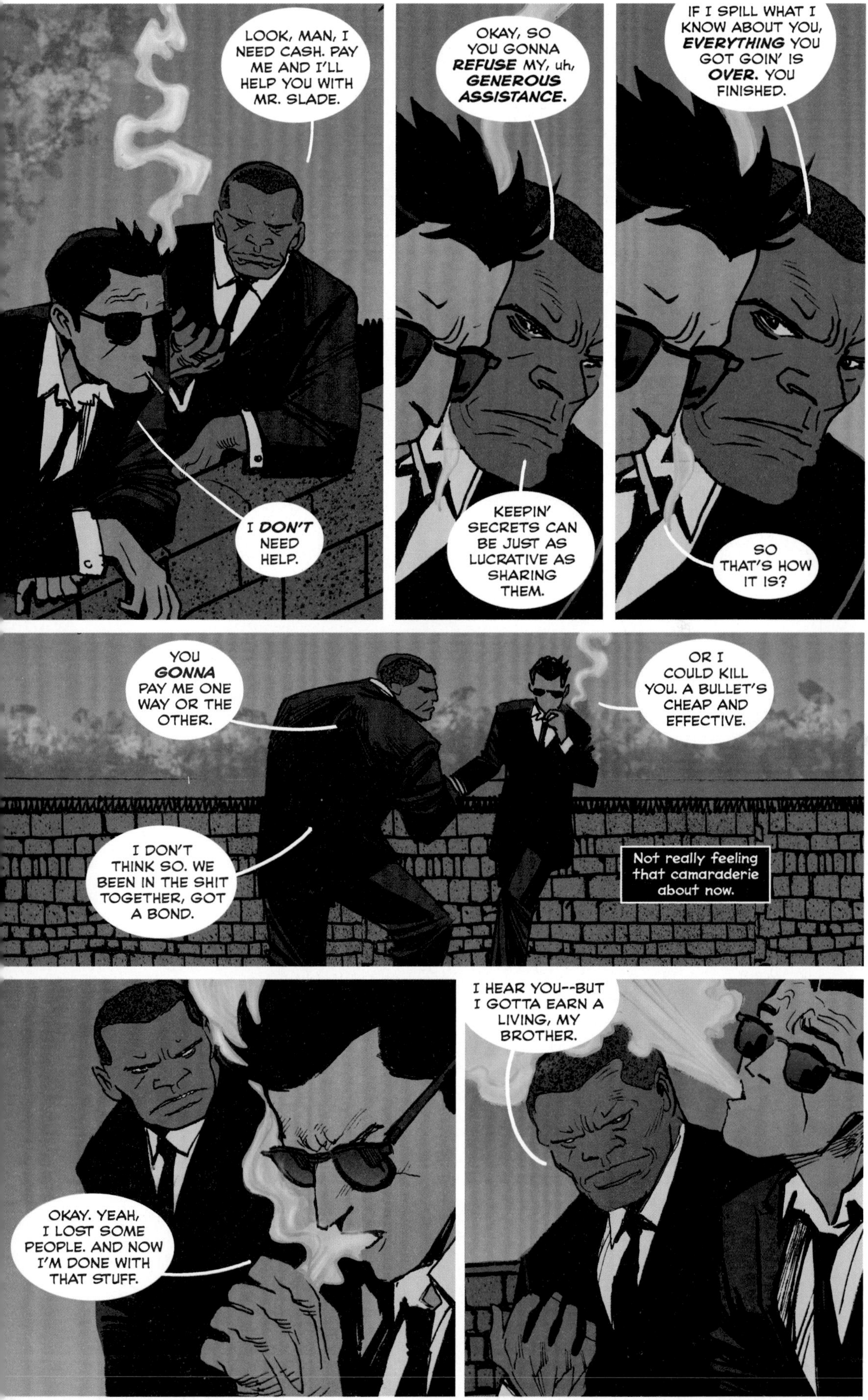
LOOK, MAN, I NEED CASH. PAY ME AND I'LL HELP YOU WITH MR. SLADE.
I DON'T NEED HELP.
OKAY, SO YOU GONNA REFUSE MY, uh, GENEROUS ASSISTANCE.
KEEPIN' SECRETS CAN BE JUST AS LUCRATIVE AS SHARING THEM.
IF I SPILL WHAT I KNOW ABOUT YOU, EVERYTHING YOU GOT GOIN' IS OVER. YOU FINISHED.
SO THAT'S HOW IT IS?
YOU GONNA PAY ME ONE WAY OR THE OTHER.
OR I COULD KILL YOU. A BULLET'S CHEAP AND EFFECTIVE.
I DON'T THINK SO. WE BEEN IN THE SHIT TOGETHER, GOT A BOND.
Not really feeling that camaraderie about now.
OKAY. YEAH, I LOST SOME PEOPLE. AND NOW I'M DONE WITH THAT STUFF.
I HEAR YOU--BUT I GOTTA EARN A LIVING, MY BROTHER.

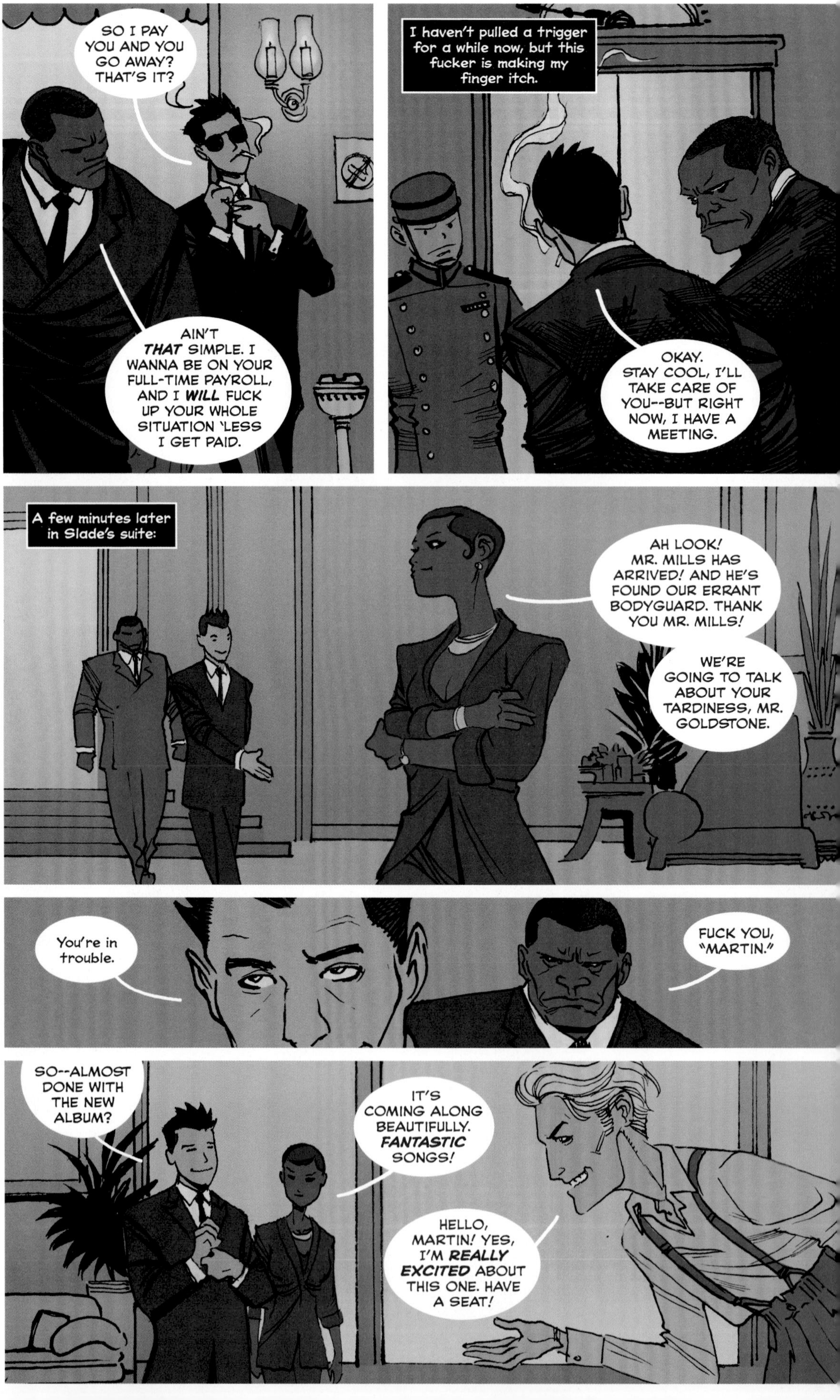
SO I PAY YOU AND YOU GO AWAY? THAT'S IT?
AIN'T THAT SIMPLE. I WANNA BE ON YOUR FULL-TIME PAYROLL, AND I WILL FUCK UP YOUR WHOLE SITUATION 'LESS I GET PAID.
I haven't pulled a trigger for a while now, but this fucker is making my finger itch.
OKAY. STAY COOL, I'LL TAKE CARE OF YOU--BUT RIGHT NOW, I HAVE A MEETING.
A few minutes later in Slade's suite:
AH LOOK! MR. MILLS HAS ARRIVED! AND HE'S FOUND OUR ERRANT BODYGUARD. THANK YOU MR. MILLS!
WE'RE GOING TO TALK ABOUT YOUR TARDINESS, MR. GOLDSTONE.
You're in trouble.
FUCK YOU, "MARTIN."
SO--ALMOST DONE WITH THE NEW ALBUM?
IT'S COMING ALONG BEAUTIFULLY. FANTASTIC SONGS!
HELLO, MARTIN! YES, I'M REALLY EXCITED ABOUT THIS ONE. HAVE A SEAT!

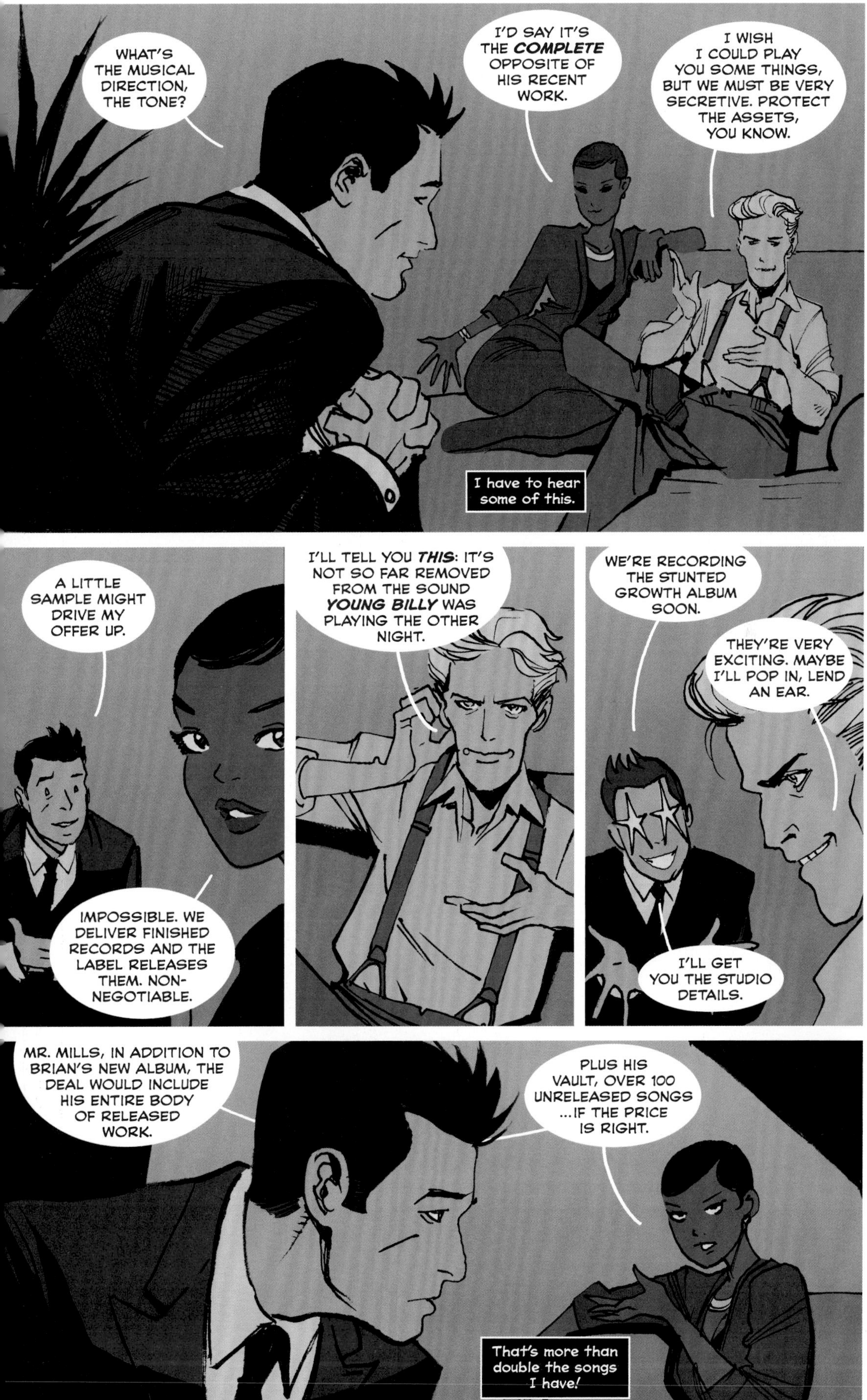
WHAT'S THE MUSICAL DIRECTION, THE TONE?
I'D SAY IT'S THE COMPLETE OPPOSITE OF HIS RECENT WORK.
I WISH I COULD PLAY YOU SOME THINGS, BUT WE MUST BE VERY SECRETIVE. PROTECT THE ASSETS, YOU KNOW.
I have to hear some of this.
A LITTLE SAMPLE MIGHT DRIVE MY OFFER UP.
IMPOSSIBLE. WE DELIVER FINISHED RECORDS AND THE LABEL RELEASES THEM. NON-NEGOTIABLE.
I'LL TELL YOU THIS: IT'S NOT SO FAR REMOVED FROM THE SOUND YOUNG BILLY WAS PLAYING THE OTHER NIGHT.
WE'RE RECORDING THE STUNTED GROWTH ALBUM SOON.
THEY'RE VERY EXCITING. MAYBE I'LL POP IN, LEND AN EAR.
I'LL GET YOU THE STUDIO DETAILS.
MR. MILLS, IN ADDITION TO BRIAN'S NEW ALBUM, THE DEAL WOULD INCLUDE HIS ENTIRE BODY OF RELEASED WORK.
PLUS HIS VAULT, OVER 100 UNRELEASED SONGS ...IF THE PRICE IS RIGHT.
That's more than double the songs I have!

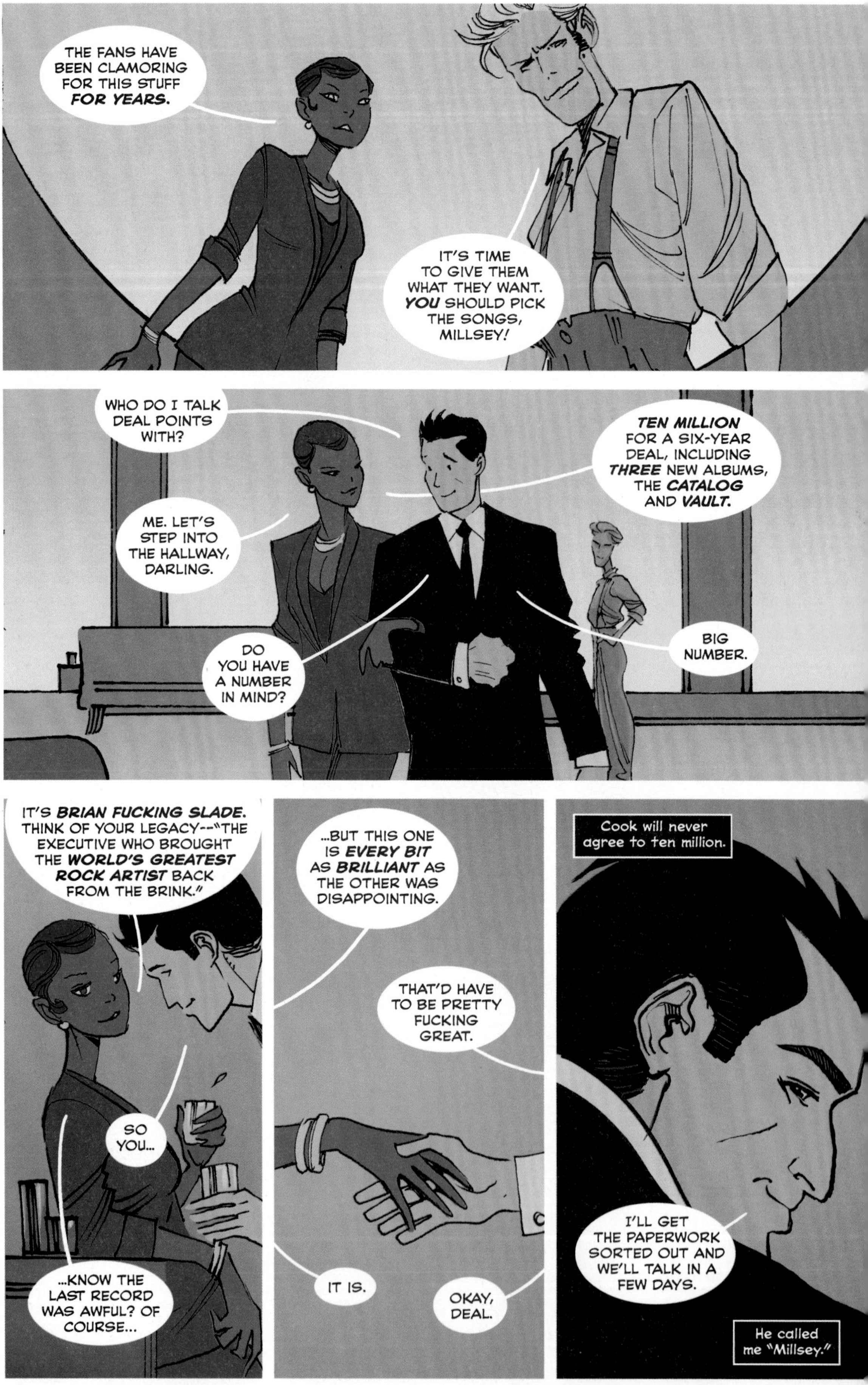
THE FANS HAVE BEEN CLAMORING FOR THIS STUFF **FOR YEARS.**
IT'S TIME TO GIVE THEM WHAT THEY WANT. ***YOU*** SHOULD PICK THE SONGS, MILLSEY!
WHO DO I TALK DEAL POINTS WITH?
TEN MILLION FOR A SIX-YEAR DEAL, INCLUDING ***THREE*** NEW ALBUMS, THE ***CATALOG*** AND ***VAULT.***
ME. LET'S STEP INTO THE HALLWAY, DARLING.
DO YOU HAVE A NUMBER IN MIND?
BIG NUMBER.
IT'S ***BRIAN FUCKING SLADE.*** THINK OF YOUR LEGACY--"THE EXECUTIVE WHO BROUGHT THE ***WORLD'S GREATEST ROCK ARTIST*** BACK FROM THE BRINK."
SO YOU...
...KNOW THE LAST RECORD WAS AWFUL? OF COURSE...
...BUT THIS ONE IS ***EVERY BIT*** AS ***BRILLIANT*** AS THE OTHER WAS DISAPPOINTING.
THAT'D HAVE TO BE PRETTY FUCKING GREAT.
IT IS.
OKAY, DEAL.
Cook will never agree to ten million.
I'LL GET THE PAPERWORK SORTED OUT AND WE'LL TALK IN A FEW DAYS.
He called me "Millsey."

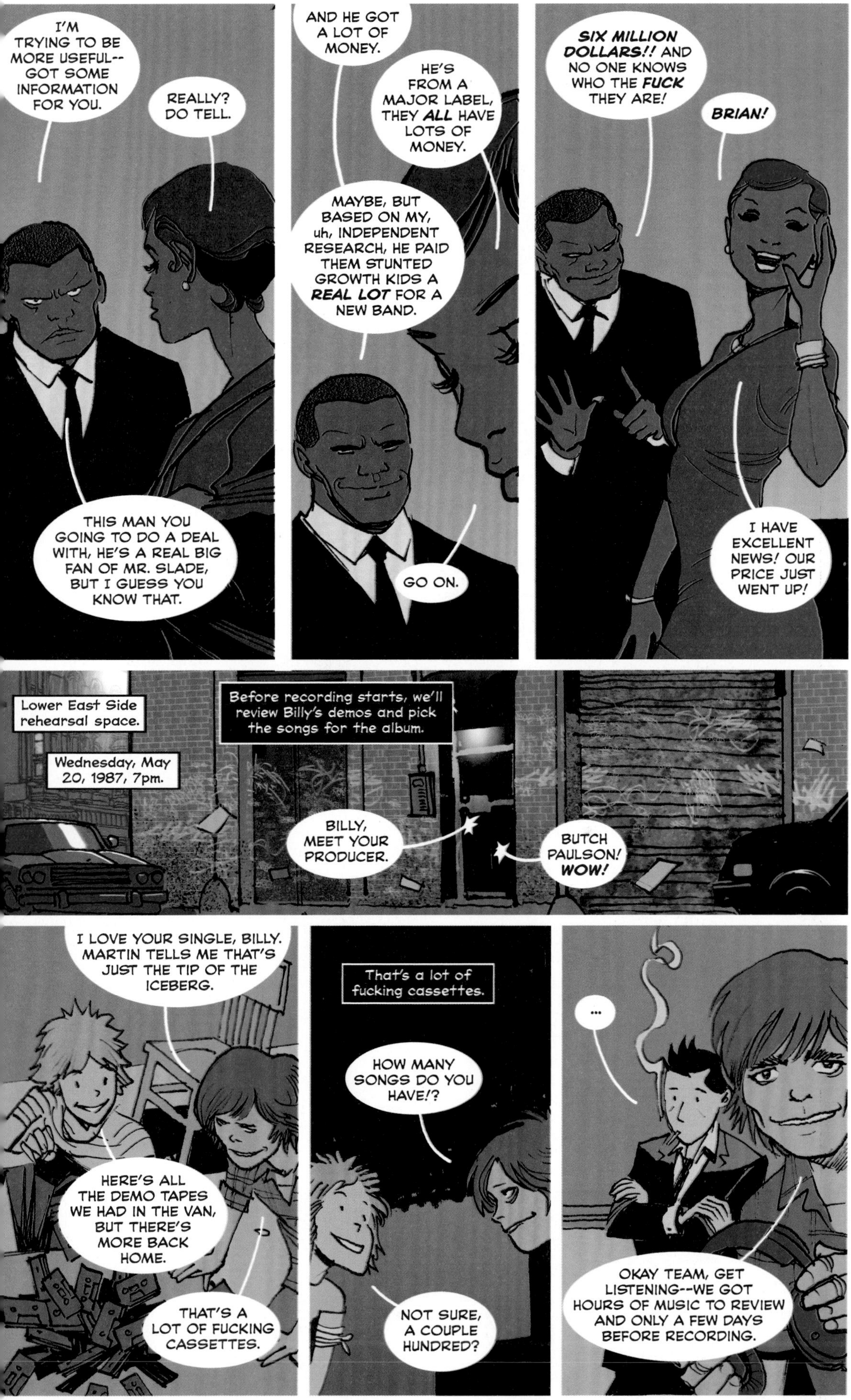
I'M TRYING TO BE MORE USEFUL--GOT SOME INFORMATION FOR YOU.
REALLY? DO TELL.
THIS MAN YOU GOING TO DO A DEAL WITH, HE'S A REAL BIG FAN OF MR. SLADE, BUT I GUESS YOU KNOW THAT.
AND HE GOT A LOT OF MONEY.
HE'S FROM A MAJOR LABEL, THEY ALL HAVE LOTS OF MONEY.
MAYBE, BUT BASED ON MY, uh, INDEPENDENT RESEARCH, HE PAID THEM STUNTED GROWTH KIDS A REAL LOT FOR A NEW BAND.
GO ON.
SIX MILLION DOLLARS!! AND NO ONE KNOWS WHO THE FUCK THEY ARE!
BRIAN!
I HAVE EXCELLENT NEWS! OUR PRICE JUST WENT UP!
Lower East Side rehearsal space.
Wednesday, May 20, 1987, 7pm.
Before recording starts, we'll review Billy's demos and pick the songs for the album.
BILLY, MEET YOUR PRODUCER.
BUTCH PAULSON! WOW!
I LOVE YOUR SINGLE, BILLY. MARTIN TELLS ME THAT'S JUST THE TIP OF THE ICEBERG.
HERE'S ALL THE DEMO TAPES WE HAD IN THE VAN, BUT THERE'S MORE BACK HOME.
THAT'S A LOT OF FUCKING CASSETTES.
That's a lot of fucking cassettes.
HOW MANY SONGS DO YOU HAVE!?
NOT SURE, A COUPLE HUNDRED?
...
OKAY TEAM, GET LISTENING--WE GOT HOURS OF MUSIC TO REVIEW AND ONLY A FEW DAYS BEFORE RECORDING.

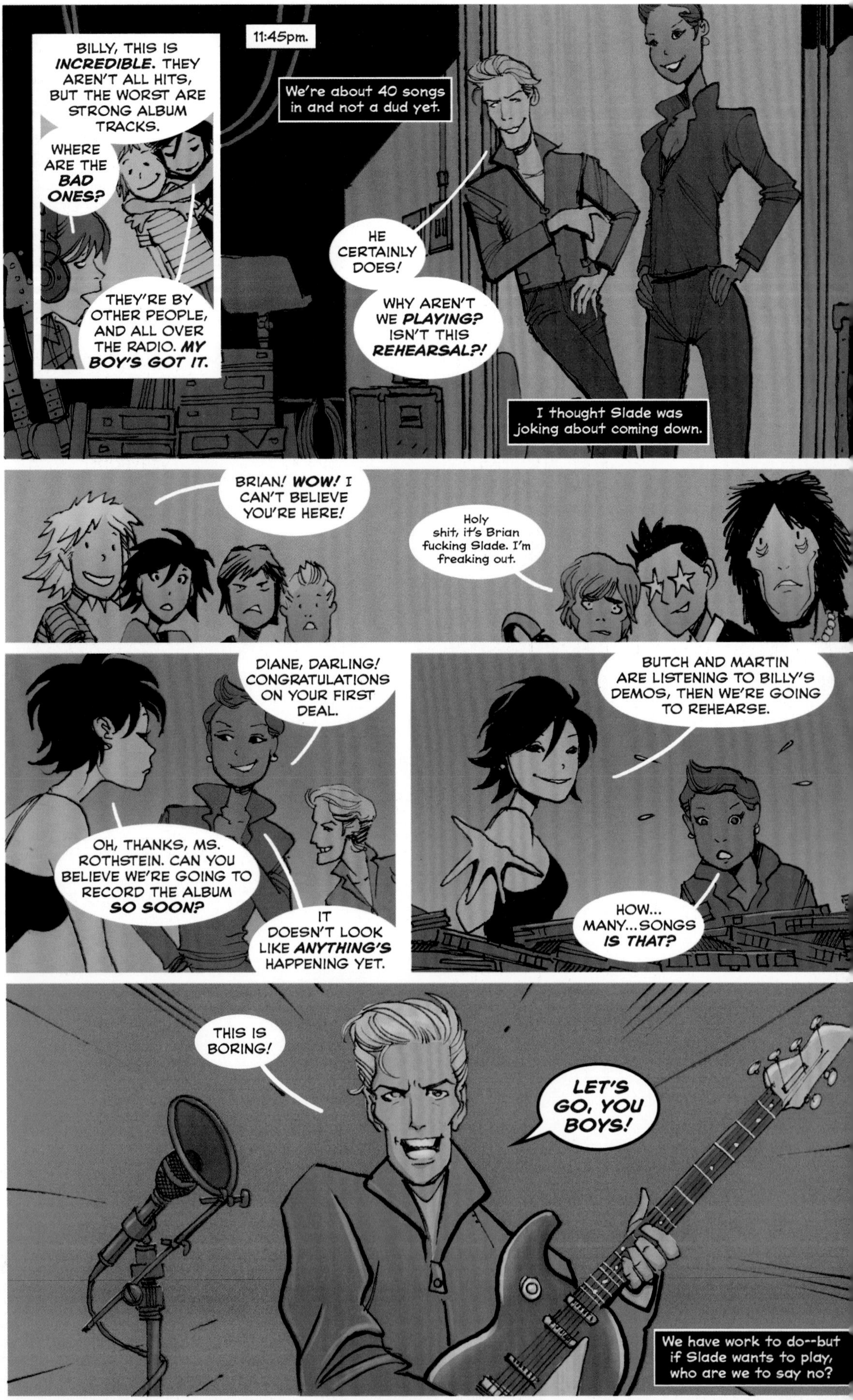

BILLY, THIS IS INCREDIBLE. THEY AREN'T ALL HITS, BUT THE WORST ARE STRONG ALBUM TRACKS.
WHERE ARE THE BAD ONES?
THEY'RE BY OTHER PEOPLE, AND ALL OVER THE RADIO. MY BOY'S GOT IT.
11:45pm.
We're about 40 songs in and not a dud yet.
HE CERTAINLY DOES!
WHY AREN'T WE PLAYING? ISN'T THIS REHEARSAL?!
I thought Slade was joking about coming down.
BRIAN! WOW! I CAN'T BELIEVE YOU'RE HERE!
Holy shit, it's Brian fucking Slade. I'm freaking out.
DIANE, DARLING! CONGRATULATIONS ON YOUR FIRST DEAL.
OH, THANKS, MS. ROTHSTEIN. CAN YOU BELIEVE WE'RE GOING TO RECORD THE ALBUM SO SOON?
IT DOESN'T LOOK LIKE ANYTHING'S HAPPENING YET.
BUTCH AND MARTIN ARE LISTENING TO BILLY'S DEMOS, THEN WE'RE GOING TO REHEARSE.
HOW... MANY...SONGS IS THAT?
THIS IS BORING!
LET'S GO, YOU BOYS!
We have work to do--but if Slade wants to play, who are we to say no?

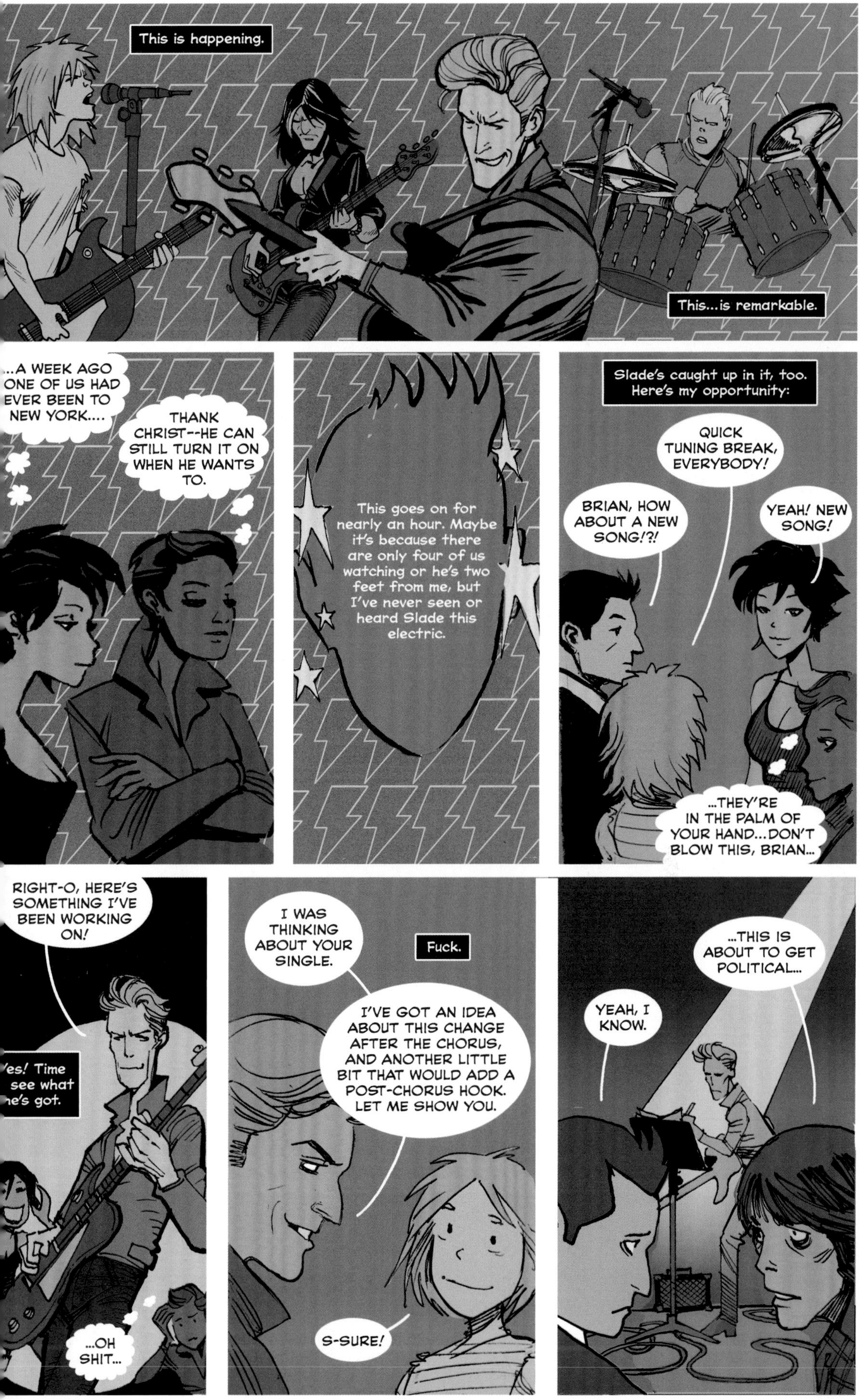
This is happening.
This...is remarkable.
...A WEEK AGO ONE OF US HAD EVER BEEN TO NEW YORK....
THANK CHRIST--HE CAN STILL TURN IT ON WHEN HE WANTS TO.
This goes on for nearly an hour. Maybe it's because there are only four of us watching or he's two feet from me, but I've never seen or heard Slade this electric.
Slade's caught up in it, too. Here's my opportunity:
QUICK TUNING BREAK, EVERYBODY!
BRIAN, HOW ABOUT A NEW SONG!?!
YEAH! NEW SONG!
...THEY'RE IN THE PALM OF YOUR HAND...DON'T BLOW THIS, BRIAN...
RIGHT-O, HERE'S SOMETHING I'VE BEEN WORKING ON!
es! Time see what e's got.
...OH SHIT...
I WAS THINKING ABOUT YOUR SINGLE.
Fuck.
I'VE GOT AN IDEA ABOUT THIS CHANGE AFTER THE CHORUS, AND ANOTHER LITTLE BIT THAT WOULD ADD A POST-CHORUS HOOK. LET ME SHOW YOU.
S-SURE!
...THIS IS ABOUT TO GET POLITICAL...
YEAH, I KNOW.

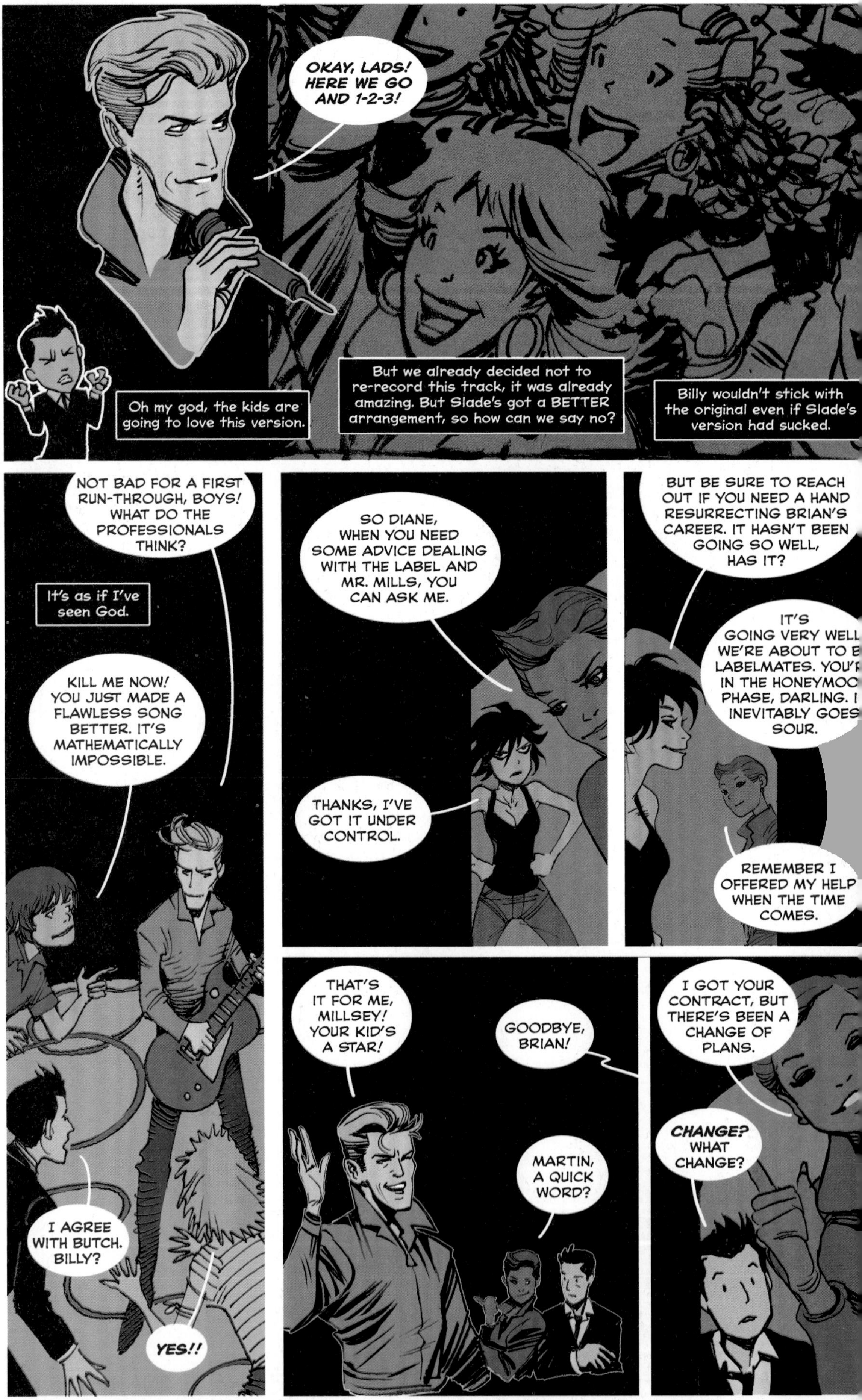
OKAY, LADS! HERE WE GO AND 1-2-3!
Oh my god, the kids are going to love this version.
But we already decided not to re-record this track, it was already amazing. But Slade's got a BETTER arrangement, so how can we say no?
Billy wouldn't stick with the original even if Slade's version had sucked.
NOT BAD FOR A FIRST RUN-THROUGH, BOYS! WHAT DO THE PROFESSIONALS THINK?
It's as if I've seen God.
KILL ME NOW! YOU JUST MADE A FLAWLESS SONG BETTER. IT'S MATHEMATICALLY IMPOSSIBLE.
I AGREE WITH BUTCH. BILLY?
YES!!
SO DIANE, WHEN YOU NEED SOME ADVICE DEALING WITH THE LABEL AND MR. MILLS, YOU CAN ASK ME.
THANKS, I'VE GOT IT UNDER CONTROL.
BUT BE SURE TO REACH OUT IF YOU NEED A HAND RESURRECTING BRIAN'S CAREER. IT HASN'T BEEN GOING SO WELL, HAS IT?
IT'S GOING VERY WELL
REMEMBER I OFFERED MY HELP WHEN THE TIME COMES.
THAT'S IT FOR ME, MILLSEY! YOUR KID'S A STAR!
GOODBYE, BRIAN!
MARTIN, A QUICK WORD?
I GOT YOUR CONTRACT, BUT THERE'S BEEN A CHANGE OF PLANS.
CHANGE? WHAT CHANGE?

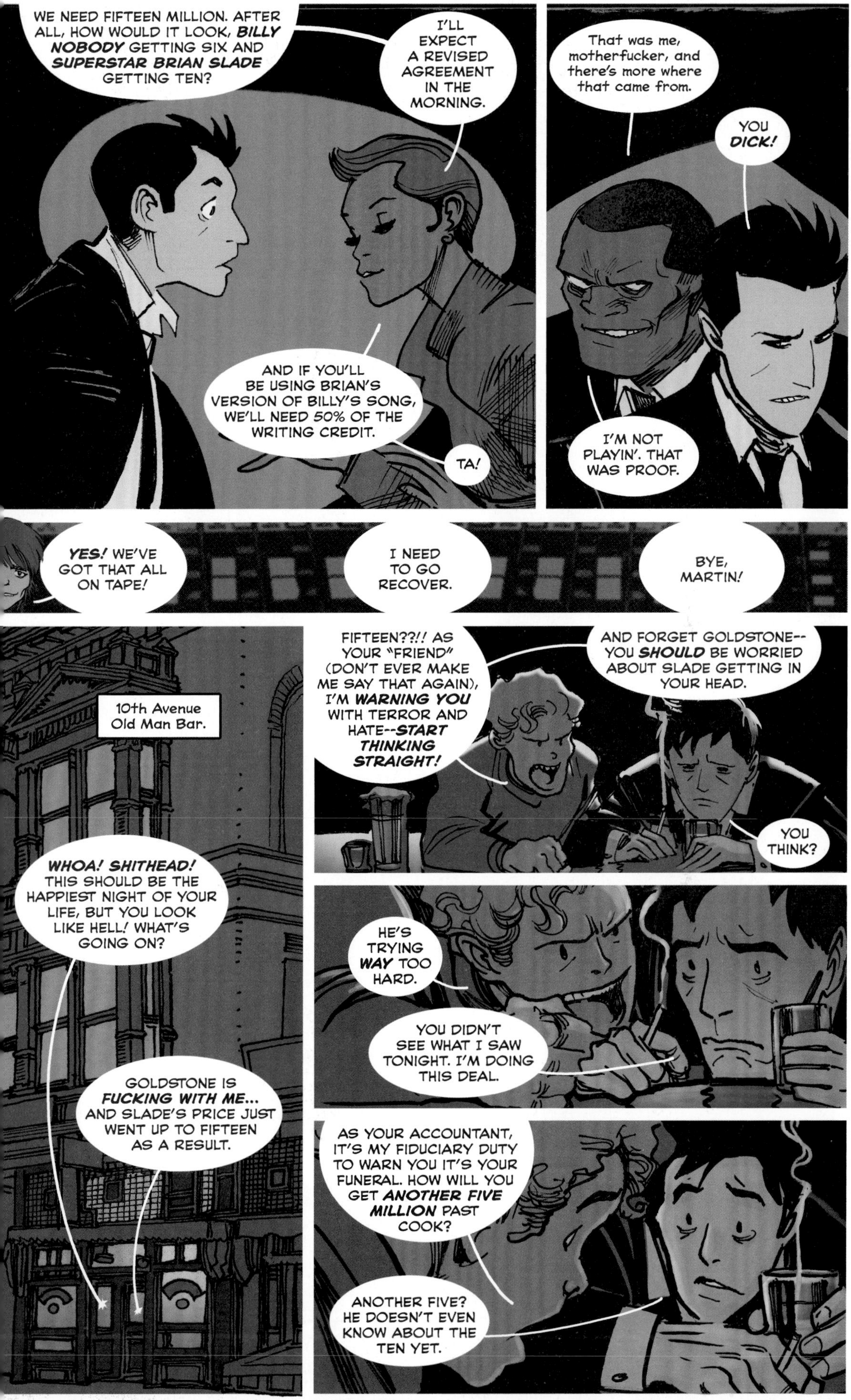
WE NEED FIFTEEN MILLION. AFTER ALL, HOW WOULD IT LOOK, BILLY NOBODY GETTING SIX AND SUPERSTAR BRIAN SLADE GETTING TEN?
I'LL EXPECT A REVISED AGREEMENT IN THE MORNING.
AND IF YOU'LL BE USING BRIAN'S VERSION OF BILLY'S SONG, WE'LL NEED 50% OF THE WRITING CREDIT.
TA!
That was me, motherfucker, and there's more where that came from.
YOU DICK!
I'M NOT PLAYIN'. THAT WAS PROOF.
YES! WE'VE GOT THAT ALL ON TAPE!
I NEED TO GO RECOVER.
BYE, MARTIN!
10th Avenue Old Man Bar.
WHOA! SHITHEAD! THIS SHOULD BE THE HAPPIEST NIGHT OF YOUR LIFE, BUT YOU LOOK LIKE HELL! WHAT'S GOING ON?
GOLDSTONE IS FUCKING WITH ME... AND SLADE'S PRICE JUST WENT UP TO FIFTEEN AS A RESULT.
FIFTEEN??!! AS YOUR "FRIEND" (DON'T EVER MAKE ME SAY THAT AGAIN), I'M WARNING YOU WITH TERROR AND HATE--START THINKING STRAIGHT!
AND FORGET GOLDSTONE-- YOU SHOULD BE WORRIED ABOUT SLADE GETTING IN YOUR HEAD.
YOU THINK?
HE'S TRYING WAY TOO HARD.
YOU DIDN'T SEE WHAT I SAW TONIGHT. I'M DOING THIS DEAL.
AS YOUR ACCOUNTANT, IT'S MY FIDUCIARY DUTY TO WARN YOU IT'S YOUR FUNERAL. HOW WILL YOU GET ANOTHER FIVE MILLION PAST COOK?
ANOTHER FIVE? HE DOESN'T EVEN KNOW ABOUT THE TEN YET.

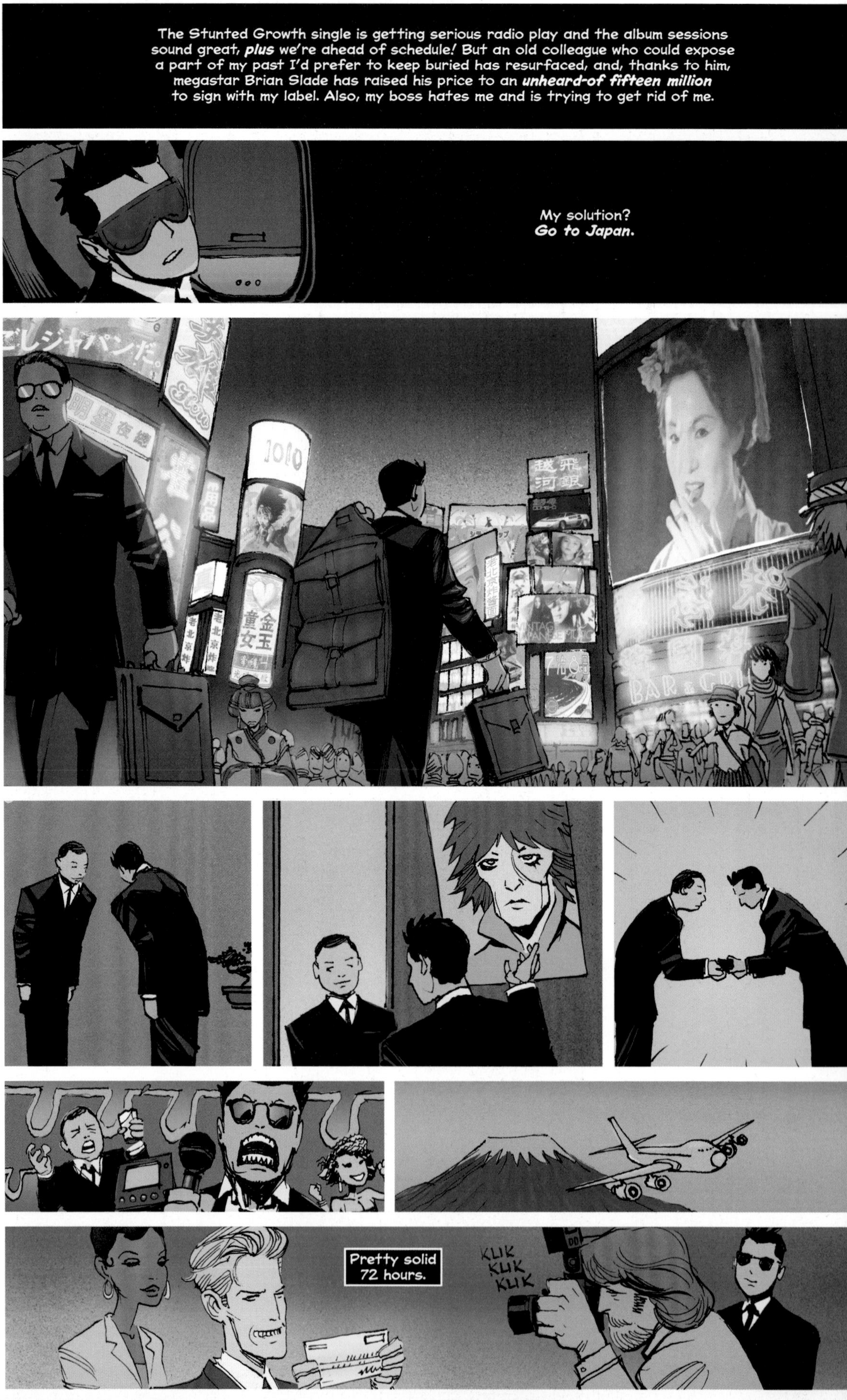
The Stunted Growth single is getting serious radio play and the album sessions sound great, ***plus*** we're ahead of schedule! But an old colleague who could expose a part of my past I'd prefer to keep buried has resurfaced, and, thanks to him, megastar Brian Slade has raised his price to an ***unheard-of fifteen million*** to sign with my label. Also, my boss hates me and is trying to get rid of me.
My solution?
Go to Japan.
Pretty solid
72 hours.
KLIK
KLIK
KLIK

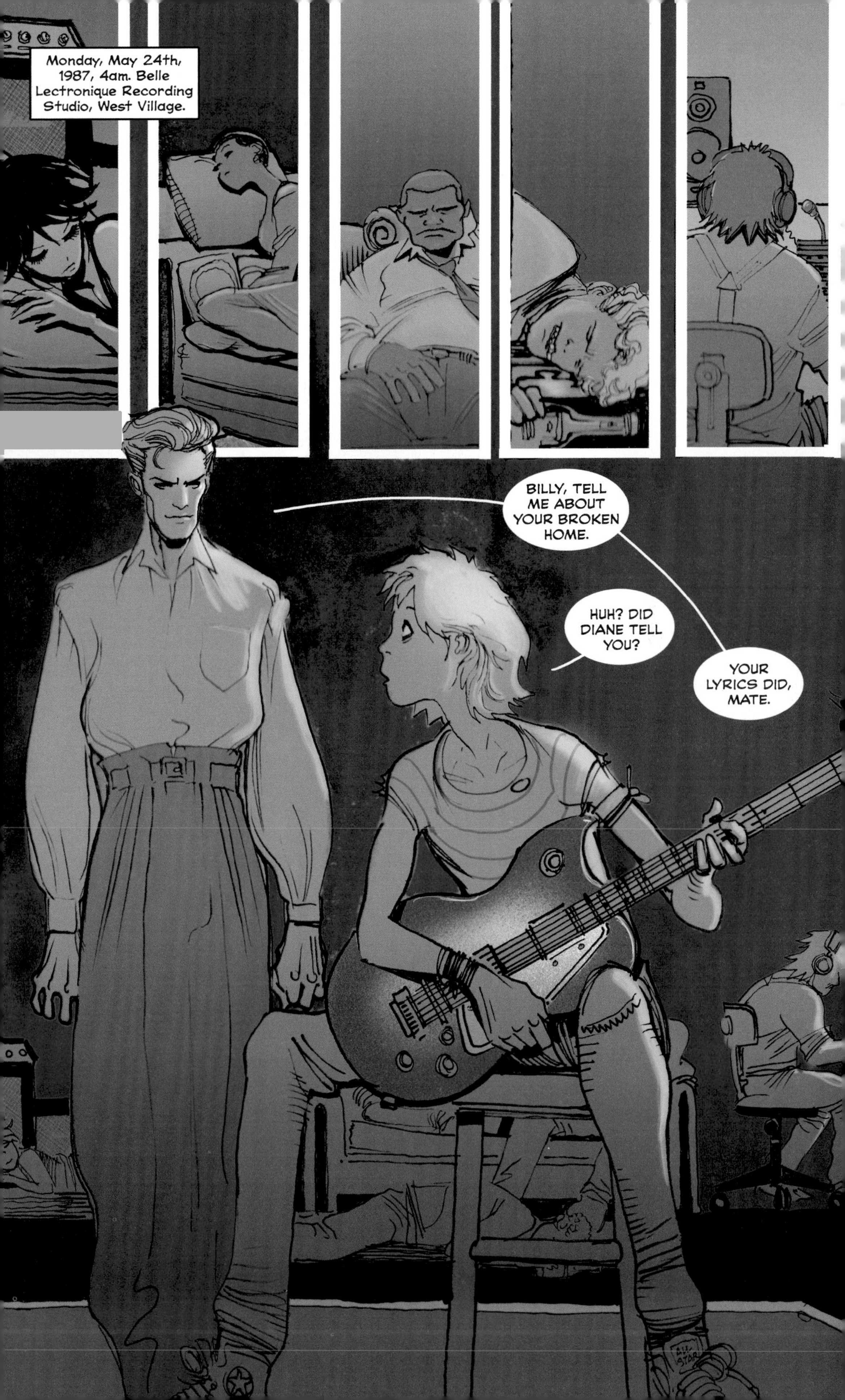
Monday, May 24th, 1987, 4am. Belle Lectronique Recording Studio, West Village.
BILLY, TELL ME ABOUT YOUR BROKEN HOME.
HUH? DID DIANE TELL YOU?
YOUR LYRICS DID, MATE.

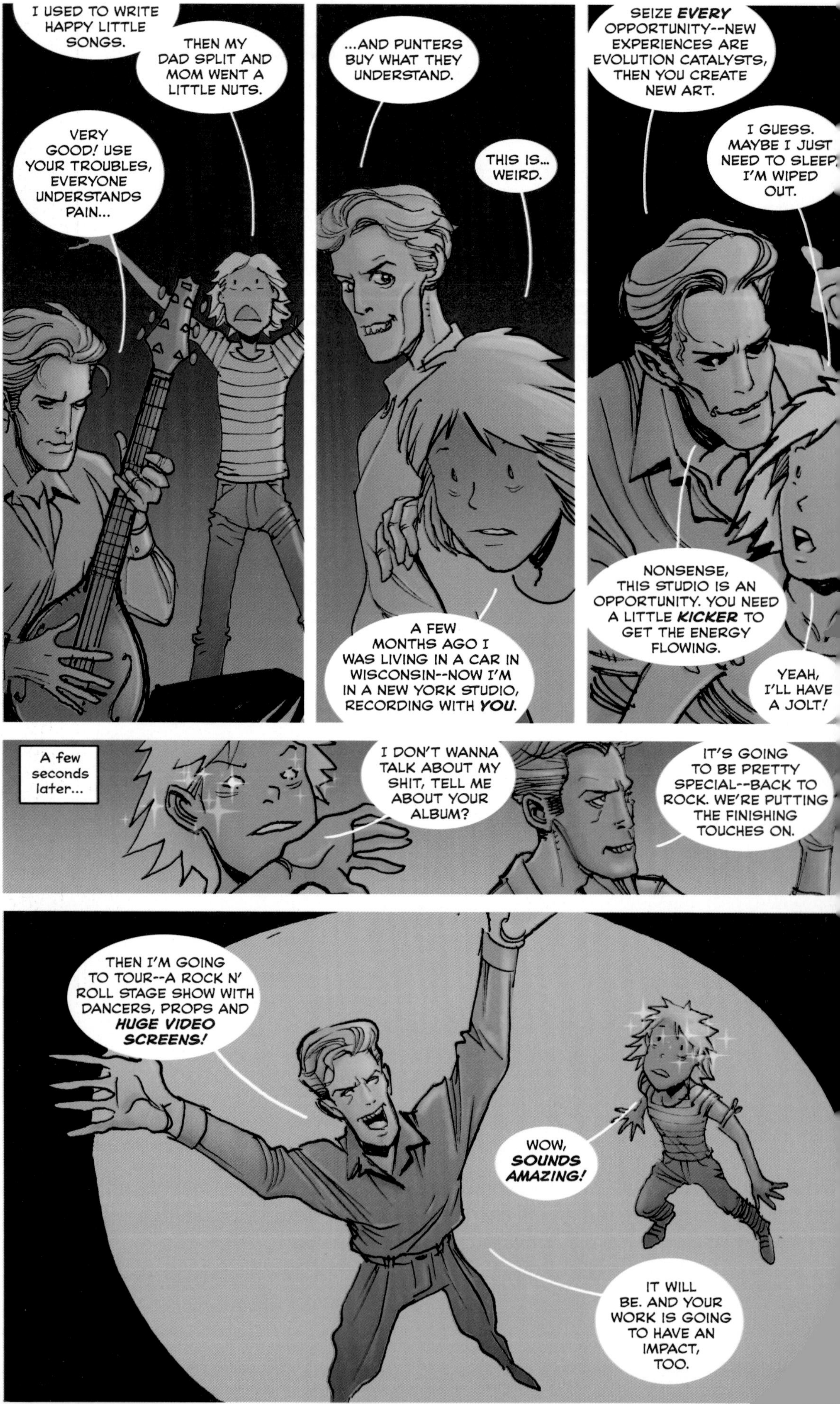
I USED TO WRITE HAPPY LITTLE SONGS.
THEN MY DAD SPLIT AND MOM WENT A LITTLE NUTS.
VERY GOOD! USE YOUR TROUBLES, EVERYONE UNDERSTANDS PAIN...
...AND PUNTERS BUY WHAT THEY UNDERSTAND.
THIS IS... WEIRD.
A FEW MONTHS AGO I WAS LIVING IN A CAR IN WISCONSIN--NOW I'M IN A NEW YORK STUDIO, RECORDING WITH ***YOU***.
SEIZE ***EVERY*** OPPORTUNITY--NEW EXPERIENCES ARE EVOLUTION CATALYSTS, THEN YOU CREATE NEW ART.
I GUESS. MAYBE I JUST NEED TO SLEEP. I'M WIPED OUT.
NONSENSE, THIS STUDIO IS AN OPPORTUNITY. YOU NEED A LITTLE ***KICKER*** TO GET THE ENERGY FLOWING.
YEAH, I'LL HAVE A JOLT!
A few seconds later...
I DON'T WANNA TALK ABOUT MY SHIT, TELL ME ABOUT YOUR ALBUM?
IT'S GOING TO BE PRETTY SPECIAL--BACK TO ROCK. WE'RE PUTTING THE FINISHING TOUCHES ON.
THEN I'M GOING TO TOUR--A ROCK N' ROLL STAGE SHOW WITH DANCERS, PROPS AND ***HUGE VIDEO SCREENS!***
WOW, ***SOUNDS AMAZING!***
IT WILL BE. AND YOUR WORK IS GOING TO HAVE AN IMPACT, TOO.

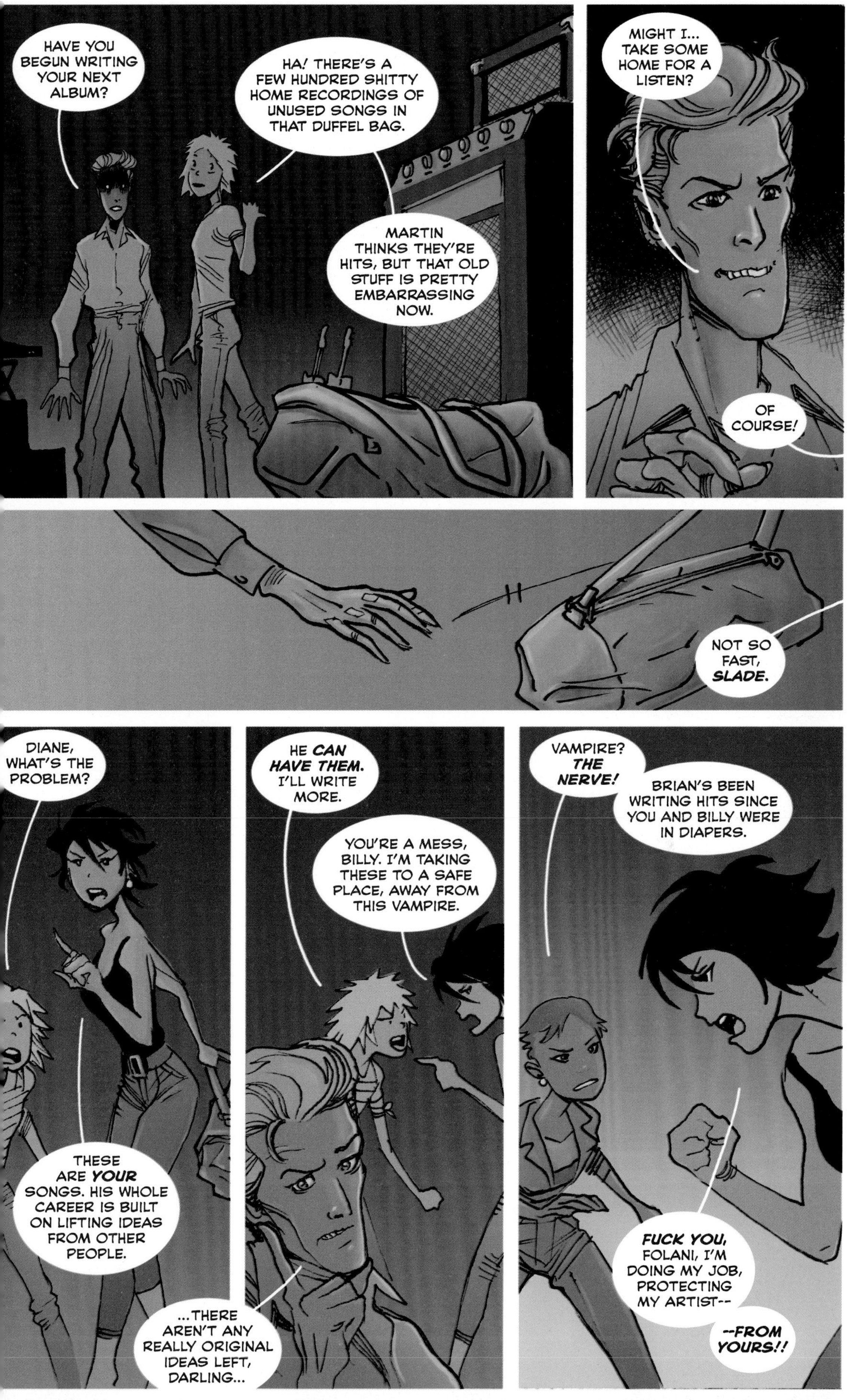
HAVE YOU BEGUN WRITING YOUR NEXT ALBUM?
HA! THERE'S A FEW HUNDRED SHITTY HOME RECORDINGS OF UNUSED SONGS IN THAT DUFFEL BAG.
MARTIN THINKS THEY'RE HITS, BUT THAT OLD STUFF IS PRETTY EMBARRASSING NOW.
MIGHT I... TAKE SOME HOME FOR A LISTEN?
OF COURSE!
NOT SO FAST, *SLADE.*
DIANE, WHAT'S THE PROBLEM?
THESE ARE *YOUR* SONGS. HIS WHOLE CAREER IS BUILT ON LIFTING IDEAS FROM OTHER PEOPLE.
HE *CAN HAVE THEM.* I'LL WRITE MORE.
YOU'RE A MESS, BILLY. I'M TAKING THESE TO A SAFE PLACE, AWAY FROM THIS VAMPIRE.
...THERE AREN'T ANY REALLY ORIGINAL IDEAS LEFT, DARLING...
VAMPIRE? *THE NERVE!*
BRIAN'S BEEN WRITING HITS SINCE YOU AND BILLY WERE IN DIAPERS.
FUCK YOU, FOLANI, I'M DOING MY JOB, PROTECTING MY ARTIST--
--FROM YOURS!!

I'LL TALK TO *YOU* BACK AT THE HOTEL.

MEEOOOWWRR

OOOH, KITTEN'S GOT CLAWS.

Wednesday, May 26th, 1987, 11:30am. St. Mark's.

TRASH AND VAUDEVILLE

BEEN MEANING TO ASK YOU, HOW'D YOU TALK DIRECTOR BALLOON-KNOT INTO THE SLADE DEAL?

DIDN'T--WENT AROUND HIM. MARITA-SAN, OUR CEO, IS A BIG SLADE FAN.

YOU SNEAKY *FUCKER!* COOK MUST BE *PISSED.*

WHAT'S HE GONNA DO, CHALLENGE HIS BOSS? BESIDES, THE SLADE DEAL'S A WINNER.

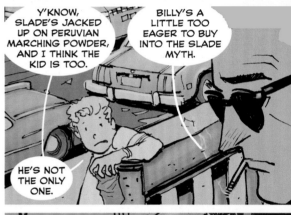

Y'KNOW, SLADE'S JACKED UP ON PERUVIAN MARCHING POWDER, AND I THINK THE KID IS TOO.

BILLY'S A LITTLE TOO EAGER TO BUY INTO THE SLADE MYTH.

HE'S NOT THE ONLY ONE.

THIS MAY BE DRUNK-MEMORY, BUT SOMETIMES THOSE TWO WAKE ME UP IN THE MORNING PLAYING AWFUL PSYCH-NOISE SHIT THAT DOESN'T SOUND LIKE THE REST OF IT...

WAIT--YOU'RE SLEEPING AT THE STUDIO?

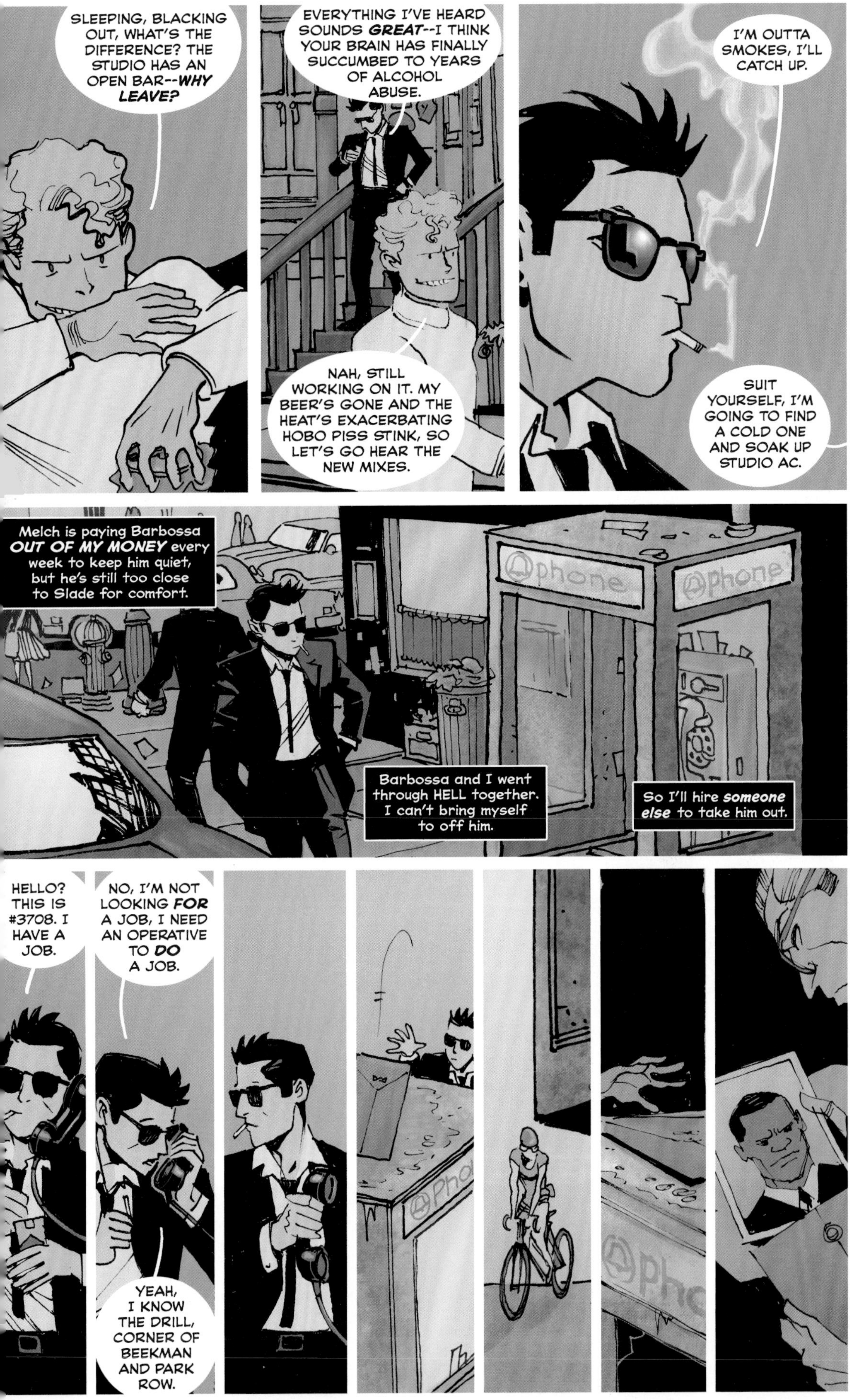
SLEEPING, BLACKING OUT, WHAT'S THE DIFFERENCE? THE STUDIO HAS AN OPEN BAR--WHY LEAVE?
EVERYTHING I'VE HEARD SOUNDS GREAT--I THINK YOUR BRAIN HAS FINALLY SUCCUMBED TO YEARS OF ALCOHOL ABUSE.
NAH, STILL WORKING ON IT. MY BEER'S GONE AND THE HEAT'S EXACERBATING HOBO PISS STINK, SO LET'S GO HEAR THE NEW MIXES.
I'M OUTTA SMOKES, I'LL CATCH UP.
SUIT YOURSELF, I'M GOING TO FIND A COLD ONE AND SOAK UP STUDIO AC.
Melch is paying Barbossa OUT OF MY MONEY every week to keep him quiet, but he's still too close to Slade for comfort.
phone
phone
Barbossa and I went through HELL together. I can't bring myself to off him.
So I'll hire someone else to take him out.
HELLO? THIS IS #3708. I HAVE A JOB.
NO, I'M NOT LOOKING FOR A JOB, I NEED AN OPERATIVE TO DO A JOB.
YEAH, I KNOW THE DRILL, CORNER OF BEEKMAN AND PARK ROW.

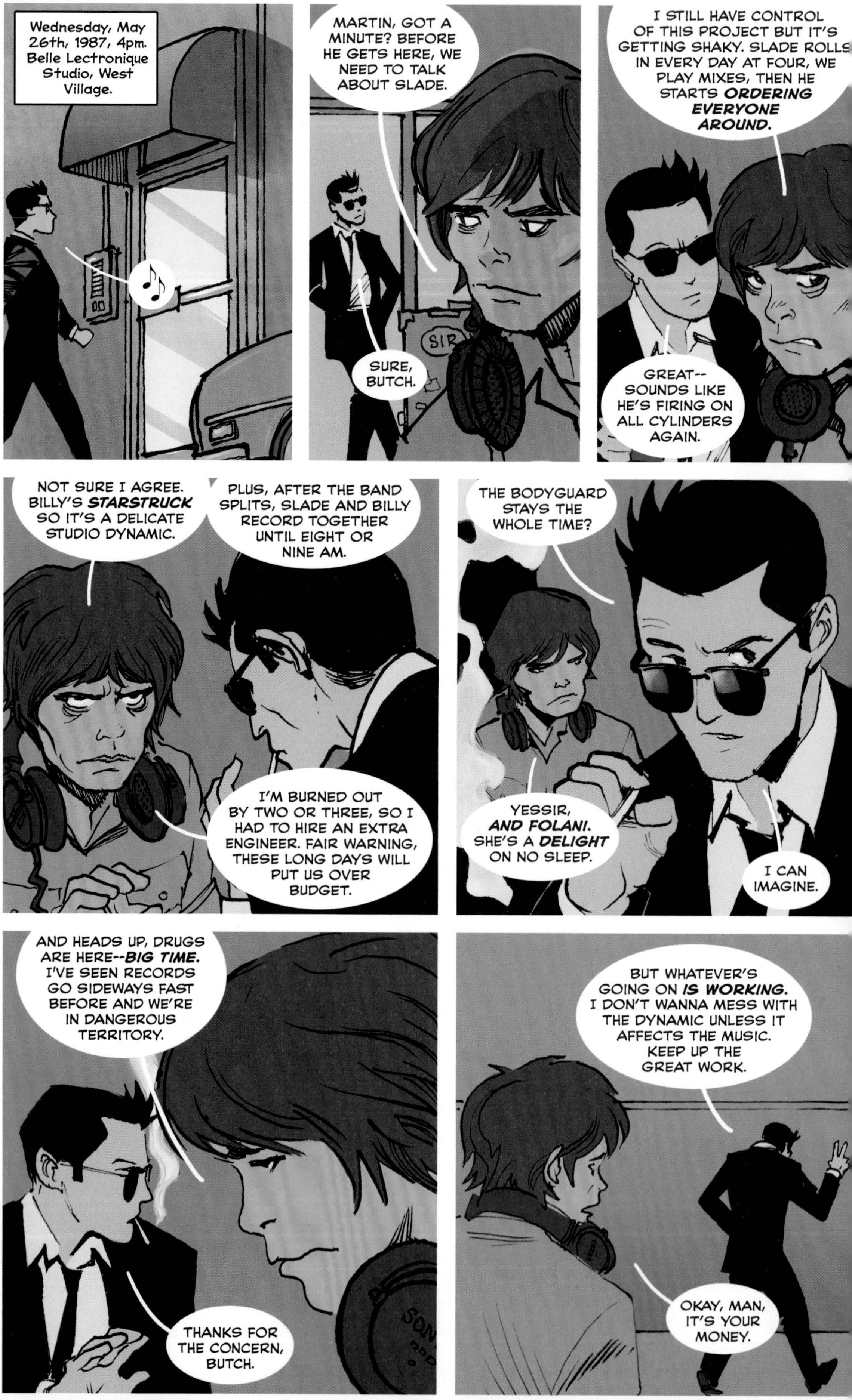
Wednesday, May 26th, 1987, 4pm. Belle Lectronique Studio, West Village.
MARTIN, GOT A MINUTE? BEFORE HE GETS HERE, WE NEED TO TALK ABOUT SLADE.
SURE, BUTCH.
SIR
I STILL HAVE CONTROL OF THIS PROJECT BUT IT'S GETTING SHAKY. SLADE ROLLS IN EVERY DAY AT FOUR, WE PLAY MIXES, THEN HE STARTS ORDERING EVERYONE AROUND.
GREAT--SOUNDS LIKE HE'S FIRING ON ALL CYLINDERS AGAIN.
NOT SURE I AGREE. BILLY'S STARSTRUCK SO IT'S A DELICATE STUDIO DYNAMIC.
PLUS, AFTER THE BAND SPLITS, SLADE AND BILLY RECORD TOGETHER UNTIL EIGHT OR NINE AM.
I'M BURNED OUT BY TWO OR THREE, SO I HAD TO HIRE AN EXTRA ENGINEER. FAIR WARNING, THESE LONG DAYS WILL PUT US OVER BUDGET.
THE BODYGUARD STAYS THE WHOLE TIME?
YESSIR, AND FOLANI. SHE'S A DELIGHT ON NO SLEEP.
I CAN IMAGINE.
AND HEADS UP, DRUGS ARE HERE--BIG TIME. I'VE SEEN RECORDS GO SIDEWAYS FAST BEFORE AND WE'RE IN DANGEROUS TERRITORY.
THANKS FOR THE CONCERN, BUTCH.
BUT WHATEVER'S GOING ON IS WORKING. I DON'T WANNA MESS WITH THE DYNAMIC UNLESS IT AFFECTS THE MUSIC. KEEP UP THE GREAT WORK.
OKAY, MAN, IT'S YOUR MONEY.

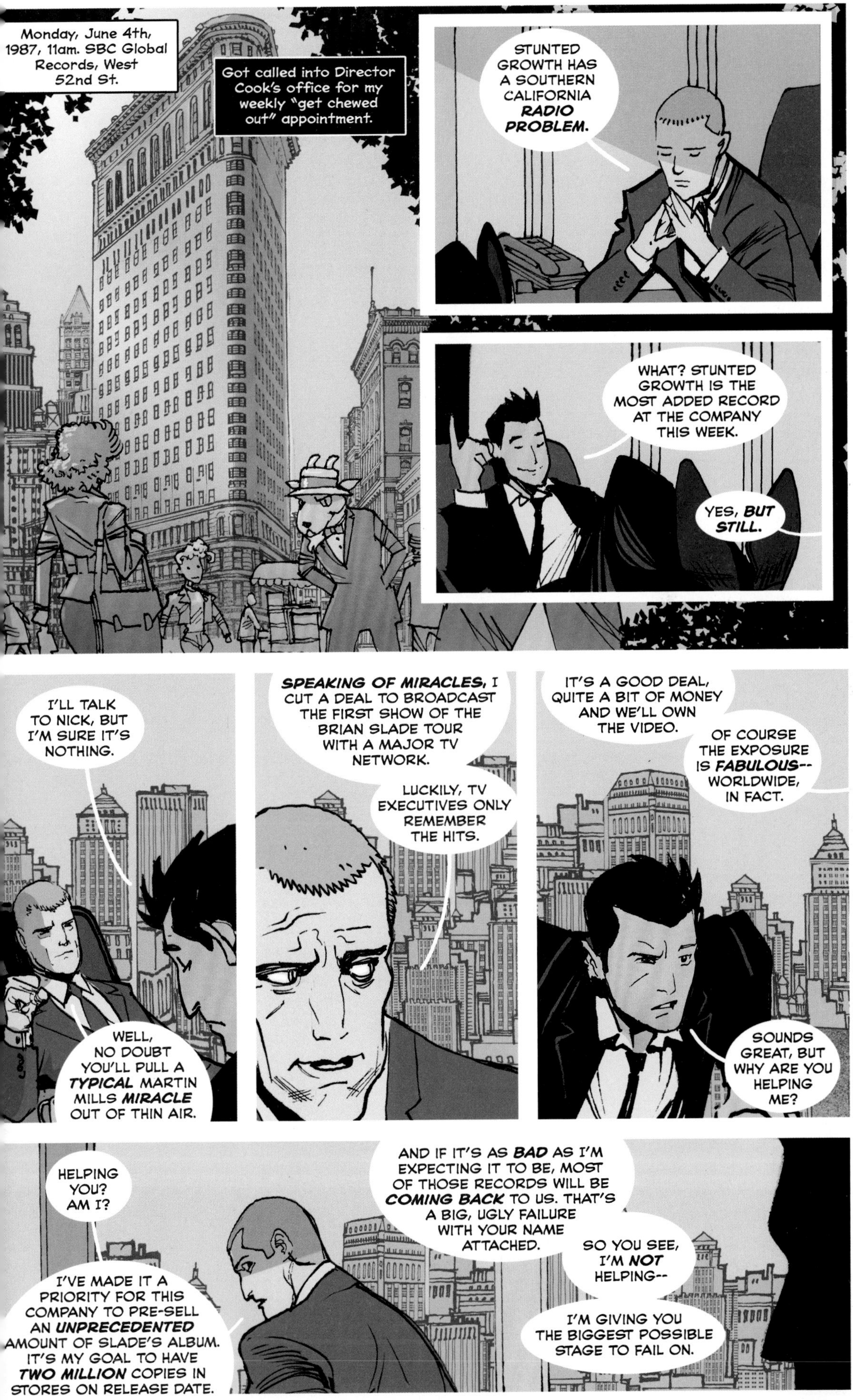
Monday, June 4th, 1987, 11am. SBC Global Records, West 52nd St.
Got called into Director Cook's office for my weekly "get chewed out" appointment.
STUNTED GROWTH HAS A SOUTHERN CALIFORNIA **RADIO PROBLEM.**
WHAT? STUNTED GROWTH IS THE MOST ADDED RECORD AT THE COMPANY THIS WEEK.
YES, **BUT STILL.**
I'LL TALK TO NICK, BUT I'M SURE IT'S NOTHING.
WELL, NO DOUBT YOU'LL PULL A **TYPICAL** MARTIN MILLS **MIRACLE** OUT OF THIN AIR.
SPEAKING OF MIRACLES, I CUT A DEAL TO BROADCAST THE FIRST SHOW OF THE BRIAN SLADE TOUR WITH A MAJOR TV NETWORK.
LUCKILY, TV EXECUTIVES ONLY REMEMBER THE HITS.
IT'S A GOOD DEAL, QUITE A BIT OF MONEY AND WE'LL OWN THE VIDEO.
OF COURSE THE EXPOSURE IS **FABULOUS**-- WORLDWIDE, IN FACT.
SOUNDS GREAT, BUT WHY ARE YOU HELPING ME?
HELPING YOU? AM I?
I'VE MADE IT A PRIORITY FOR THIS COMPANY TO PRE-SELL AN **UNPRECEDENTED** AMOUNT OF SLADE'S ALBUM. IT'S MY GOAL TO HAVE **TWO MILLION** COPIES IN STORES ON RELEASE DATE.
AND IF IT'S AS **BAD** AS I'M EXPECTING IT TO BE, MOST OF THOSE RECORDS WILL BE **COMING BACK** TO US. THAT'S A BIG, UGLY FAILURE WITH YOUR NAME ATTACHED.
SO YOU SEE, I'M **NOT** HELPING--
I'M GIVING YOU THE BIGGEST POSSIBLE STAGE TO FAIL ON.

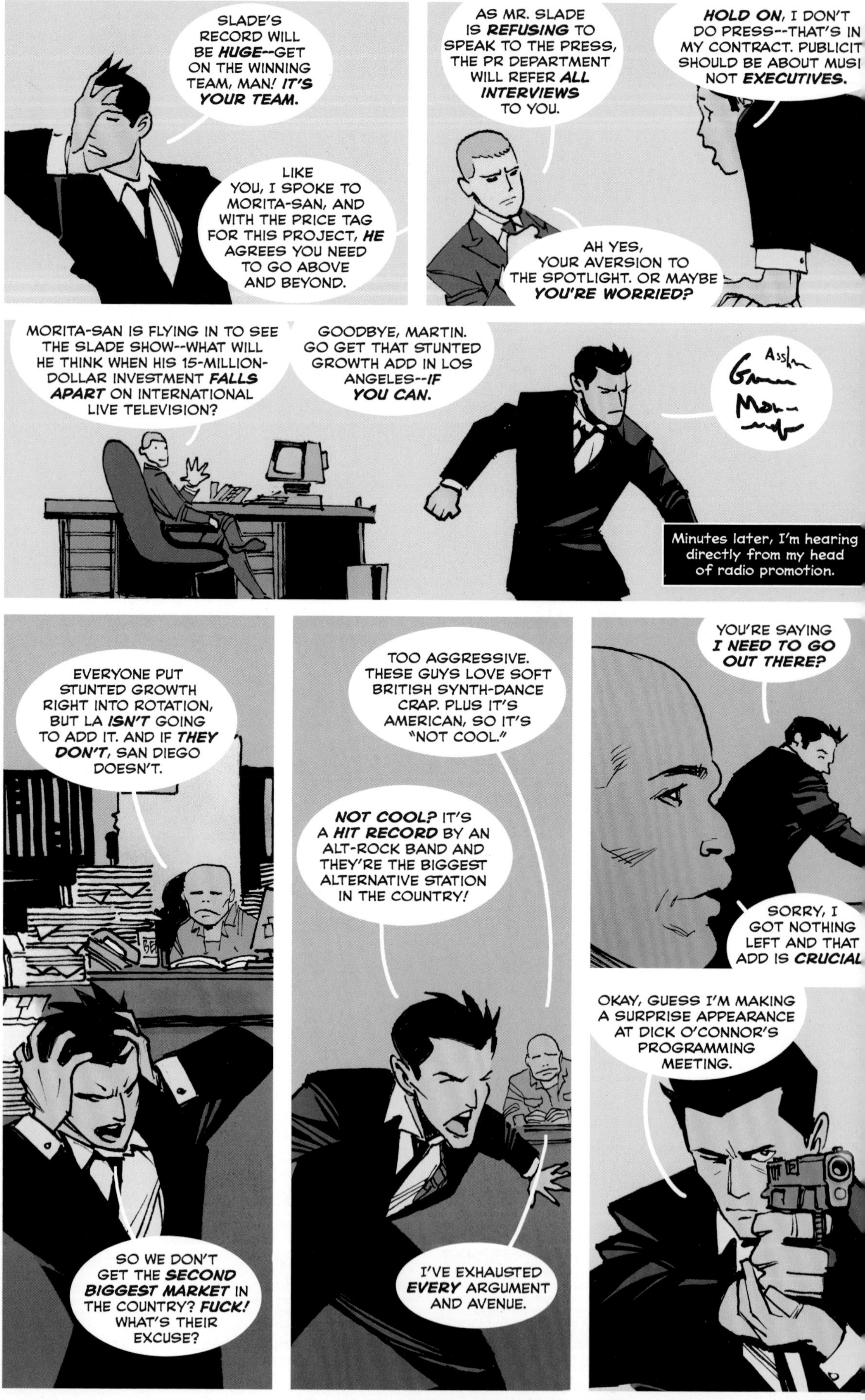

SLADE'S RECORD WILL BE HUGE--GET ON THE WINNING TEAM, MAN! IT'S YOUR TEAM.
LIKE YOU, I SPOKE TO MORITA-SAN, AND WITH THE PRICE TAG FOR THIS PROJECT, HE AGREES YOU NEED TO GO ABOVE AND BEYOND.
AS MR. SLADE IS REFUSING TO SPEAK TO THE PRESS, THE PR DEPARTMENT WILL REFER ALL INTERVIEWS TO YOU.
HOLD ON, I DON'T DO PRESS--THAT'S IN MY CONTRACT. PUBLICIT SHOULD BE ABOUT MUSI NOT EXECUTIVES.
AH YES, YOUR AVERSION TO THE SPOTLIGHT. OR MAYBE YOU'RE WORRIED?
MORITA-SAN IS FLYING IN TO SEE THE SLADE SHOW--WHAT WILL HE THINK WHEN HIS 15-MILLION-DOLLAR INVESTMENT FALLS APART ON INTERNATIONAL LIVE TELEVISION?
GOODBYE, MARTIN. GO GET THAT STUNTED GROWTH ADD IN LOS ANGELES--IF YOU CAN.
Minutes later, I'm hearing directly from my head of radio promotion.
EVERYONE PUT STUNTED GROWTH RIGHT INTO ROTATION, BUT LA ISN'T GOING TO ADD IT. AND IF THEY DON'T, SAN DIEGO DOESN'T.
SO WE DON'T GET THE SECOND BIGGEST MARKET IN THE COUNTRY? FUCK! WHAT'S THEIR EXCUSE?
TOO AGGRESSIVE. THESE GUYS LOVE SOFT BRITISH SYNTH-DANCE CRAP. PLUS IT'S AMERICAN, SO IT'S "NOT COOL."
NOT COOL? IT'S A HIT RECORD BY AN ALT-ROCK BAND AND THEY'RE THE BIGGEST ALTERNATIVE STATION IN THE COUNTRY!
I'VE EXHAUSTED EVERY ARGUMENT AND AVENUE.
YOU'RE SAYING I NEED TO GO OUT THERE?
SORRY, I GOT NOTHING LEFT AND THAT ADD IS CRUCIAL
OKAY, GUESS I'M MAKING A SURPRISE APPEARANCE AT DICK O'CONNOR'S PROGRAMMING MEETING.

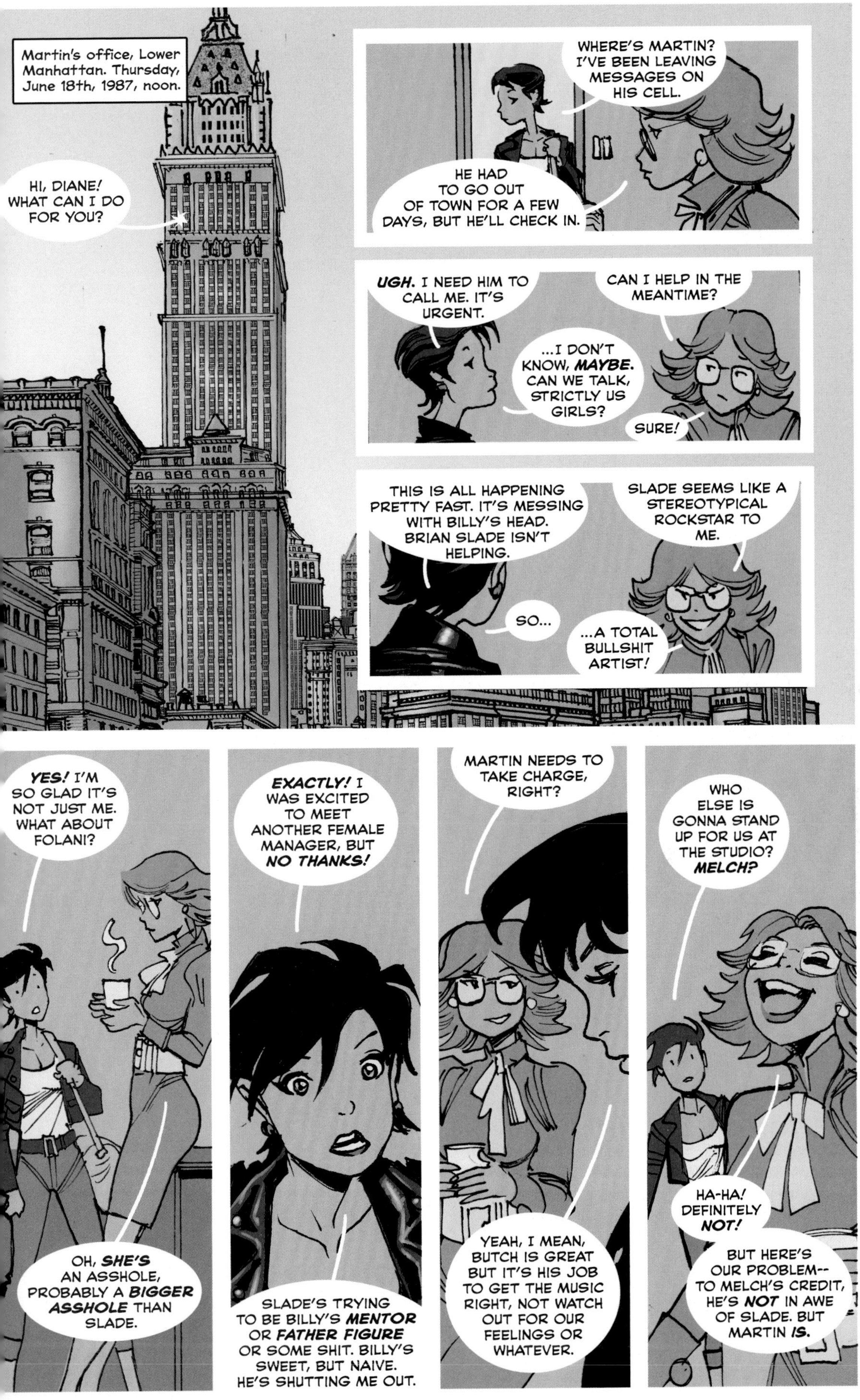

Martin's office, Lower Manhattan. Thursday, June 18th, 1987, noon.
HI, DIANE! WHAT CAN I DO FOR YOU?
WHERE'S MARTIN? I'VE BEEN LEAVING MESSAGES ON HIS CELL.
HE HAD TO GO OUT OF TOWN FOR A FEW DAYS, BUT HE'LL CHECK IN.
UGH. I NEED HIM TO CALL ME. IT'S URGENT.
CAN I HELP IN THE MEANTIME?
...I DON'T KNOW, MAYBE. CAN WE TALK, STRICTLY US GIRLS?
SURE!
THIS IS ALL HAPPENING PRETTY FAST. IT'S MESSING WITH BILLY'S HEAD. BRIAN SLADE ISN'T HELPING.
SLADE SEEMS LIKE A STEREOTYPICAL ROCKSTAR TO ME.
SO...
...A TOTAL BULLSHIT ARTIST!
YES! I'M SO GLAD IT'S NOT JUST ME. WHAT ABOUT FOLANI?
OH, SHE'S AN ASSHOLE, PROBABLY A BIGGER ASSHOLE THAN SLADE.
EXACTLY! I WAS EXCITED TO MEET ANOTHER FEMALE MANAGER, BUT NO THANKS!
SLADE'S TRYING TO BE BILLY'S MENTOR OR FATHER FIGURE OR SOME SHIT. BILLY'S SWEET, BUT NAIVE. HE'S SHUTTING ME OUT.
MARTIN NEEDS TO TAKE CHARGE, RIGHT?
YEAH, I MEAN, BUTCH IS GREAT BUT IT'S HIS JOB TO GET THE MUSIC RIGHT, NOT WATCH OUT FOR OUR FEELINGS OR WHATEVER.
WHO ELSE IS GONNA STAND UP FOR US AT THE STUDIO? MELCH?
HA-HA! DEFINITELY NOT!
BUT HERE'S OUR PROBLEM-- TO MELCH'S CREDIT, HE'S NOT IN AWE OF SLADE. BUT MARTIN IS.

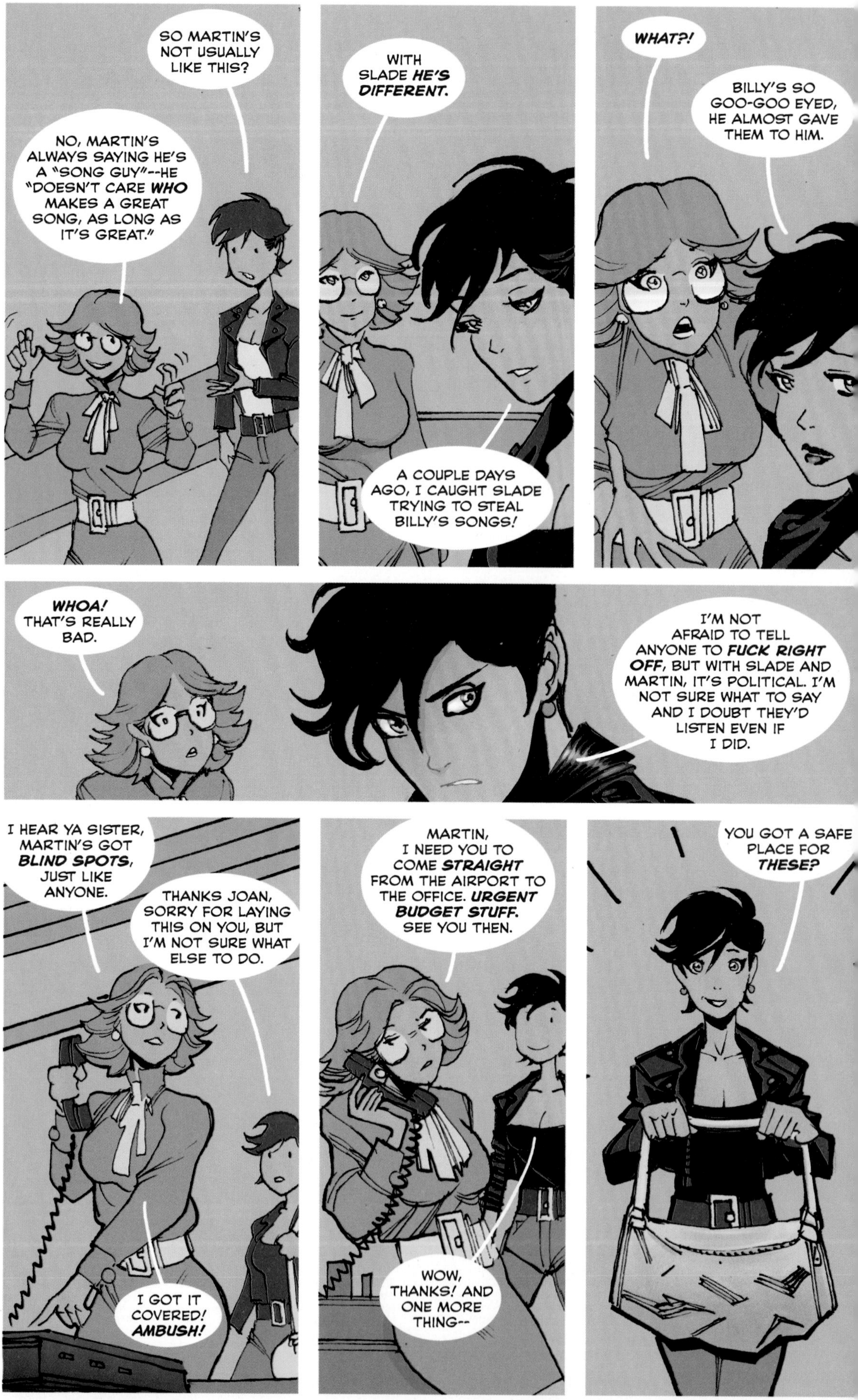
SO MARTIN'S NOT USUALLY LIKE THIS?
NO, MARTIN'S ALWAYS SAYING HE'S A "SONG GUY"--HE "DOESN'T CARE WHO MAKES A GREAT SONG, AS LONG AS IT'S GREAT."
WITH SLADE HE'S DIFFERENT.
A COUPLE DAYS AGO, I CAUGHT SLADE TRYING TO STEAL BILLY'S SONGS!
WHAT?!
BILLY'S SO GOO-GOO EYED, HE ALMOST GAVE THEM TO HIM.
WHOA! THAT'S REALLY BAD.
I'M NOT AFRAID TO TELL ANYONE TO FUCK RIGHT OFF, BUT WITH SLADE AND MARTIN, IT'S POLITICAL. I'M NOT SURE WHAT TO SAY AND I DOUBT THEY'D LISTEN EVEN IF I DID.
I HEAR YA SISTER, MARTIN'S GOT BLIND SPOTS, JUST LIKE ANYONE.
THANKS JOAN, SORRY FOR LAYING THIS ON YOU, BUT I'M NOT SURE WHAT ELSE TO DO.
I GOT IT COVERED! AMBUSH!
MARTIN, I NEED YOU TO COME STRAIGHT FROM THE AIRPORT TO THE OFFICE. URGENT BUDGET STUFF. SEE YOU THEN.
WOW, THANKS! AND ONE MORE THING--
YOU GOT A SAFE PLACE FOR THESE?

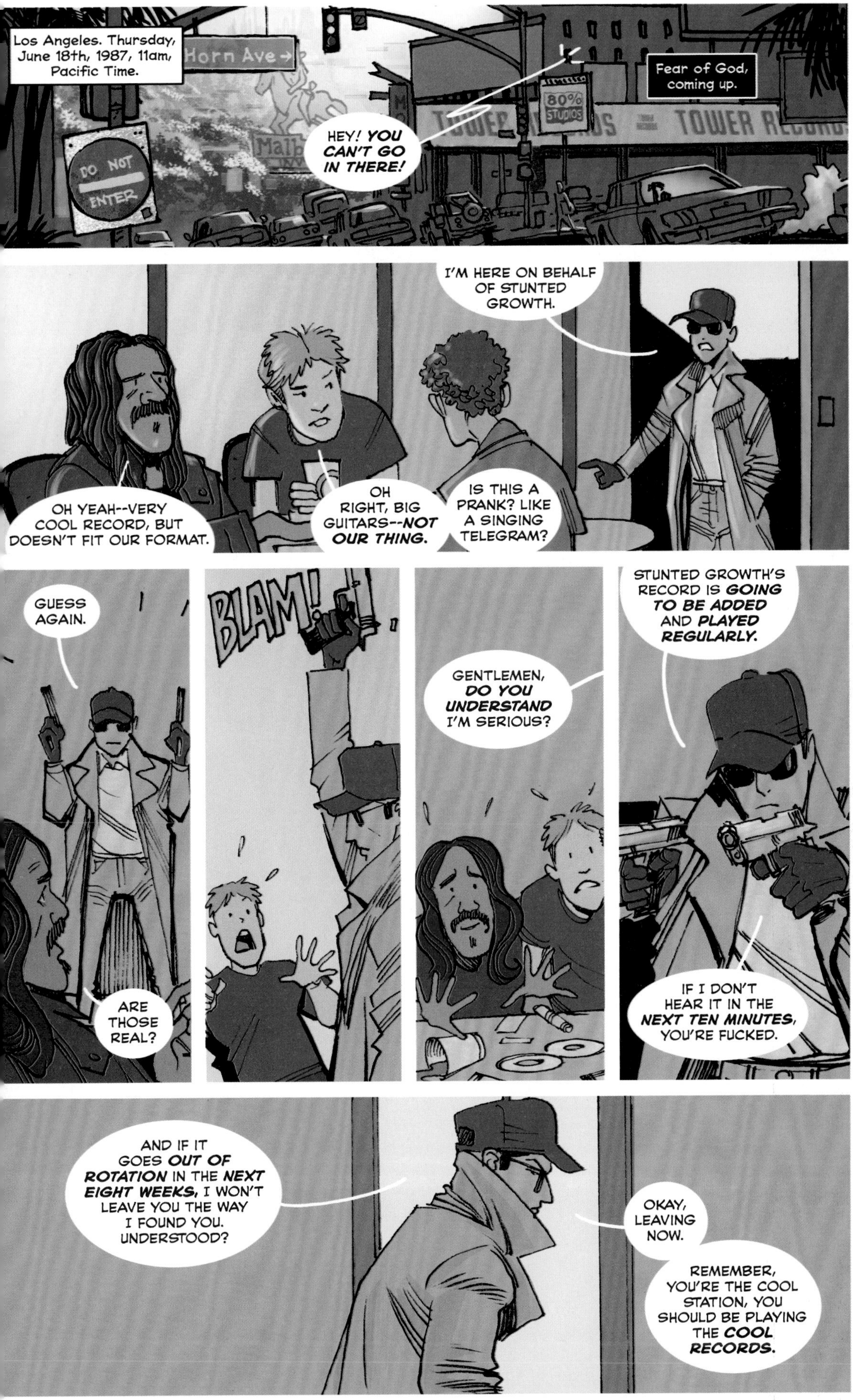
Los Angeles. Thursday, June 18th, 1987, 11am, Pacific Time.
Horn Ave
DO NOT ENTER
80% STUDIOS
TOWER RECORDS
Fear of God, coming up.
HEY! YOU CAN'T GO IN THERE!
I'M HERE ON BEHALF OF STUNTED GROWTH.
OH YEAH--VERY COOL RECORD, BUT DOESN'T FIT OUR FORMAT.
OH RIGHT, BIG GUITARS--NOT OUR THING.
IS THIS A PRANK? LIKE A SINGING TELEGRAM?
GUESS AGAIN.
ARE THOSE REAL?
BLAM!
GENTLEMEN, DO YOU UNDERSTAND I'M SERIOUS?
STUNTED GROWTH'S RECORD IS GOING TO BE ADDED AND PLAYED REGULARLY.
IF I DON'T HEAR IT IN THE NEXT TEN MINUTES, YOU'RE FUCKED.
AND IF IT GOES OUT OF ROTATION IN THE NEXT EIGHT WEEKS, I WON'T LEAVE YOU THE WAY I FOUND YOU. UNDERSTOOD?
OKAY, LEAVING NOW.
REMEMBER, YOU'RE THE COOL STATION, YOU SHOULD BE PLAYING THE COOL RECORDS.

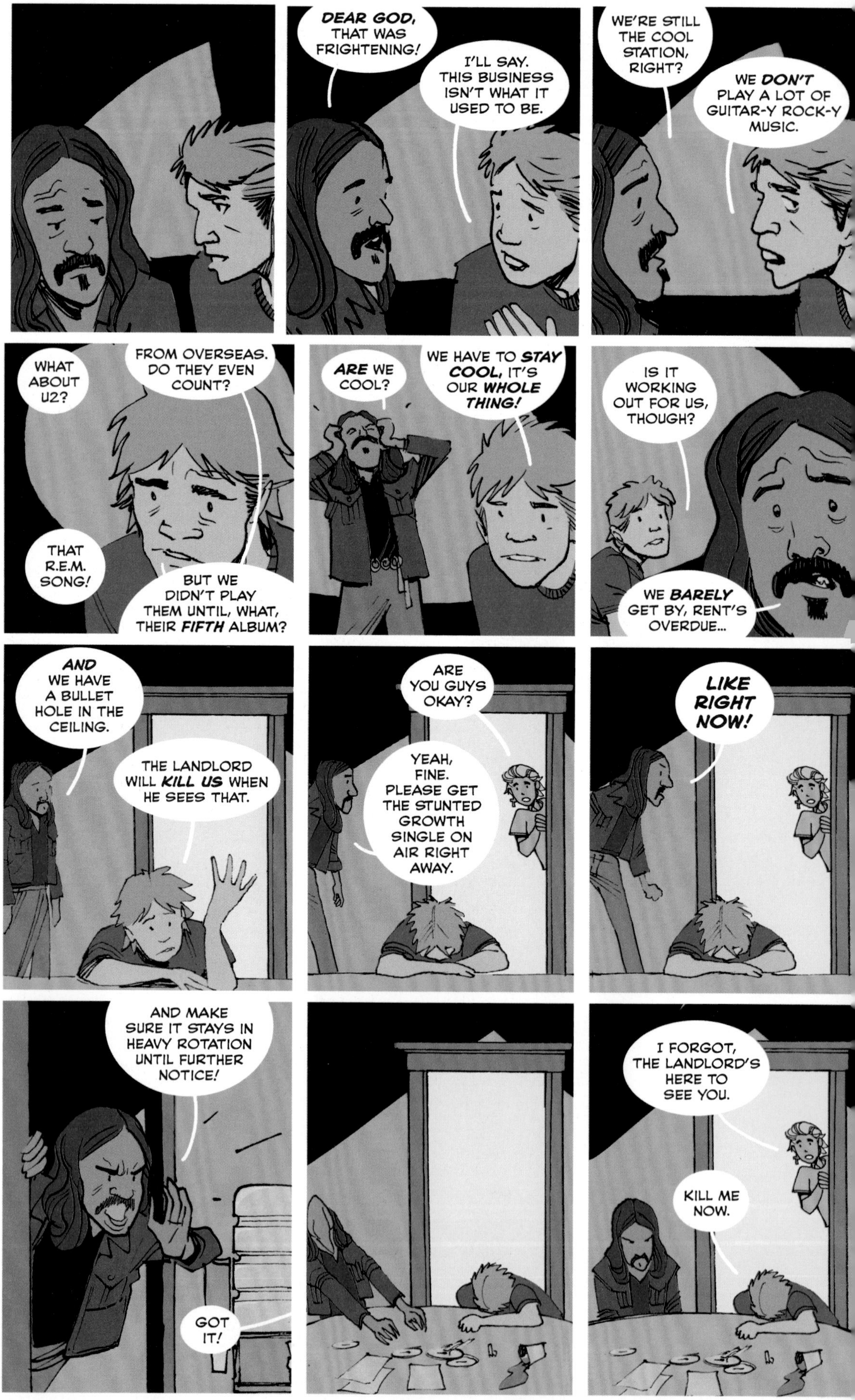
DEAR GOD, THAT WAS FRIGHTENING!
I'LL SAY. THIS BUSINESS ISN'T WHAT IT USED TO BE.
WE'RE STILL THE COOL STATION, RIGHT?
WE DON'T PLAY A LOT OF GUITAR-Y ROCK-Y MUSIC.
WHAT ABOUT U2?
FROM OVERSEAS. DO THEY EVEN COUNT?
THAT R.E.M. SONG!
BUT WE DIDN'T PLAY THEM UNTIL, WHAT, THEIR FIFTH ALBUM?
ARE WE COOL?
WE HAVE TO STAY COOL, IT'S OUR WHOLE THING!
IS IT WORKING OUT FOR US, THOUGH?
WE BARELY GET BY, RENT'S OVERDUE...
AND WE HAVE A BULLET HOLE IN THE CEILING.
THE LANDLORD WILL KILL US WHEN HE SEES THAT.
ARE YOU GUYS OKAY?
YEAH, FINE. PLEASE GET THE STUNTED GROWTH SINGLE ON AIR RIGHT AWAY.
LIKE RIGHT NOW!
AND MAKE SURE IT STAYS IN HEAVY ROTATION UNTIL FURTHER NOTICE!
GOT IT!
I FORGOT, THE LANDLORD'S HERE TO SEE YOU.
KILL ME NOW.

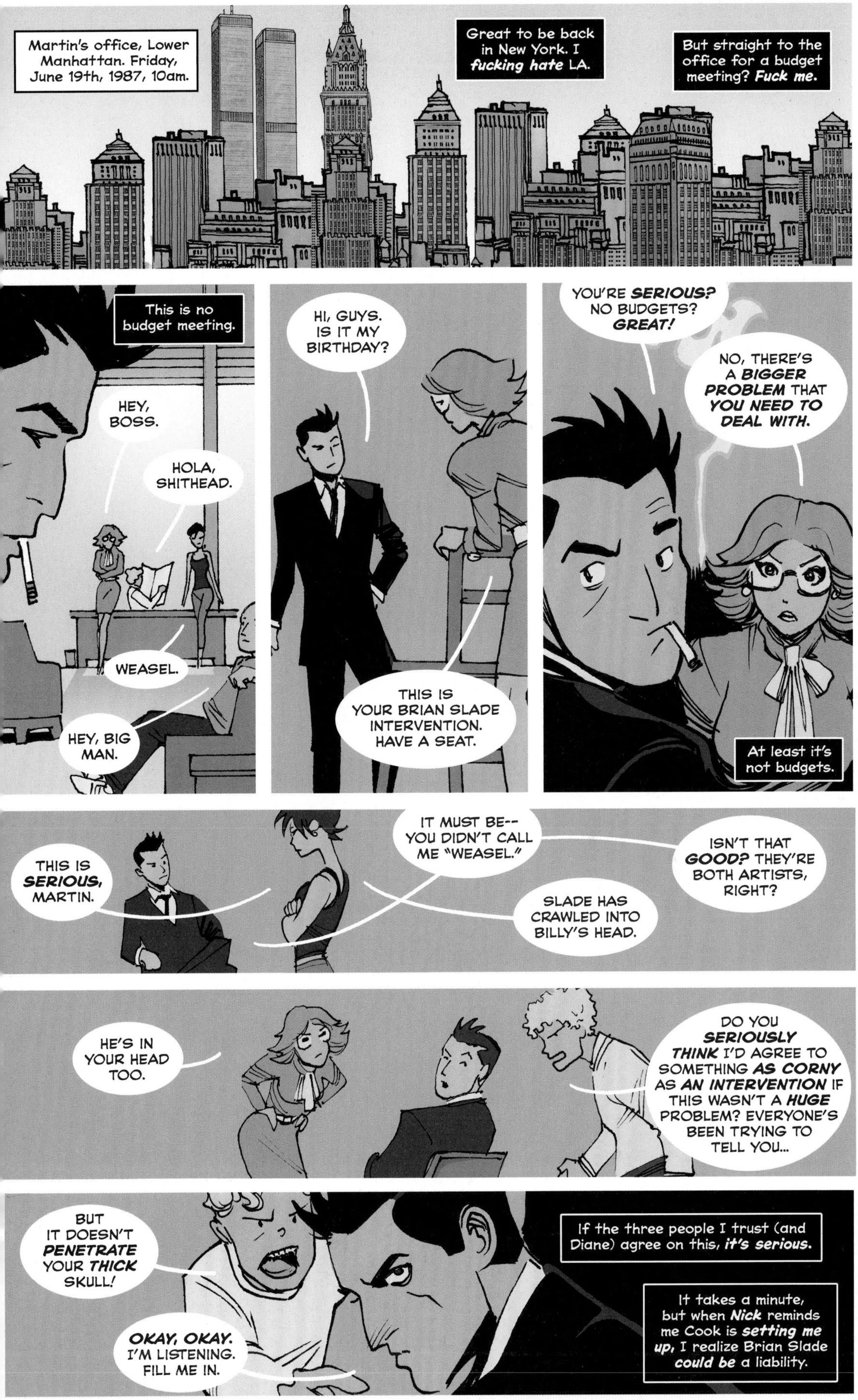

Martin's office, Lower Manhattan. Friday, June 19th, 1987, 10am.
Great to be back in New York. I *fucking hate* LA.
But straight to the office for a budget meeting? *Fuck me.*
This is no budget meeting.
HEY, BOSS.
HOLA, SHITHEAD.
WEASEL.
HEY, BIG MAN.
HI, GUYS. IS IT MY BIRTHDAY?
THIS IS YOUR BRIAN SLADE INTERVENTION. HAVE A SEAT.
YOU'RE *SERIOUS?* NO BUDGETS? *GREAT!*
NO, THERE'S A *BIGGER PROBLEM* THAT *YOU NEED TO DEAL WITH.*
At least it's not budgets.
THIS IS *SERIOUS,* MARTIN.
IT MUST BE-- YOU DIDN'T CALL ME "WEASEL."
SLADE HAS CRAWLED INTO BILLY'S HEAD.
ISN'T THAT *GOOD?* THEY'RE BOTH ARTISTS, RIGHT?
HE'S IN YOUR HEAD TOO.
DO YOU *SERIOUSLY THINK* I'D AGREE TO SOMETHING *AS CORNY* AS *AN INTERVENTION* IF THIS WASN'T A *HUGE* PROBLEM? EVERYONE'S BEEN TRYING TO TELL YOU...
BUT IT DOESN'T *PENETRATE* YOUR *THICK* SKULL!
OKAY, OKAY. I'M LISTENING. FILL ME IN.
If the three people I trust (and Diane) agree on this, *it's serious.*
It takes a minute, but when *Nick* reminds me Cook is *setting me up,* I realize Brian Slade *could be* a liability.

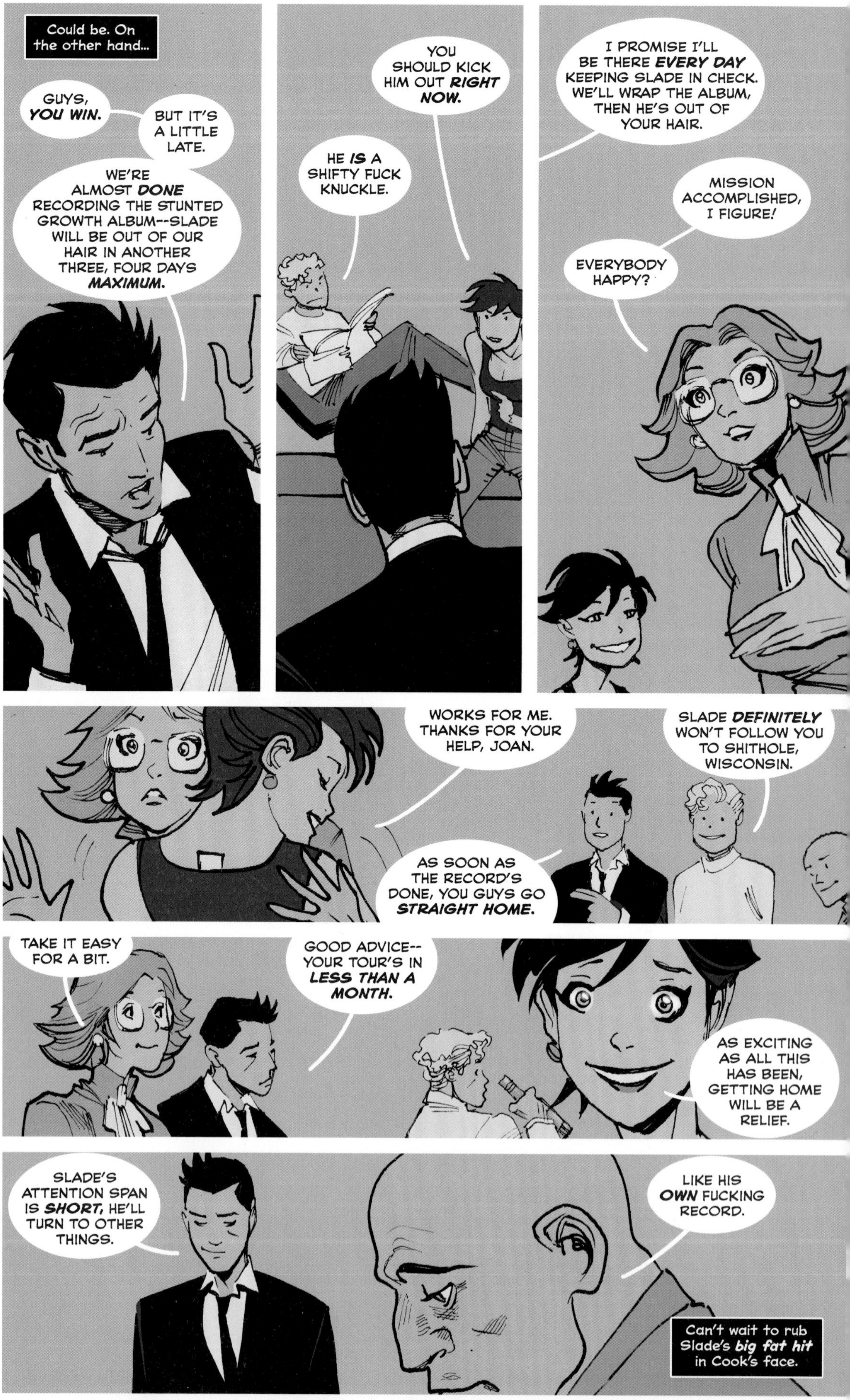

Could be. On the other hand...
GUYS, YOU WIN.
BUT IT'S A LITTLE LATE.
WE'RE ALMOST DONE RECORDING THE STUNTED GROWTH ALBUM--SLADE WILL BE OUT OF OUR HAIR IN ANOTHER THREE, FOUR DAYS MAXIMUM.
YOU SHOULD KICK HIM OUT RIGHT NOW.
HE IS A SHIFTY FUCK KNUCKLE.
I PROMISE I'LL BE THERE EVERY DAY KEEPING SLADE IN CHECK. WE'LL WRAP THE ALBUM, THEN HE'S OUT OF YOUR HAIR.
MISSION ACCOMPLISHED, I FIGURE!
EVERYBODY HAPPY?
WORKS FOR ME. THANKS FOR YOUR HELP, JOAN.
SLADE DEFINITELY WON'T FOLLOW YOU TO SHITHOLE, WISCONSIN.
AS SOON AS THE RECORD'S DONE, YOU GUYS GO STRAIGHT HOME.
TAKE IT EASY FOR A BIT.
GOOD ADVICE-- YOUR TOUR'S IN LESS THAN A MONTH.
AS EXCITING AS ALL THIS HAS BEEN, GETTING HOME WILL BE A RELIEF.
SLADE'S ATTENTION SPAN IS SHORT, HE'LL TURN TO OTHER THINGS.
LIKE HIS OWN FUCKING RECORD.
Can't wait to rub Slade's big fat hit in Cook's face.

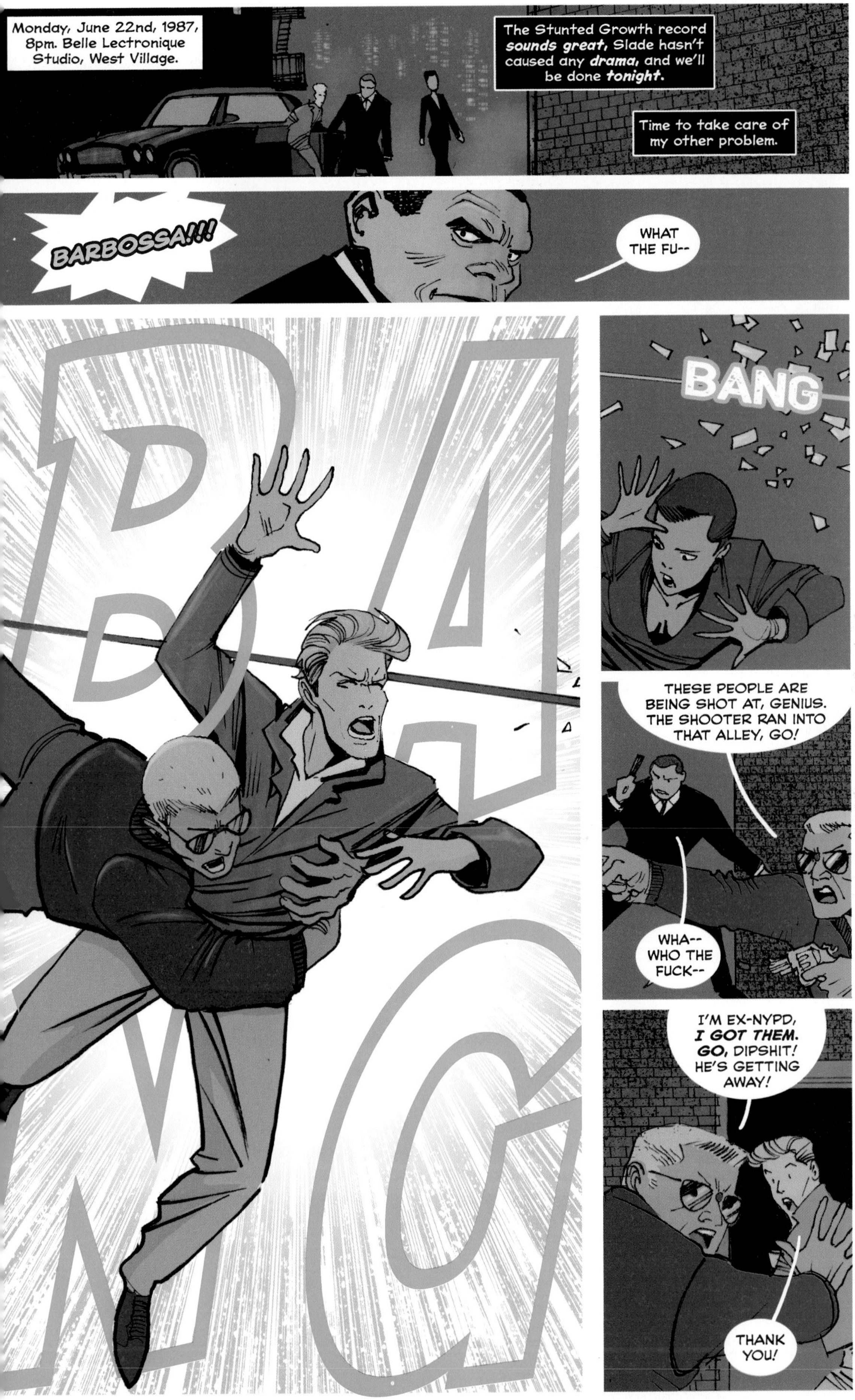
Monday, June 22nd, 1987, 8pm. Belle Lectronique Studio, West Village.
The Stunted Growth record ***sounds great,*** Slade hasn't caused any ***drama,*** and we'll be done ***tonight.***
Time to take care of my other problem.
BARBOSSA!!!
WHAT THE FU--
BANG
BANG
THESE PEOPLE ARE BEING SHOT AT, GENIUS. THE SHOOTER RAN INTO THAT ALLEY, GO!
WHA-- WHO THE FUCK--
I'M EX-NYPD, ***I GOT THEM. GO,*** DIPSHIT! HE'S GETTING AWAY!
THANK YOU!

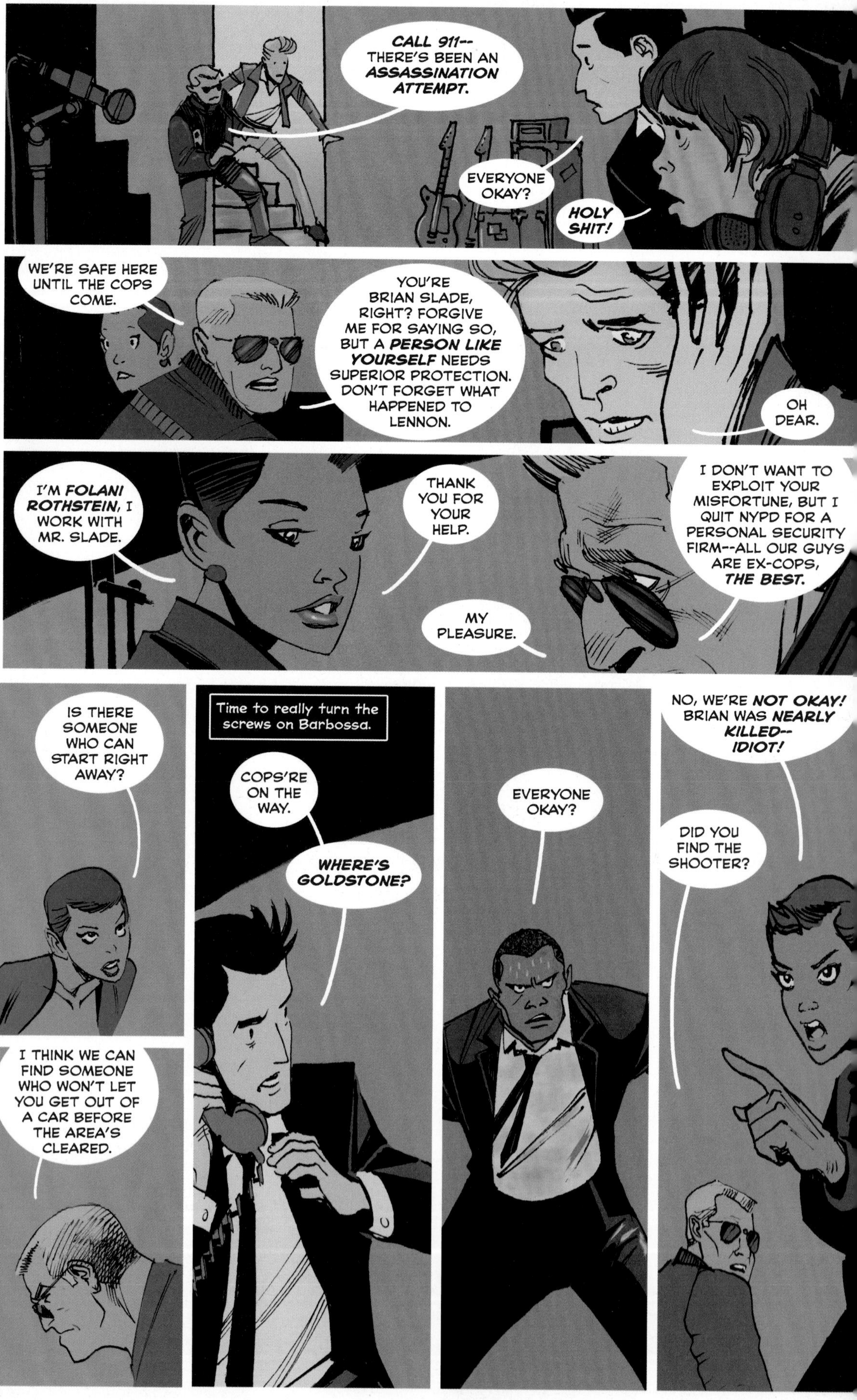
CALL 911-- THERE'S BEEN AN ASSASSINATION ATTEMPT.
EVERYONE OKAY?
HOLY SHIT!
WE'RE SAFE HERE UNTIL THE COPS COME.
YOU'RE BRIAN SLADE, RIGHT? FORGIVE ME FOR SAYING SO, BUT A PERSON LIKE YOURSELF NEEDS SUPERIOR PROTECTION. DON'T FORGET WHAT HAPPENED TO LENNON.
OH DEAR.
I'M FOLANI ROTHSTEIN, I WORK WITH MR. SLADE.
THANK YOU FOR YOUR HELP.
MY PLEASURE.
I DON'T WANT TO EXPLOIT YOUR MISFORTUNE, BUT I QUIT NYPD FOR A PERSONAL SECURITY FIRM--ALL OUR GUYS ARE EX-COPS, THE BEST.
IS THERE SOMEONE WHO CAN START RIGHT AWAY?
I THINK WE CAN FIND SOMEONE WHO WON'T LET YOU GET OUT OF A CAR BEFORE THE AREA'S CLEARED.
Time to really turn the screws on Barbossa.
COPS'RE ON THE WAY.
WHERE'S GOLDSTONE?
EVERYONE OKAY?
NO, WE'RE NOT OKAY! BRIAN WAS NEARLY KILLED-- IDIOT!
DID YOU FIND THE SHOOTER?

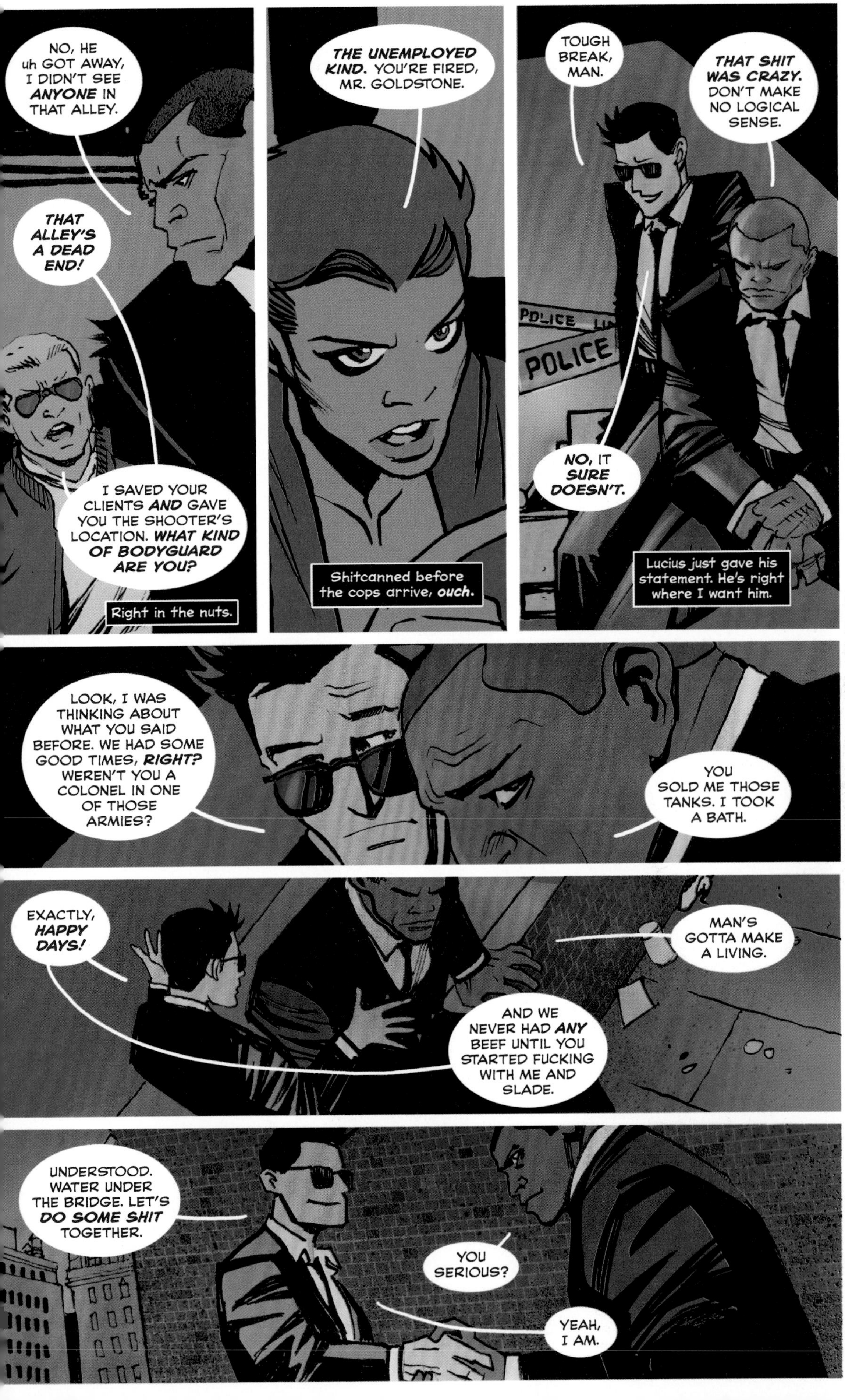
NO, HE uh GOT AWAY, I DIDN'T SEE ANYONE IN THAT ALLEY.
THAT ALLEY'S A DEAD END!
I SAVED YOUR CLIENTS AND GAVE YOU THE SHOOTER'S LOCATION. WHAT KIND OF BODYGUARD ARE YOU?
Right in the nuts.
THE UNEMPLOYED KIND. YOU'RE FIRED, MR. GOLDSTONE.
Shitcanned before the cops arrive, ouch.
TOUGH BREAK, MAN.
THAT SHIT WAS CRAZY. DON'T MAKE NO LOGICAL SENSE.
POLICE
POLICE
NO, IT SURE DOESN'T.
Lucius just gave his statement. He's right where I want him.
LOOK, I WAS THINKING ABOUT WHAT YOU SAID BEFORE. WE HAD SOME GOOD TIMES, RIGHT? WEREN'T YOU A COLONEL IN ONE OF THOSE ARMIES?
YOU SOLD ME THOSE TANKS. I TOOK A BATH.
EXACTLY, HAPPY DAYS!
MAN'S GOTTA MAKE A LIVING.
AND WE NEVER HAD ANY BEEF UNTIL YOU STARTED FUCKING WITH ME AND SLADE.
UNDERSTOOD. WATER UNDER THE BRIDGE. LET'S DO SOME SHIT TOGETHER.
YOU SERIOUS?
YEAH, I AM.

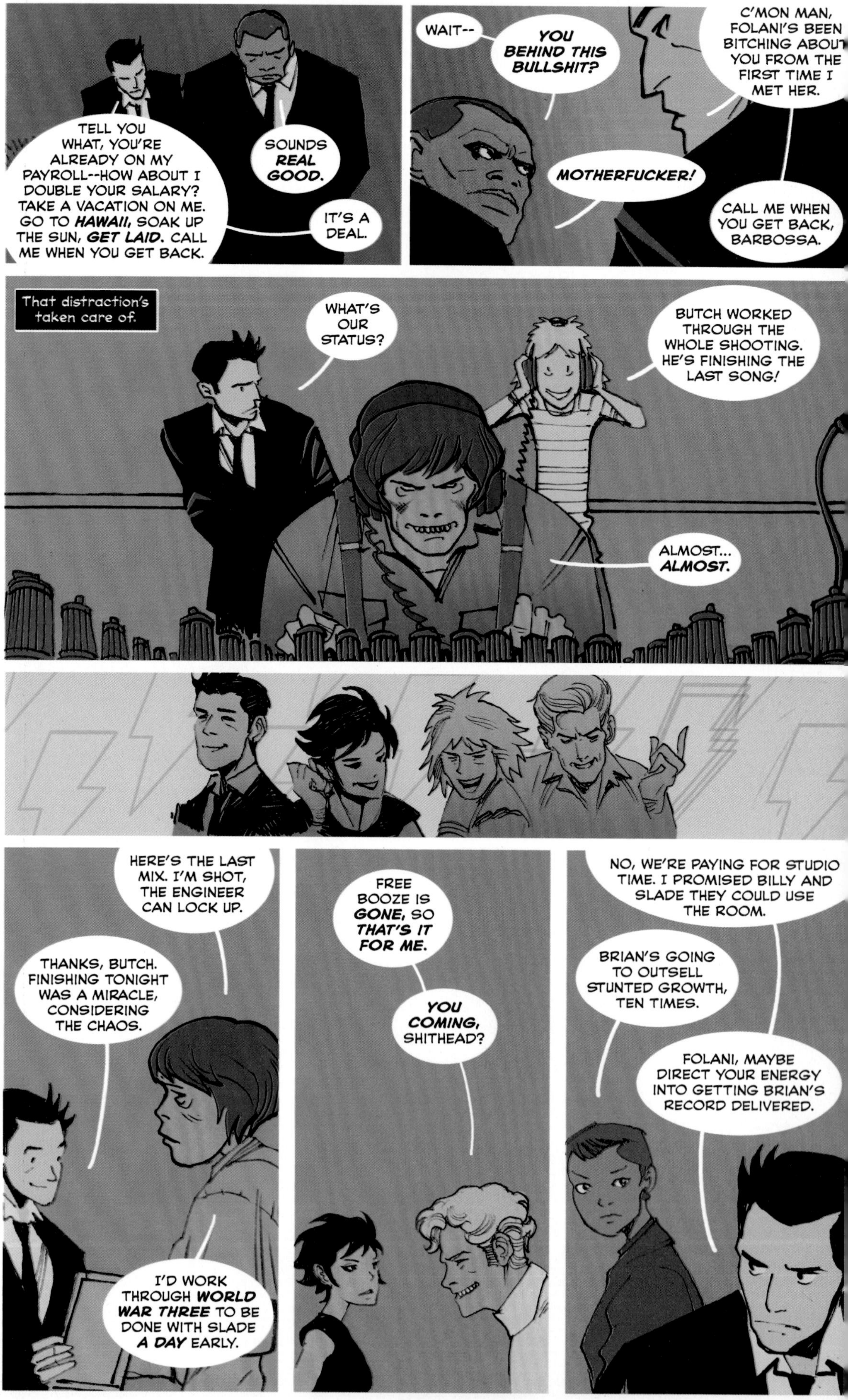
TELL YOU WHAT, YOU'RE ALREADY ON MY PAYROLL--HOW ABOUT I DOUBLE YOUR SALARY? TAKE A VACATION ON ME. GO TO HAWAII, SOAK UP THE SUN, GET LAID. CALL ME WHEN YOU GET BACK.
SOUNDS REAL GOOD.
IT'S A DEAL.
WAIT--
YOU BEHIND THIS BULLSHIT?
C'MON MAN, FOLANI'S BEEN BITCHING ABOUT YOU FROM THE FIRST TIME I MET HER.
MOTHERFUCKER!
CALL ME WHEN YOU GET BACK, BARBOSSA.
That distraction's taken care of.
WHAT'S OUR STATUS?
BUTCH WORKED THROUGH THE WHOLE SHOOTING. HE'S FINISHING THE LAST SONG!
ALMOST... ALMOST.
HERE'S THE LAST MIX. I'M SHOT, THE ENGINEER CAN LOCK UP.
THANKS, BUTCH. FINISHING TONIGHT WAS A MIRACLE, CONSIDERING THE CHAOS.
I'D WORK THROUGH WORLD WAR THREE TO BE DONE WITH SLADE A DAY EARLY.
FREE BOOZE IS GONE, SO THAT'S IT FOR ME.
YOU COMING, SHITHEAD?
NO, WE'RE PAYING FOR STUDIO TIME. I PROMISED BILLY AND SLADE THEY COULD USE THE ROOM.
BRIAN'S GOING TO OUTSELL STUNTED GROWTH, TEN TIMES.
FOLANI, MAYBE DIRECT YOUR ENERGY INTO GETTING BRIAN'S RECORD DELIVERED.

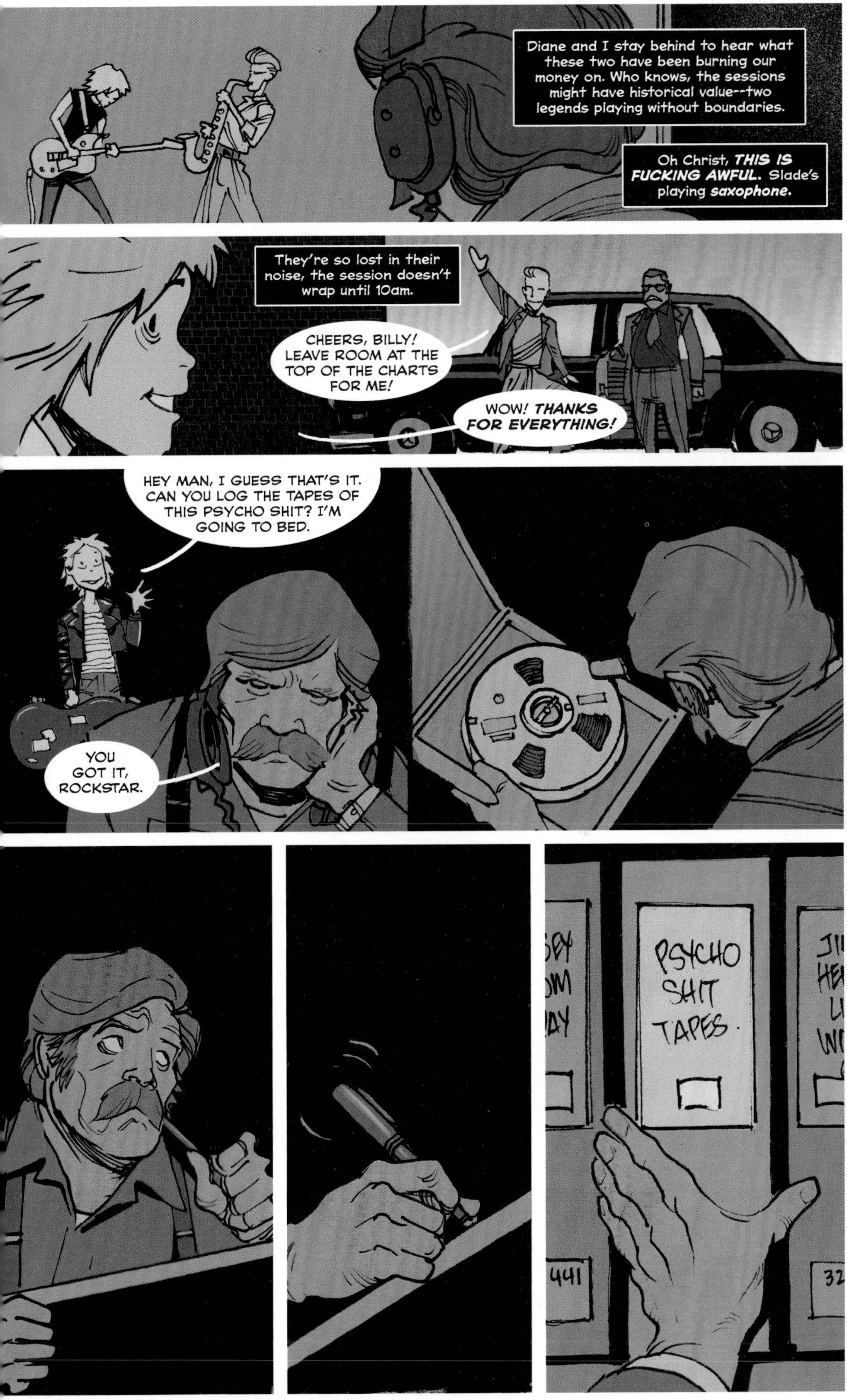

Diane and I stay behind to hear what these two have been burning our money on. Who knows, the sessions might have historical value--two legends playing without boundaries.
Oh Christ, **THIS IS FUCKING AWFUL.** Slade's playing ***saxophone.***
They're so lost in their noise, the session doesn't wrap until 10am.
CHEERS, BILLY! LEAVE ROOM AT THE TOP OF THE CHARTS FOR ME!
WOW! ***THANKS FOR EVERYTHING!***
HEY MAN, I GUESS THAT'S IT. CAN YOU LOG THE TAPES OF THIS PSYCHO SHIT? I'M GOING TO BED.
YOU GOT IT, ROCKSTAR.
PSYCHO SHIT TAPES.
441

HIGH HOPES FOR STUNTED GROWTH

STUNTED STUNS IN NYC DEBUT; GLAM MAN FAN OF BAND

BY GEOFF VOGEUR

NEW YORK   The much-anticipated NYC debut by the Wisconsin 4-piece act was a raucous and energetic 16-song set, packed with strong material, swagger and personality. The future would appear to be anything but inhibited for punk / glam / rock hybrid Stunted Growth, based on their set this week in lower Manhattan.

As impressive as the performance was, the crowd nearly overshadowed it, filled as it was with hipster actors, writers and just as many hopeful A&Rs and label Prezzies whose dreams of signing the act were dashed when SBC hitmaker Martin Mills opened the ticket booth minutes before the show started.

Industry superstars and their entourages were virtually ignored when Brian Slade, not seen publicly for years, was heard to be in the house. Indeed, Slade watched the band from the soundboard and has taken an interest in the act. In the meantime, their current chart-climbing single moves to SBC and will be marketed by Mills' team.

Rumors are swirling as to who will be brought on to produce their forthcoming album, but the rumor mill includes Rick Rubin, Madonna and, according to his representative, Folani Rothstein, the aforementioned Brian Slade. "Brian thinks they're brilliant and is hoping to be very involved going forward," Rothstein said. If true, this would be Slade's first production for an artist (other than himself) since the 70s.

Tongues are further wagging over the rumored cost of the deal, a supposedly multimillion-dollar signing that apparently took place at an unscheduled gig in Southern Connecticut, further illustrating hitmaker Mill's ability to stay ahead of his competition.

During the 40-minute set, the boisterous crowd was treated to a number of undeniable future hits, although this writer was unable to discern song titles. If SBC label head Director Cook knew any of them himself, he kept his cards close to the vest, saying only "We're very excited to be in the Stunted Growth business," before jumping into a waiting car.

An associate of Mills, who identified himself only as "Melch" said one of the songs was called "Goat F***er", and was likely to be first single. When pressed on the problematic nature of the title, the representative vomited on this writer's shoes. Mills, as per usual, didn't make his presence known during the show and could not be located afterwards.

Monday, July 27th, noon, Old Man Bar, 10th Avenue.
I'm catching Melch up on my day so far.
It started all wrong, with a meeting in Director Cook's midtown office.
THIS IS A PIECE OF SHIT.
NTED ROWTH
Then he tells me Stunted Growth is an insult to the label's integrity.

SO YOU REPLY...?

FAIR POINT.

IT'S A RECORD COMPANY--IT DOESN'T HAVE INTEGRITY.

A CROWD WAS GATHERING OUTSIDE HIS OFFICE.

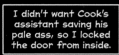

I didn't want Cook's assistant saving his pale ass, so I locked the door from inside.

...WE'VE SHIPPED OVER A MILLION, AND HAVE ORDERS FOR ANOTHER HALF MILLION. WE CAN'T MAKE THEM FAST ENOUGH!

IT'S A HUGE RADIO HIT, EVERY TOUR DATE IS SOLD OUT AND THEY'VE MOVED UP TO STADIUM GIGS.

THE VIDEO IS ALL OVER MTV AND BILLY'S RECORDING A NEW ALBUM ON THE ROAD.

IT'S RAINING MONEY, AND YOU'RE THE ONLY GUY ON EARTH WHO CAN FIND SOMETHING TO BITCH ABOUT.

So he says--

I DON'T LIKE YOU, MARTIN.

ALERT THE MEDIA.

YOU THINK YOU HAVE THE UPPER HAND?! I DICTATE THE PRIORITIES!

NO, YOU DON'T.

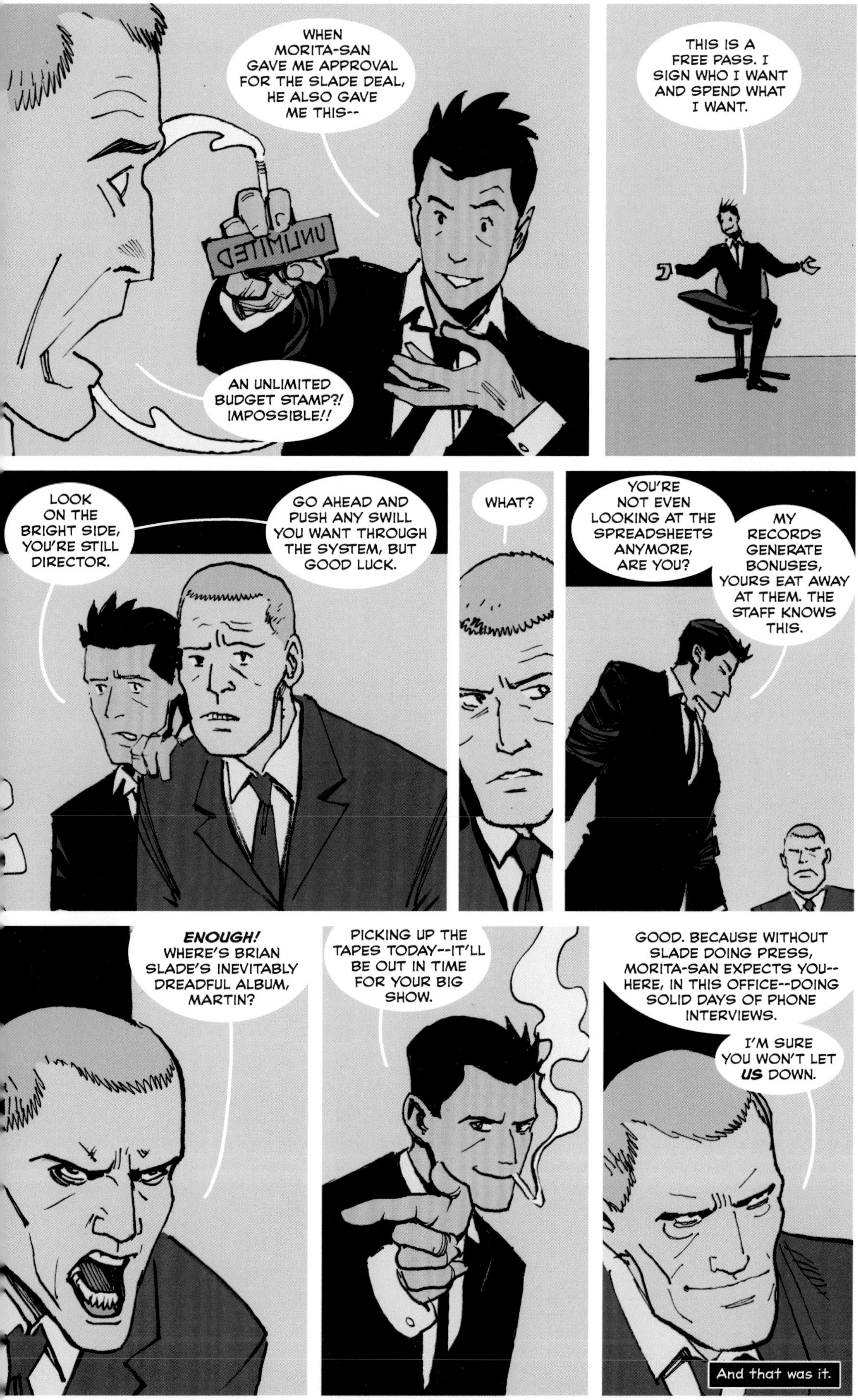
WHEN MORITA-SAN GAVE ME APPROVAL FOR THE SLADE DEAL, HE ALSO GAVE ME THIS--
UNLIMITED
AN UNLIMITED BUDGET STAMP?! IMPOSSIBLE!!
THIS IS A FREE PASS. I SIGN WHO I WANT AND SPEND WHAT I WANT.
LOOK ON THE BRIGHT SIDE, YOU'RE STILL DIRECTOR.
GO AHEAD AND PUSH ANY SWILL YOU WANT THROUGH THE SYSTEM, BUT GOOD LUCK.
WHAT?
YOU'RE NOT EVEN LOOKING AT THE SPREADSHEETS ANYMORE, ARE YOU?
MY RECORDS GENERATE BONUSES, YOURS EAT AWAY AT THEM. THE STAFF KNOWS THIS.
ENOUGH! WHERE'S BRIAN SLADE'S INEVITABLY DREADFUL ALBUM, MARTIN?
PICKING UP THE TAPES TODAY--IT'LL BE OUT IN TIME FOR YOUR BIG SHOW.
GOOD. BECAUSE WITHOUT SLADE DOING PRESS, MORITA-SAN EXPECTS YOU--HERE, IN THIS OFFICE--DOING SOLID DAYS OF PHONE INTERVIEWS.
I'M SURE YOU WON'T LET US DOWN.
And that was it.

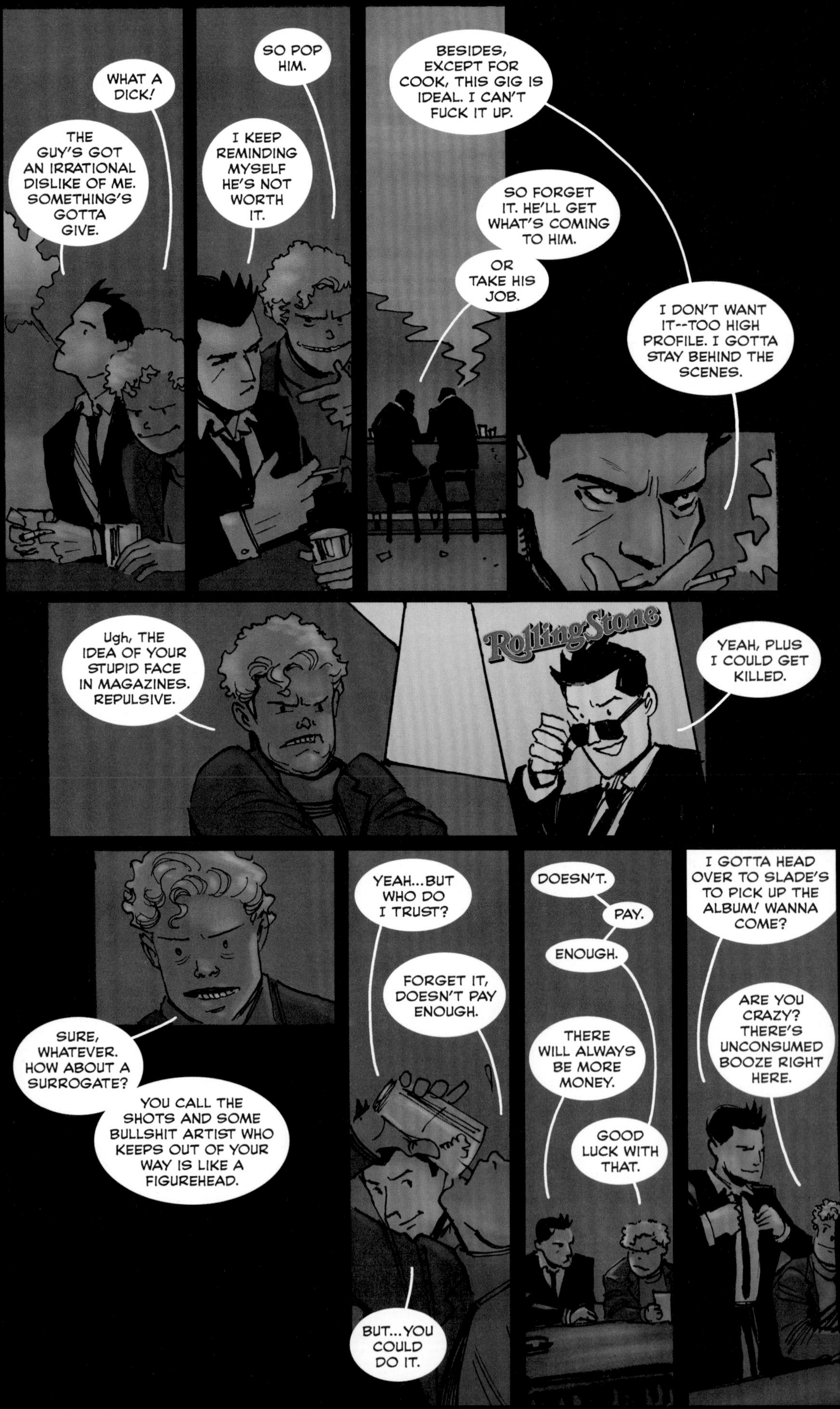
WHAT A DICK!
THE GUY'S GOT AN IRRATIONAL DISLIKE OF ME. SOMETHING'S GOTTA GIVE.
SO POP HIM.
I KEEP REMINDING MYSELF HE'S NOT WORTH IT.
BESIDES, EXCEPT FOR COOK, THIS GIG IS IDEAL. I CAN'T FUCK IT UP.
SO FORGET IT. HE'LL GET WHAT'S COMING TO HIM.
OR TAKE HIS JOB.
I DON'T WANT IT--TOO HIGH PROFILE. I GOTTA STAY BEHIND THE SCENES.
Ugh, THE IDEA OF YOUR STUPID FACE IN MAGAZINES. REPULSIVE.
RollingStone
YEAH, PLUS I COULD GET KILLED.
SURE, WHATEVER. HOW ABOUT A SURROGATE?
YOU CALL THE SHOTS AND SOME BULLSHIT ARTIST WHO KEEPS OUT OF YOUR WAY IS LIKE A FIGUREHEAD.
YEAH...BUT WHO DO I TRUST?
FORGET IT, DOESN'T PAY ENOUGH.
BUT...YOU COULD DO IT.
DOESN'T.
PAY.
ENOUGH.
THERE WILL ALWAYS BE MORE MONEY.
GOOD LUCK WITH THAT.
I GOTTA HEAD OVER TO SLADE'S TO PICK UP THE ALBUM! WANNA COME?
ARE YOU CRAZY? THERE'S UNCONSUMED BOOZE RIGHT HERE.

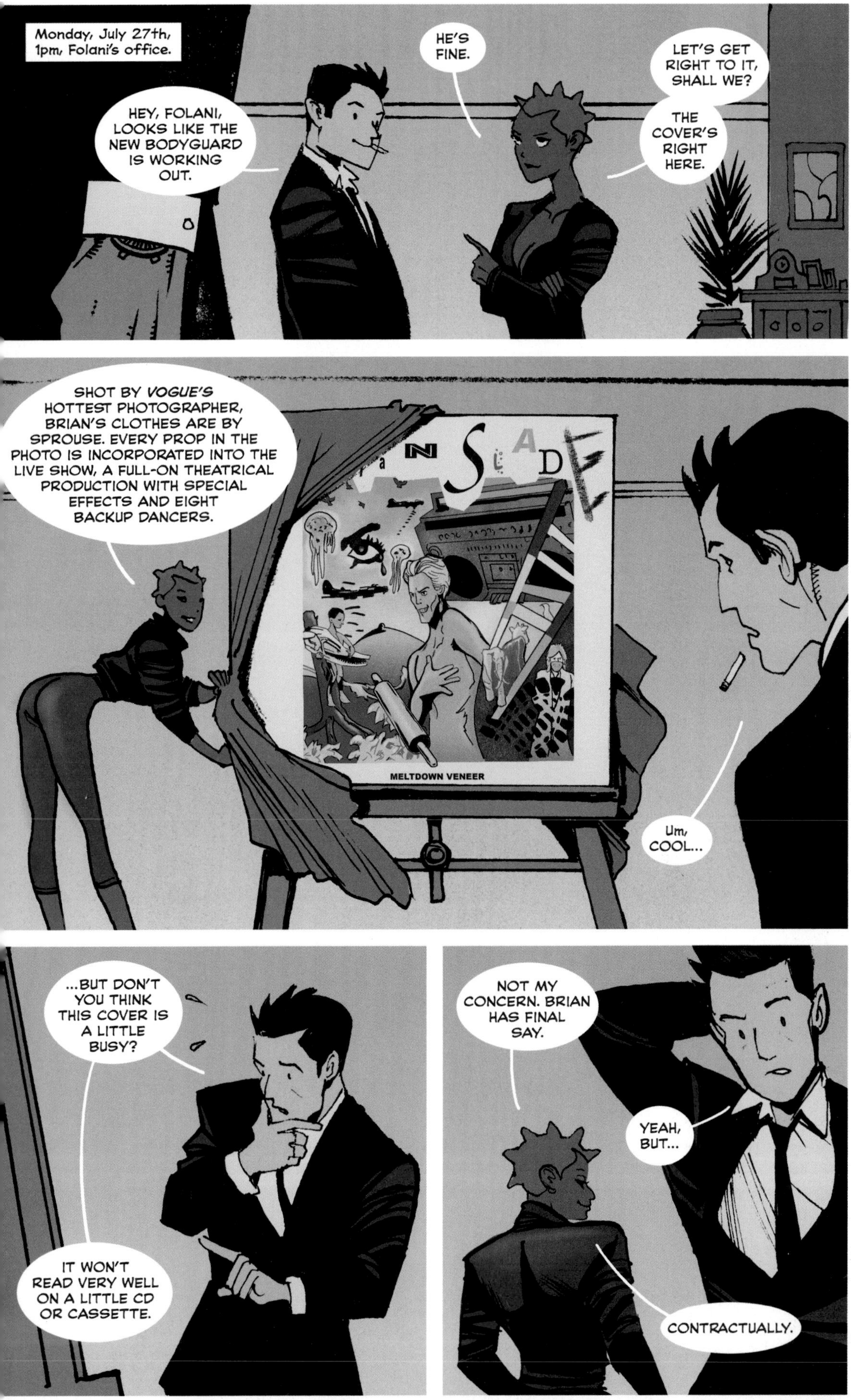

Monday, July 27th, 1pm, Folani's office.
HEY, FOLANI, LOOKS LIKE THE NEW BODYGUARD IS WORKING OUT.
HE'S FINE.
LET'S GET RIGHT TO IT, SHALL WE?
THE COVER'S RIGHT HERE.
SHOT BY *VOGUE'S* HOTTEST PHOTOGRAPHER, BRIAN'S CLOTHES ARE BY SPROUSE. EVERY PROP IN THE PHOTO IS INCORPORATED INTO THE LIVE SHOW, A FULL-ON THEATRICAL PRODUCTION WITH SPECIAL EFFECTS AND EIGHT BACKUP DANCERS.
MELTDOWN VENEER
Um, COOL...
...BUT DON'T YOU THINK THIS COVER IS A LITTLE BUSY?
IT WON'T READ VERY WELL ON A LITTLE CD OR CASSETTE.
NOT MY CONCERN. BRIAN HAS FINAL SAY.
YEAH, BUT...
CONTRACTUALLY.

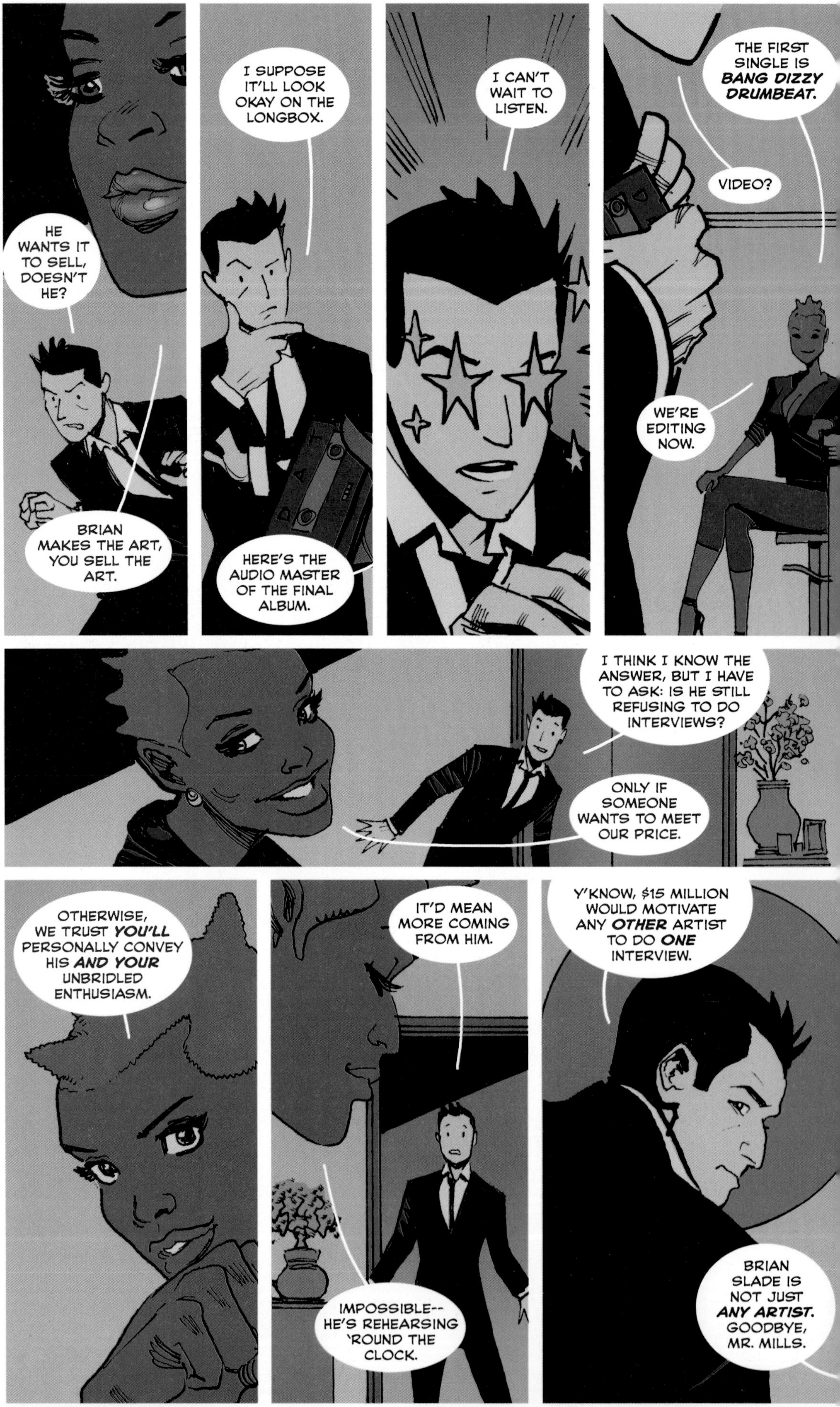

HE WANTS IT TO SELL, DOESN'T HE?
BRIAN MAKES THE ART, YOU SELL THE ART.
I SUPPOSE IT'LL LOOK OKAY ON THE LONGBOX.
HERE'S THE AUDIO MASTER OF THE FINAL ALBUM.
I CAN'T WAIT TO LISTEN.
THE FIRST SINGLE IS ***BANG DIZZY DRUMBEAT.***
VIDEO?
WE'RE EDITING NOW.
I THINK I KNOW THE ANSWER, BUT I HAVE TO ASK: IS HE STILL REFUSING TO DO INTERVIEWS?
ONLY IF SOMEONE WANTS TO MEET OUR PRICE.
OTHERWISE, WE TRUST ***YOU'LL*** PERSONALLY CONVEY HIS ***AND YOUR*** UNBRIDLED ENTHUSIASM.
IT'D MEAN MORE COMING FROM HIM.
IMPOSSIBLE-- HE'S REHEARSING 'ROUND THE CLOCK.
Y'KNOW, $15 MILLION WOULD MOTIVATE ANY ***OTHER*** ARTIST TO DO ***ONE*** INTERVIEW.
BRIAN SLADE IS NOT JUST ***ANY ARTIST.*** GOODBYE, MR. MILLS.

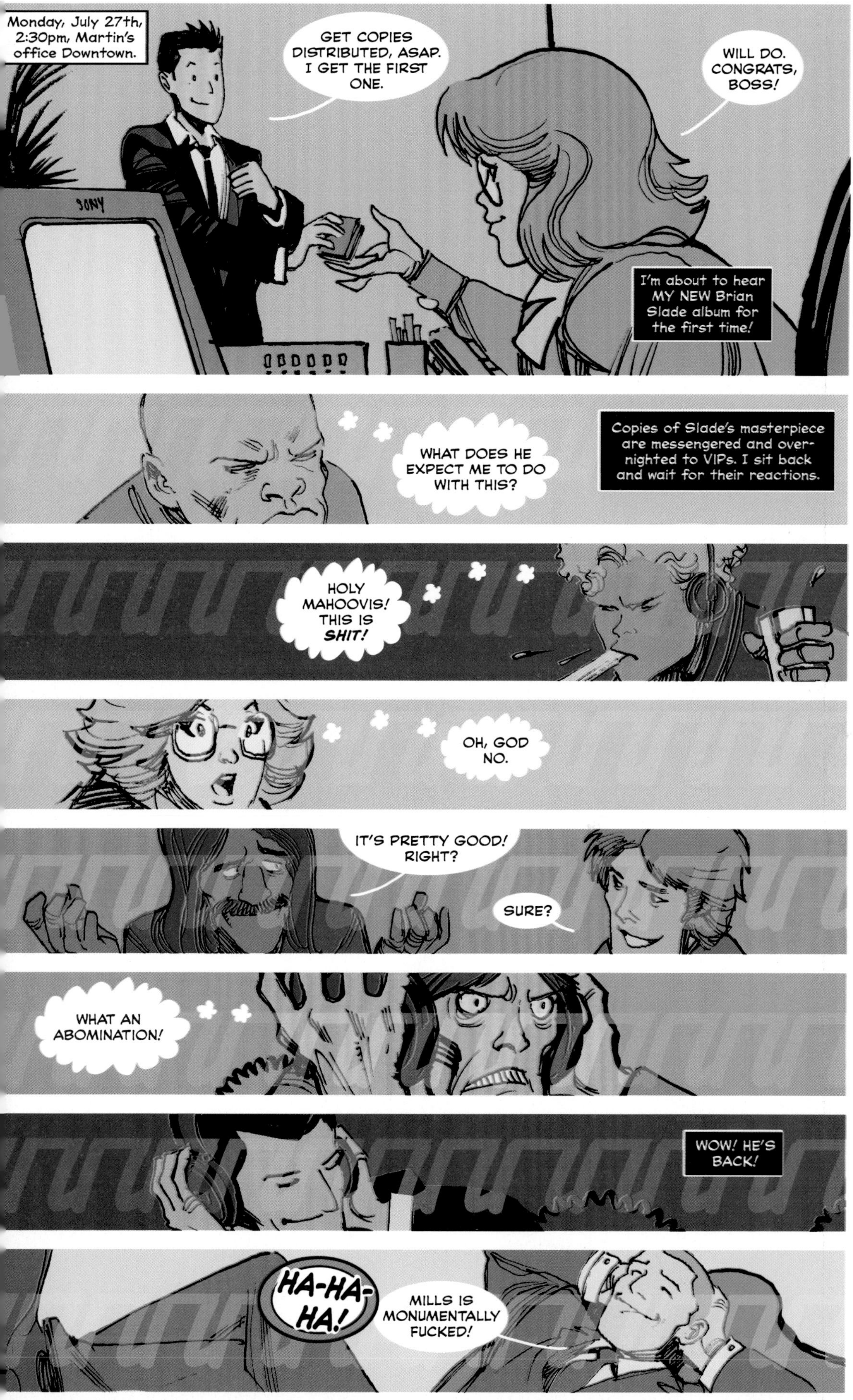
Monday, July 27th, 2:30pm, Martin's office Downtown.
GET COPIES DISTRIBUTED, ASAP. I GET THE FIRST ONE.
WILL DO. CONGRATS, BOSS!
SONY
I'm about to hear MY NEW Brian Slade album for the first time!
Copies of Slade's masterpiece are messengered and over-nighted to VIPs. I sit back and wait for their reactions.
WHAT DOES HE EXPECT ME TO DO WITH THIS?
HOLY MAHOOVIS! THIS IS SHIT!
OH, GOD NO.
IT'S PRETTY GOOD! RIGHT?
SURE?
WHAT AN ABOMINATION!
WOW! HE'S BACK!
HA-HA-HA!
MILLS IS MONUMENTALLY FUCKED!

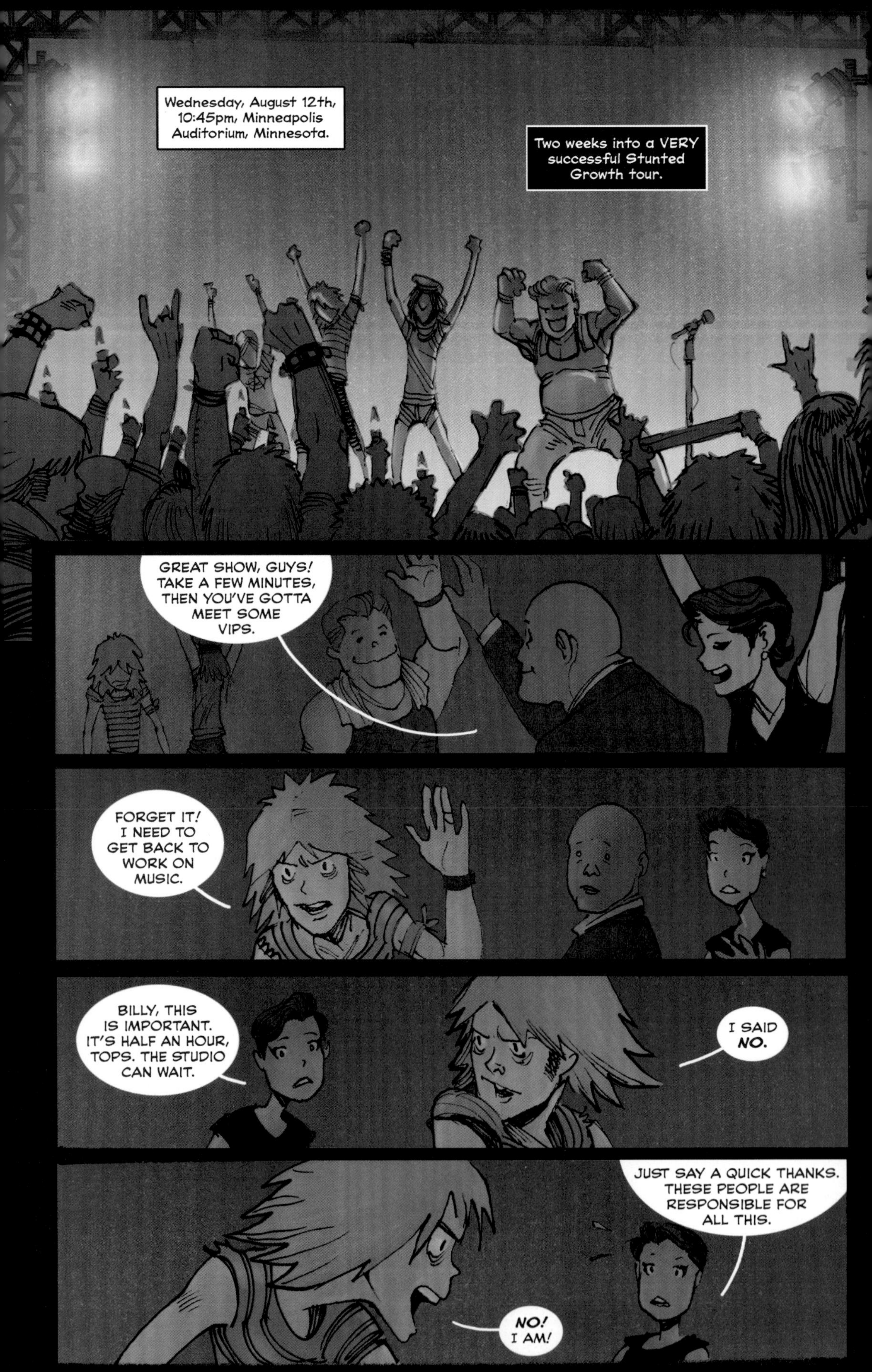
Wednesday, August 12th, 10:45pm, Minneapolis Auditorium, Minnesota.
Two weeks into a VERY successful Stunted Growth tour.
GREAT SHOW, GUYS! TAKE A FEW MINUTES, THEN YOU'VE GOTTA MEET SOME VIPS.
FORGET IT! I NEED TO GET BACK TO WORK ON MUSIC.
BILLY, THIS IS IMPORTANT. IT'S HALF AN HOUR, TOPS. THE STUDIO CAN WAIT.
I SAID NO.
JUST SAY A QUICK THANKS. THESE PEOPLE ARE RESPONSIBLE FOR ALL THIS.
NO! I AM!

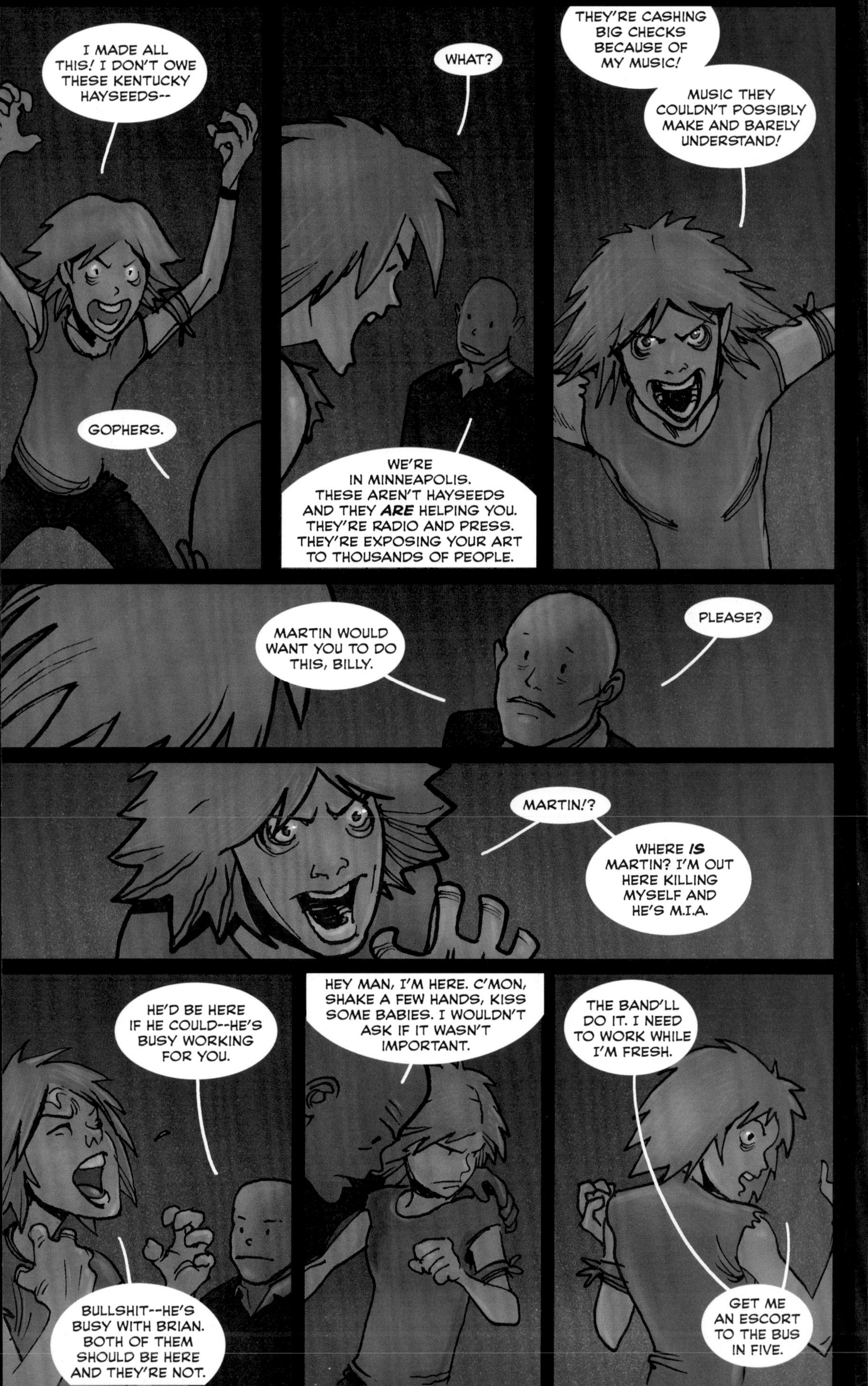
I MADE ALL THIS! I DON'T OWE THESE KENTUCKY HAYSEEDS--
GOPHERS.
WHAT?
WE'RE IN MINNEAPOLIS. THESE AREN'T HAYSEEDS AND THEY **ARE** HELPING YOU. THEY'RE RADIO AND PRESS. THEY'RE EXPOSING YOUR ART TO THOUSANDS OF PEOPLE.
THEY'RE CASHING BIG CHECKS BECAUSE OF MY MUSIC!
MUSIC THEY COULDN'T POSSIBLY MAKE AND BARELY UNDERSTAND!
MARTIN WOULD WANT YOU TO DO THIS, BILLY.
PLEASE?
MARTIN!?
WHERE **IS** MARTIN? I'M OUT HERE KILLING MYSELF AND HE'S M.I.A.
HE'D BE HERE IF HE COULD--HE'S BUSY WORKING FOR YOU.
BULLSHIT--HE'S BUSY WITH BRIAN. BOTH OF THEM SHOULD BE HERE AND THEY'RE NOT.
HEY MAN, I'M HERE. C'MON, SHAKE A FEW HANDS, KISS SOME BABIES. I WOULDN'T ASK IF IT WASN'T IMPORTANT.
THE BAND'LL DO IT. I NEED TO WORK WHILE I'M FRESH.
GET ME AN ESCORT TO THE BUS IN FIVE.

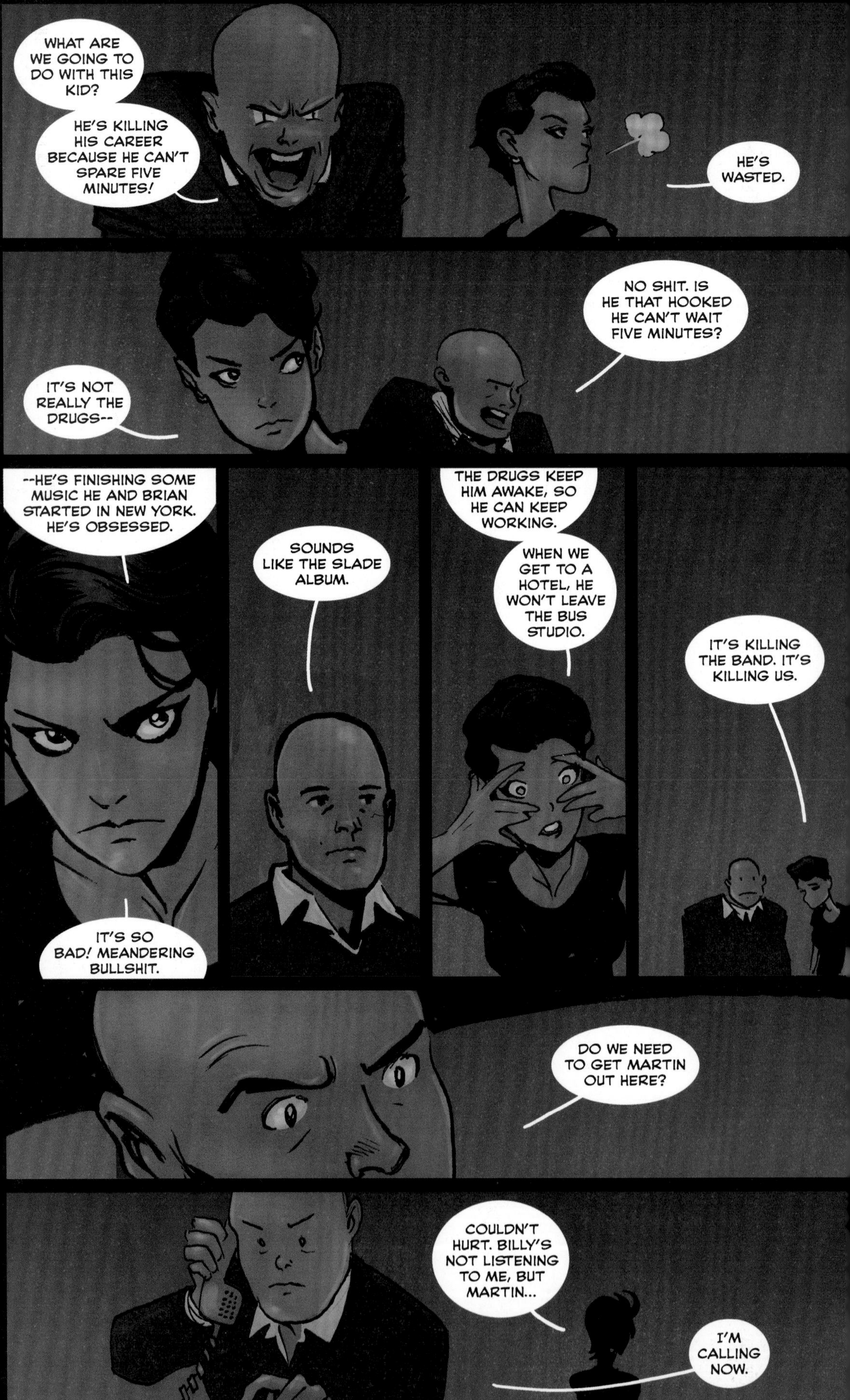
WHAT ARE WE GOING TO DO WITH THIS KID?
HE'S KILLING HIS CAREER BECAUSE HE CAN'T SPARE FIVE MINUTES!
HE'S WASTED.
NO SHIT. IS HE THAT HOOKED HE CAN'T WAIT FIVE MINUTES?
IT'S NOT REALLY THE DRUGS--
--HE'S FINISHING SOME MUSIC HE AND BRIAN STARTED IN NEW YORK. HE'S OBSESSED.
IT'S SO BAD! MEANDERING BULLSHIT.
SOUNDS LIKE THE SLADE ALBUM.
THE DRUGS KEEP HIM AWAKE, SO HE CAN KEEP WORKING.
WHEN WE GET TO A HOTEL, HE WON'T LEAVE THE BUS STUDIO.
IT'S KILLING THE BAND. IT'S KILLING US.
DO WE NEED TO GET MARTIN OUT HERE?
COULDN'T HURT. BILLY'S NOT LISTENING TO ME, BUT MARTIN...
I'M CALLING NOW.

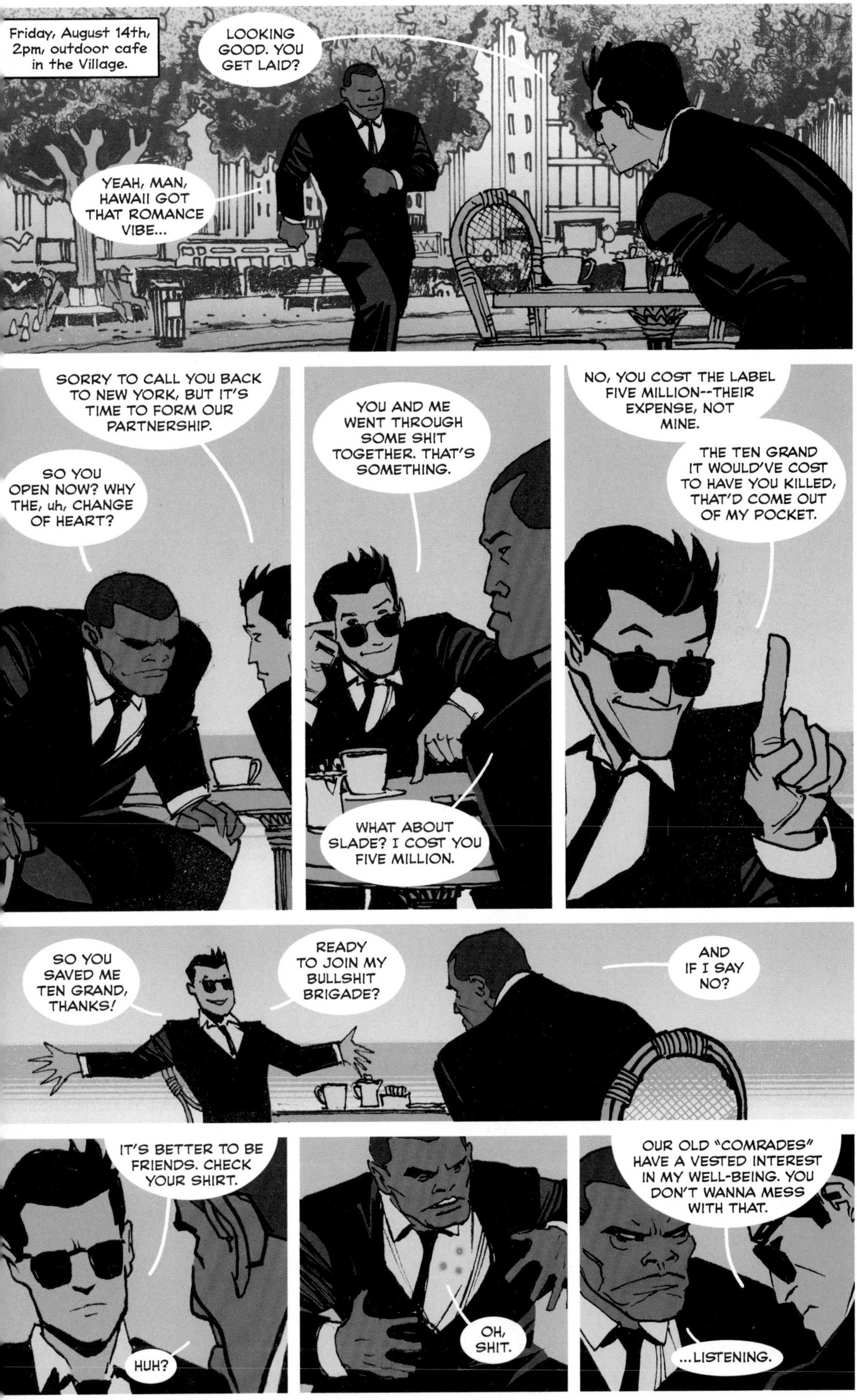
Friday, August 14th, 2pm, outdoor cafe in the Village.
LOOKING GOOD. YOU GET LAID?
YEAH, MAN, HAWAII GOT THAT ROMANCE VIBE...
SORRY TO CALL YOU BACK TO NEW YORK, BUT IT'S TIME TO FORM OUR PARTNERSHIP.
SO YOU OPEN NOW? WHY THE, uh, CHANGE OF HEART?
YOU AND ME WENT THROUGH SOME SHIT TOGETHER. THAT'S SOMETHING.
WHAT ABOUT SLADE? I COST YOU FIVE MILLION.
NO, YOU COST THE LABEL FIVE MILLION--THEIR EXPENSE, NOT MINE.
THE TEN GRAND IT WOULD'VE COST TO HAVE YOU KILLED, THAT'D COME OUT OF MY POCKET.
SO YOU SAVED ME TEN GRAND, THANKS!
READY TO JOIN MY BULLSHIT BRIGADE?
AND IF I SAY NO?
IT'S BETTER TO BE FRIENDS. CHECK YOUR SHIRT.
HUH?
OH, SHIT.
OUR OLD "COMRADES" HAVE A VESTED INTEREST IN MY WELL-BEING. YOU DON'T WANNA MESS WITH THAT.
...LISTENING.

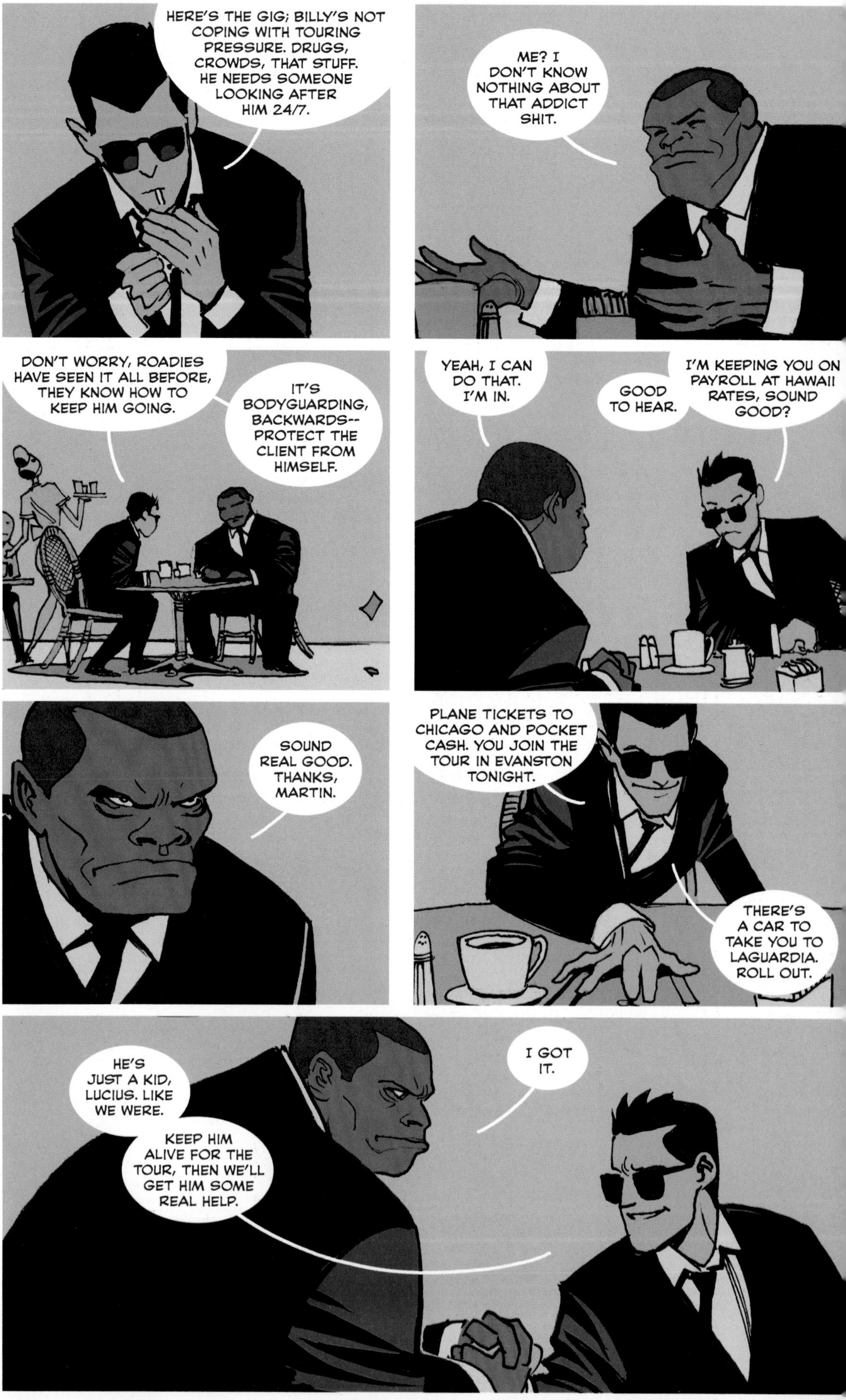
HERE'S THE GIG; BILLY'S NOT COPING WITH TOURING PRESSURE. DRUGS, CROWDS, THAT STUFF. HE NEEDS SOMEONE LOOKING AFTER HIM 24/7.
ME? I DON'T KNOW NOTHING ABOUT THAT ADDICT SHIT.
DON'T WORRY, ROADIES HAVE SEEN IT ALL BEFORE, THEY KNOW HOW TO KEEP HIM GOING.
IT'S BODYGUARDING, BACKWARDS-- PROTECT THE CLIENT FROM HIMSELF.
YEAH, I CAN DO THAT. I'M IN.
GOOD TO HEAR.
I'M KEEPING YOU ON PAYROLL AT HAWAII RATES, SOUND GOOD?
SOUND REAL GOOD. THANKS, MARTIN.
PLANE TICKETS TO CHICAGO AND POCKET CASH. YOU JOIN THE TOUR IN EVANSTON TONIGHT.
THERE'S A CAR TO TAKE YOU TO LAGUARDIA. ROLL OUT.
HE'S JUST A KID, LUCIUS. LIKE WE WERE.
KEEP HIM ALIVE FOR THE TOUR, THEN WE'LL GET HIM SOME REAL HELP.
I GOT IT.

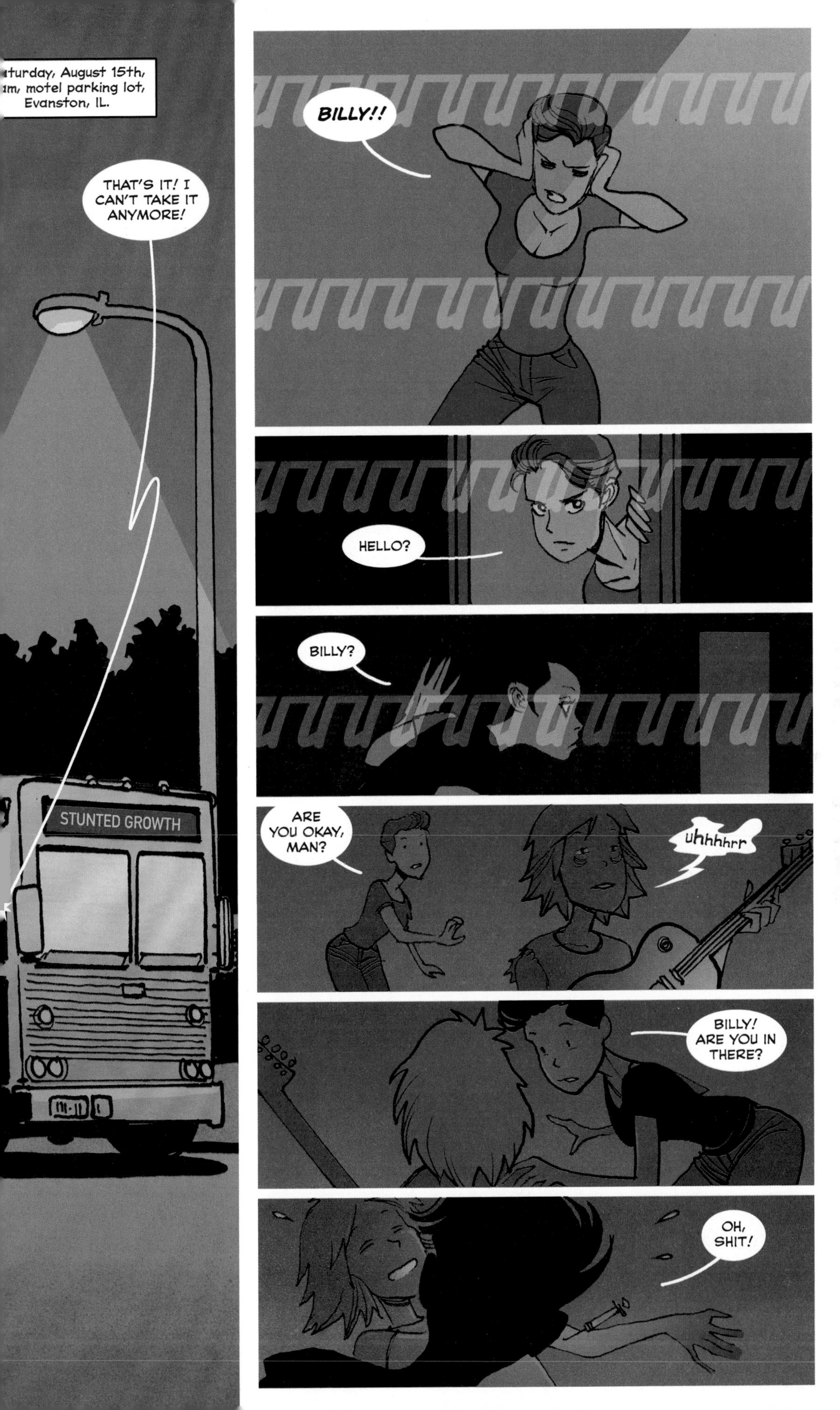

aturday, August 15th, am, motel parking lot, Evanston, IL.
THAT'S IT! I CAN'T TAKE IT ANYMORE!
STUNTED GROWTH
BILLY!!
HELLO?
BILLY?
ARE YOU OKAY, MAN?
uhhhhrr
BILLY! ARE YOU IN THERE?
OH, SHIT!

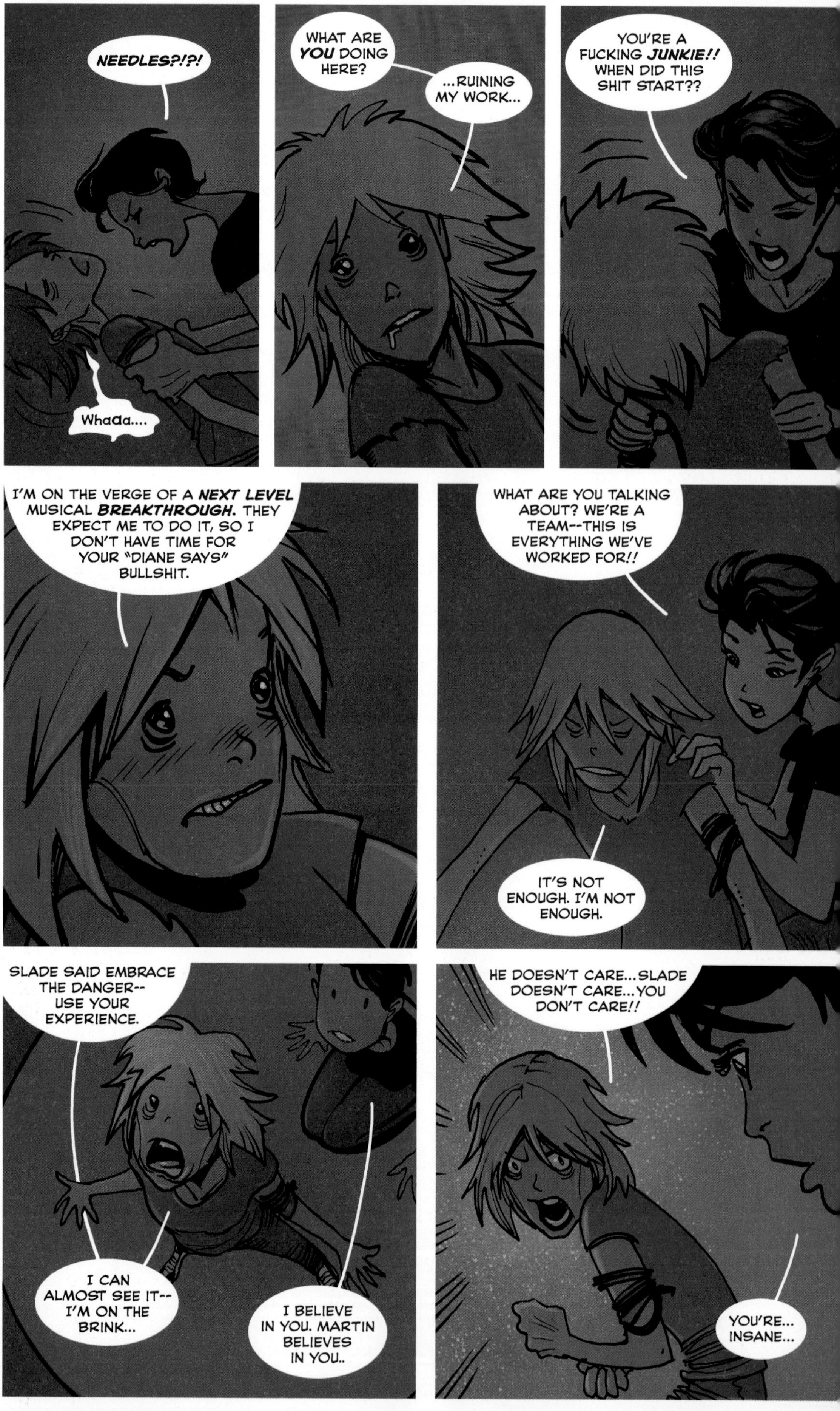
NEEDLES?!?!
Whaaa....
WHAT ARE YOU DOING HERE?
...RUINING MY WORK...
YOU'RE A FUCKING JUNKIE!! WHEN DID THIS SHIT START??
I'M ON THE VERGE OF A NEXT LEVEL MUSICAL BREAKTHROUGH. THEY EXPECT ME TO DO IT, SO I DON'T HAVE TIME FOR YOUR "DIANE SAYS" BULLSHIT.
WHAT ARE YOU TALKING ABOUT? WE'RE A TEAM--THIS IS EVERYTHING WE'VE WORKED FOR!!
IT'S NOT ENOUGH. I'M NOT ENOUGH.
SLADE SAID EMBRACE THE DANGER-- USE YOUR EXPERIENCE.
I CAN ALMOST SEE IT-- I'M ON THE BRINK...
I BELIEVE IN YOU. MARTIN BELIEVES IN YOU..
HE DOESN'T CARE...SLADE DOESN'T CARE...YOU DON'T CARE!!
YOU'RE... INSANE...

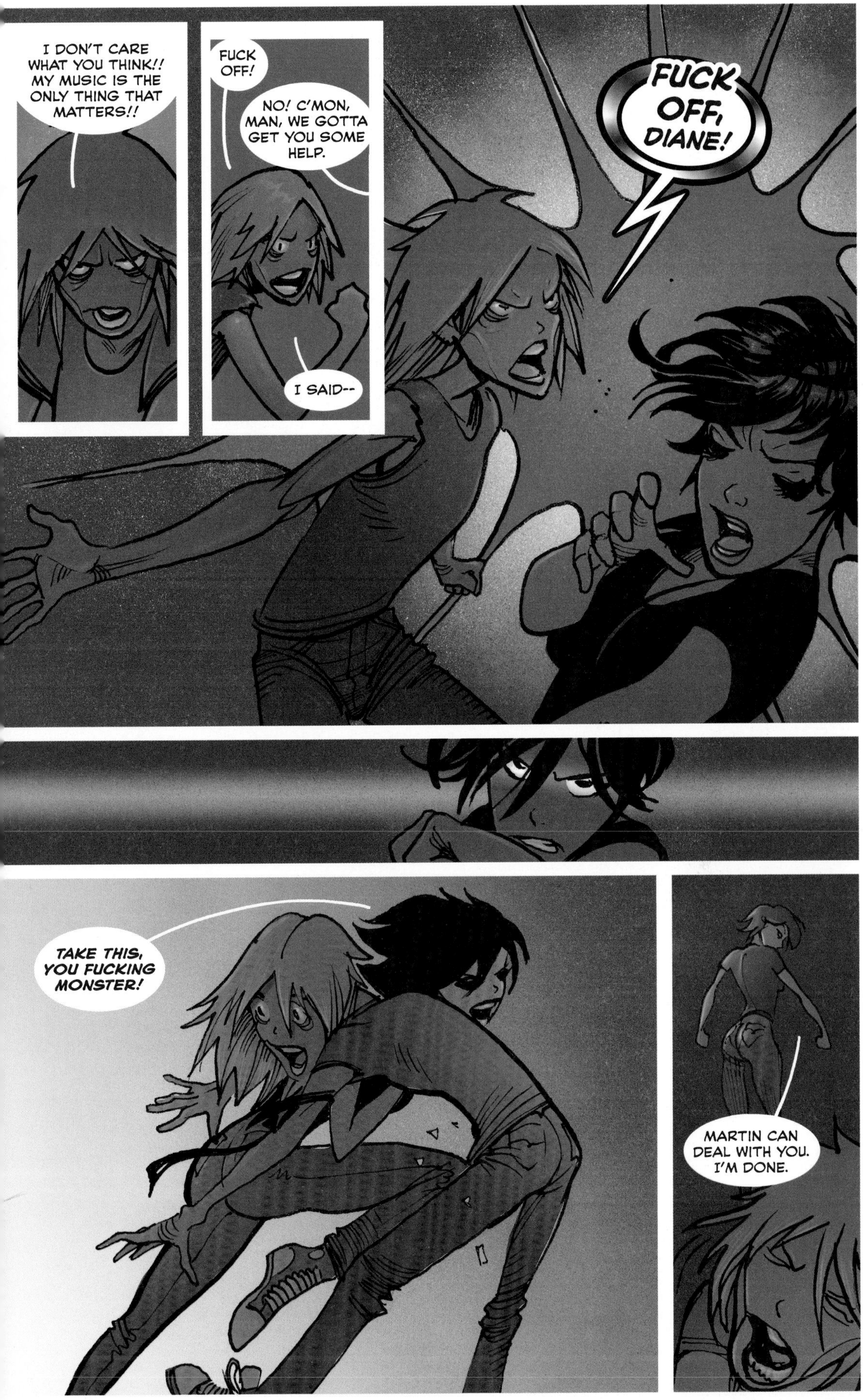

I DON'T CARE WHAT YOU THINK!! MY MUSIC IS THE ONLY THING THAT MATTERS!!
FUCK OFF!
NO! C'MON, MAN, WE GOTTA GET YOU SOME HELP.
I SAID--
FUCK OFF, DIANE!
TAKE THIS, YOU FUCKING MONSTER!
MARTIN CAN DEAL WITH YOU. I'M DONE.

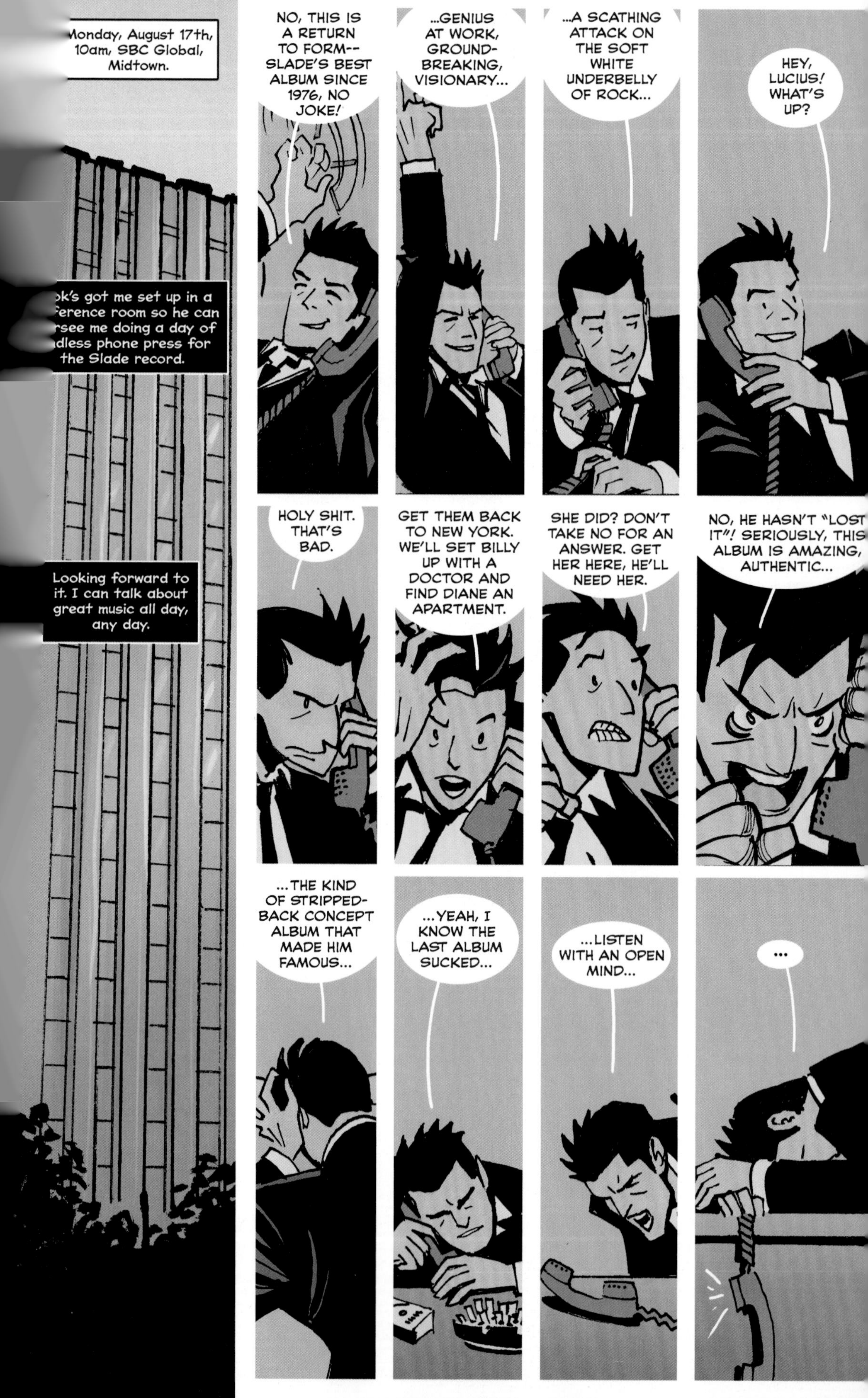
Monday, August 17th, 10am, SBC Global, Midtown.
ok's got me set up in a ference room so he can rsee me doing a day of dless phone press for the Slade record.
Looking forward to it. I can talk about great music all day, any day.
NO, THIS IS A RETURN TO FORM-- SLADE'S BEST ALBUM SINCE 1976, NO JOKE!
...GENIUS AT WORK, GROUND-BREAKING, VISIONARY...
...A SCATHING ATTACK ON THE SOFT WHITE UNDERBELLY OF ROCK...
HEY, LUCIUS! WHAT'S UP?
HOLY SHIT. THAT'S BAD.
GET THEM BACK TO NEW YORK. WE'LL SET BILLY UP WITH A DOCTOR AND FIND DIANE AN APARTMENT.
SHE DID? DON'T TAKE NO FOR AN ANSWER. GET HER HERE, HE'LL NEED HER.
NO, HE HASN'T "LOST IT"! SERIOUSLY, THIS ALBUM IS AMAZING, AUTHENTIC...
...THE KIND OF STRIPPED-BACK CONCEPT ALBUM THAT MADE HIM FAMOUS...
...YEAH, I KNOW THE LAST ALBUM SUCKED...
...LISTEN WITH AN OPEN MIND...
...

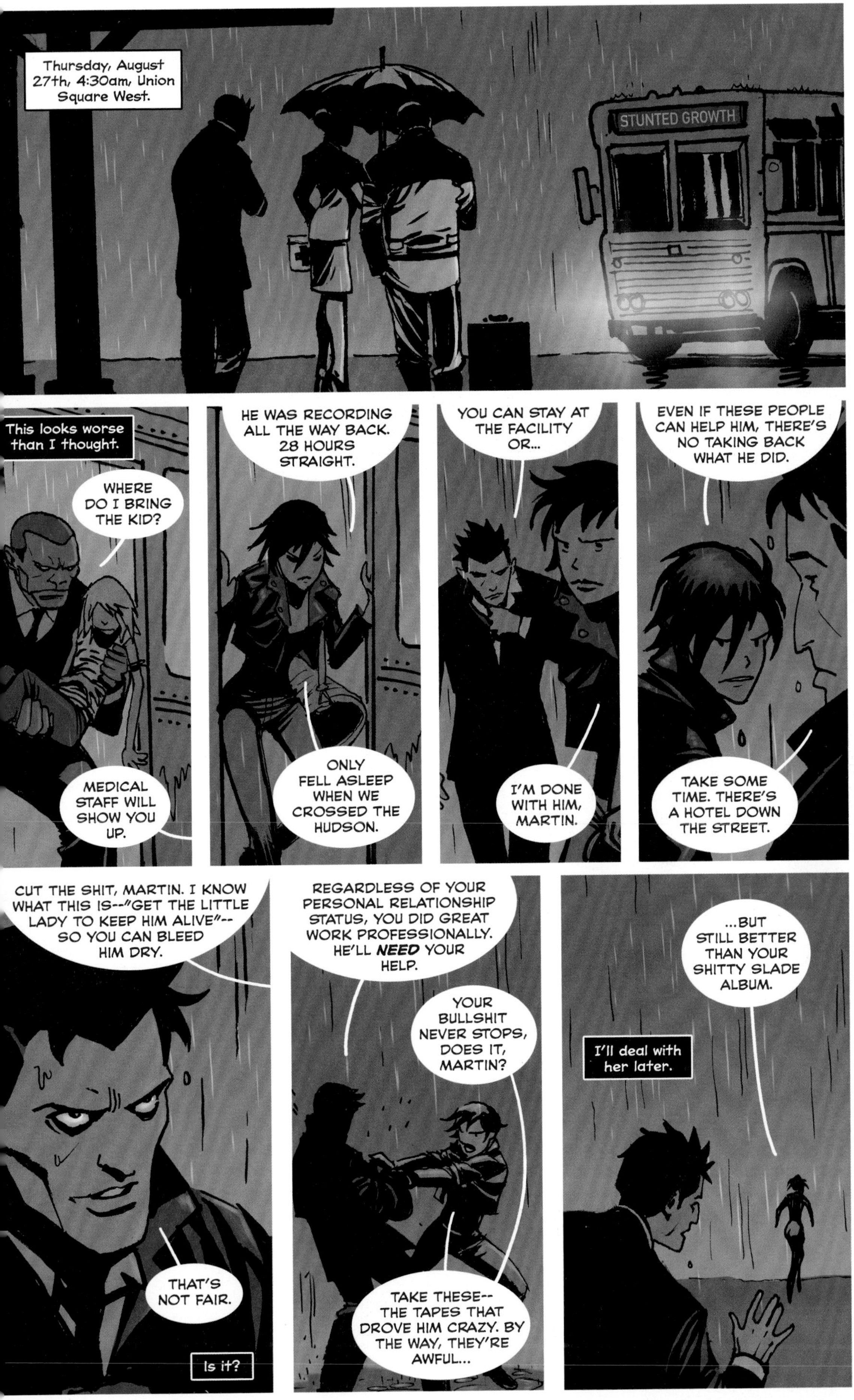
Thursday, August 27th, 4:30am, Union Square West.
STUNTED GROWTH
This looks worse than I thought.
WHERE DO I BRING THE KID?
MEDICAL STAFF WILL SHOW YOU UP.
HE WAS RECORDING ALL THE WAY BACK. 28 HOURS STRAIGHT.
ONLY FELL ASLEEP WHEN WE CROSSED THE HUDSON.
YOU CAN STAY AT THE FACILITY OR...
I'M DONE WITH HIM, MARTIN.
EVEN IF THESE PEOPLE CAN HELP HIM, THERE'S NO TAKING BACK WHAT HE DID.
TAKE SOME TIME. THERE'S A HOTEL DOWN THE STREET.
CUT THE SHIT, MARTIN. I KNOW WHAT THIS IS--"GET THE LITTLE LADY TO KEEP HIM ALIVE"--SO YOU CAN BLEED HIM DRY.
THAT'S NOT FAIR.
Is it?
REGARDLESS OF YOUR PERSONAL RELATIONSHIP STATUS, YOU DID GREAT WORK PROFESSIONALLY. HE'LL NEED YOUR HELP.
YOUR BULLSHIT NEVER STOPS, DOES IT, MARTIN?
TAKE THESE--THE TAPES THAT DROVE HIM CRAZY. BY THE WAY, THEY'RE AWFUL...
...BUT STILL BETTER THAN YOUR SHITTY SLADE ALBUM.
I'll deal with her later.

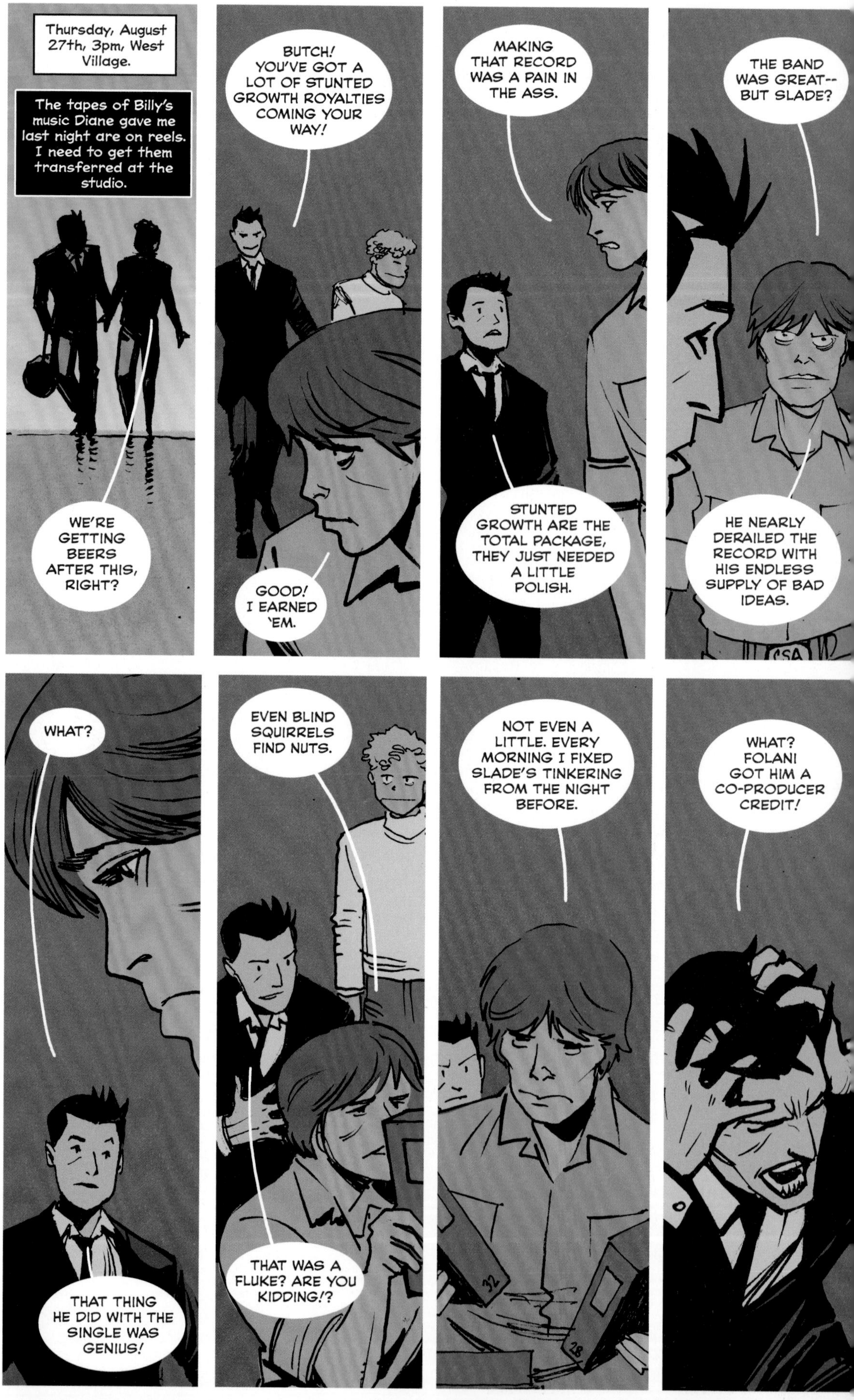
Thursday, August 27th, 3pm, West Village.
The tapes of Billy's music Diane gave me last night are on reels. I need to get them transferred at the studio.
WE'RE GETTING BEERS AFTER THIS, RIGHT?
BUTCH! YOU'VE GOT A LOT OF STUNTED GROWTH ROYALTIES COMING YOUR WAY!
GOOD! I EARNED 'EM.
MAKING THAT RECORD WAS A PAIN IN THE ASS.
STUNTED GROWTH ARE THE TOTAL PACKAGE, THEY JUST NEEDED A LITTLE POLISH.
THE BAND WAS GREAT--BUT SLADE?
HE NEARLY DERAILED THE RECORD WITH HIS ENDLESS SUPPLY OF BAD IDEAS.
WHAT?
THAT THING HE DID WITH THE SINGLE WAS GENIUS!
EVEN BLIND SQUIRRELS FIND NUTS.
THAT WAS A FLUKE? ARE YOU KIDDING!?
NOT EVEN A LITTLE. EVERY MORNING I FIXED SLADE'S TINKERING FROM THE NIGHT BEFORE.
WHAT? FOLANI GOT HIM A CO-PRODUCER CREDIT!

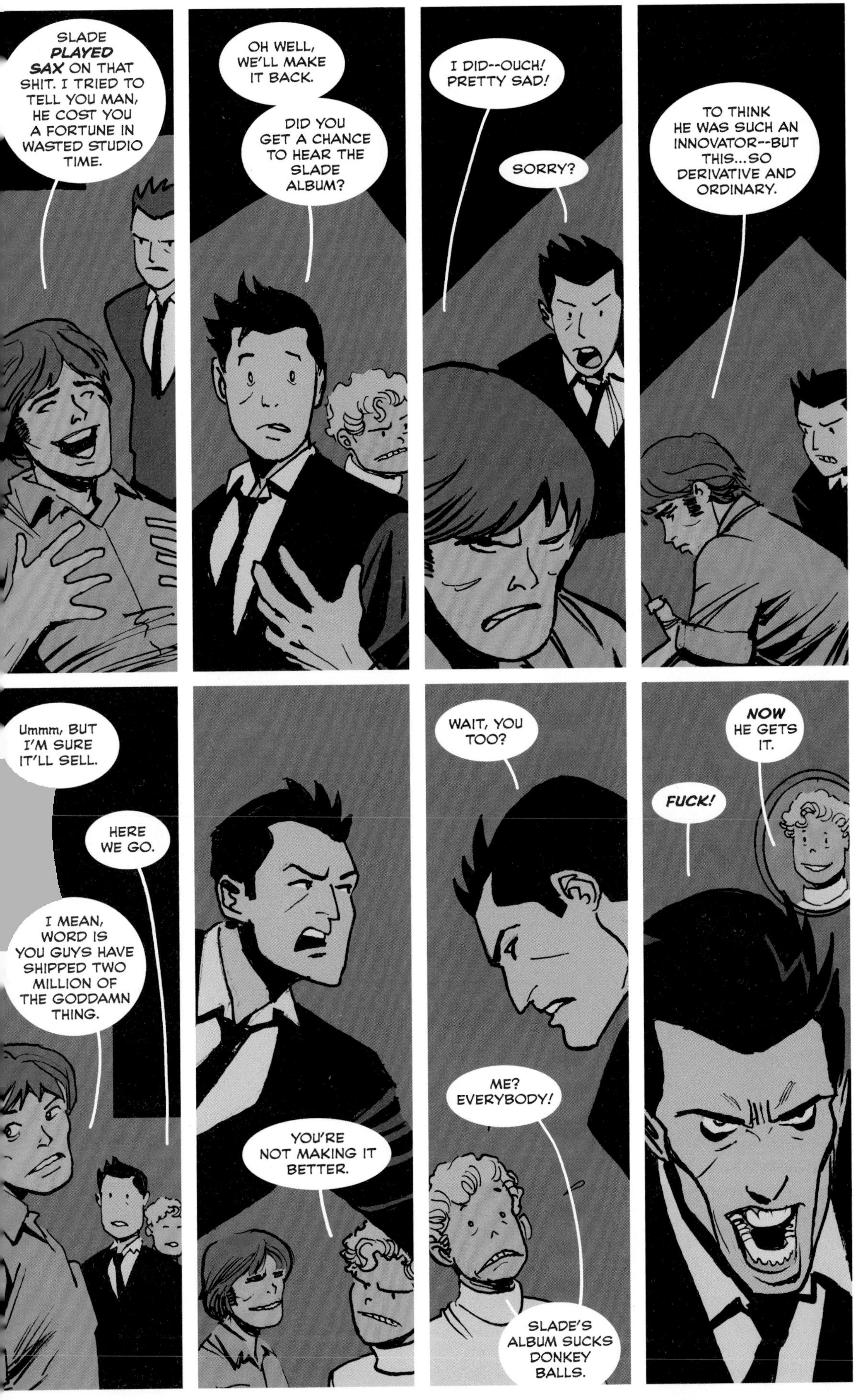
SLADE PLAYED SAX ON THAT SHIT. I TRIED TO TELL YOU MAN, HE COST YOU A FORTUNE IN WASTED STUDIO TIME.
OH WELL, WE'LL MAKE IT BACK.
DID YOU GET A CHANCE TO HEAR THE SLADE ALBUM?
I DID--OUCH! PRETTY SAD!
SORRY?
TO THINK HE WAS SUCH AN INNOVATOR--BUT THIS...SO DERIVATIVE AND ORDINARY.
Ummm, BUT I'M SURE IT'LL SELL.
HERE WE GO.
I MEAN, WORD IS YOU GUYS HAVE SHIPPED TWO MILLION OF THE GODDAMN THING.
YOU'RE NOT MAKING IT BETTER.
WAIT, YOU TOO?
ME? EVERYBODY!
SLADE'S ALBUM SUCKS DONKEY BALLS.
NOW HE GETS IT.
FUCK!

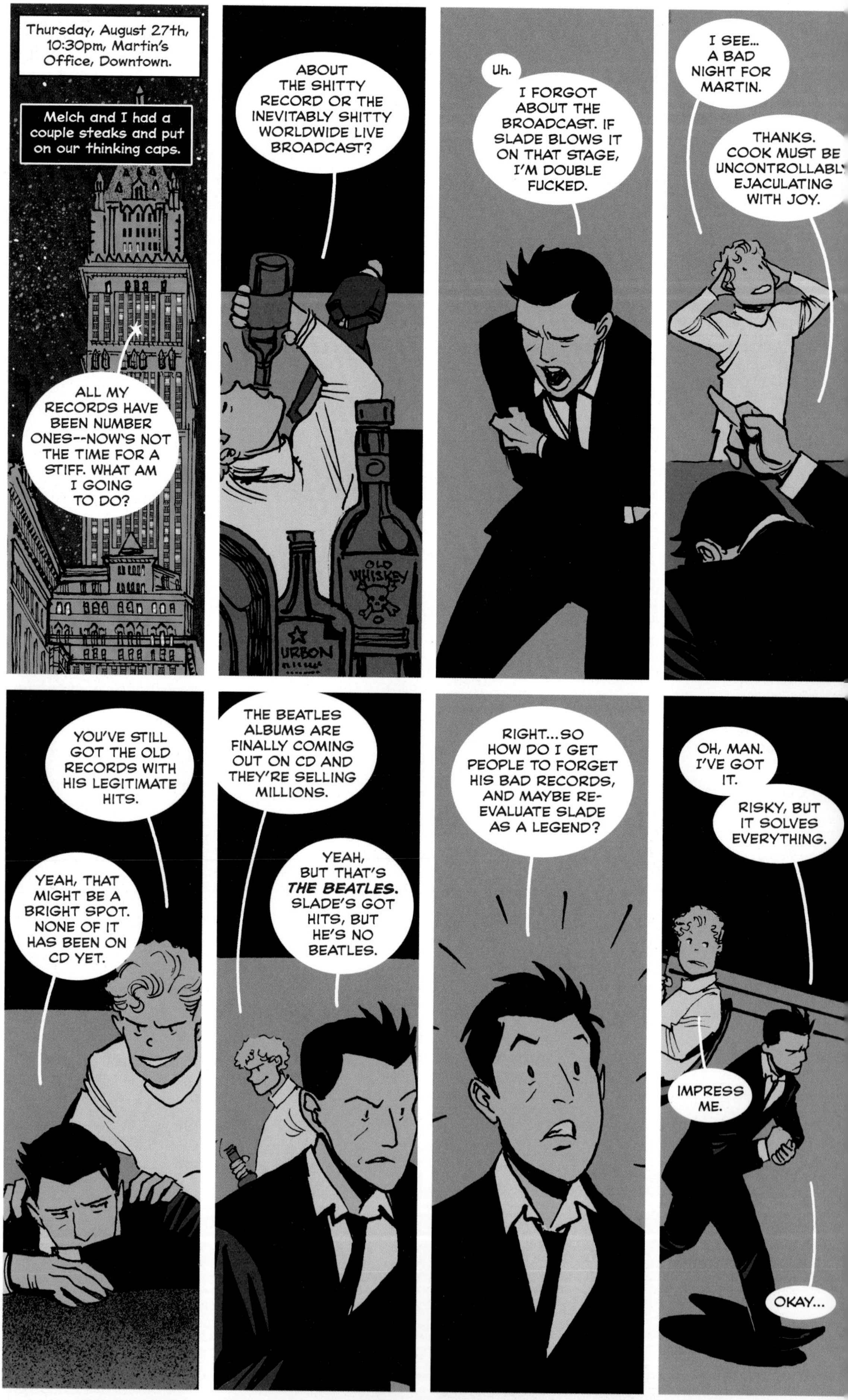
Thursday, August 27th, 10:30pm, Martin's Office, Downtown.
Melch and I had a couple steaks and put on our thinking caps.
ALL MY RECORDS HAVE BEEN NUMBER ONES--NOW'S NOT THE TIME FOR A STIFF. WHAT AM I GOING TO DO?
ABOUT THE SHITTY RECORD OR THE INEVITABLY SHITTY WORLDWIDE LIVE BROADCAST?
Uh.
I FORGOT ABOUT THE BROADCAST. IF SLADE BLOWS IT ON THAT STAGE, I'M DOUBLE FUCKED.
I SEE... A BAD NIGHT FOR MARTIN.
THANKS. COOK MUST BE UNCONTROLLABLY EJACULATING WITH JOY.
YOU'VE STILL GOT THE OLD RECORDS WITH HIS LEGITIMATE HITS.
YEAH, THAT MIGHT BE A BRIGHT SPOT. NONE OF IT HAS BEEN ON CD YET.
THE BEATLES ALBUMS ARE FINALLY COMING OUT ON CD AND THEY'RE SELLING MILLIONS.
YEAH, BUT THAT'S *THE BEATLES.* SLADE'S GOT HITS, BUT HE'S NO BEATLES.
RIGHT...SO HOW DO I GET PEOPLE TO FORGET HIS BAD RECORDS, AND MAYBE RE-EVALUATE SLADE AS A LEGEND?
OH, MAN. I'VE GOT IT.
RISKY, BUT IT SOLVES EVERYTHING.
IMPRESS ME.
OKAY...

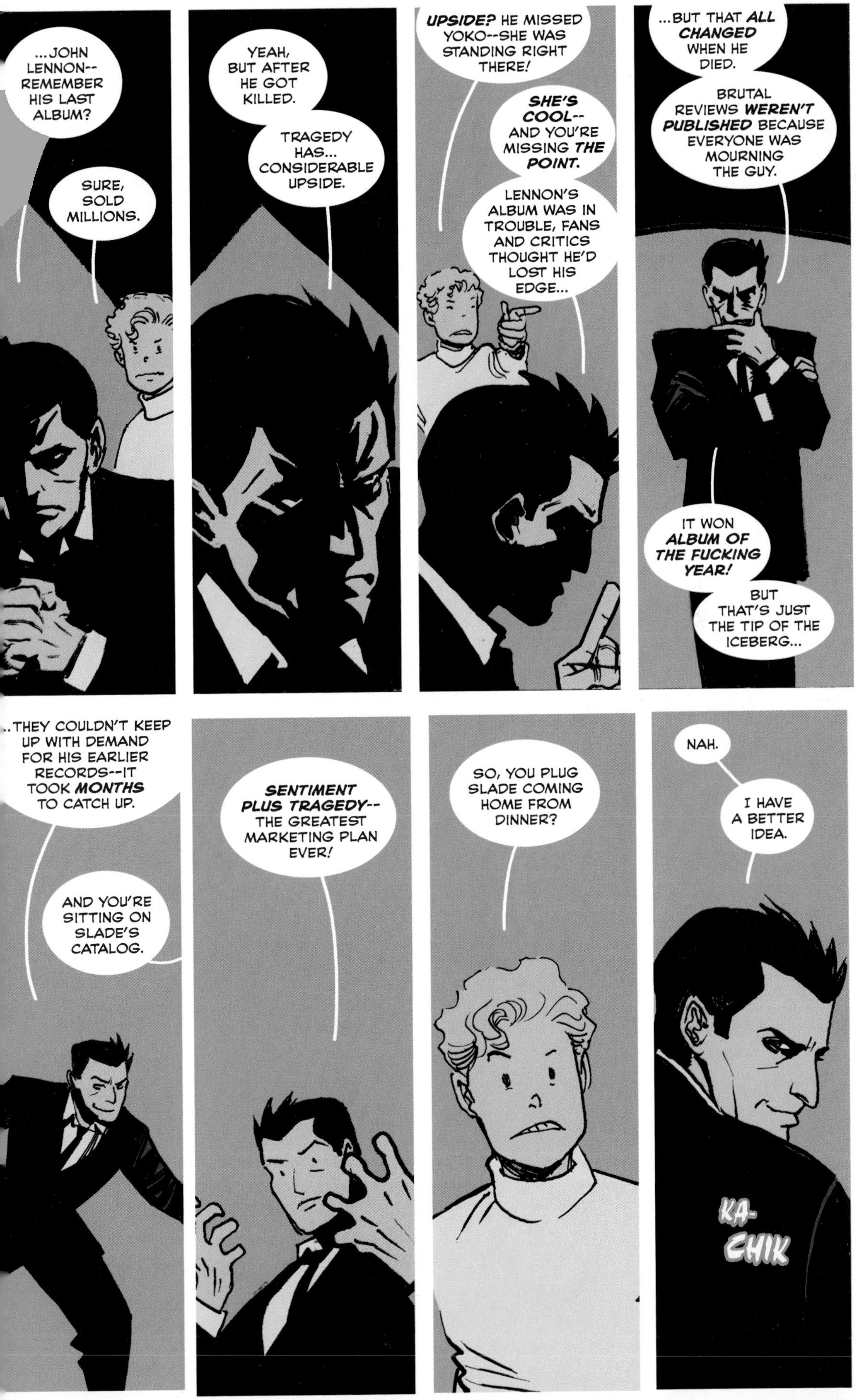
...JOHN LENNON--REMEMBER HIS LAST ALBUM?
SURE, SOLD MILLIONS.
YEAH, BUT AFTER HE GOT KILLED.
TRAGEDY HAS... CONSIDERABLE UPSIDE.
UPSIDE? HE MISSED YOKO--SHE WAS STANDING RIGHT THERE!
SHE'S COOL--AND YOU'RE MISSING THE POINT.
LENNON'S ALBUM WAS IN TROUBLE, FANS AND CRITICS THOUGHT HE'D LOST HIS EDGE...
...BUT THAT ALL CHANGED WHEN HE DIED.
BRUTAL REVIEWS WEREN'T PUBLISHED BECAUSE EVERYONE WAS MOURNING THE GUY.
IT WON ALBUM OF THE FUCKING YEAR!
BUT THAT'S JUST THE TIP OF THE ICEBERG...
...THEY COULDN'T KEEP UP WITH DEMAND FOR HIS EARLIER RECORDS--IT TOOK MONTHS TO CATCH UP.
AND YOU'RE SITTING ON SLADE'S CATALOG.
SENTIMENT PLUS TRAGEDY--THE GREATEST MARKETING PLAN EVER!
SO, YOU PLUG SLADE COMING HOME FROM DINNER?
NAH.
I HAVE A BETTER IDEA.
KA-CHIK

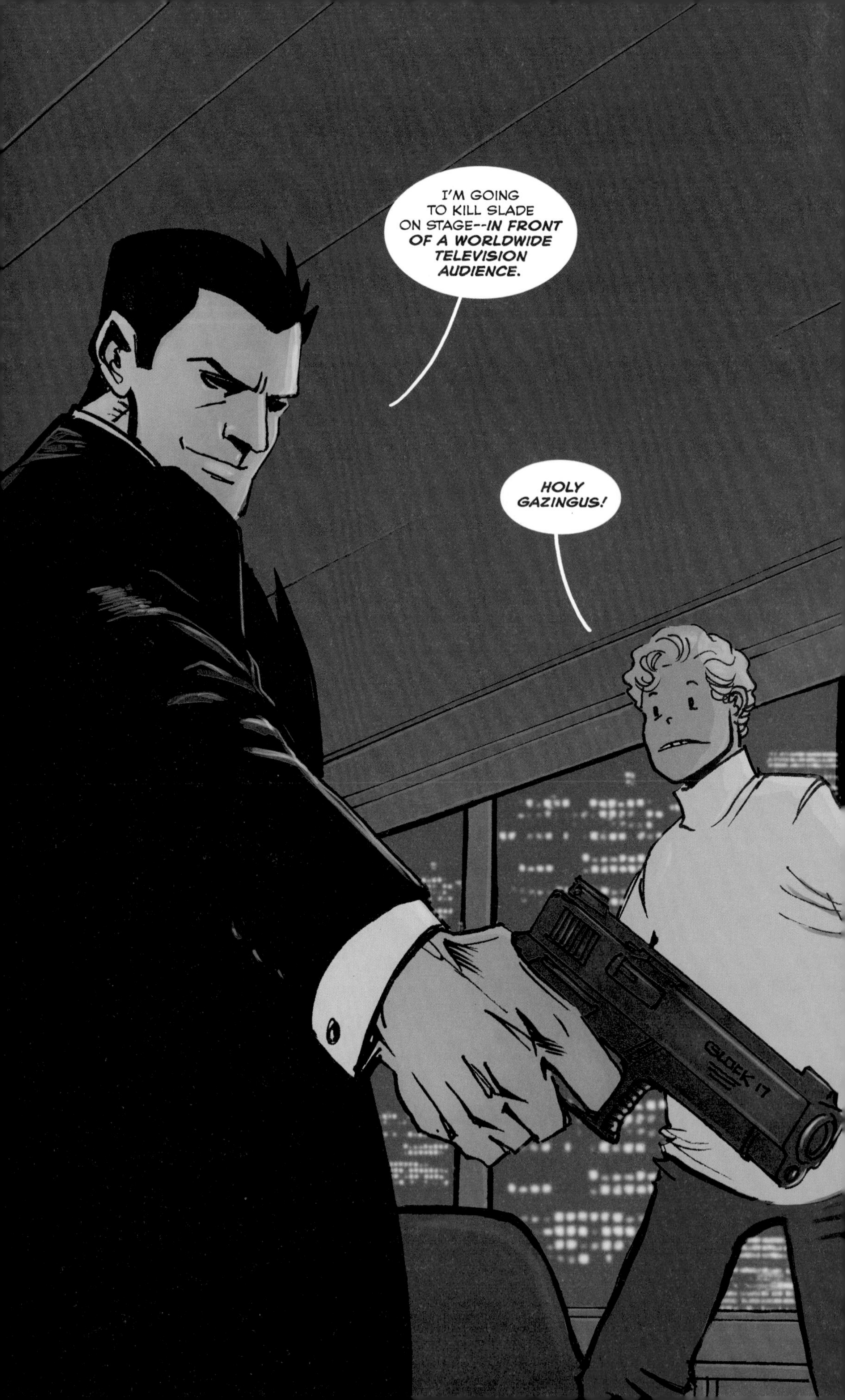
I'M GOING TO KILL SLADE ON STAGE--*IN FRONT OF A WORLDWIDE TELEVISION AUDIENCE.*
HOLY GAZINGUS!
GLOCK 17

BRIAN SLADE : NEW ALBUM!
FOR IMMEDIATE RELEASE

SBC Global is delighted to announce the release of a brand-new Brian Slade studio album, *Meltdown Veneer*, on August 31st, 1987.

Meltdown Veneer is the 17th studio album from the critically acclaimed art-rocker. It follows his 1983 worldwide commercial breakthrough *Some Kinda Fun*, which yielded four Top Forty singles and earned multiple platinum certifications and its successor, *After Dark*, which also went Platinum.

Recorded in secret in multiple studios around New York City, *Meltdown Veneer* is Slade's longest album to date, with a running time of nearly 72 minutes, and was specifically designed for the CD format.

The ever-mysterious Slade said this of the album: "*Meltdown Veneer* is the sum total of all I am and have been, and the North Star for where I'm headed next."

"Bang Dizzy Drum," the first single from the album, is already off to a huge start at radio, being added across a variety of formats (encompassing pop, dance, alternative and AOR), and the video, featuring elements from Slade's upcoming groundbreaking worldwide multi-media tour, is already a smash, in heavy rotation.

The tour will commence in New York on September 19th, with the most extravagant launch party ever seen. Millions around the globe are invited to attend via a worldwide TV simulcast from the legendary Monroe Coliseum on the CBN network.

Slade was signed to a worldwide deal with SBC via Martin Mills' 3100 Records imprint. Mills, who signed mega-stars Mechatroika and Stunted Growth, said "We are very excited to be in the Brian Slade business. This may be the greatest album of Brian's storied career."

Furthermore, Slade's classic catalog is included in the deal and will be rolled out during the tour, re-packaged with bonus tracks from the artist's legendary vault.

Mr. Slade will not be doing interviews.

-7706-

Please contact Joan Andreas at 3100 Records for review copies.

52 West 52nd Street, New York, New York 10019

1000 Park West, Los Angeles, California 90076

YANN—
you should PAY ME
TRIPLE RATE TO
Review SHIT This BAD
—GLEN

LOVE IT!! MAKE THIS OUR
LEAD REVIEW IN THE NEXT
ISSUE + MAKE SURE YOU
FIND A BAD PICTURE OF SLADE
TO GO WITH IT! ABOUT
TIME WE TOOK DOWN
THIS POMPOUS ASS!!
—Y

Meltdown Right Here: Welcome to Brian Slade's Creative Nadir
The Emperor Has No Songs

The most iconic and influential active artist in rock has been backsliding for a bit. Here we have the (inevitable?) crash.

Throughout the previous decade, Brian Slade redirected the very path of popular culture and metamorphosized himself again and again, reinventing himself with the same ease his rivals changed their denims, all the while seemingly leading the pack, ahead of the curve of our very lives.

But was he anticipating the future or dictating his version of it to us, his slavish fans? That conundrum's always been lurking in the background of Slade's career arc.

With the release of his new album, the positively tone-deaf "Meltdown Veneer," his perch as a visionary is more debatable than ever. Slade's 70s work felt weighty and interesting; he gave us hundreds of talking points to unravel. Weighing the mysteries surrounding them, was a process often as frustrating as it was rewarding.

It's near-impossible to buy he's predicting the future of pop when he sports a Bono haircut (all business to the front, party in the back) and writes lyrics that reference, of all things, the banal "Crocodile Dundee," apparently without irony.

Slade albums work best when he's crafted a sturdy concept or persona to build on; the alien rock star, a totalitarian future, some soulless Germanic Count run amuck. Here, as with his last few albums, there's no thematic coherence to hold the proceedings together - although he seems desperate for us to think there is.

Since the early 80s, when Slade ditched his personas, we are
left with an empty shell that desperately needs a new character
to inhabit it. When he released "Some Kinda Fun," It was a cal-
culated effort to synch up with the sound of today, rather than
the sound of tomorrow. Simply put, it was his attempt to engineer a hit.

And to his credit it did the job. The worldwide success of the
album vaulted him from an art-rock cult figure with to a
multi-platinum worldwide superstar, a pyrrhic vindication for
outsider fans who endured the taunts of thick-headed denim and
leather rock artists and their succubi.

The novelty of Brian Slade dropping the persona and (presumably) being himself for a change, was, in itself, exciting.
After all, it was a role he'd seemingly never played before -
and perhaps this would lead us to understand a hitherto fascinating artist in greater depth.

Slade fans debated whether "Some Kinda Fun" was a stylistic
triumph, a pop sellout, or just another pit-stop on the way to
future glories. It's safe to say nobody imagined it'd serve as
Slade's last stand.

Since "going norm," Slade's productivity is positively glacial
by his previous standards. This wouldn't be so bad if each of the
three albums weren't considerably worse than the one immedi-
ately preceding it. During the 70s he'd have released five or
six masterpieces in the same timeframe. (Note: I'm not counting
some positively horrifying work for film soundtracks that he
must be taking on strictly for the money). His artistic arc here
is positively leaden.

Earlier this year Slade turned 40, placing him firmly in rock's
"old fogey" territory. If "Some Kinda Fun" was his retirement
fund cash-in, okay, it well-earned and forgivable. But its follow-up, "After Dark," was a contract-dictated quickie with a
preponderance of dull cover versions; a massive disappoint-
ment. I regret to inform you that "Meltdown Veneer" is even
worse, this time thanks to a preponderance of terrible originals.

Slade's lingered in place before, but then he was mining themes
with purpose. His Zurich trilogy, for instance, yielded some of
the most compelling work in his career. In comparison to his
recent work, those albums were released in quick succession
and, more importantly, showed a line of evolution.

Now Slade's adrift, banging out the thinnest of ideas in the form of embryonic, under-developed songs. In the sparse promotional materials surrounding the release, there's but one quote from Slade (who is not doing interviews for the album), "This is the sum total of everything that has come before."

That's the problem in a nutshell. Without an overarching idea to explore for two albums in a row, Slade over-compensates by stuffing his third with everything-but-the-kitchen-sink. It doesn't work.

"Meltdown Veneer" proudly broadcasts Slade's decision to quit switching guises with each album. Perhaps sensing the artistic inertia of his last two LPs, here he over-compensates by switching character from song to song. The effect is as jarring and annoying as the worn out stereotypes these poorly-sketched figures represent.

He's the unapologetically horny middle-aged man, the war-fearing citizen of the world (someone's finally told him Reagan's been elected, apparently), the homeless advocate (ironically living in a gilded palace), and, apparently, the spawn of some sort of crystalline arachnid (?).

The latter at least suggests an intriguing, ominous premise, but Slade fails to capitalize by linking it to the other tracks (maybe these songs all are connected in his head, but the web he spins here - if he has spun one - is imperceptible). And yes, he namechecks some of his older creations, but it feels like a stunt, with no motive other than to compel his hardcore fanbase to continue to pay attention - akin to destroying a universe only to recreate it with no discernable improvement under the guise of something new and better.

His newfound financial success may be responsible for Slade losing touch so completely that he's reduced to cannibalizing himself just when he has a rabid worldwide audience eager to lock step with him and and revel in a truly groundbreaking shift in his chameleonic career.

So with no seeming artistic or philosophical redeeming social value, it surely holds up as pop collection, right?

"Meltdown Veneer" is devoid of anything approaching a hit, but not for lack of trying. Its booming percussion, cluttered synth arrangements and languid guitars are unsubtle, obvious and wholly unsuccessful attempts at stadium rock - each element over-fussed with and overproduced to the point where it suffocates under the weight of its (too) many components.

very track overstays its welcome, bloating an already inter-
inable running time. The CD era has allowed artists the freedom to create longer albums, but just because the format can
old 72 minutes doesn't mean you have to use all of them - espe-
ially when the length of songs here only serves to highlight
he acute shortage of good ideas in attendance.

he album opener, Get-In Get-Out, is Slade's take on the home-
ess problem, feeling entirely forced and insincere. Sappy,
ing-song lyrics are overstuffed with obvious lachrymosities; a
ecidedly cookie-cutter attempt to stir the heartstrings. You'd
hink a man used to taking on guises could stay on theme for
he length of a single song, yet throughout the track's intermi-
able playing time Slade's position seems to shift from one of
ympathy to viewing these unfortunates an inconvenience that
hould be swept from his sidewalk so the man can get from the
imo to his penthouse without being troubled by their bodies im-
eding his journey.

ocus remains problematic for Slade throughout the sprawling
71 minute running time of "Meltdown Veneer." How We War is
ure 80s excess, a shambling, recondite exploration of... some-
hing, heralded by a blaring synth lick and buried by the most
rtificial and oppressive drum sound ever committed to disc.

eauty Rod Forum is something to do with sex (he's still mad for
t, shockingly) with incessant guitar solos played faster,
arder, shriller and as often as possible for the song's nearly
3 minute running time. It is laughably un-erotic; the aural
quivalent of saltpeter.

he album's first single, Bang Dizzy Drum, sees Slade as the
echerous dad driving the babysitter home, whilst complaining
MTV did not play a video from his last album (?). As is all the
rage, this is choreographed to synchronized interpretative
ance in the song's video, currently causing eyes to bleed
worldwide as it pumps out from the cathode tube with shocking,
relentless, mind-numbing regularity. This, like many of the
tracks here seems written to exist as a video, not a song. You
an literally hear where the Michael Jackson-dictated "Thriller" choreography is supposed to land.

he title track, with its flabby melody and naive analysis of
nuclear anxiety, is positively banal in both concept and execution. Maybe lyrics like "just outside the heart wall / we hold
our breath / pray the core won't collapse" work in the context
of dance music, where bad lyrics seem to be considered a sign
of good taste, but they miss the mark by a wide mile when ac-
companied by screeching guitars.

Zombos is one of the most gruesome compositions Slade's ever committed to tape. I'll leave it there.

It's followed up by Insect Bone Mother, the spoken-word track intended to tie the whole enterprise together, which, as noted earlier, it fails to do and spectacularly so. A vague horror / science fiction narrative, it lives in a world well outside the rest of the compositions, inasmuch as they are at least grounded in reality. While a flight from Slade's ill-informed blue-collar Springsteen-esque screeds should be a welcome relief, it's instead a startling, jaw-dropping bump in the road.

It gets worse. Sing A Song (Fakin' My Love), starts out as a silky mid-tempo Earth Wind and Fire knock-off. The string-laden, between-the-sheets love ballad is nothing new, but doesn't cause offense. All hope is lost when Ah-nold (!!!), making a cameo, mumbles a barely comprehensible and frankly, embarrassing, rap about an apocalyptic wasteland in the wake of geopolitical strife. The Austrian's star power adds nothing, although it does remind the listener they could watch the better part of a good film on their VCR in the time it takes to listen to this album.

Manhattan's Gone Mad is unbearably cluttered, and while claustrophobic production may be great for conveying the insanity of the big apple, that's not the point here. It's a love song to the New York Sanitation Department.

We're well past the 50-minute mark, and, as most artists do, Slade's saved the worst for last. Suffice to say, the titles '87 But Why? and Cut Me are ill-considered under the circumstances. "Why" and "cut," indeed. Album closer Happy Man sounds like it was tossed off in an afternoon and would not be out of place on a Peter Cetera record.

Even the artwork is shit, featuring Slade gesticulating luxuriously in repose in an entirely artificial setting, amidst images we're told "hold special relevance" to the music within. The cover suggests the mindset of Slade circa 1987 is an earnest emptiness and 100% creatively drained (I'm not sure how the rolling pin fits in, as there are no "Andy Capp" references, at least that I can hear).

Sure, it'll be big: Slade is going on tour, his tours are events, and events sell records. He's spun gold from mediocre records in the past; in fact, he's attained an out-of-kilter level of influence and status with a mere handful of truly groundbreaking records. He helped bring glitter rock, Detroit soul and Teutonic-techno-prog to a wider audience. But for every brilliant album, he's released two dogs. Slade's greatest achievement is getting the rock press to warmly embrace a handful of iconic images and characters as important creations in pop history. Musically, he's only gotten by making sure even the duff albums have a memorable hit single or two.

If "Meltdown Veneer" is the sum of all Slade is — a sort of foppish highbrow Bryan Adams — then it's time to look back on his previous work with a more critical eye, one I'm quite sure it will not withstand. For those who've eagerly anticipated this long overdue battering of one of rock's flimsiest sacred cows, you have much to look forward to as Slade's catalog will be re-released during his forthcoming year-long world tour.

Brian, we fell for the pomp, swagger and swing of your days gone by, but now we know there was nothing there all along. Your work, packed with glib literary references and falsely forward-looking musical diversions was, in the end, Oz's emerald curtain. In reality, you have all the substance of a cardboard cutout of Huey Lewis in a strip mall record shop.

Meltdown, indeed. This is the greatest betrayal in rock and roll.

Shame on you, Brian Slade.

- Glen Basters

Friday, September 11, 1987.

HAPPY FRIDAY, EVERYBODY! THE COLISEUM IS LIT UP TONIGHT TO CELEBRATE THE RETURN OF THE LEGENDARY BRIAN SLADE! HE'LL BE TAKING THE STAGE HERE IN NEW YORK ONE WEEK FROM TONIGHT!

IT'S BEEN *FIVE YEARS* SINCE HIS LAST LIVE APPEARANCE AND WE'RE CO-BROADCASTING THIS HISTORIC PERFORMANCE WORLDWIDE ON SEPTEMBER 19TH AT 8PM EASTERN!

THAT'S RIGHT, JEM! FANS ARE LOOKING FORWARD TO HEARING HIS GREATEST HITS, ALONG WITH SONGS FROM HIS NEW ALBUM! STUNTED GROWTH WERE TO OPEN THE SHOW, BUT HAD TO CANCEL DUE TO EXHAUSTION. THEY JUST CAME OFF A GRUELING U.S. TOUR, AND THEIR HIGH-ENERGY PERFORMANCES TOOK A TOLL ON THE BAND'S LEAD SINGER.

HE'S SAID TO BE GETTING SOME WELL-DESERVED REST AND RELAXATION BEFORE EMBARKING ON A EUROPEAN STADIUM TOUR LATER THIS FALL.

SORRY TO WAKE YOU, KID. TIME FOR YOUR MEDS.

...SURE...

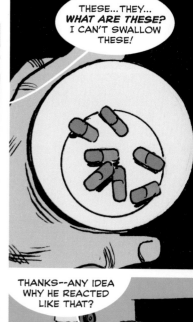

THESE...THEY... *WHAT ARE THESE?* I CAN'T SWALLOW THESE!

NO NO NO. THEY NEED TO *HEAR* THESE...

KID, WHAT'S WRONG?

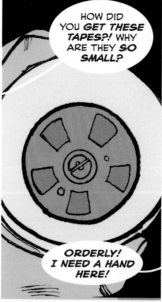

HOW DID YOU *GET THESE TAPES?!* WHY ARE THEY *SO SMALL?*

ORDERLY! I NEED A HAND HERE!

THANKS--ANY IDEA WHY HE REACTED LIKE THAT?

GOTTA... GET... TAPES...

LOOK AT THE PAPERWORK. MEDS COME IN ON TRAYS, CIRCLES SET HIM OFF.

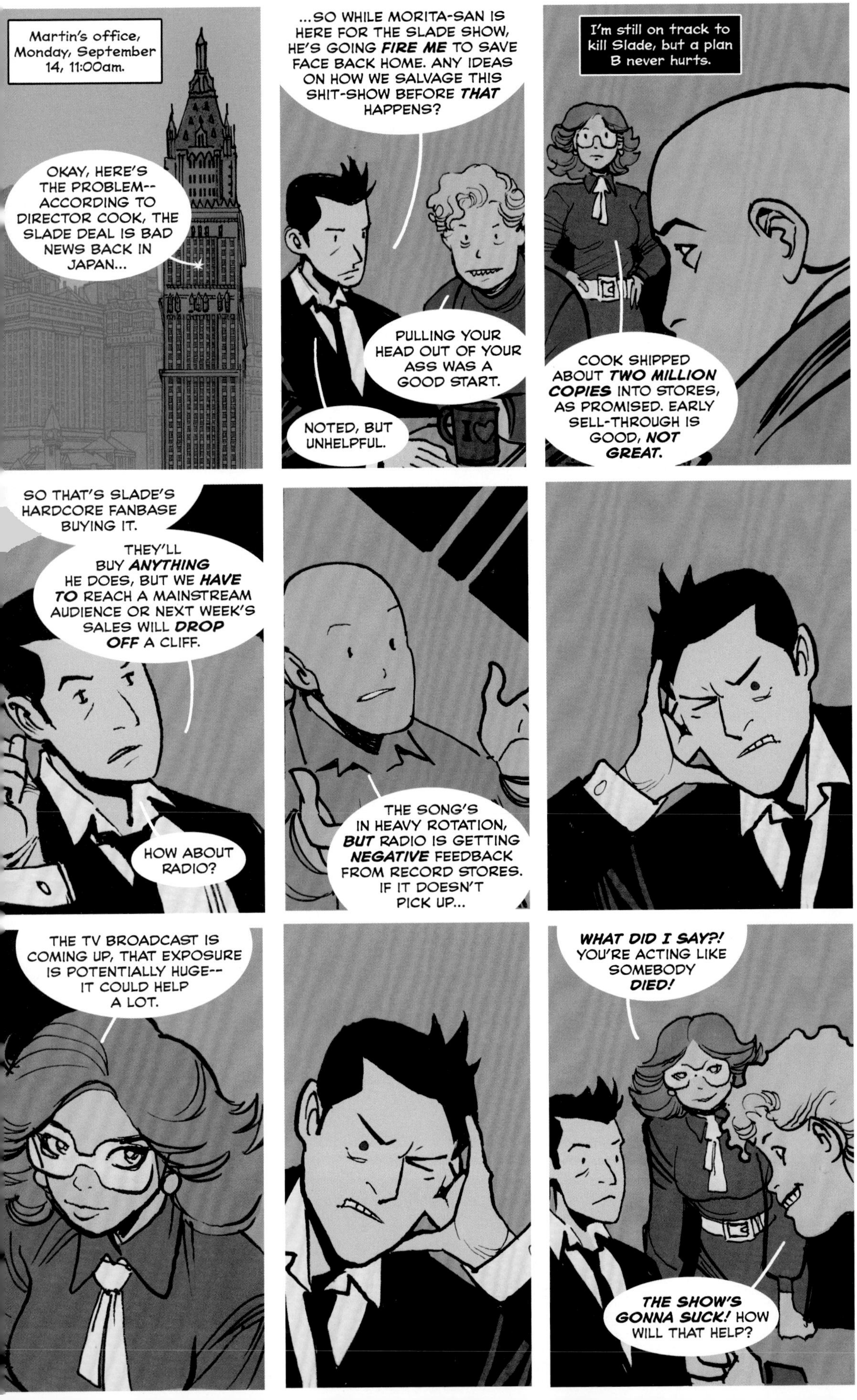

Martin's office, Monday, September 14, 11:00am.
OKAY, HERE'S THE PROBLEM-- ACCORDING TO DIRECTOR COOK, THE SLADE DEAL IS BAD NEWS BACK IN JAPAN...
...SO WHILE MORITA-SAN IS HERE FOR THE SLADE SHOW, HE'S GOING FIRE ME TO SAVE FACE BACK HOME. ANY IDEAS ON HOW WE SALVAGE THIS SHIT-SHOW BEFORE THAT HAPPENS?
PULLING YOUR HEAD OUT OF YOUR ASS WAS A GOOD START.
NOTED, BUT UNHELPFUL.
I'm still on track to kill Slade, but a plan B never hurts.
COOK SHIPPED ABOUT TWO MILLION COPIES INTO STORES, AS PROMISED. EARLY SELL-THROUGH IS GOOD, NOT GREAT.
SO THAT'S SLADE'S HARDCORE FANBASE BUYING IT.
THEY'LL BUY ANYTHING HE DOES, BUT WE HAVE TO REACH A MAINSTREAM AUDIENCE OR NEXT WEEK'S SALES WILL DROP OFF A CLIFF.
HOW ABOUT RADIO?
THE SONG'S IN HEAVY ROTATION, BUT RADIO IS GETTING NEGATIVE FEEDBACK FROM RECORD STORES. IF IT DOESN'T PICK UP...
THE TV BROADCAST IS COMING UP, THAT EXPOSURE IS POTENTIALLY HUGE-- IT COULD HELP A LOT.
WHAT DID I SAY?! YOU'RE ACTING LIKE SOMEBODY DIED!
THE SHOW'S GONNA SUCK! HOW WILL THAT HELP?

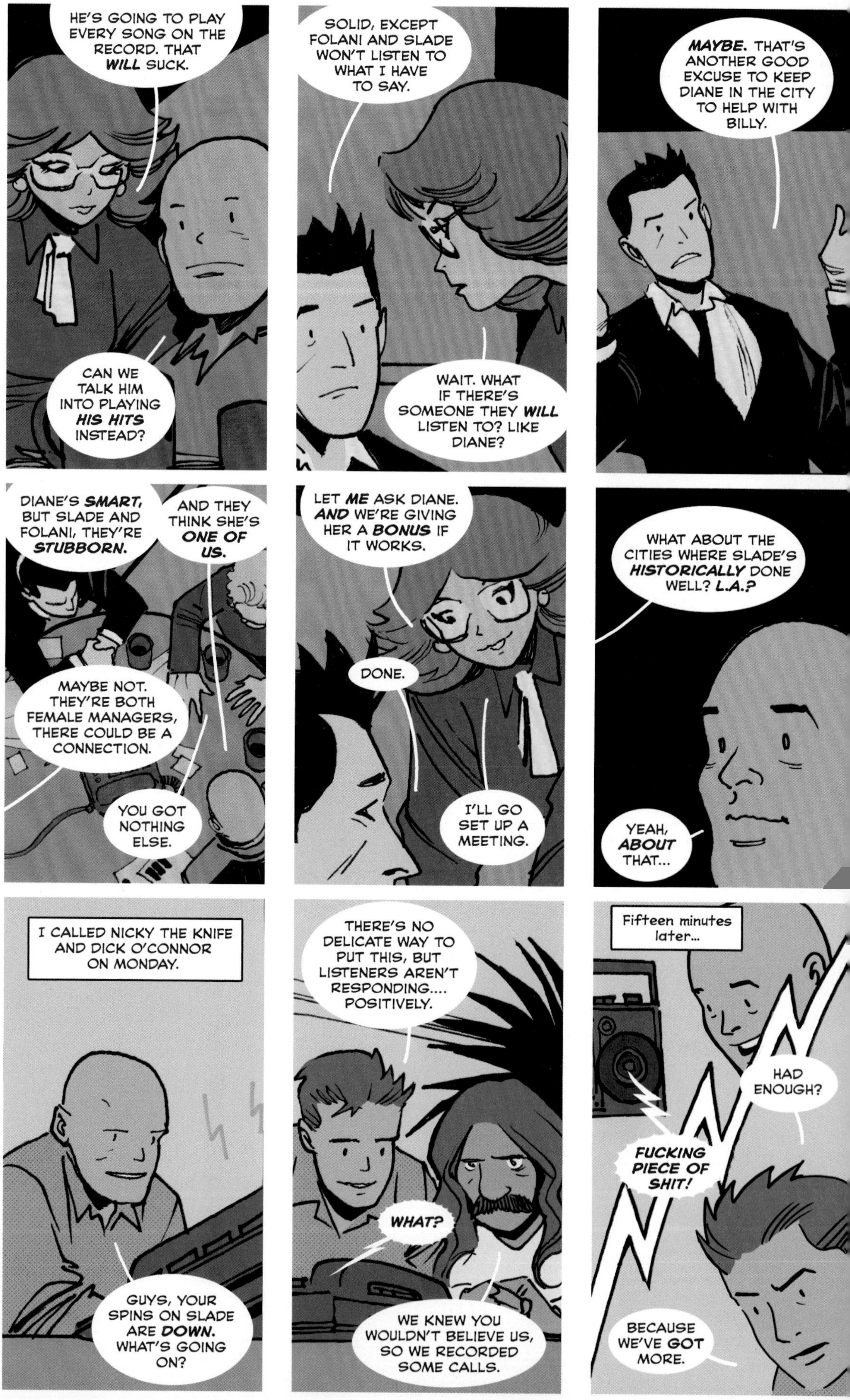
HE'S GOING TO PLAY EVERY SONG ON THE RECORD. THAT WILL SUCK.
CAN WE TALK HIM INTO PLAYING HIS HITS INSTEAD?
SOLID, EXCEPT FOLANI AND SLADE WON'T LISTEN TO WHAT I HAVE TO SAY.
WAIT. WHAT IF THERE'S SOMEONE THEY WILL LISTEN TO? LIKE DIANE?
MAYBE. THAT'S ANOTHER GOOD EXCUSE TO KEEP DIANE IN THE CITY TO HELP WITH BILLY.
DIANE'S SMART, BUT SLADE AND FOLANI, THEY'RE STUBBORN.
AND THEY THINK SHE'S ONE OF US.
MAYBE NOT. THEY'RE BOTH FEMALE MANAGERS, THERE COULD BE A CONNECTION.
YOU GOT NOTHING ELSE.
LET ME ASK DIANE. AND WE'RE GIVING HER A BONUS IF IT WORKS.
DONE.
I'LL GO SET UP A MEETING.
WHAT ABOUT THE CITIES WHERE SLADE'S HISTORICALLY DONE WELL? L.A.?
YEAH, ABOUT THAT...
I CALLED NICKY THE KNIFE AND DICK O'CONNOR ON MONDAY.
GUYS, YOUR SPINS ON SLADE ARE DOWN. WHAT'S GOING ON?
THERE'S NO DELICATE WAY TO PUT THIS, BUT LISTENERS AREN'T RESPONDING.... POSITIVELY.
WHAT?
WE KNEW YOU WOULDN'T BELIEVE US, SO WE RECORDED SOME CALLS.
Fifteen minutes later...
HAD ENOUGH?
FUCKING PIECE OF SHIT!
BECAUSE WE'VE GOT MORE.

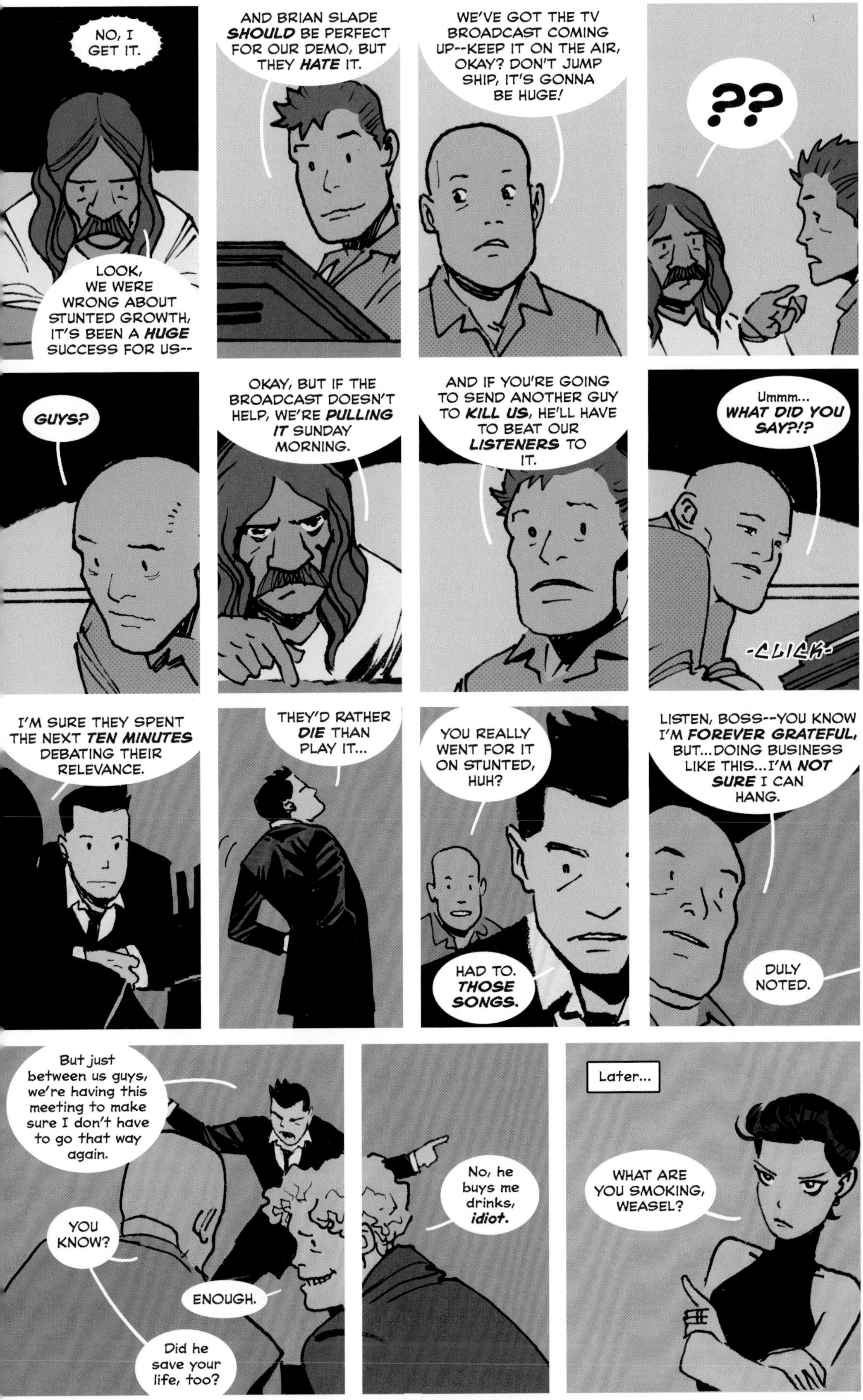
NO, I GET IT.
LOOK, WE WERE WRONG ABOUT STUNTED GROWTH, IT'S BEEN A HUGE SUCCESS FOR US--
AND BRIAN SLADE SHOULD BE PERFECT FOR OUR DEMO, BUT THEY HATE IT.
WE'VE GOT THE TV BROADCAST COMING UP--KEEP IT ON THE AIR, OKAY? DON'T JUMP SHIP, IT'S GONNA BE HUGE!
??
GUYS?
OKAY, BUT IF THE BROADCAST DOESN'T HELP, WE'RE PULLING IT SUNDAY MORNING.
AND IF YOU'RE GOING TO SEND ANOTHER GUY TO KILL US, HE'LL HAVE TO BEAT OUR LISTENERS TO IT.
Ummm... WHAT DID YOU SAY?!?
-CLICK-
I'M SURE THEY SPENT THE NEXT TEN MINUTES DEBATING THEIR RELEVANCE.
THEY'D RATHER DIE THAN PLAY IT...
YOU REALLY WENT FOR IT ON STUNTED, HUH?
HAD TO. THOSE SONGS.
LISTEN, BOSS--YOU KNOW I'M FOREVER GRATEFUL, BUT...DOING BUSINESS LIKE THIS...I'M NOT SURE I CAN HANG.
DULY NOTED.
But just between us guys, we're having this meeting to make sure I don't have to go that way again.
YOU KNOW?
ENOUGH.
Did he save your life, too?
No, he buys me drinks, idiot.
Later...
WHAT ARE YOU SMOKING, WEASEL?

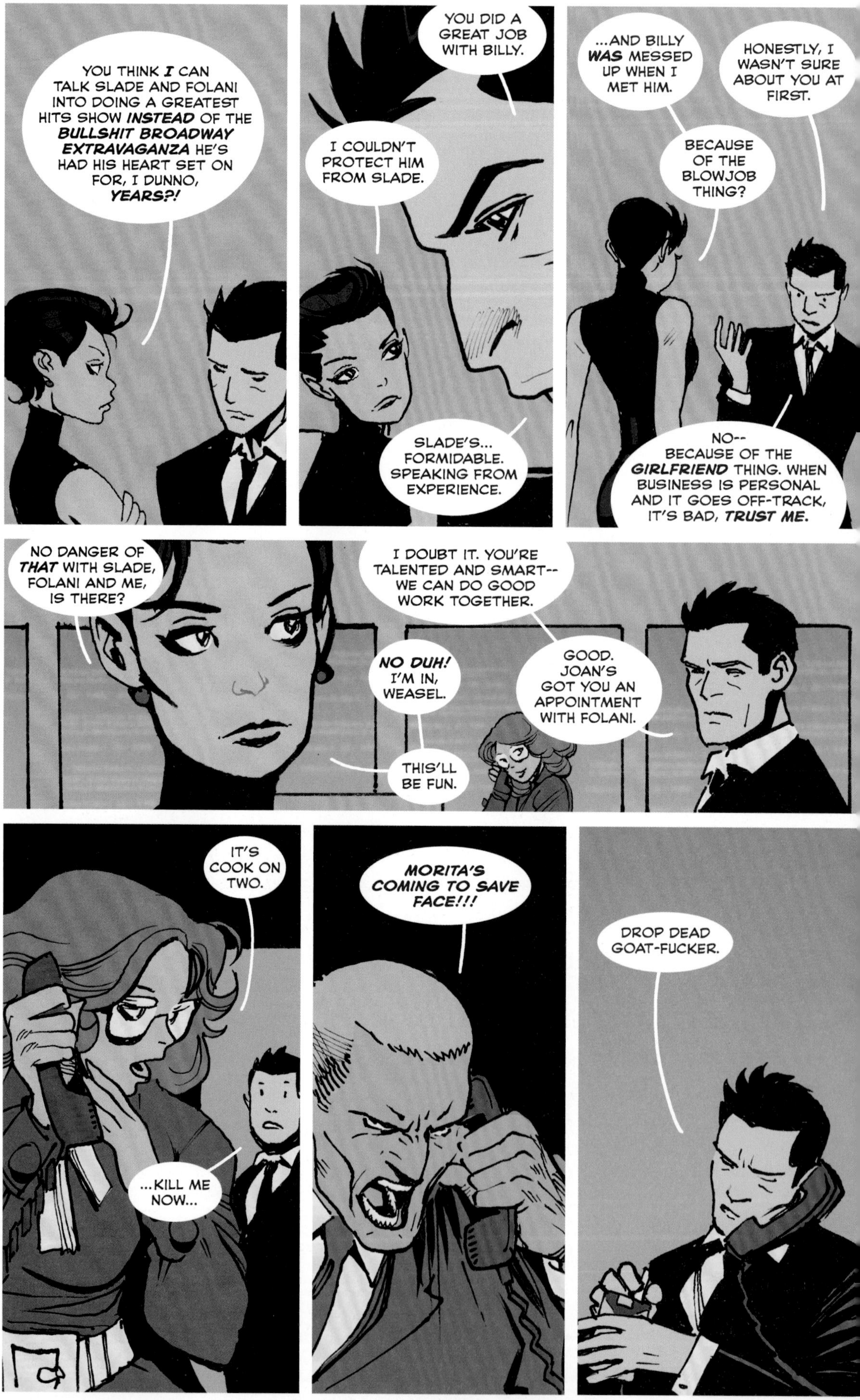
YOU THINK *I* CAN TALK SLADE AND FOLANI INTO DOING A GREATEST HITS SHOW *INSTEAD* OF THE *BULLSHIT BROADWAY EXTRAVAGANZA* HE'S HAD HIS HEART SET ON FOR, I DUNNO, *YEARS?!*
YOU DID A GREAT JOB WITH BILLY.
I COULDN'T PROTECT HIM FROM SLADE.
SLADE'S... FORMIDABLE. SPEAKING FROM EXPERIENCE.
...AND BILLY *WAS* MESSED UP WHEN I MET HIM.
HONESTLY, I WASN'T SURE ABOUT YOU AT FIRST.
BECAUSE OF THE BLOWJOB THING?
NO-- BECAUSE OF THE *GIRLFRIEND* THING. WHEN BUSINESS IS PERSONAL AND IT GOES OFF-TRACK, IT'S BAD, *TRUST ME.*
NO DANGER OF *THAT* WITH SLADE, FOLANI AND ME, IS THERE?
I DOUBT IT. YOU'RE TALENTED AND SMART-- WE CAN DO GOOD WORK TOGETHER.
GOOD. JOAN'S GOT YOU AN APPOINTMENT WITH FOLANI.
NO DUH! I'M IN, WEASEL.
THIS'LL BE FUN.
IT'S COOK ON TWO.
...KILL ME NOW...
MORITA'S COMING TO SAVE FACE!!!
DROP DEAD GOAT-FUCKER.

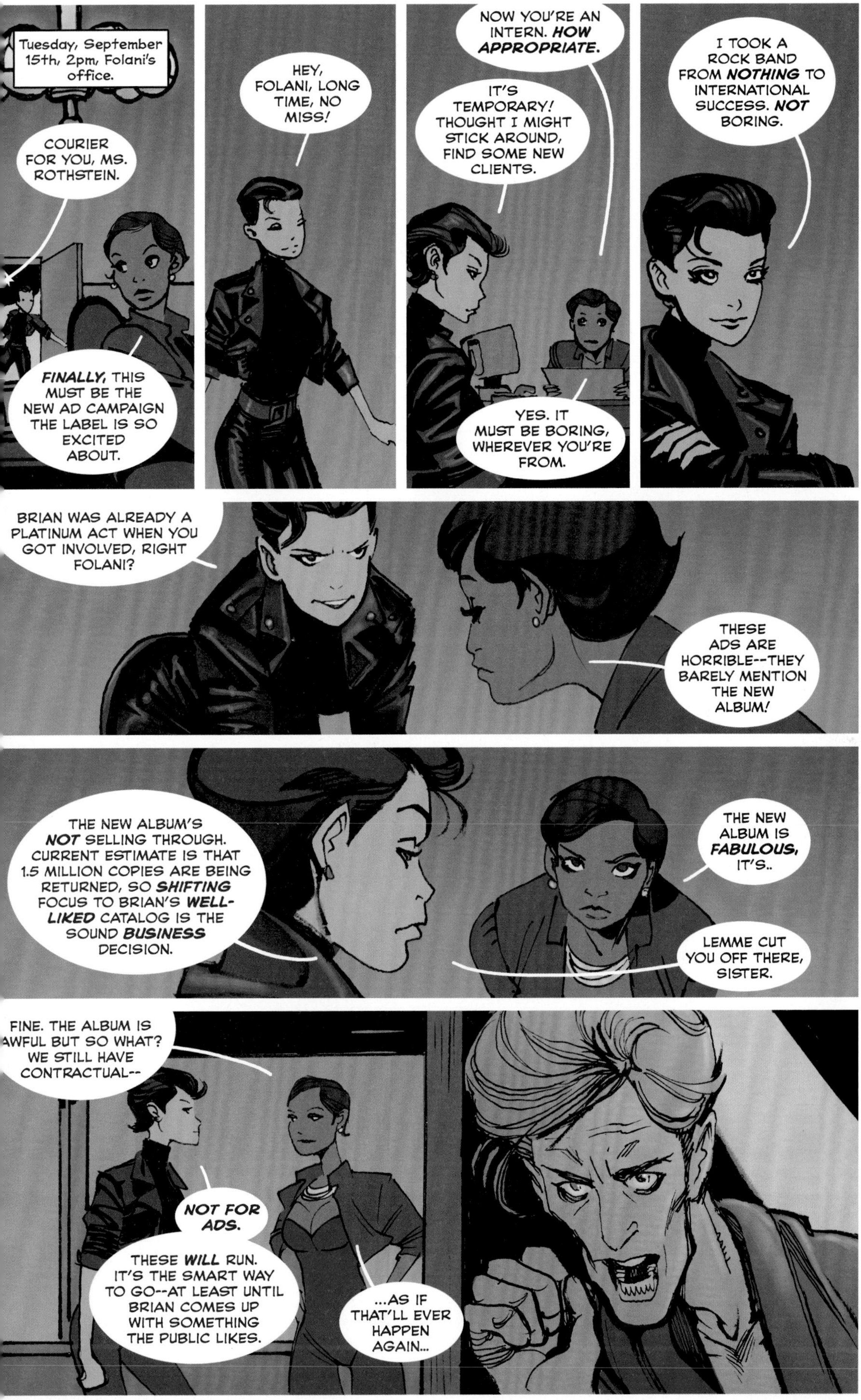
Tuesday, September 15th, 2pm, Folani's office.
COURIER FOR YOU, MS. ROTHSTEIN.
FINALLY, THIS MUST BE THE NEW AD CAMPAIGN THE LABEL IS SO EXCITED ABOUT.
HEY, FOLANI, LONG TIME, NO MISS!
NOW YOU'RE AN INTERN. HOW APPROPRIATE.
IT'S TEMPORARY! THOUGHT I MIGHT STICK AROUND, FIND SOME NEW CLIENTS.
YES. IT MUST BE BORING, WHEREVER YOU'RE FROM.
I TOOK A ROCK BAND FROM NOTHING TO INTERNATIONAL SUCCESS. NOT BORING.
BRIAN WAS ALREADY A PLATINUM ACT WHEN YOU GOT INVOLVED, RIGHT FOLANI?
THESE ADS ARE HORRIBLE--THEY BARELY MENTION THE NEW ALBUM!
THE NEW ALBUM IS FABULOUS, IT'S..
LEMME CUT YOU OFF THERE, SISTER.
THE NEW ALBUM'S NOT SELLING THROUGH. CURRENT ESTIMATE IS THAT 1.5 MILLION COPIES ARE BEING RETURNED, SO SHIFTING FOCUS TO BRIAN'S WELL-LIKED CATALOG IS THE SOUND BUSINESS DECISION.
FINE. THE ALBUM IS AWFUL BUT SO WHAT? WE STILL HAVE CONTRACTUAL--
NOT FOR ADS.
THESE WILL RUN. IT'S THE SMART WAY TO GO--AT LEAST UNTIL BRIAN COMES UP WITH SOMETHING THE PUBLIC LIKES.
...AS IF THAT'LL EVER HAPPEN AGAIN...

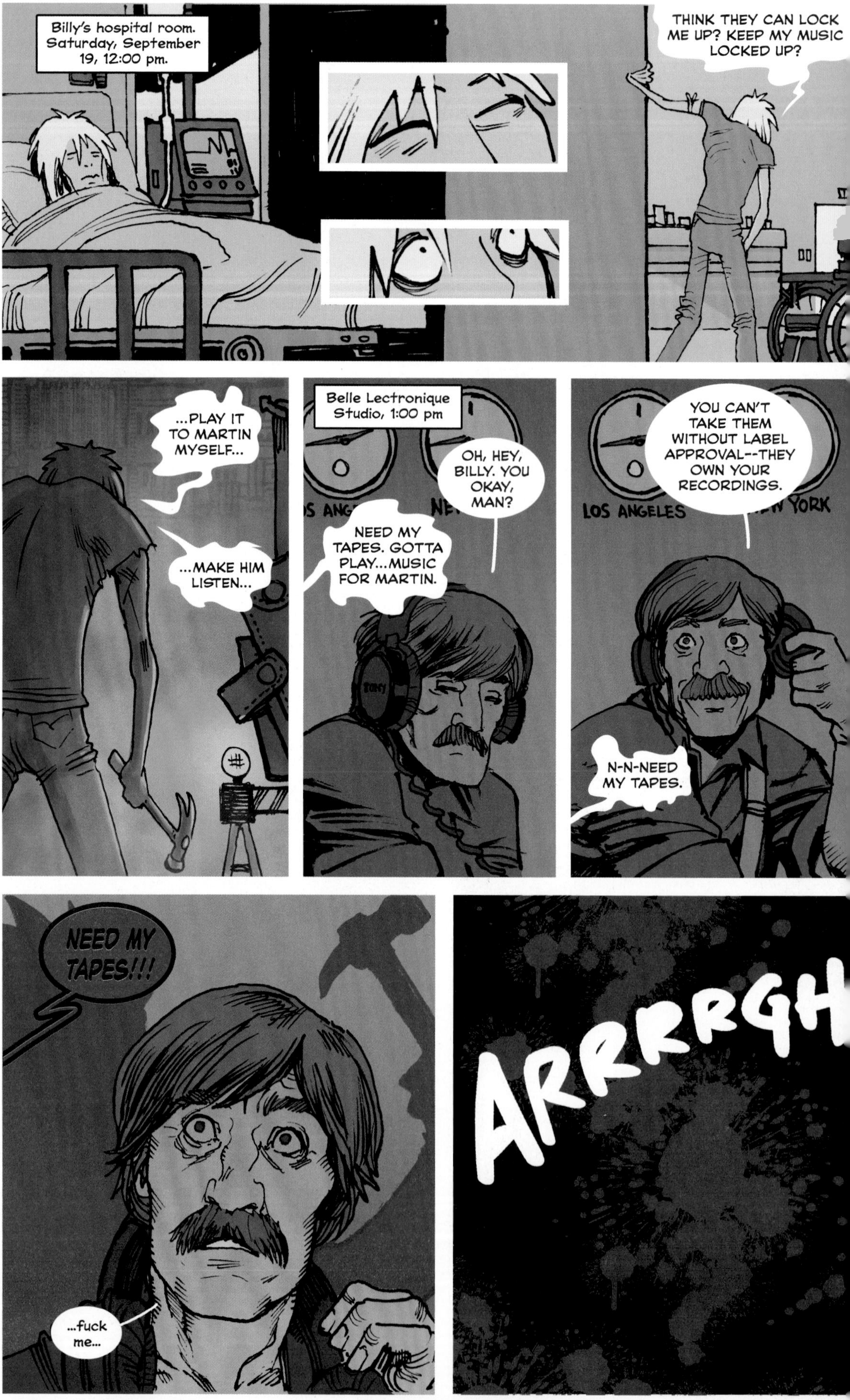
Billy's hospital room. Saturday, September 19, 12:00 pm.
THINK THEY CAN LOCK ME UP? KEEP MY MUSIC LOCKED UP?
...PLAY IT TO MARTIN MYSELF...
...MAKE HIM LISTEN...
Belle Lectronique Studio, 1:00 pm
OH, HEY, BILLY. YOU OKAY, MAN?
NEED MY TAPES. GOTTA PLAY...MUSIC FOR MARTIN.
LOS ANGELES
YOU CAN'T TAKE THEM WITHOUT LABEL APPROVAL--THEY OWN YOUR RECORDINGS.
N-N-NEED MY TAPES.
NEED MY TAPES!!!
...fuck me...
ARRRRGH

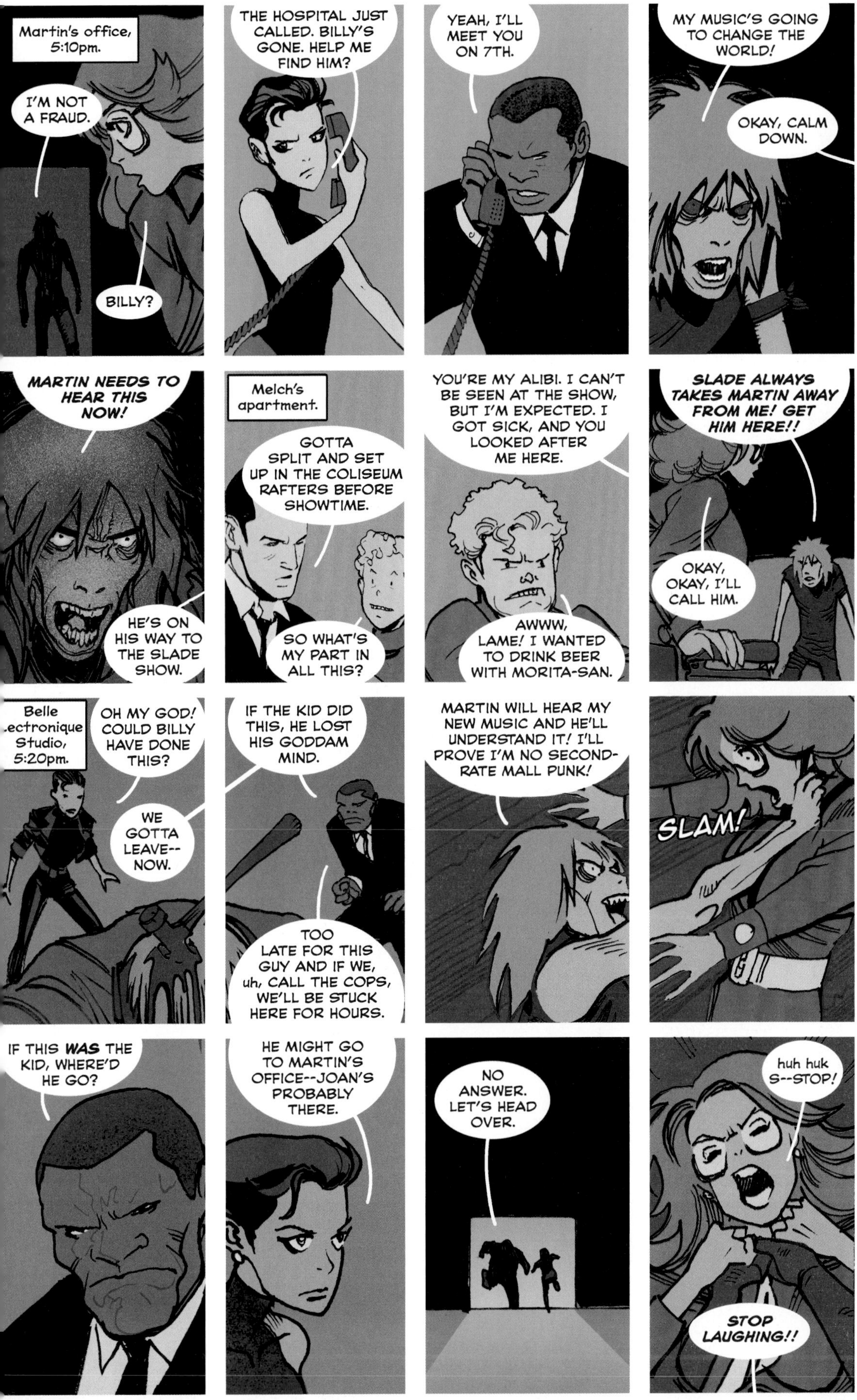
Martin's office, 5:10pm.
I'M NOT A FRAUD.
BILLY?
THE HOSPITAL JUST CALLED. BILLY'S GONE. HELP ME FIND HIM?
YEAH, I'LL MEET YOU ON 7TH.
MY MUSIC'S GOING TO CHANGE THE WORLD!
OKAY, CALM DOWN.
MARTIN NEEDS TO HEAR THIS NOW!
HE'S ON HIS WAY TO THE SLADE SHOW.
Melch's apartment.
GOTTA SPLIT AND SET UP IN THE COLISEUM RAFTERS BEFORE SHOWTIME.
SO WHAT'S MY PART IN ALL THIS?
YOU'RE MY ALIBI. I CAN'T BE SEEN AT THE SHOW, BUT I'M EXPECTED. I GOT SICK, AND YOU LOOKED AFTER ME HERE.
AWWW, LAME! I WANTED TO DRINK BEER WITH MORITA-SAN.
SLADE ALWAYS TAKES MARTIN AWAY FROM ME! GET HIM HERE!!
OKAY, OKAY, I'LL CALL HIM.
Belle
.ectronique
Studio,
5:20pm.
OH MY GOD! COULD BILLY HAVE DONE THIS?
WE GOTTA LEAVE-- NOW.
IF THE KID DID THIS, HE LOST HIS GODDAM MIND.
TOO LATE FOR THIS GUY AND IF WE, uh, CALL THE COPS, WE'LL BE STUCK HERE FOR HOURS.
MARTIN WILL HEAR MY NEW MUSIC AND HE'LL UNDERSTAND IT! I'LL PROVE I'M NO SECOND-RATE MALL PUNK!
SLAM!
IF THIS WAS THE KID, WHERE'D HE GO?
HE MIGHT GO TO MARTIN'S OFFICE--JOAN'S PROBABLY THERE.
NO ANSWER. LET'S HEAD OVER.
huh huk S--STOP!
STOP LAUGHING!!

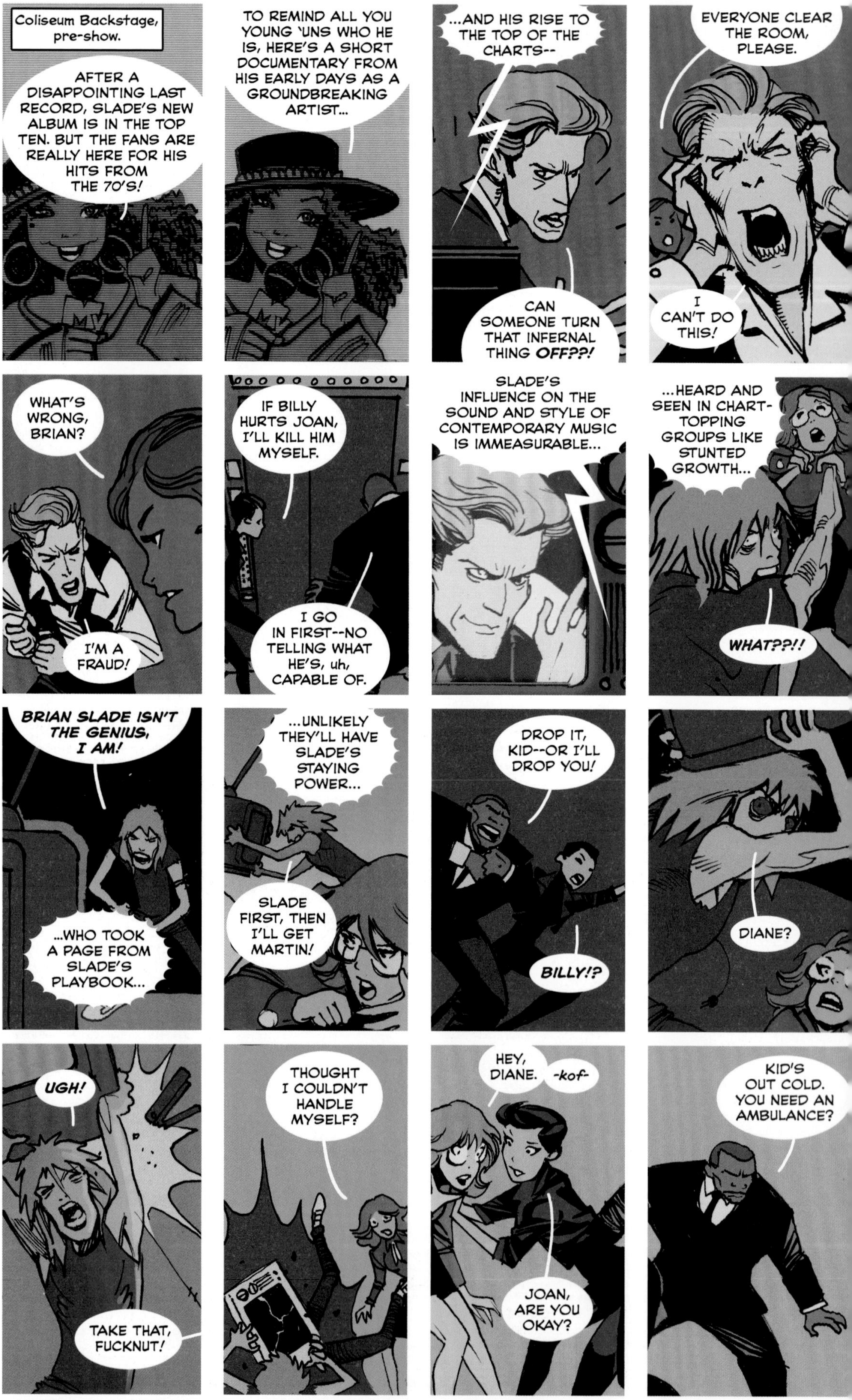

Coliseum Backstage, pre-show.
AFTER A DISAPPOINTING LAST RECORD, SLADE'S NEW ALBUM IS IN THE TOP TEN. BUT THE FANS ARE REALLY HERE FOR HIS HITS FROM THE 70'S!
TO REMIND ALL YOU YOUNG 'UNS WHO HE IS, HERE'S A SHORT DOCUMENTARY FROM HIS EARLY DAYS AS A GROUNDBREAKING ARTIST...
...AND HIS RISE TO THE TOP OF THE CHARTS--
CAN SOMEONE TURN THAT INFERNAL THING OFF??!
EVERYONE CLEAR THE ROOM, PLEASE.
I CAN'T DO THIS!
WHAT'S WRONG, BRIAN?
I'M A FRAUD!
IF BILLY HURTS JOAN, I'LL KILL HIM MYSELF.
I GO IN FIRST--NO TELLING WHAT HE'S, uh, CAPABLE OF.
SLADE'S INFLUENCE ON THE SOUND AND STYLE OF CONTEMPORARY MUSIC IS IMMEASURABLE...
...HEARD AND SEEN IN CHART-TOPPING GROUPS LIKE STUNTED GROWTH...
WHAT??!!
BRIAN SLADE ISN'T THE GENIUS, I AM!
...WHO TOOK A PAGE FROM SLADE'S PLAYBOOK...
...UNLIKELY THEY'LL HAVE SLADE'S STAYING POWER...
SLADE FIRST, THEN I'LL GET MARTIN!
DROP IT, KID--OR I'LL DROP YOU!
BILLY!?
DIANE?
UGH!
TAKE THAT, FUCKNUT!
THOUGHT I COULDN'T HANDLE MYSELF?
HEY, DIANE.
-kof-
JOAN, ARE YOU OKAY?
KID'S OUT COLD. YOU NEED AN AMBULANCE?

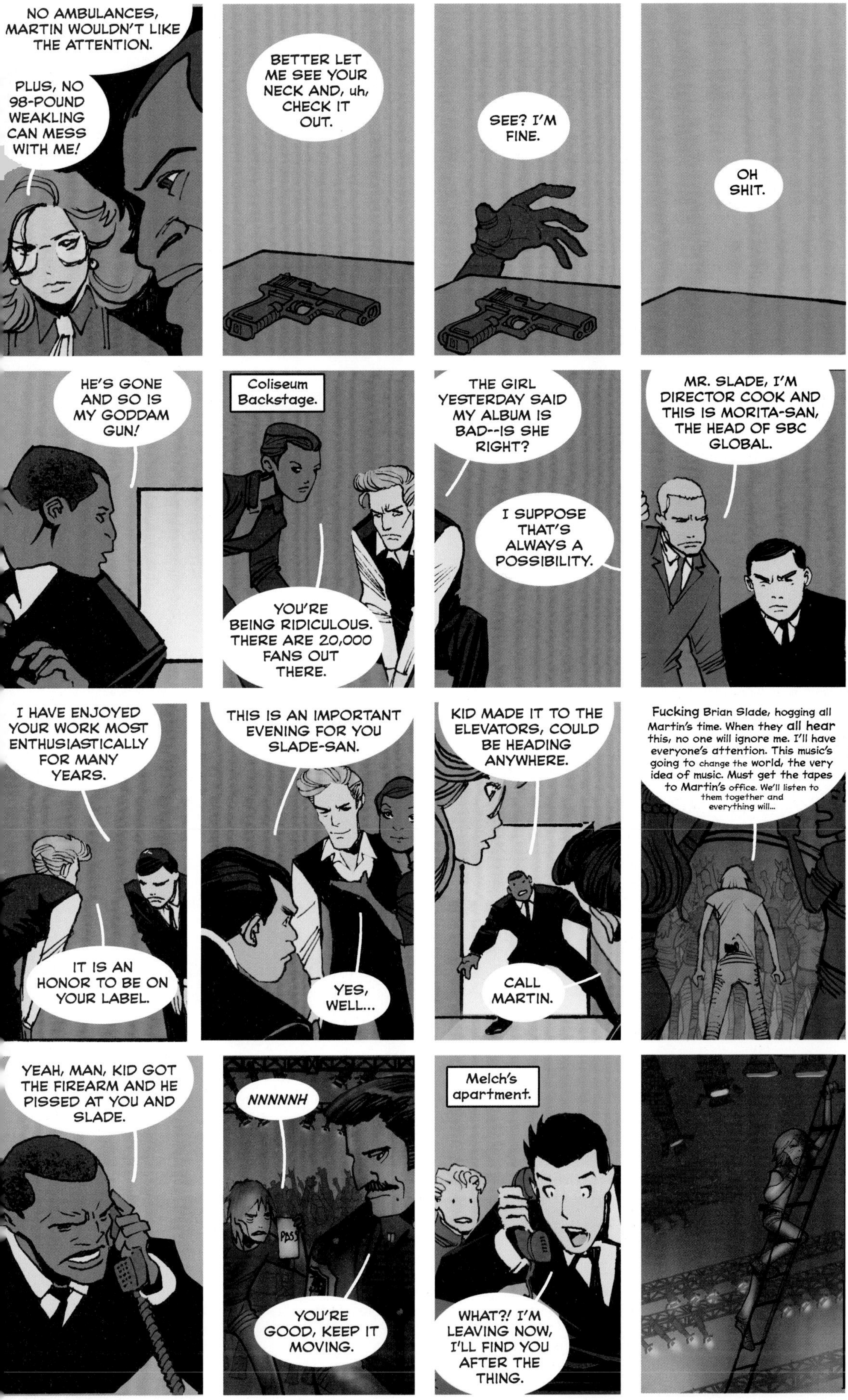
NO AMBULANCES, MARTIN WOULDN'T LIKE THE ATTENTION.
PLUS, NO 98-POUND WEAKLING CAN MESS WITH ME!
BETTER LET ME SEE YOUR NECK AND, uh, CHECK IT OUT.
SEE? I'M FINE.
OH SHIT.
HE'S GONE AND SO IS MY GODDAM GUN!
Coliseum Backstage.
YOU'RE BEING RIDICULOUS. THERE ARE 20,000 FANS OUT THERE.
THE GIRL YESTERDAY SAID MY ALBUM IS BAD--IS SHE RIGHT?
I SUPPOSE THAT'S ALWAYS A POSSIBILITY.
MR. SLADE, I'M DIRECTOR COOK AND THIS IS MORITA-SAN, THE HEAD OF SBC GLOBAL.
I HAVE ENJOYED YOUR WORK MOST ENTHUSIASTICALLY FOR MANY YEARS.
IT IS AN HONOR TO BE ON YOUR LABEL.
THIS IS AN IMPORTANT EVENING FOR YOU SLADE-SAN.
YES, WELL...
KID MADE IT TO THE ELEVATORS, COULD BE HEADING ANYWHERE.
CALL MARTIN.
Fucking Brian Slade, hogging all Martin's time. When they all hear this, no one will ignore me. I'll have everyone's attention. This music's going to change the world, the very idea of music. Must get the tapes to Martin's office. We'll listen to them together and everything will...
YEAH, MAN, KID GOT THE FIREARM AND HE PISSED AT YOU AND SLADE.
NNNNNH
PASS
YOU'RE GOOD, KEEP IT MOVING.
Melch's apartment.
WHAT?! I'M LEAVING NOW, I'LL FIND YOU AFTER THE THING.

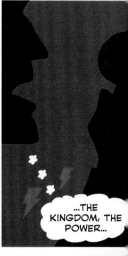

Coliseum, SHOWTIME!

WHEN YOU GET TO THE RAINBOW'S END AND ALL THAT'S LEFT...

IS HOPE...

...THE KINGDOM, THE POWER...

BRIAN SLADE

NO, I *HAVEN'T* SEEN BILLY-- OR *MARTIN MILLS!* DISGRACEFUL TREATMENT!

MARTIN, um, HE GOT *DELAYED.*

IF YOU'LL EXCUSE ME, *I* HAVE A CONCERT TO SEE.

WE GOTTA SEARCH THIS BUILDING. KID'S DANGEROUS.

COULDN'T WAIT FOR THAT BITCH TO LEAVE. I'LL TAKE THE FLOOR.

FUCK, HE'S GOT A CLEAR SHOT AT SLADE.

...GONNA KILL YOU, BRIAN...

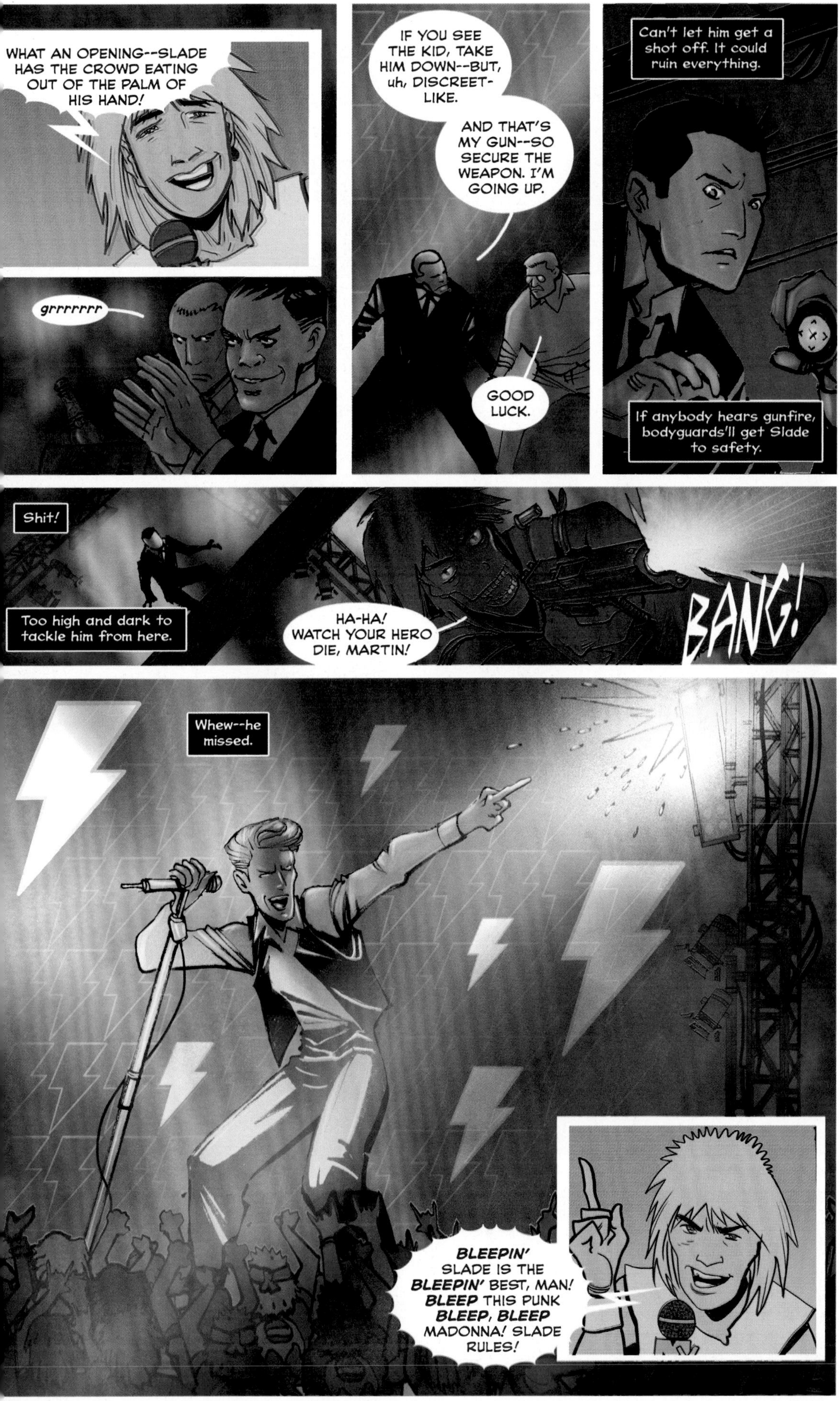
WHAT AN OPENING--SLADE HAS THE CROWD EATING OUT OF THE PALM OF HIS HAND!
grrrrrrr
IF YOU SEE THE KID, TAKE HIM DOWN--BUT, uh, DISCREET-LIKE.
AND THAT'S MY GUN--SO SECURE THE WEAPON. I'M GOING UP.
GOOD LUCK.
Can't let him get a shot off. It could ruin everything.
If anybody hears gunfire, bodyguards'll get Slade to safety.
Shit!
Too high and dark to tackle him from here.
HA-HA! WATCH YOUR HERO DIE, MARTIN!
BANG!
Whew--he missed.
BLEEPIN' SLADE IS THE BLEEPIN' BEST, MAN! BLEEP THIS PUNK BLEEP, BLEEP MADONNA! SLADE RULES!

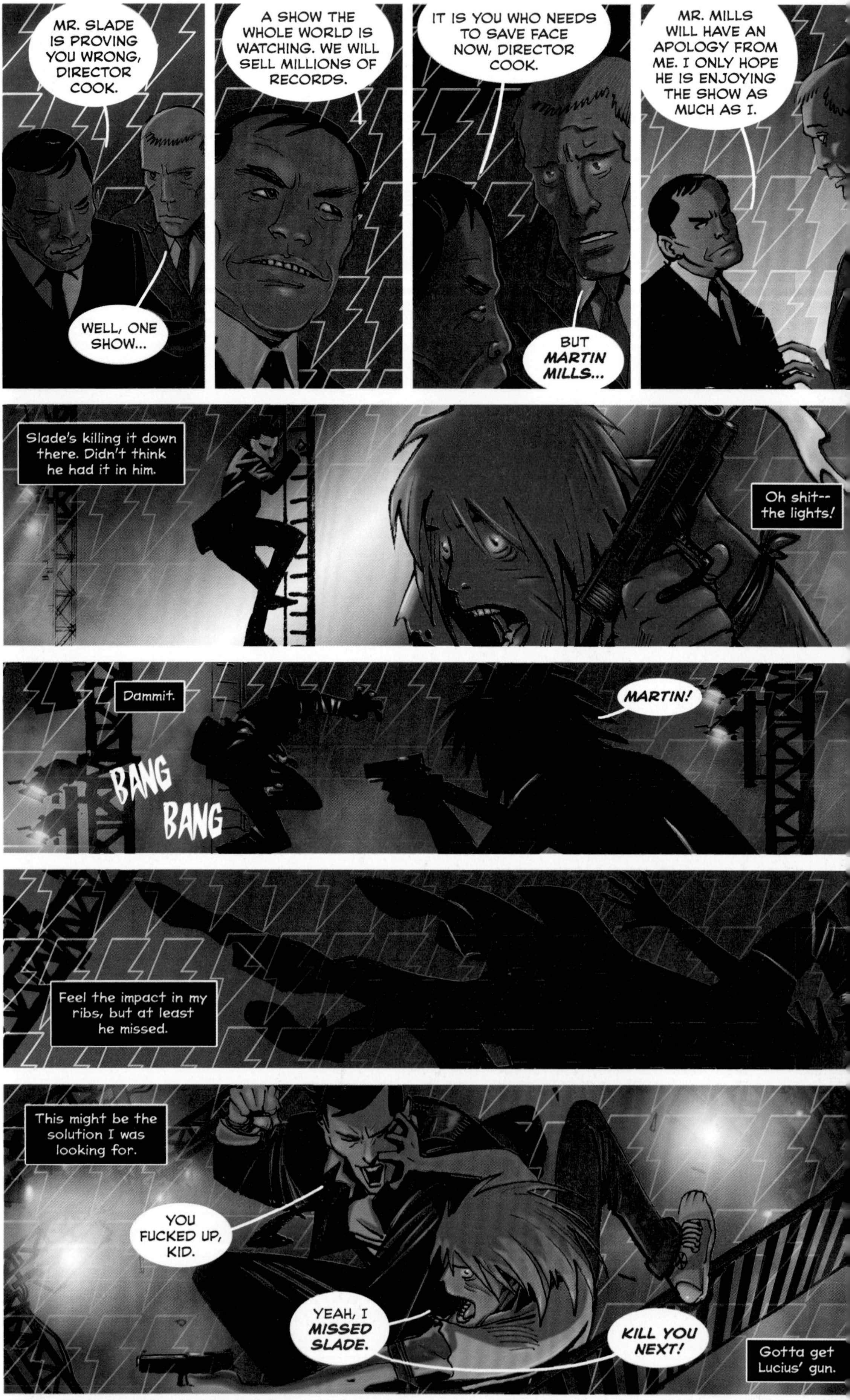
MR. SLADE IS PROVING YOU WRONG, DIRECTOR COOK.
WELL, ONE SHOW...
A SHOW THE WHOLE WORLD IS WATCHING. WE WILL SELL MILLIONS OF RECORDS.
IT IS YOU WHO NEEDS TO SAVE FACE NOW, DIRECTOR COOK.
BUT *MARTIN MILLS*...
MR. MILLS WILL HAVE AN APOLOGY FROM ME. I ONLY HOPE HE IS ENJOYING THE SHOW AS MUCH AS I.
Slade's killing it down there. Didn't think he had it in him.
Oh shit--the lights!
Dammit.
MARTIN!
BANG
BANG
Feel the impact in my ribs, but at least he missed.
This might be the solution I was looking for.
YOU FUCKED UP, KID.
YEAH, I *MISSED SLADE.*
KILL YOU NEXT!
Gotta get Lucius' gun.

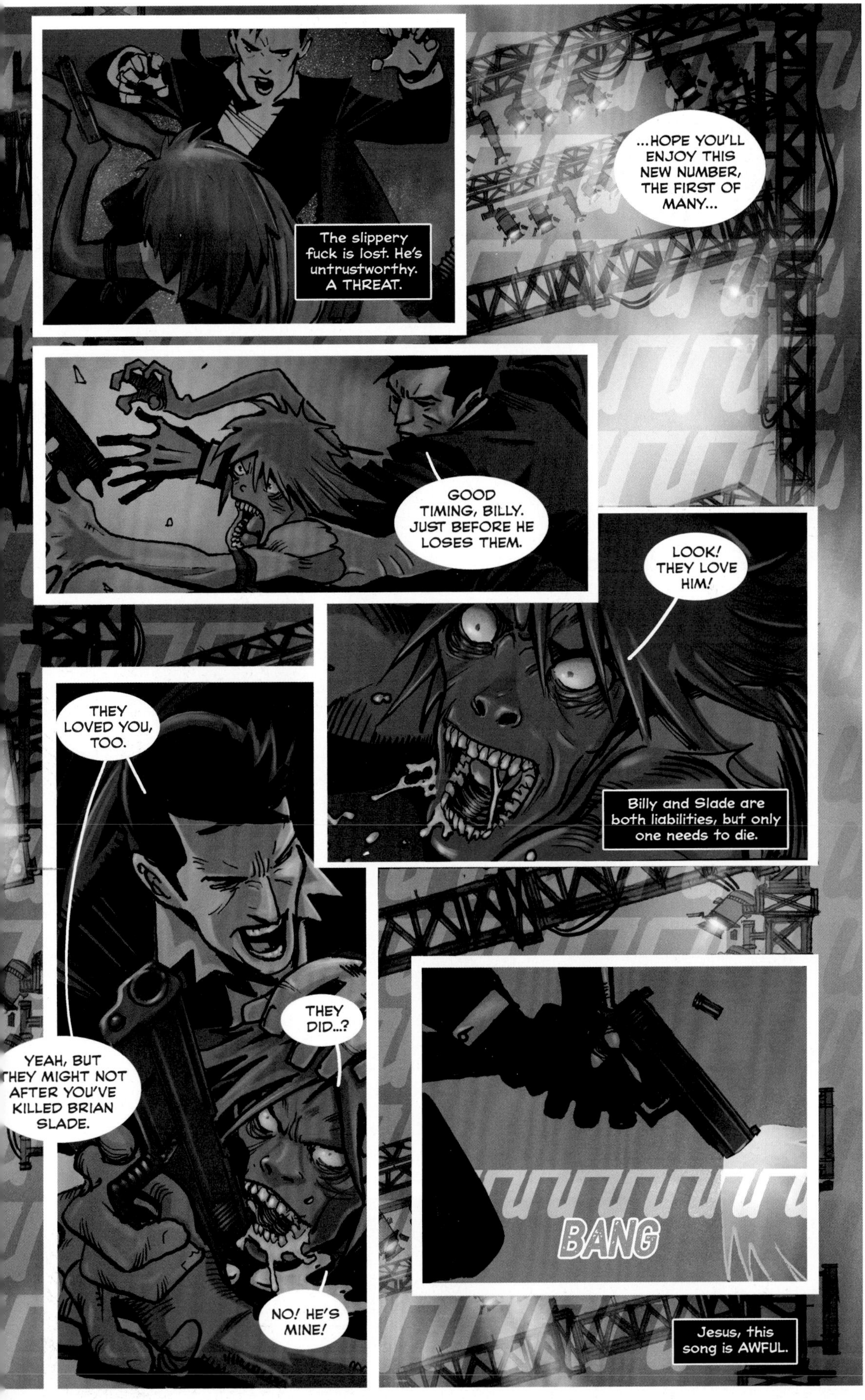
The slippery fuck is lost. He's untrustworthy. A THREAT.
...HOPE YOU'LL ENJOY THIS NEW NUMBER, THE FIRST OF MANY...
GOOD TIMING, BILLY. JUST BEFORE HE LOSES THEM.
LOOK! THEY LOVE HIM!
Billy and Slade are both liabilities, but only one needs to die.
THEY LOVED YOU, TOO.
THEY DID...?
YEAH, BUT THEY MIGHT NOT AFTER YOU'VE KILLED BRIAN SLADE.
NO! HE'S MINE!
BANG
Jesus, this song is AWFUL.

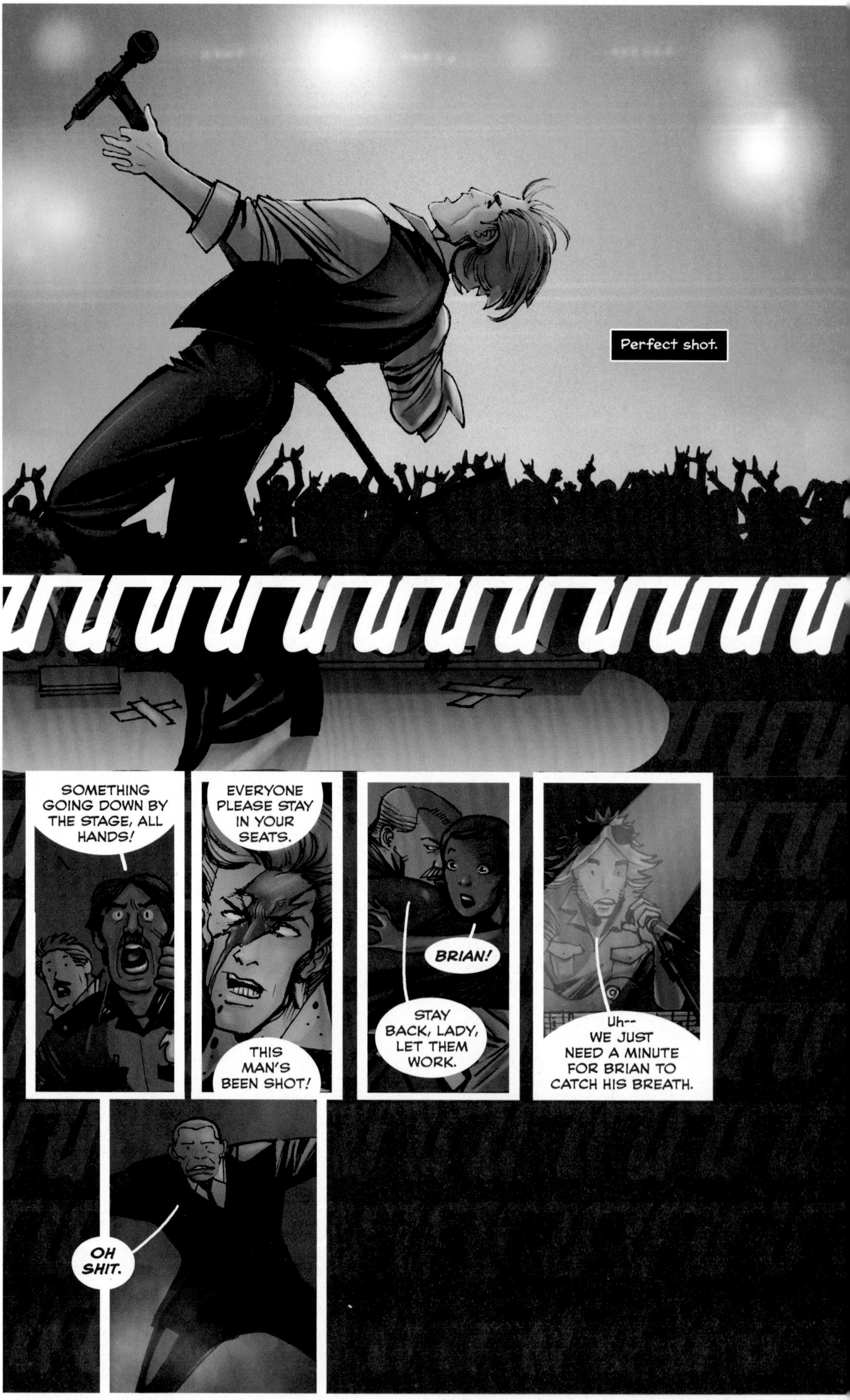
Perfect shot.
SOMETHING GOING DOWN BY THE STAGE, ALL HANDS!
EVERYONE PLEASE STAY IN YOUR SEATS.
THIS MAN'S BEEN SHOT!
BRIAN!
STAY BACK, LADY, LET THEM WORK.
Uh-- WE JUST NEED A MINUTE FOR BRIAN TO CATCH HIS BREATH.
OH SHIT.

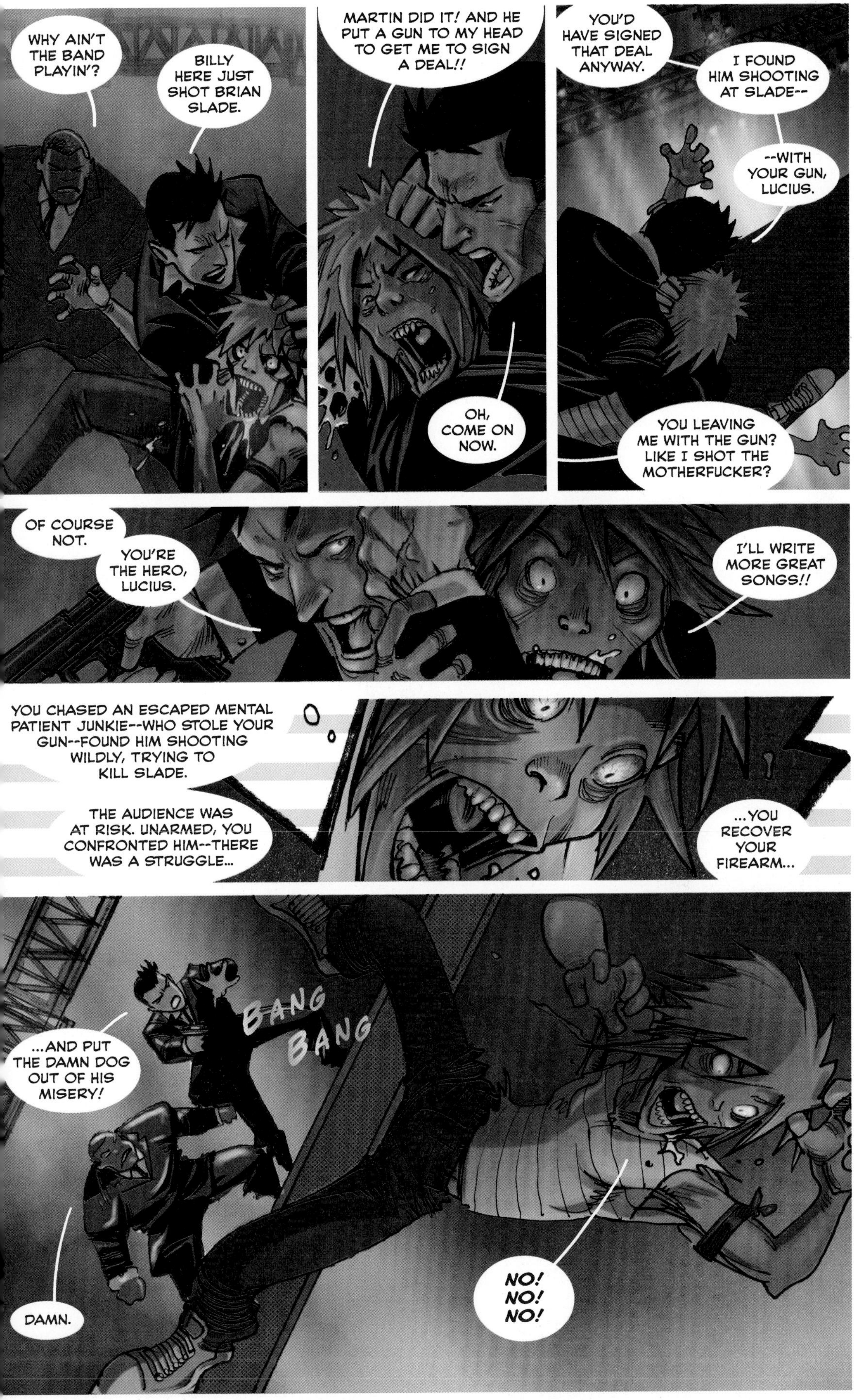
WHY AIN'T THE BAND PLAYIN'?
BILLY HERE JUST SHOT BRIAN SLADE.
MARTIN DID IT! AND HE PUT A GUN TO MY HEAD TO GET ME TO SIGN A DEAL!!
OH, COME ON NOW.
YOU'D HAVE SIGNED THAT DEAL ANYWAY.
I FOUND HIM SHOOTING AT SLADE--
--WITH YOUR GUN, LUCIUS.
YOU LEAVING ME WITH THE GUN? LIKE I SHOT THE MOTHERFUCKER?
OF COURSE NOT.
YOU'RE THE HERO, LUCIUS.
I'LL WRITE MORE GREAT SONGS!!
YOU CHASED AN ESCAPED MENTAL PATIENT JUNKIE--WHO STOLE YOUR GUN--FOUND HIM SHOOTING WILDLY, TRYING TO KILL SLADE.
THE AUDIENCE WAS AT RISK. UNARMED, YOU CONFRONTED HIM--THERE WAS A STRUGGLE...
...YOU RECOVER YOUR FIREARM...
...AND PUT THE DAMN DOG OUT OF HIS MISERY!
BANG
BANG
DAMN.
NO! NO! NO!

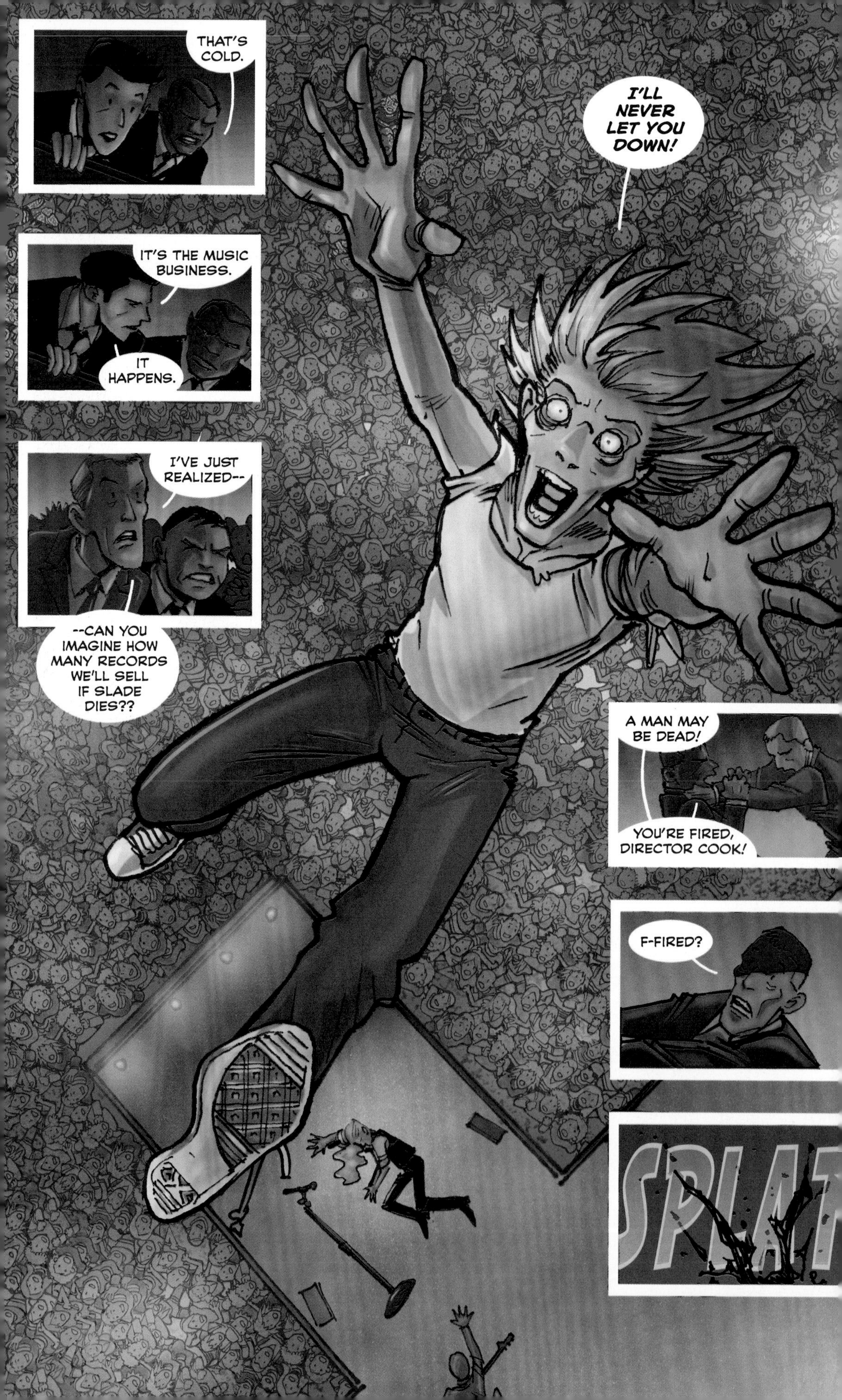
THAT'S COLD.
IT'S THE MUSIC BUSINESS.
IT HAPPENS.
I'VE JUST REALIZED--
--CAN YOU IMAGINE HOW MANY RECORDS WE'LL SELL IF SLADE DIES??
I'LL NEVER LET YOU DOWN!
A MAN MAY BE DEAD!
YOU'RE FIRED, DIRECTOR COOK!
F-FIRED?
SPLAT

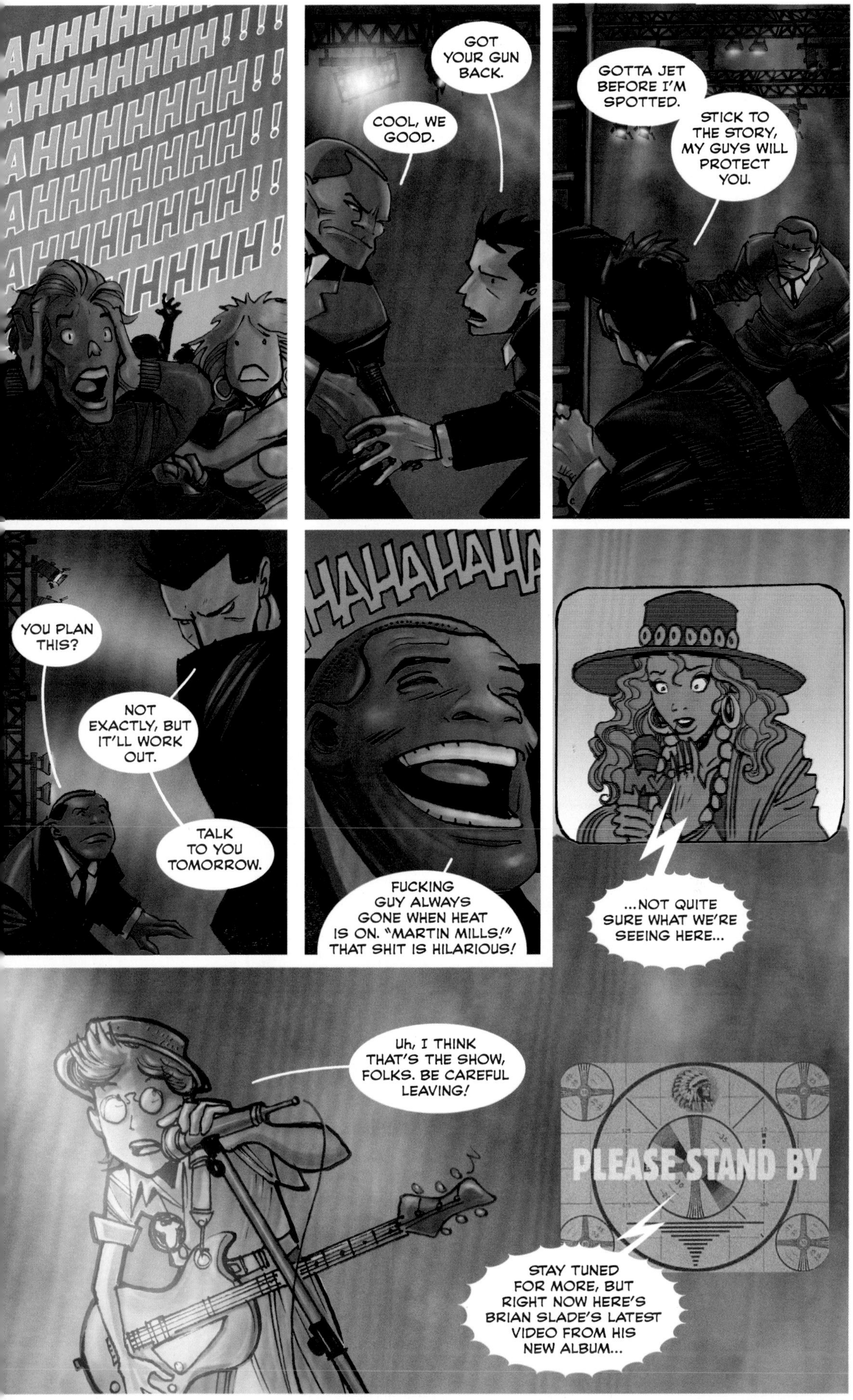
AHHHHHHHH!!!!
AHHHHHHHH!!
AHHHHHHHH!!
AHHHHHHHH!!
AHHHHHHHH!
GOT YOUR GUN BACK.
COOL, WE GOOD.
GOTTA JET BEFORE I'M SPOTTED.
STICK TO THE STORY, MY GUYS WILL PROTECT YOU.
YOU PLAN THIS?
NOT EXACTLY, BUT IT'LL WORK OUT.
TALK TO YOU TOMORROW.
HAHAHAHA
FUCKING GUY ALWAYS GONE WHEN HEAT IS ON. "MARTIN MILLS!" THAT SHIT IS HILARIOUS!
...NOT QUITE SURE WHAT WE'RE SEEING HERE...
Uh, I THINK THAT'S THE SHOW, FOLKS. BE CAREFUL LEAVING!
PLEASE STAND BY
STAY TUNED FOR MORE, BUT RIGHT NOW HERE'S BRIAN SLADE'S LATEST VIDEO FROM HIS NEW ALBUM...

30 CENTS · © 1983 News Group Publications Inc. · Vol. 182, No. 129
30 cents beyond 50 mile zone, except L.I.
AMERICA'S FASTEST-GROWING NEWSPAPER
ABC AVERAG[E] SALES EXCEE[D]

BRIAN SLADE SHO[T] AT GARDEN

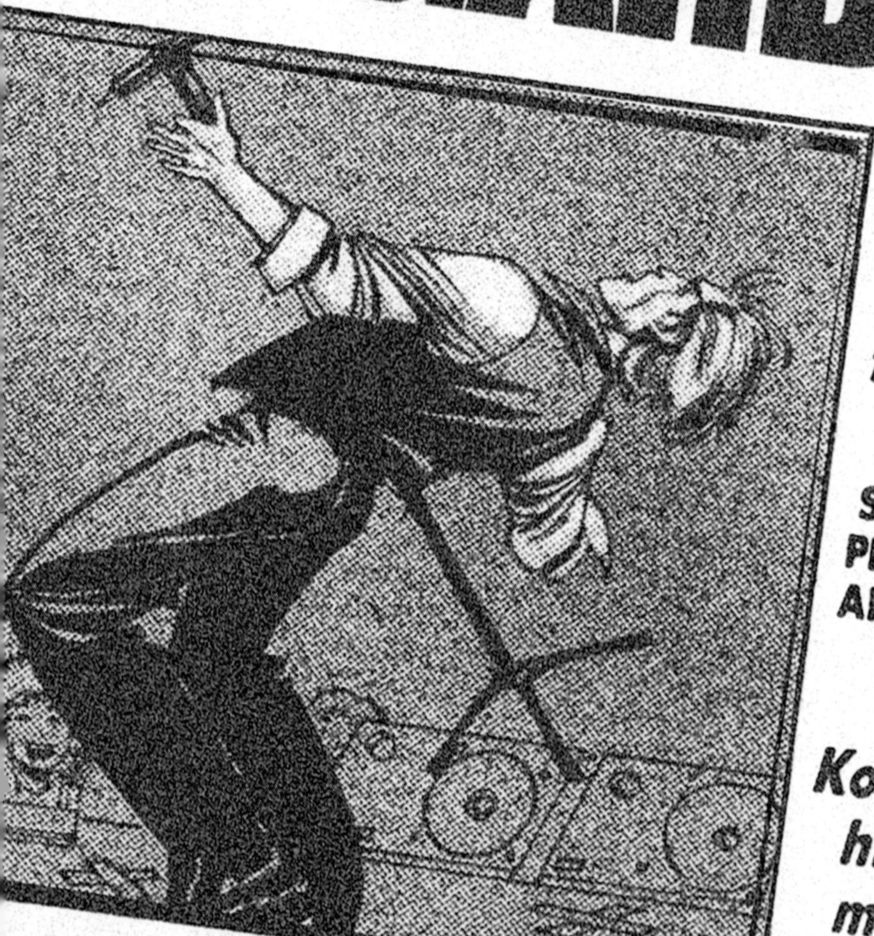

kickin' [scr]eamin'

An angry Juan Emilio Robles tries to kick a photographer yesterday as detectives took him in to be booked for the murder last year of Chase Manhattan exec Kathleen Williams. Robles, a hulking 28-year-old ex-con, is accused of stabbing the 30-year-old victim during a bungled robbery attempt on a stairway in the Waldorf-Astoria Hotel in midtown. Story on Page 14.

Gunman for[ces] woman to decapitate tavern owne[r]

PAGE TWO

SENATE OKAYS PREZ'S PICK FOR ARMS CONTROL

PAGE FIVE

Koch plans to hire 1,000 more cops

PAGE THREE

TAXING DAY FOR 1 MILLION IN N.Y.

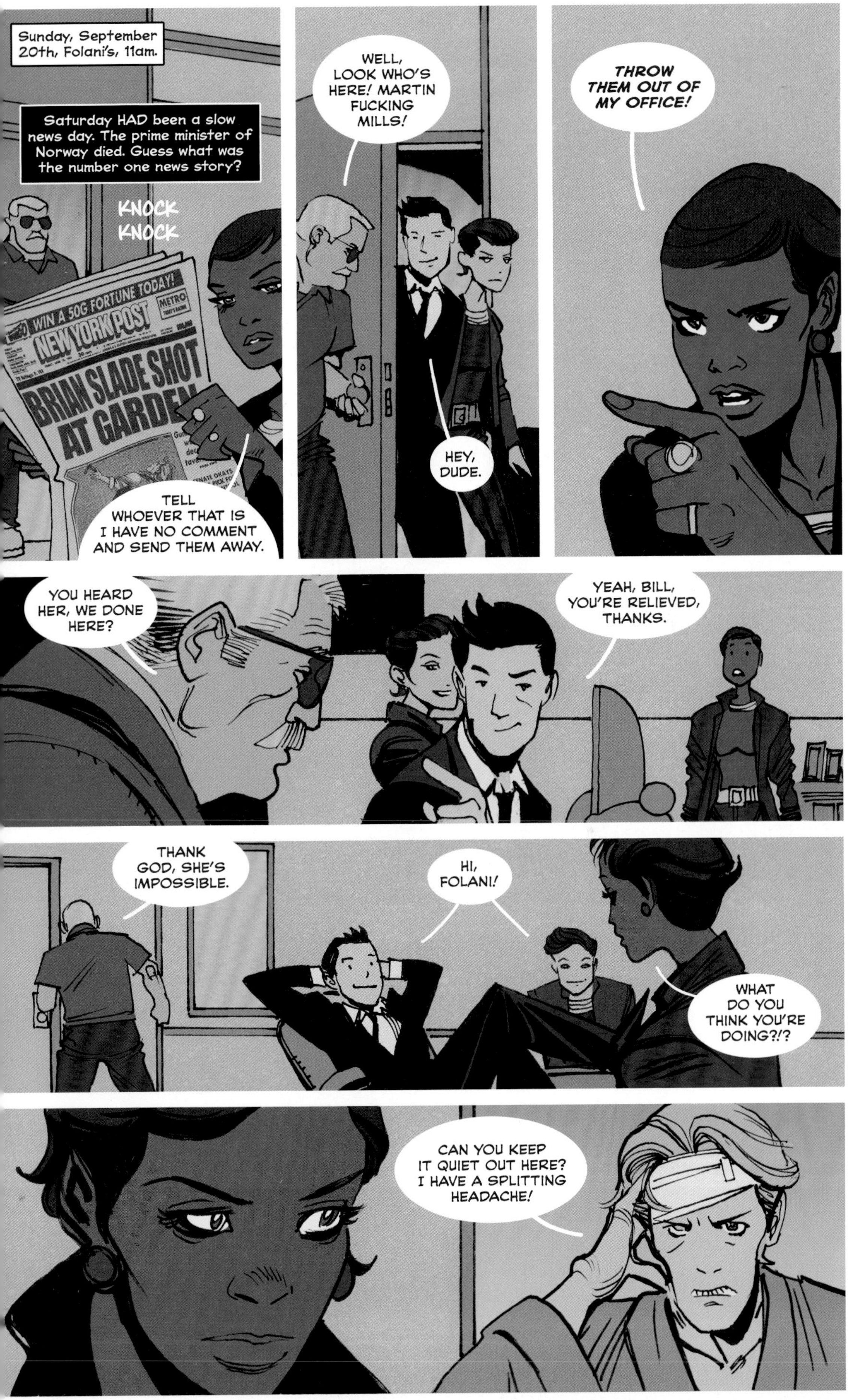
Sunday, September 20th, Folani's, 11am.
Saturday HAD been a slow news day. The prime minister of Norway died. Guess what was the number one news story?
KNOCK KNOCK
WIN A 50G FORTUNE TODAY!
NEW YORK POST
METRO
BRIAN SLADE SHOT AT GARDEN
TELL WHOEVER THAT IS I HAVE NO COMMENT AND SEND THEM AWAY.
WELL, LOOK WHO'S HERE! MARTIN FUCKING MILLS!
HEY, DUDE.
THROW THEM OUT OF MY OFFICE!
YOU HEARD HER, WE DONE HERE?
YEAH, BILL, YOU'RE RELIEVED, THANKS.
THANK GOD, SHE'S IMPOSSIBLE.
HI, FOLANI!
WHAT DO YOU THINK YOU'RE DOING?!?
CAN YOU KEEP IT QUIET OUT HERE? I HAVE A SPLITTING HEADACHE!

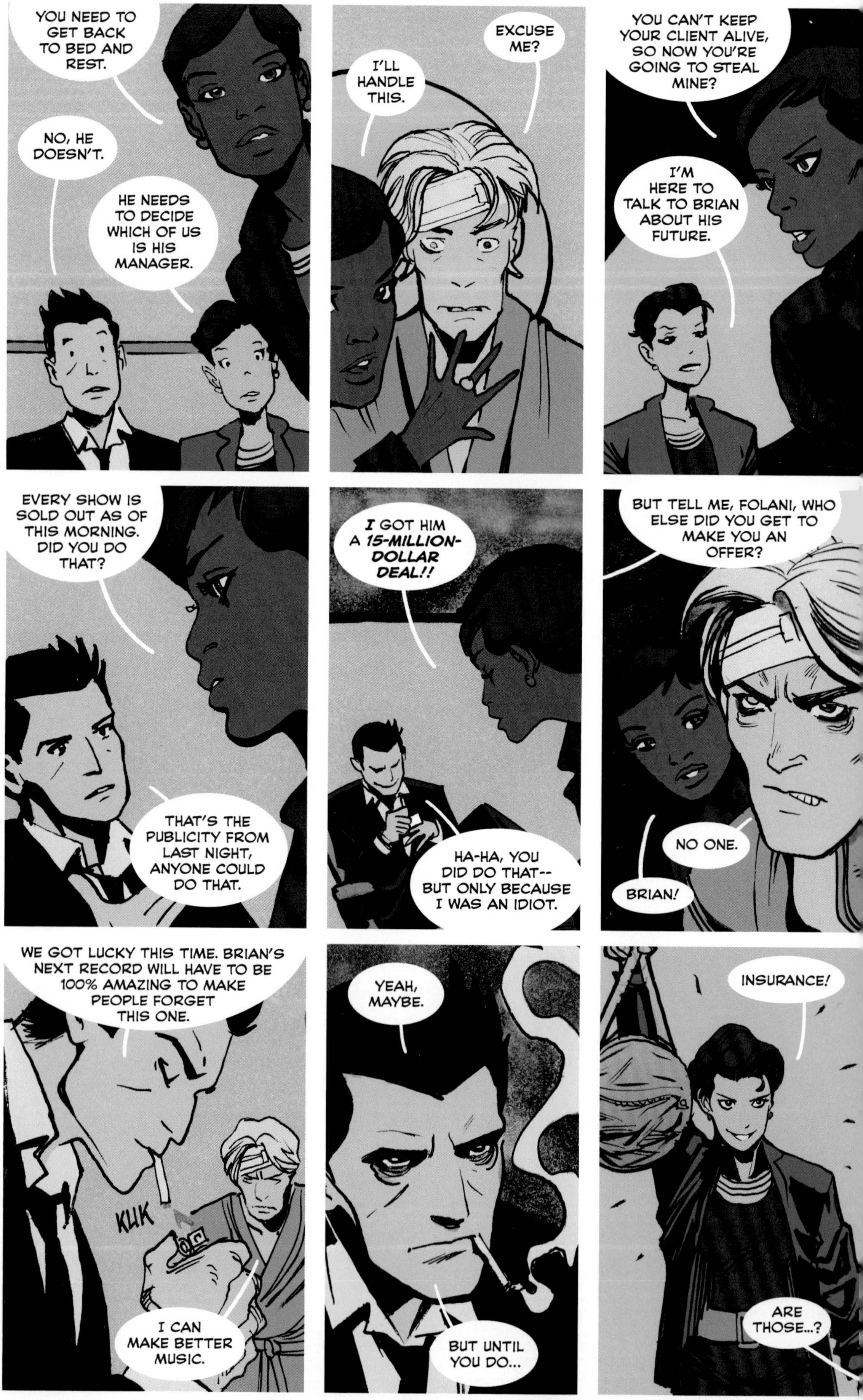
YOU NEED TO GET BACK TO BED AND REST.
NO, HE DOESN'T.
HE NEEDS TO DECIDE WHICH OF US IS HIS MANAGER.
EXCUSE ME?
I'LL HANDLE THIS.
YOU CAN'T KEEP YOUR CLIENT ALIVE, SO NOW YOU'RE GOING TO STEAL MINE?
I'M HERE TO TALK TO BRIAN ABOUT HIS FUTURE.
EVERY SHOW IS SOLD OUT AS OF THIS MORNING. DID YOU DO THAT?
THAT'S THE PUBLICITY FROM LAST NIGHT, ANYONE COULD DO THAT.
I GOT HIM A 15-MILLION-DOLLAR DEAL!!
HA-HA, YOU DID DO THAT-- BUT ONLY BECAUSE I WAS AN IDIOT.
BUT TELL ME, FOLANI, WHO ELSE DID YOU GET TO MAKE YOU AN OFFER?
NO ONE.
BRIAN!
WE GOT LUCKY THIS TIME. BRIAN'S NEXT RECORD WILL HAVE TO BE 100% AMAZING TO MAKE PEOPLE FORGET THIS ONE.
KUK
I CAN MAKE BETTER MUSIC.
YEAH, MAYBE.
BUT UNTIL YOU DO...
INSURANCE!
ARE THOSE...?

THEY ARE. ENOUGH MATERIAL FOR BRIAN TO RECORD UNTIL THE DAY HE DIES.

BILLY'S DEMOS!

UH-HUH. HUNDREDS OF AMAZING SONGS.

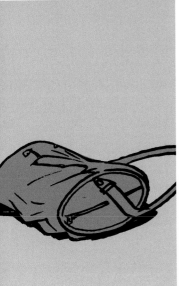

BRIAN?

YOU'RE FIRED. GET OUT.

WHAT?? I'LL SUE!

Pfff--I'VE BEEN SUED BEFORE.

I'LL SEE YOU IN COURT, ASSHOLE!

WHAT'S UP WITH YOUR EYE?

I BELIEVE IT'S CALLED ANACONDAS-TORIA-SOMETHING. FROM THE BULLET GRAZE.

THAT'S FREAKY, MAN. WE CAN USE THAT.

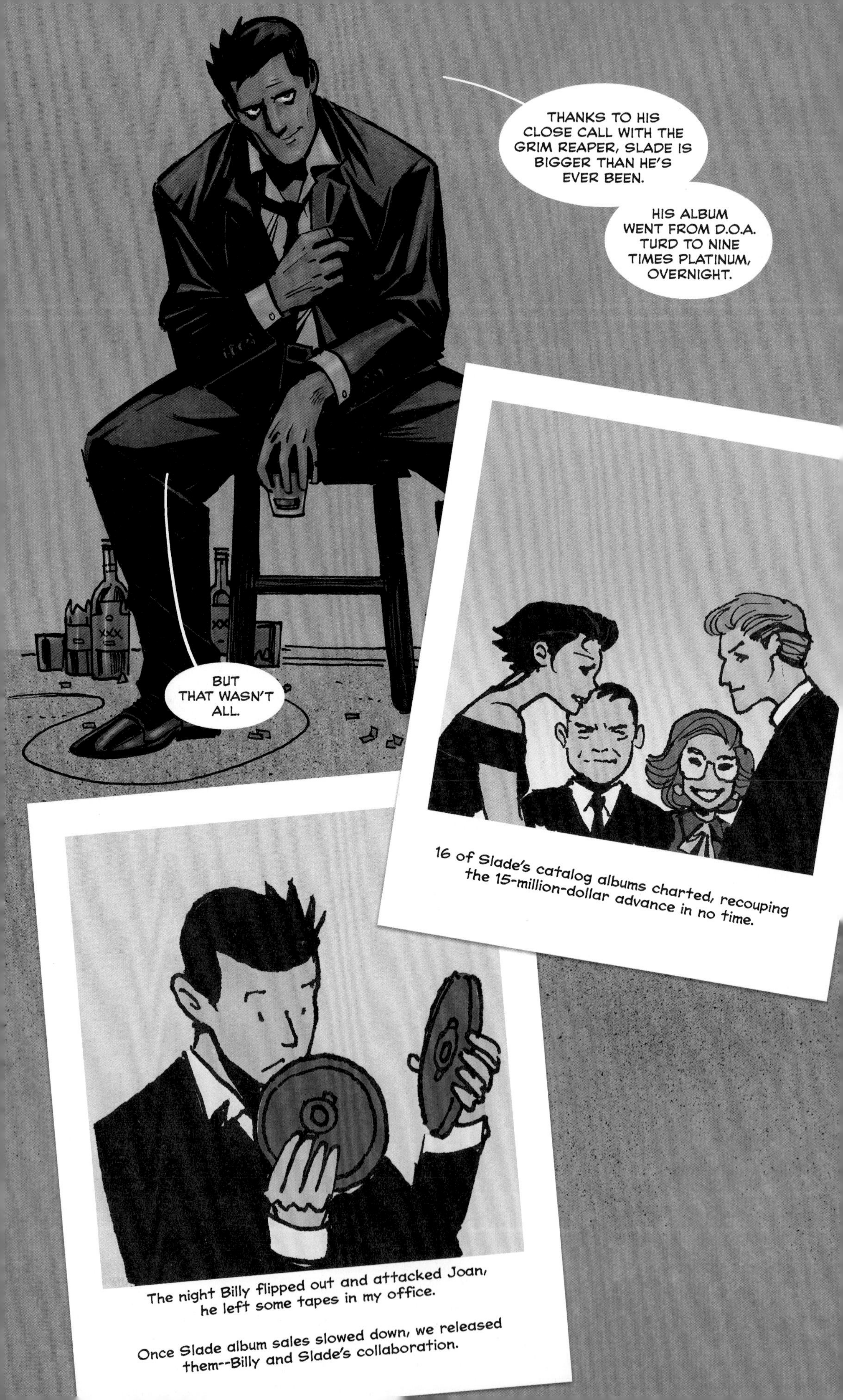
THANKS TO HIS CLOSE CALL WITH THE GRIM REAPER, SLADE IS BIGGER THAN HE'S EVER BEEN.
HIS ALBUM WENT FROM D.O.A. TURD TO NINE TIMES PLATINUM, OVERNIGHT.
BUT THAT WASN'T ALL.
16 of Slade's catalog albums charted, recouping the 15-million-dollar advance in no time.
The night Billy flipped out and attacked Joan, he left some tapes in my office.
Once Slade album sales slowed down, we released them--Billy and Slade's collaboration.

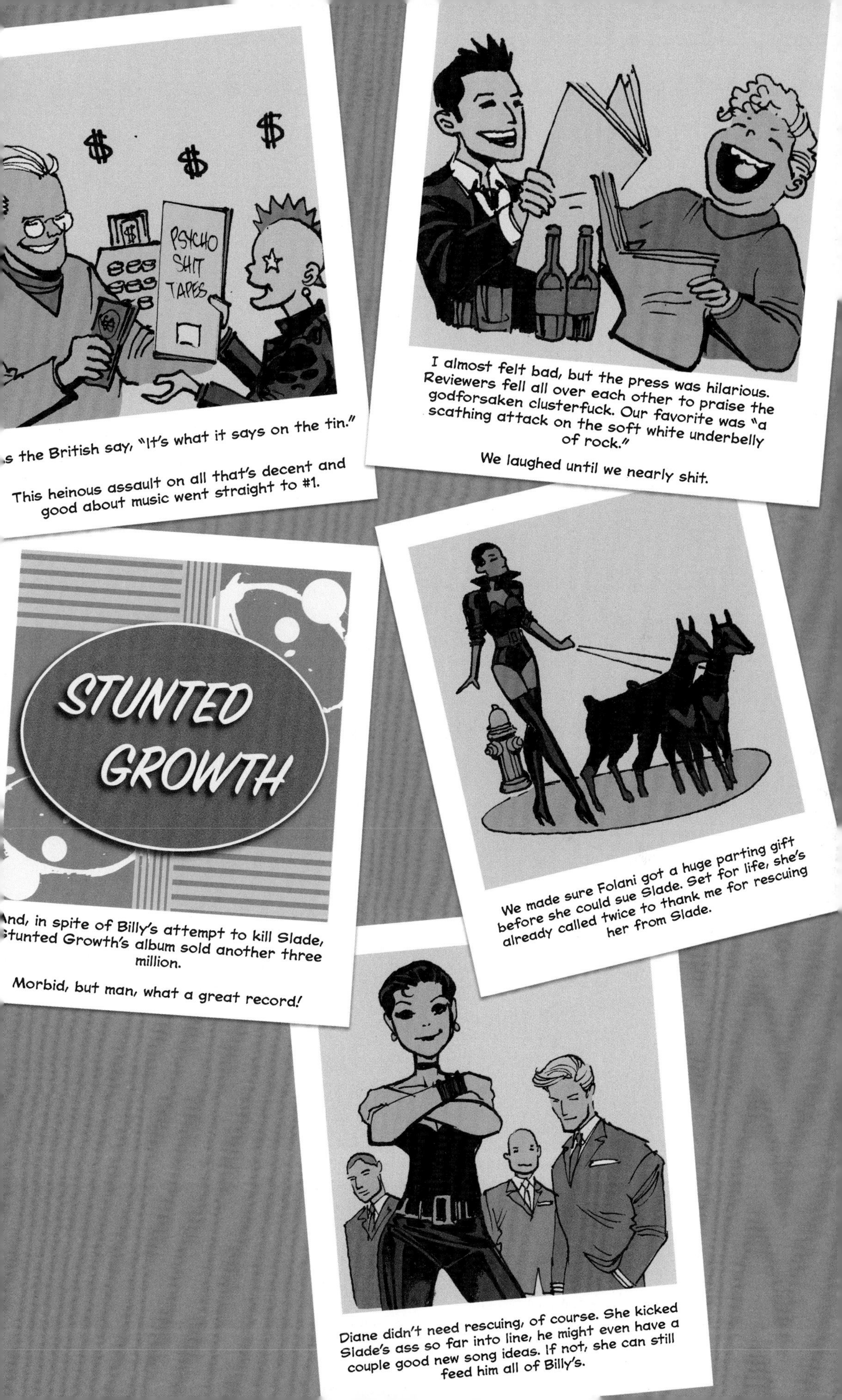

PSYCHO SHIT TAPES
s the British say, "It's what it says on the tin."
This heinous assault on all that's decent and good about music went straight to #1.
I almost felt bad, but the press was hilarious. Reviewers fell all over each other to praise the godforsaken clusterfuck. Our favorite was "a scathing attack on the soft white underbelly of rock."
We laughed until we nearly shit.
STUNTED GROWTH
nd, in spite of Billy's attempt to kill Slade, tunted Growth's album sold another three million.
Morbid, but man, what a great record!
We made sure Folani got a huge parting gift before she could sue Slade. Set for life, she's already called twice to thank me for rescuing her from Slade.
Diane didn't need rescuing, of course. She kicked Slade's ass so far into line, he might even have a couple good new song ideas. If not, she can still feed him all of Billy's.

The mayor of New York held a press conference to thank Lucius for saving the lives of countless concert-goers, and Slade publicly hired Lucius as his new personal bodyguard at the ceremony.

With Slade's records selling like crazy, Morita-san's rep was restored. Cook was an asshole, but as he proved the hard way, executives come and go, sometimes painfully.

Morita-san offered me the director job. I didn't want it, but I couldn't let him hire any old shitheel to be my new boss.

So I got to pick my very own shitheel.

At first, Melch had no interest, but once he realized he'd have another office to escape his yuppie scum banking co-workers, he was in. His first act as director? Free beer Fridays.

Of course, he's not going to devote any time to a label he doesn't know shit about running.

He's just a beard for the best-qualified person--

Yeah, it's sexist bullshit, but promoting someone (especially a woman) from assistant to director wasn't going to fly with Japan, at least not yet.

Joan's getting Melch's pay, and she'll transition into his job once they realize what an enormous liability he is.

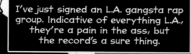

I've just signed an L.A. gangsta rap group. Indicative of everything L.A., they're a pain in the ass, but the record's a sure thing.

Nick's tipped me off to a hot new rock act from fucking Florida--big local following, very theatrical, semi-industrial. Great stuff.

Institutions go on. Royalties dry up. Fads end. But songs matter and artistic vindication is elusive--unless you've got me on your side.

I mean, yeah, he's dead, but Billy got his in the end.

MARTIN MILLS WILL RETURN IN:

GANGSTAS, GOTH AND GUNS

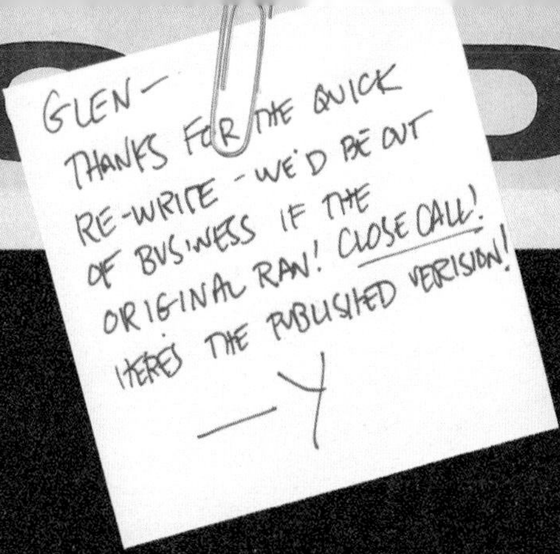
GLEN—
THANKS FOR THE QUICK
RE-WRITE - WE'D BE OUT
OF BUSINESS IF THE
ORIGINAL RAN! CLOSE CALL!
HERE'S THE PUBLISHED VERISION!
—Y

Meltdown Averted: Welcome to Brian Slade's Creative Renaissance The Emperor's Triumphant Return

By Glen Basters

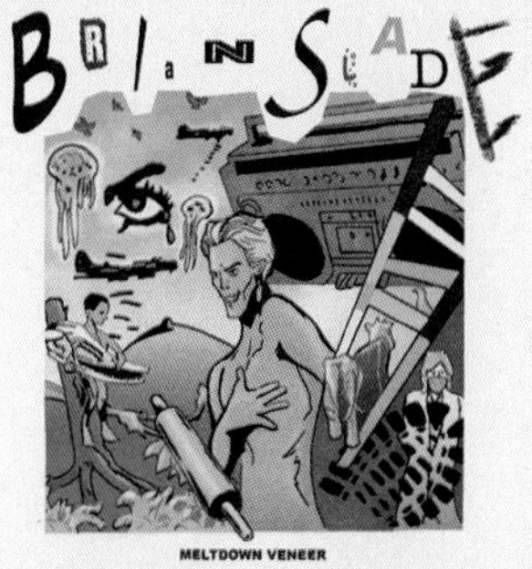
BRIAN SLADE
MELTDOWN VENEER

MELTDOWN VENEER
Brian Slade

The whispered consensus amongst rock critics is that Brian Slade, the most iconic and influential living artist in rock was backsliding in recent years. We were wrong.

In *Meltdown Veneer* we have the most remarkable return to form of the rock era, which (I'm humbled to say) vindicates years of work we collectively misinterpreted.

Slade's ability to dictate the future to his legions of slavish fans has always been one of the most remarkable aspects of his storied career. Throughout the previous decade, Brian Slade forged the very path of popular culture, metamorphosizing again and again, reinventing his persona with the same casual ease his rivals changed their denims.

The release of *Meltdown Veneer,* his new, positively earth-shattering album, Slade's legacy as a rock 'n roll visionary is more assured than ever.

Slade's 70s work brought intellectual, literary concepts to the form; planting hundreds of fascinating clues to unravel, a joy; as entertaining as it was rewarding. *Meltdown Veneer* is a puzzle box that'll have fans debating the mysteries of its creator for years to come.

Slade albums have historically featured a carefully crafted surrogate for the artist, deftly fleshed out with each successive song until the personas themselves become legends. Rock fans and critics alike have grown to embrace them; the alien rock star, the wild boy of our inevitable totalitarian future, the heartless, fascinating Germanic Count run amuck. Here, he's created a thematic coherence to hold the proceedings together – by pulling seemingly disparate creations into one credible universe, where they co-habituate with new characters and ideas, every bit as fascinating as those that came before.

Since the early 80s, when Slade seemingly ditched his personas, we were left guessing where he'd go next. When he released *Some Kinda Fun,* it was an effortless synch-up with the sound of today, rather than his usual predictive conjuring of tomorrow's new sound.

To his credit, it did the job. The worldwide success of the album vaulted him from an art-rock cult figure with to a multi-platinum worldwide superstar, a pyrrhic vindication for outsider fans who long endured the taunts of thick-headed denim and leather rock artists and their succubi.

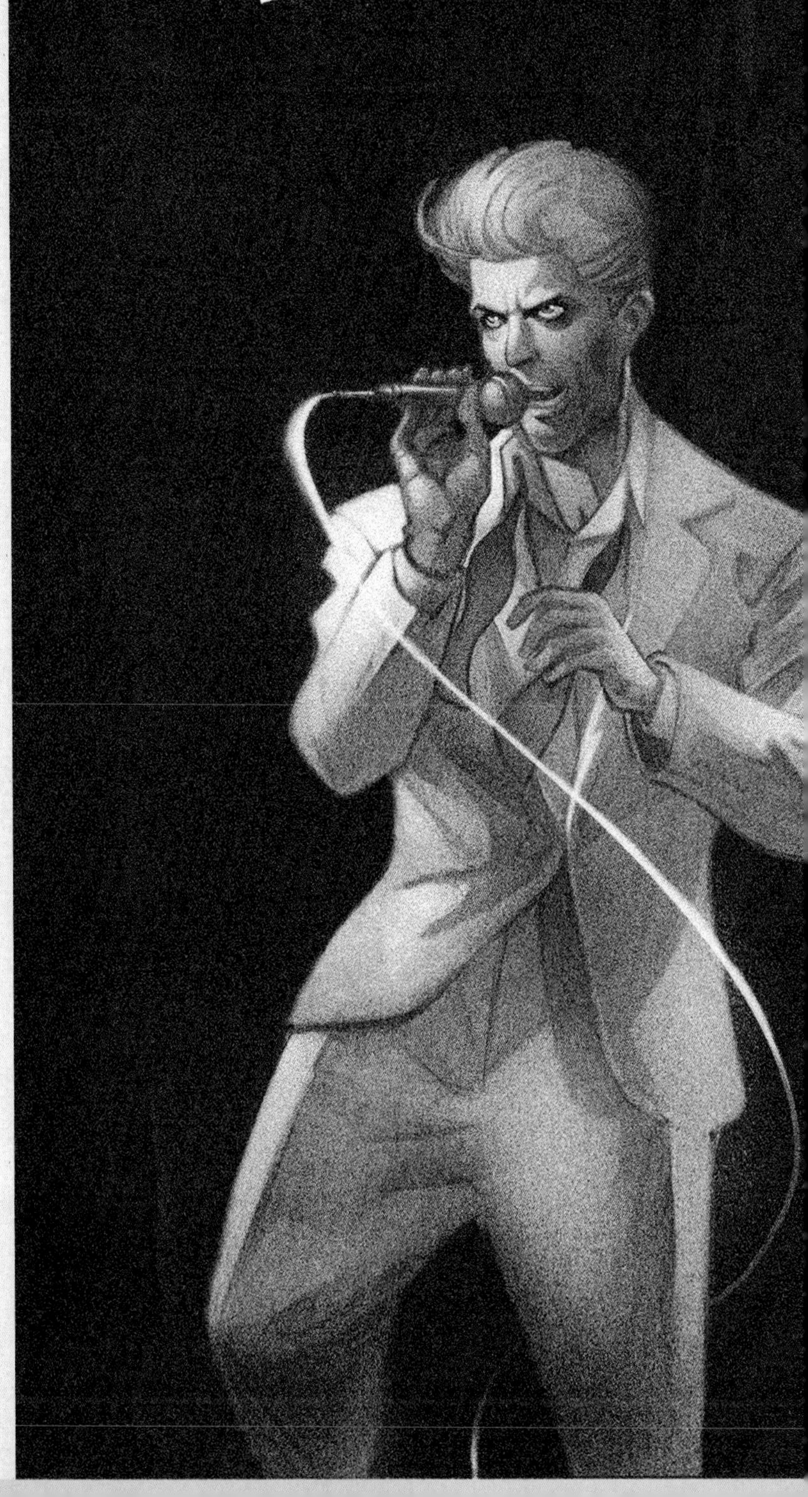

The novelty of Brian Slade dropping the persona and (presumably) being himself for a change, was, in itself, exciting. After all, it was a role he'd seemingly never played before – but no one was sure where he would go from there.

Slade fans can stop debating whether *Some Kinda Fun* was a stylistic triumph, a pop sellout, or just another pit-stop on the way to future glories. It's safe to say nobody imagined it'd serve as the gateway to Slade's overarching master plan. Its follow-up, *After Dark*, was even more subversive; a brilliant sleight of hand utilizing cover versions to convey deeper themes.

Since the early 80s fans noted his reduced productivity with distress. During the 70s he'd have released five or six albums in the same period. Earlier this year, Slade turned 40, worryingly placing him firmly in rock's elder statesman territory, and sparking debate as to if he was creatively dry.

I am beyond pleased to inform you that *Meltdown Veneer* exposes a secret master plan executed with painstaking precision. The destination is worth the journey; it is the greatest record of an unequalled career, thanks to a preponderance of instantly unforgettable originals.

It's easy to understand how this complex creation took longer to orchestrate with such fulfilling resonance. It is something entirely new, mining contemporary and classic themes with a deft and assured hand. In comparison to older work, this album shines as a fully realized, coherent summary of all that's gone before while showing a glorious path forward to the next evolution.

Slade's two previous albums added millions of new, young, MTV-generation fanatics to his already adoring fanbase, but it was all part of a master plan to invite them, on the journey to this, his greatest, most ambitious and--most successful--work. Slade's newly expanded fanbase means he's got the power to unite millions of devotees in lock step with his worthy ideas. It'll be a joy to see the world impact of this album.

The sparse promotional materials surrounding the release include a single quote from Slade: "This is the sum total of everything that has come before."

That may qualify as understatement of the year. For two albums in a row, Slade lulled us into a state of happy pop complacency, in the service of blowing our minds with his third--a record that pulls together all the threads of his life and works with a depth previously considered unachievable in contemporary music.

Meltdown Veneer decisively vindicates Slade's decision to quit switching guises. Perhaps sensing the need to pick up the pace to match the quick-cut world of the go-go 80s, here he responds to ever-shorter attention spans by switching character from song to song. The effect is as exciting and innovative as the fresh new ideas these fully realized characters represent.

This conceit allows him to namecheck some of his most notorious creations, but it never feels like a stunt. Slade's noble motive is to unify and enhance the universe his followers have invested more than a decade in. Unprecedented in rock, he's created something familiar but improved/evolved them into something new and challenging.

Slade savages the state of current rock acts with razor-sharp wit. Sporting what is clearly a parody of Bono's haircut (except in this case it's all business to the front, revolution in the brain) he writes scathing lyrics that skewers mainstream drivel like *Crocodile Dundee*--by name--with rapier-like wit.

He deflates the self-centered mentality of horny middle-aged men, represents all good war-fearing world citizens in a vicious, witty takedown of Reagan's Presidency, is a powerful advocate for the homeless (showing he's fully engaged with societal ills), and, most incredibly, morphs

into the spawn of some magnificent crystalline arachnid with the same ease he tackles real world concerns.

The latter is perhaps his most intriguingly brilliant premise yet, but you MUST hear it for yourself. These songs are all connected, but the web he spins here--and boy, has he has spun one! It is impossible to describe in a review, but surely scholars will write tomes dissecting it in the near future.

I know you're asking yourself: imbued as it is with all this revolutionary artistic and philosophical social value, *Meltdown Veneer* surely can't hold up as pop collection, right? Wrong. *Meltdown Veneer* is devoid of anything approaching a dud, but not at the expense of experimentation. Its booming percussion, tasteful synth arrangements and expressive guitars are subtle, subversive and wholly successful stabs at bloated stadium rock--each element carefully executed and produced with a complementary finesse to the point where it suffocates under the weight of its (too) many components.

Despite the generous running time, every track leaves the listener hungry for more. The CD era has allowed artists the freedom to create longer albums. While others have abused the format's 72 minutes running time by padding out albums with filler, the length of songs here only serves to highlight the cornucopia of good ideas in attendance.

It's hard to pick a favorite song, but album opener "Get-In Get-Out," Slade's incisive look at the homeless, is a nuanced and wholly sincere viewpoint that may actually solve the issue if only governments would listen. Never pandering, Slade welds an incredible hook to a decidedly pointed lyric, bringing it all home with a vocal performance that could stir the heartstrings of the dead. Of course a man used to taking on guises could imagine himself in the place of those less fortunate convincingly. But, if rumors are true, Slade spent a few nights sleeping on the New York streets, all in service of accurately and respectfully representing the plight of those living rough. It feels like it. In the course of a single song, Slade's executed one of the year's perfect singles and evoked grand empathy for the homeless.

"How We War" is a driving, mystical exploration of otherworldliness, heralded by a wonderful synth lick, sugar-coated by the most revolutionary drum sound ever committed to disc.

"Beauty Rod Forum" is a study on lust and sex (he's still mad for it, naturally) with sparse guitar solos playing out the seduction in stylish urgency for the song's nearly 8-minute running time. It is stunningly effective erotica; Prince and Madonna would blush.

The album's first single, "Bang Dizzy Drum," sees Slade confronting middle age, rightfully castigating MTV for staying blandly neutral in a world where caring for the rights of all people requires choosing sides. Showing solidarity with contemporary R&B acts who are routinely underserved by the network, the video is impeccably choreographed, incorporating native dance. Slade uses his platform of fame to broadcast a message of racial harmony around the world. This track perfects the balance of video with song, a superb encapsulation of all we demand from our music in the eighties, sticking the landing effortlessly.

The title track, with its zippy melody and insightful analysis of nuclear anxiety, is positively revolutionary in both concept and execution. Lyrics like "just outside the heart wall / we hold our breath / pray the core won't collapse" hit the target perfectly when embellished by screeching guitars.

"Zombos" is one of the greatest compositions Slade's ever committed to tape. I'll leave it there.

It's followed up by "Insect Bone Mother," the spoken-word track that ties Slade's whole career trajectory and purpose together. An utterly stunning horror / science fiction narrative, it lives in a world well outside any previous Slade composition, inasmuch as it is well beyond the grounded reality we inhabit. A flight of Slade's genius is a welcome relief, a startling, jaw-dropping sea-change in a world populated by blue-collar Bon Jovi and Huey Lewis clones.

As noted earlier, it is impossible to deconstruct in a single review. Any attempt to do so would fail, and spectacularly so. It gets better.

"Sing A Song (Fakin' My Love)," starts out as a silky mid-tempo Earth Wind and Fire-style ballad. The string-laden, between-the-sheets love jam is deceptively seductive, but takes a stunning turn when Ah-nold (!!!), making a cameo, delivers a stark, chilling spoken word piece about an apocalyptic wasteland in the wake of geopolitical strife. The Austrian's star power adds a winking layer of crass commercialism while his performance reminds listeners that the theater of the mind is far more impactful than watching a glossy special effects film on their VCR.

"Manhattan's Gone Mad" is almost unbelievably cluttered, perfect for conveying the insanity the fight to keep your head above water in the vicious seas of of the Big Apple. It's a love song to the New Yorkers who persevere.

We're well past the 50-minute mark, and, while most artists save the lesser material for last, Slade's done the opposite. Suffice to say it would be treasonous for me to ruin the delight of discovering what awaits listeners on "'87 But Why?" and "Cut Me."

Closer "Happy Man" pulls all the threads together in an optimistic album topper that can't help but leave you smiling, filled with hope.

Even the artwork is a new high, featuring a naked Slade luxuriating in repose in a carefully curated artificial setting featuring key images from his career, each revealing special clues about the music within.

In addition to providing hours of entertainment for dedicated fans, the cover suggests the mindset of Slade circa 1987 is one of boundless creativity, powered by a sense of his own history (I'm filled with anticipation to learn how the rolling pin fits in, but no doubt it's pure magic). No matter what critics say, it'll be big: Slade is going on tour, his tours are events, and events sell records.

He's attained a well-earned degree of influence and status through a career filled with undeniably earth-shattering records. He helped bring glitter rock, Detroit soul and Teutonic-techno-prog to a wider audience. Slade's greatest achievement is getting the world to warmly embrace deep philosophical concepts through iconic imagery and characters, musically triumphing by making sure his albums never have a single duff track.

If *Meltdown Veneer* is the sum of all Slade is--the shimmering antidote to the meat and potatoes Bryan Adams and his ilk--then now is the perfect time to look back on his previous work with fresh eyes. In light of this latest masterpiece, no doubt spelunking through his back pages will be filled with new revelations. For those who've eagerly anticipated the redemption of one of rock's greatest artists, you have much to look forward to as Slade's catalog will be re-released during his forthcoming year-long world tour.

Brian, we embraced the pomp, swagger and swing of your days gone by, but now we know something even sexier lurked beneath the surface. The Oscar Wilde of rock is back. Meltdown, my ass. This is the greatest payoff in rock and roll.

Long may you rock, Brian Slade.

DON'T YOU WONDER SOMETIMES?

The Intersection and Potential of Infinite David Bowies, Brian Slades,
Comics and GUNNING FOR HITS

This essay was originally going to be about either a) David Bowie's methods of connecting, or b) his influence on and appearances in comics, or c) how that got us to GUNNING FOR HITS.

GUNNING FOR HITS has been designed as a layered, immersive piece that functions as a commentary on many aspects of human existence; especially how we interact with our world and each other.

I'm not crazy about explaining every aspect of the work, preferring to let the reader take their own unique experience from it. That said, a few questions have been raised that should be clarified.

This piece addresses all those topics, as they intersect anyway. Strap yourself in!

"I'm not an original thinker. What I'm best at doing is synthesizing those things in society or culture, refracting those things, and producing some kind of a glob of how it is that we live at this particular time." —David Bowie

Two questions I'm frequently asked about GUNNING FOR HITS are "Is Brian Slade David Bowie?" or "Is Brian Slade that Brian Slade?" Both are about the character in the comic, but the latter also refers to the Bowie-esque figure of *Velvet Goldmine*, Todd Haynes' 1998 cult film about the 70s British glam scene.

The answers are complicated but hang in there; I promise I'll get to them.

If you're not familiar, *Velvet Goldmine* is a near-verbatim re-telling of Bowie's early 70s, complete with recreations of real events and people. It features a character named Brian Slade as Bowie's stand-in. To its credit, *Velvet Goldmine* amplifies the queer-positive / outsider subtext present in much glam rock, and mostly looks amazing doing it. Yet it is surprisingly dull, especially considering the subject.

That's the best I can say about the film. Here's the worst; its structure is clumsily copped from *Citizen Kane*. The soundtrack is largely 90s bands feigning 70s glam. Point being, it's someone else's story, on someone else's framework, with watered-down versions of someone else's music, with a few strands of tinsel tossed on.

The Slade character is depicted as aloof and cruel, displaying no intelligence whatsoever. In other words, he's portrayed as a dumb, selfish Bowie. Adding insult to injury, Haynes implies Bowie became a right-wing shill in the 80s. Regardless of what you think about Bowie's music, this is an unnecessarily nasty assault on his truly decent character.

Haynes dismisses criticism of the portrayal on *Velvet Goldmine's* commentary track, citing Bowie's own disparagement of his 80s output as a rationale / excuse. It's defensive and disingenuous. In the early stages of the commentary, Haynes tries to distance his Slade character from Bowie (for legal reasons, no doubt). By the time the commentary wraps, Haynes has dropped that pretense. It's clear that in Haynes' mind at least, Slade is Bowie and Bowie is Slade.

This is where *Velvet Goldmine* really fails; it doesn't do anything imaginative with Haynes' Slade / Bowie. It's not only a wasted opportunity but an insult to Bowie's imaginative mash-up aesthetic.

Notoriously, Bowie refused to license his music to Haynes, supposedly infuriating the director. This rejection may have triggered angry retaliatory script revisions. Even so, it's a particularly petty bitchiness that causes a filmmaker to trash the person whose story he's telling verbatim, without the subject's permission.

Despite the film's shortcomings, the idea of Bowie fiction remains intriguing.

This is because Bowie lived and worked through a succession of characters that helped him understand his true self and the bigger world. As an artist, every persona was an opportunity, not only for Bowie's to accumulate new perspective but also for new fans to discover him. Every successive character was a new shade in an expanding palette of gateway Bowies he kept throwing at them until they found one that best suited their tastes. Successfully shifting his work across different mediums, Bowie had far greater reach than most musicians did when collecting new fans.

Beyond his own creations, the range of his roles is pretty spectacular: the Elephant Man, Baal, Colliers in *Merry Christmas*, Mr. Lawrence, Jareth in *Labyrinth* (the one film that included his likeness rights for merchandising, hence the only Bowie action figures), Andy Warhol in *Basquiat*, the vampire John Blaylock in *The Hunger*, Pontius Pilate in Scorcese's *Last Temptation of Christ*, and Phillip Jeffries in *Twin Peaks*.

There are a plethora of cameos, some showing he was as adept at comedy as drama; *Extras*, *Zoolander*, and *Spongebob*. There are more, although none as shocking as his appearance on *Bing Crosby's Christmas Special* (Bing was a fan and personally requested him!).

As with anyone so prolific, Bowie appeared in some trash, too. Take *The Linguini Incident*, re-titled *Shag-O-Rama* on its brief turn-of-the-century DVD release, hoping to capitalize on Austin Powers-fever. The rebranding made a bad film seem even worse. And there were straight-up baffling roles, like the unfortunately named Sir Roland Moorecock in *Dream On*, a softcore HBO sex comedy.

His most important role, the alien Thomas Jerome Newton of *The Man Who Fell To Earth*, resonated most with Bowie. Towards the end of his life, he revisited Newton via the *Lazarus* stage musical, a contemporary, less linear take on the *MWFTE* story. It's a rare case of Bowie looking back. Of all his personas, only Major Tom had as many outings.

No matter which Bowies you like or hate, every one of them is someone's favorite Bowie.

Considering his penchant for alter egos, Bowie seems like a natural fit with comics, but his relationship with the medium was fractured, at best.

David's friend and fellow glam star, Marc Bolan of T-Rex, was a Marvel fanatic in the 60s. Bolan referenced Dr. Strange in lyrics and interviewed Stan Lee. He certainly would've shared his comics interest with David, but aside from one early Bowie song, "Uncle Arthur" — in which the titular character is said to "still read comics" and "follows Batman" — Bowie never seemed to gravitate to or reference comics. By his own admission, he was precious about his reading.

In the 70s, Stan Lee wrote that Bowie and his then-wife, Angie, had visited Marvel's offices to discuss an upcoming project. Eventually, it was revealed this wasn't a David Bowie comic, but a proposed Black Widow TV series, starring Angie. The show never happened, although there are some spectacularly 70s photos of Angie as Natasha with an unknown actor in period-unfortunate Daredevil gear. David finally appeared legitimately in a Marvel comic in the 80s, their adaption of *Labyrinth*.

Still, Bowie's influence is everywhere, including comics. Jim Starlin's Warlock is a "cosmic messiah." Much of the Metal Hurlant / Heavy Metal axis has roots that lead to Bowie. Frank Miller channeled Bowie into his *Dark Knight* Joker. Years later, Grant Morrison's Joker was similarly Bowie-infused. Alan Moore referenced him. In *Sandman*, Neil Gaiman specified his Lucifer should visually reference late-60s hippie Bowie.

I've been a Bowie fan since the mid-70s, almost as long as I've been a comic reader. In 1989, I was fortunate enough to work for Rykodisc, a then-tiny independent record label. We had just made a huge (for us) investment to re-release Bowie's 1969-1989 catalog, and it was my job to produce the re-release campaign, encompassing *Space Oddity* to *Scary Monsters*, arguably his most-well regarded work.

When I started working with him, he was pulling himself out of a self-proclaimed artistic slump. David rarely looked back on his body of work, always planning the next project. Because of our campaign, I had the job of walking him through his past. With many common interests, we got on well. He later told me he was dreading the exercise of listening to old recordings, but ultimately found it refreshing and energizing.

"If you feel safe in the area you're working in, you're not working in the right area. Always go a little further into the water than you feel you're capable of being in. Go a little bit out of your depth. And when you don't feel that your feet are quite touching the bottom, you're just about in the right place to do something exciting." —David Bowie

His last major tour had been a grind, supporting an album he'd realized he didn't like very much. With a mix of glee and regret, he described the joy he felt burning the Glass Spider tour staging in a field in New Zealand, relieved he'd never have to perform that particular set again.

Bowie was 100% committed to his newest project, the rock band Tin Machine, of which he was (impossibly) supposed to be accepted as "just another member." A lackluster reception resulted in a bitter split with his label. Undeterred, he made two more albums with the band. It ultimately fell apart, no doubt in part because the project's momentum was interrupted by a massive solo Bowie greatest hits tour.

David would've preferred to focus on Tin Machine, but used the solo tour to create another challenge for himself, announcing this would be last time he played his best-known songs live.

Abandoning crowd-pleasers like "Space Oddity" and "Fame" was an unprecedented risk, showing a deadly serious commitment to his artistic reinvention. A decade later, he reneged on this promise, but in 1989, the announcement generated unprecedented heights of rock FOMO.

Ryko had faith Bowie would turn his career around, but there was always the possibility he may not. If Bowie's star had faded, the company could've folded. That seed of concern inspired the idea that eventually became GUNNING FOR HITS.

Luckily, the Bowie campaign was a success, resulting in a rewarding, friendly relationship that coaxed many gems out his vault and helped introduce him to a new generation of fans. David forged ahead, and my career in the music business continued on. The idea for GFH continued to stew in my head for a few decades.

To answer the original question, yes, the GFH Brian Slade has elements of Bowie, and, by extension, his cinema counterpart, but he's definitely not either character. I used David's 1989 predicament as a jumping-off point, but in GFH, my Slade's path is a commentary on the cynical major label practice of reinventing acts they considered washed-up in the 80s.

Focused on new fresh artists, MTV had passed a lot of huge 70s acts by, and MTV drove sales. Naturally, the labels turned their attention to whatever was selling, leaving many artists who'd sold millions just a few years earlier without support. Faced with declining sales, labels threatened to drop them unless they'd work with assigned songwriters and producers. After a visual makeover, including the requisite big budget video, they'd get a huge push, MTV play and — voila!, they were platinum again!

The strategy was repeatedly employed because it was easier (and more cost-effective) to polish and sell an act with name recognition than break a new one. The artists enjoyed renewed success, but at a price.

This was a new kind of relationship between artist and label, treating musicians more like brands than bands. It's emblematic of the shift in music in the 80s, where corporate product strategy infiltrated not just the selling of music, but the music itself. It's a compromised form of reinvention – the very opposite of Bowie's.

"I'm fully confident that copyright, for instance, will no longer exist in 10 years, and authorship and intellectual property is in for such a bashing... It's terribly exciting. But on the other hand, it doesn't matter if you think it's exciting

or not; it's what's going to happen." —David Bowie, ahead of the curve, 2002

Full disclosure: much in the same way Bowie cobbled ideas together, I hijacked the name Brian Slade. After all, Haynes stole Bowie's story and Bowie shamelessly mashed-up other people's ideas with his. Considering all this, I have no moral qualms and it's all pleasingly meta. Brian Slade is simply a brilliant rock n' roll name.

Another question I get is "do you dislike Bowie?" This is probably because my Slade character is a calculating, manipulative and creatively burnt-out shell of his former self. It couldn't help that my protagonist is plotting to murder Slade, just for making a shit album.

The idea of killing the doppelgänger is a commentary on how we, as fans, have been trained to react to grief as consumers.

To this day, I vividly recall how upset my mother was when Elvis died. It was as if a close relative had passed, and millions of others felt the same.

I was older when Lennon was gunned down, working at a little record store. Seeing the resulting sales provided profound and shocking psychological insight into morbid human irrationality. It was bizarre to see customers buying multiple copies of albums that were obviously never going out of print as "investments." The irony was they were made by a guy who famously sang "imagine no possessions."

If you ask any label exec that's ever watched the effect of an artist's passing, they'll confirm death is the ultimate publicity stunt, and no promotion you could ever buy would generate anywhere near the income. It's grim and sounds cynical, but also true.

To answer how I felt about David, let me be clear, I loved him. He was fascinating, friendly, and always wonderful to talk to. He'd be sartorially resplendent in a crisp suit, while I came to meetings scruffy, in sweatpants (seriously, what was I thinking?). To his credit, he never looked down on me. When not talking business, we happily discussed music and art.

As a lifelong comics reader myself, I tried to engage him on the topic of comics more than once. It seemed like a world he should be interested in, especially as there were so many interesting things happening in that period. Sadly, it was a non-starter, and I assumed we'd never get an official Bowie comic.

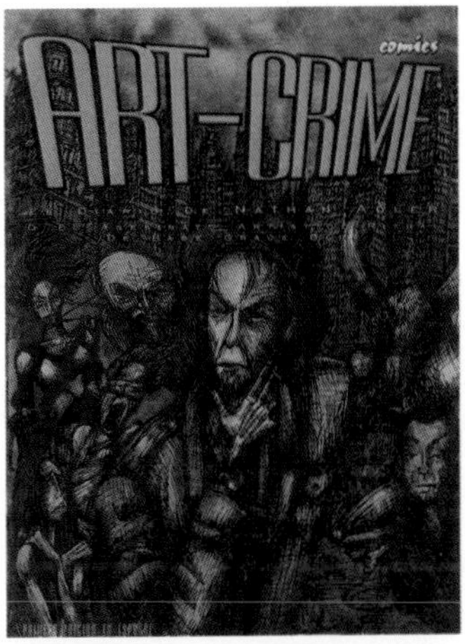
comics
ART-CRIME

In 1995, apparently without Bowie's knowledge or approval, the Mexican branch of his label commissioned a comic book to accompany his then-current album, *Outside*. David had written an excerpt of the diary of Nathan Adler, the protagonist of the album, which appeared in the packaging. This was adapted into the comic Art Crime. Published only in Mexico as a promotional freebie, it was produced in very limited numbers and is now worth hundreds of dollars.

Although amateurishly illustrated, it's a clever attempt to make the complicated concept album more understandable. David liked it. Remembering my interest in comics, he kindly sent me one. He knew the Adler story was a lot for the casual listener and sensed he wasn't going to continue telling it on future albums. He'd considered translating it into other media, including animation.

In 1994, Marvel launched a Marvel Music line of comics with an Alice Cooper series written by Neil Gaiman. They followed it up with a plethora of other titles, including a Rolling Stones *Voodoo Lounge* book by Dave McKean. Bowie and Jagger maintained a friendly competitive relationship, and David considered comics as a medium to tell his remaining Adler stories. He and I briefly discussed the project. My (possibly inaccurate) recollection was Marvel Music hoped Gaiman would be writing, but the imprint was axed before anything came of it.

Despite an official Bowie comic being a near-miss, his presence continued to be felt in great comics. Matt Fraction and Mike Allred created "inspired by" characters. In developing WICKED & DIVINE, Kieron Gillen considered basing each of the young gods on a different Bowie persona, before settling on Lucifer being the sole Bowie-based character (why are the Bowie characters always Lucifers?).

Which brings us to a recent announcement and the resulting proposition, one full of promise. Following the success of *Bohemian Rhapsody*, *The Dirt*, and presumably more of the same with the imminent *Rocketman*, of course there'll be an onslaught of rock biofilms.

One of the first to be announced was a Bowie project. The Internet lit up with opinion, as it does. Bowie's son, Duncan Jones — himself a successful filmmaker — shared that it's an unauthorized biopic focusing on David's pre-stardom years. The estate hasn't approved it, and they won't license any Bowie music to the film.

I'm personally opposed to the idea. The problem with any attempt to chronicle Bowie in film is he's too big a character to be contained in a straight biographical movie. Frankly, he would've found that approach incredibly boring. We've had three authorized Bowie docs in recent years. I'm guessing those reflect almost exactly what he wanted you to know.

In my view, far more interesting than the biopic announcement was an alternative proposition from Duncan, who's involved in a wide-range of nerd-culture, having directed *Moon*, *Source Code*, *Warcraft*, *Mute*, and the forthcoming *Rogue Trooper*, based on *2000 A.D.'s* iconic character.

When Jones took to Twitter to address the biopic, he proposed an alternative idea worthy of Bowie's legacy, tagging writer Neil Gaiman and Peter Ramsey (director of *Spider-man: Into The Spiderverse*) and suggesting they collaborate on an animated Bowie project, utilizing David's characters.

Jaws dropped, and Jones tantalizingly left them to it, signing off with, "you know where to find me." Both men have comic pedigrees, and, as noted before this wouldn't be Gaiman's first flirtation with Bowie, even onscreen, as Media from *American Gods* manifested as "Life On Mars" video-era Bowie in the television adaptation, played by Gillian Anderson.

Duncan's nailed it. Without David here to do the job, I think he'd enjoy creators taking inspiration from his work and fashioning new Bowies. While it remains to be seen if Gaiman and Ramsey's interest and schedules will align to make this real, no doubt the result would be spectacular and worthy of David's legacy.

I'm going to sit right down, hoping for this gift of Sound and Vision from Gaiman and Ramsey. In the meantime, I hope you've enjoyed my little Bowie variation.

For those of you who read the backmatter in monthly issues of GFH, I apologize for repeating a few small chunks of information here (and if you didn't read the individual issues, 1-4 all have extensive backmatter not in this volume).

I'm going to repeat myself once more, but it's worth repeating because it's an important part of creative life many of us forget.

Most people don't realize it, but David got his ass handed to him in the London music business for nearly a solid decade before breaking through. He was signed to multiple labels, played in loads of bands, had many managers, chased a variety of styles, and honed his skills. Even after "Space Oddity" was a hit, he was considered washed-up, over. But he picked himself and tried again. The only time he seriously considered giving up music, his career choice was mime. He was apparently a really good mime, but I'm glad he focused on music instead.

As noted previously, David's success didn't translate into daily perfection. He experienced challenges and tackled them with grace and fearlessness that's truly inspirational in scope.

Knowing he was on short time, Bowie made *Blackstar* — his greatest album since the 70s — an inspired, defiant collection of music that spits life in the face of death. In the same brief period, he co-created a theatrical musical, his lifelong dream. There is one takeaway — we only get so much time and must make the most of it.

"The worst thing would be to...look back and think of all the things that one could have tried and could have done, and think — why didn't I do that?" —David Bowie

David's passing inspired me to return to a dream I'd abandoned when my music career came along. I wanted to make comics all my life. Now I have. I'm going to make more and (hopefully!) my work will continue to develop and improve. For me, storytelling isn't about churning out product, but about reflecting on the world we live in. So my comics may not come fast and furious, but they'll come.

If you take nothing else away from this book, I hope you'll remember this: art rules and we should make and enjoy as much of it as we can before the clock runs out. Forge ahead, and make something you are passionate about even if it seems impossible. Ridicule and failure are nothing to be afraid of. They will make you stronger and better. Go for it.

ROCK!!

JR2

"The very meaninglessness of life forces man to create his own meaning."
—Stanley Kubrick

COVER GALLERY

When I wasn't driving my collaborators crazy, agonizing over minutiae and tweaking scripts up till the last possible moment, the process of making GFH was pretty painless – except for covers.

Month after month, our cover deadline snuck up on us like a ninja, appearing out of nowhere and forcing us to think and act fast. Luckily, Casey Silver would make us get them done on time (thanks Casey!) and Moritat could knock out great stuff on short notice (thanks Moritat!). We were generally mindful, but covers are due earlier than interiors, for solicitation purposes. Despite the importance of covers, their priority in our workflow inevitably seemed to slip down the food chain.

Early on we'd agreed not to go 'full 80s" for the interior art, no obvious neons or Nagel-style. On the other hand, I was more than willing to whore out our covers with garish 80s colors and referential images.

I had an A&R buddy who was totally dedicated to jazz. He would only sign pure jazz acts, no light-jazz, no pop-jazz. On the other hand, while he signed many credible rock acts, he would also sign schlock if he saw hit potential. Google "Baby I Love Your Way / Freebird Medley" by Will To Power – he signed that garbage. It was massive and he laughed his ass all the way to the bank, which helped him sign more pure jazz acts.

My position on the comic is the interiors were our jazz but our covers could be Will To Power medleys, where no color was too garish, as long as that approach would serve its purpose; getting people to pick the damn thing up and look at it.

ISSUE ONE

cover by Moritat

Suddenly, our first cover deadline was upon us. We had nothing planned. I mocked up a design in Photoshop and Moritat whipped up a clean, simple drawing, which I fell in love with. Easy, right? Sure, except he'd intended it as a placeholder for a more elaborate version. When his more refined take appeared, I was torn. I went so far as to glue printouts of both covers to comics and place them on the racks at my local comic shop. I still waffled.

This is called "demo-itis" in the music business. It's when you fall in love with an early recording of a song and fail to recognize an improved version when it's right in front of you. Both covers have their charms, but I was leaning towards the simpler version. Everyone told me I was wrong. Unsure, I shared both images with a group of artists. Their feedback helped show me the error of my ways. Thanks to Rev. Dave Johnston, Chris Samnee, Matthew Southworth, Coop, Jimmy Palmiotti, and especially Jesse Hamm, who found a clever trick reconciling aspects I liked from both versions. This is a solid example of social media gone right, and indisputable proof they are all swell people.

ISSUE TWO

cover by Moritat

This *Station To Station* riff came together quickly - perfectly executed by Moritat in an afternoon or less(!). I was thrilled and the type treatment sealed the deal. Perfect, right?

Nope. It was suggested that, since most music consumption is via streaming services where few pay attention to album artwork, who'd get the reference? I pointed out if we could sell this comic to 1% of 1% of the people who DID know the source image, we'd have the best-selling comic of the year. As far as I was concerned, that ended the debate.

ISSUE THREE

cover by Moritat

I envisioned this as a painted tribute to Bob Larkin's 1978 KISS *Marvel Super Special* cover. I asked Moritat who we could get to paint it, and he offered his services (I was unaware this style of painting was in his skill set, but color me impressed!). Unfortunately, we ran out of time again and utilized a line art version. It's an effective cover, but I assume most people familiar with the iconic Kiss cover didn't make the connection without the pulp-y painting style to drive it home.

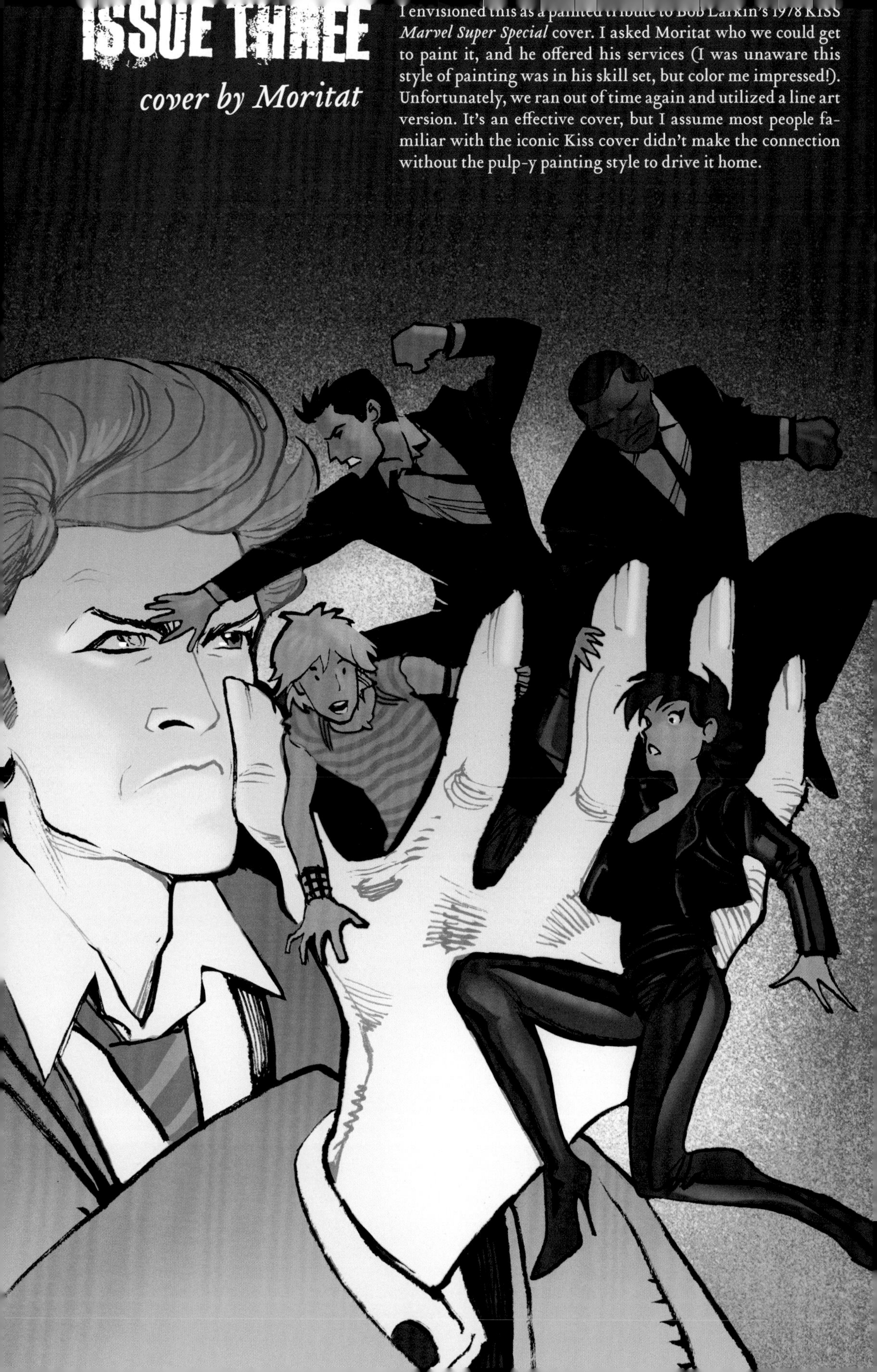

When the deadline loomed again, Moritat magically whipped out this great cover for issue four. He'd managed to achieve one of our goals for the series, creating a credible challenger to a classic Jaime Hernandez Love & Rockets piece we'd identified early on as our white whale of rock comic illustrations. Many fans expressed the same sentiment, which is high praise indeed. That said, from a "matching the contents" standpoint, it's probably more suited to issue five.

ISSUE FOUR

cover by Moritat

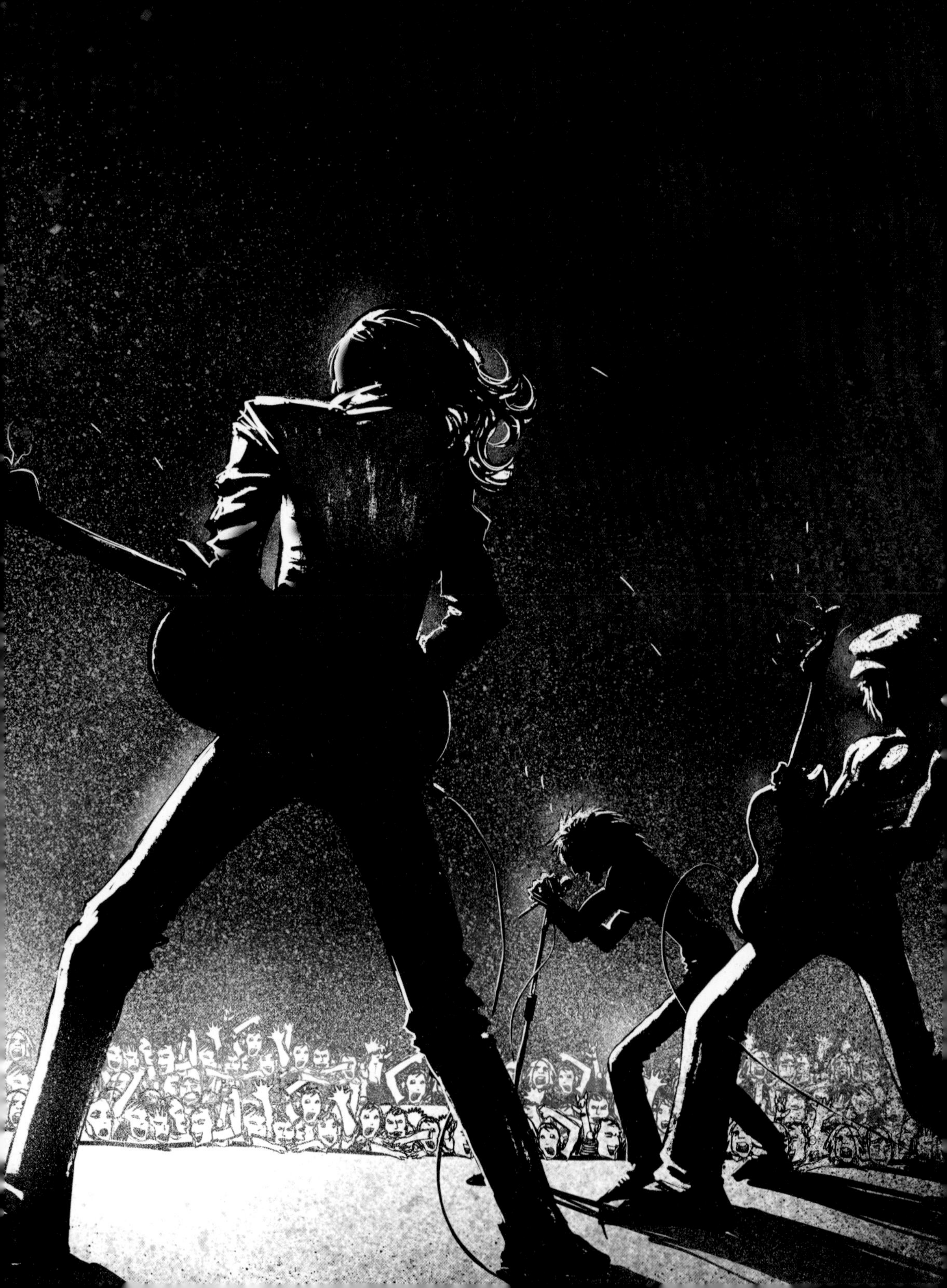

ISSUE FIVE

cover by Dan Veesenmeyer

My sketch for this cover was based on John Woo's *The Killer*, one of my favorite Hong Kong films. It's a relevant touchstone; Martin sees himself as a noble warrior, yet he's a murderer, much in the same way the titular "hero" of the film is. Moritat, Casey and I were all dealing with tons of pressure, and our communication wasn't the best. A cover appeared, but I felt it didn't have the intensity of the rough. With no time, that cover had to go off to solicitation.

I hastily reached out to my longtime pal Dan Veesenmeyer, a talented artist who'd worked on the *X-Men* and *Batman Animated* cartoons in the 90's, and had previously drawn an issue of the *WildCATS* animated spin-off comic in the early days of Image. Dan just finished a year-long assignment and was ready to take a much-needed break from drawing. I can't thank him enough for picking up his pen and delivering this cover in striking neon colors, with the gold and platinum records really popping!

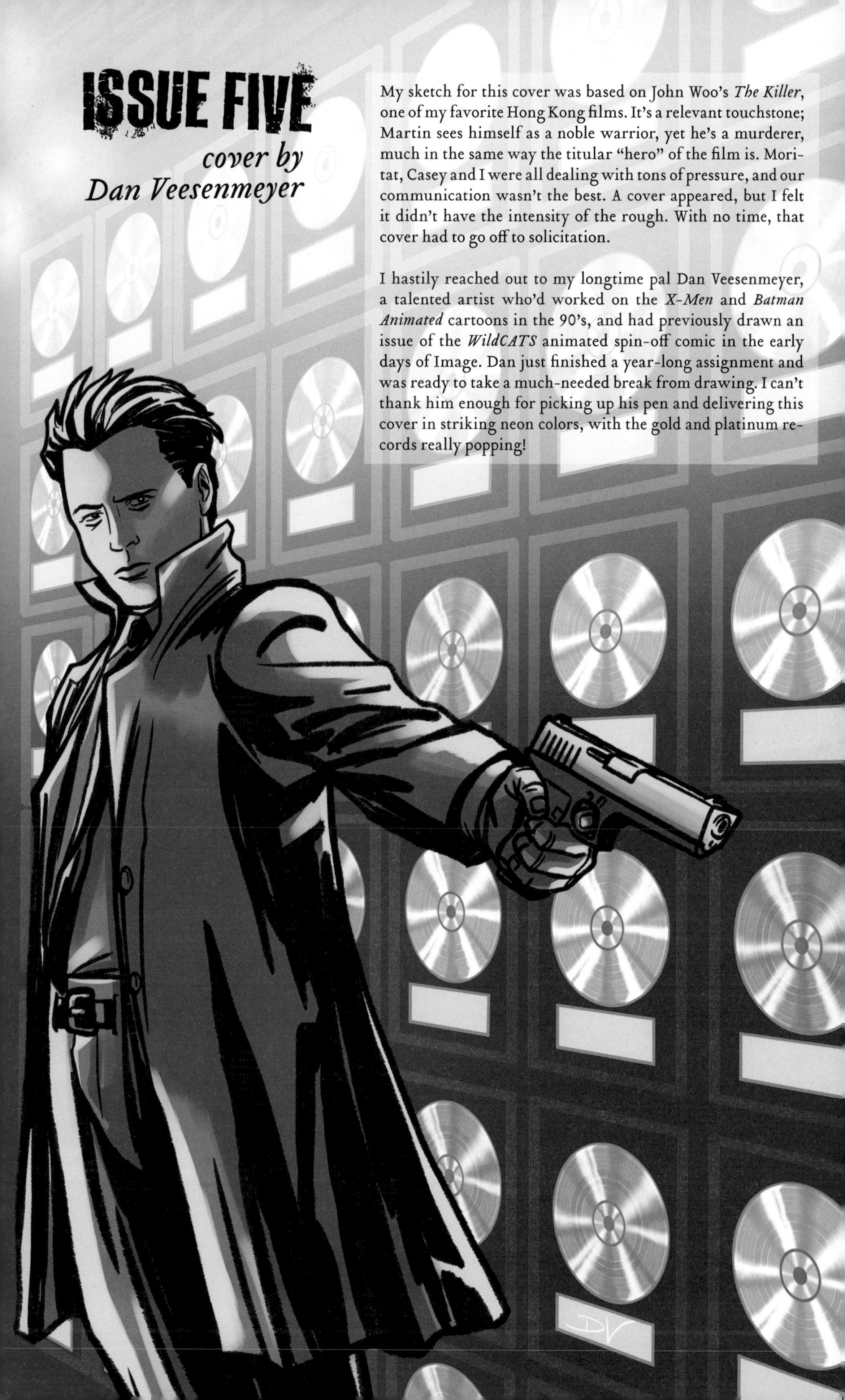

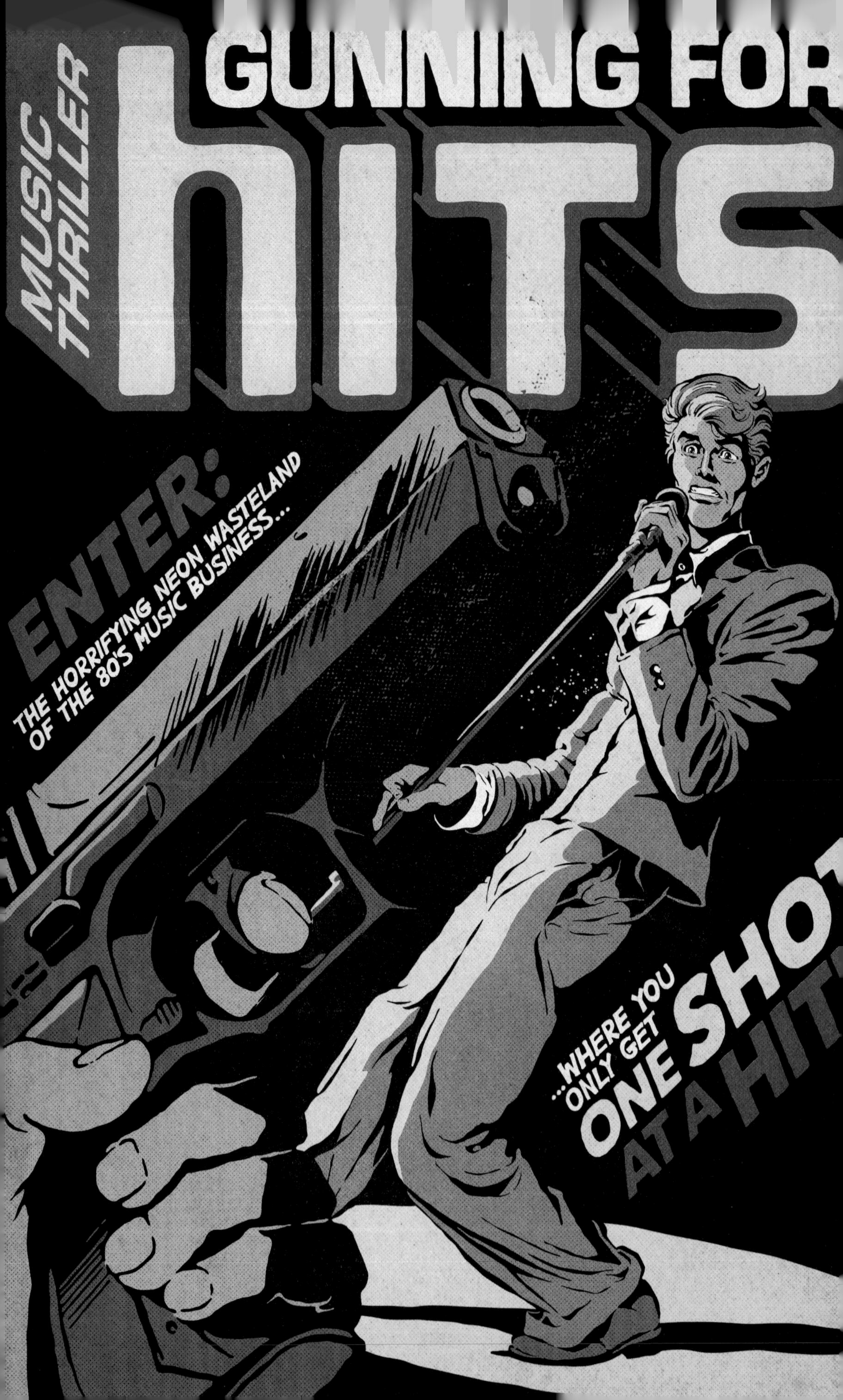

MUSIC THRILLER
GUNNING FOR
HITS
ENTER:
THE HORRIFYING NEON WASTELAND OF THE 80'S MUSIC BUSINESS...
...WHERE YOU ONLY GET
ONE SHOT
AT A HIT

ISSUE SIX

cover by
Butcher Billy

I'd done a half-assed sketch / paste-up based on the cover of *Low*, featuring Slade's head on a target. This was intended as a single element of a larger image, which would've shown multiple Brian Slades on one of those "shoot the ducks" carnival games, in the crosshairs of a gun sight, possibly with Billy & Martin shooting at them. It was an overly complicated idea for a cover. A failure to communicate resulted in a nicely cleaned up version of my drawing, but without the additional context, it didn't work. As much as I'd like to have a cover art credit to my name, this wasn't it. We covered the art up with what looked like crime scene tape emblazoned with a disclaimer saying this wasn't the final cover and off it went to solicitation.

I'd originally intended to have all GFH's covers done by the brilliant Brazilian, Butcher Billy, my favorite contemporary pop artist. Moritat offered to draw them, and it made sense to have the interiors match the covers. By the time we got issue 6, Moritat was too busy to revise an idea I'd soured on anyway.

I dialed the Butcher, who came through with a thoroughly appropriate, brightly colored mash-up of two of his favorite subjects, retro comics and, um, Brian Slade. It's deliberately retro - the series is set in 1987, after all. Most importantly, the flat bold colors really make it stand out from the over-rendered coloring that causes a lot of covers on the new release wall to blur together.

GUNNING FOR
hITS
MUSIC THRILLER
ISSUE ONE
image
ROUGVIE
MORITAT
SILVER

GUNNING FOR
hITS
MUSIC THRILLER

GUNNING FOR
hITS
MUSIC THRILLER
NOT FINAL COVER
SPOILERS!
SPOILERS!

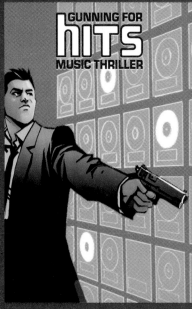

Jeff Rougvie (writer, creator) is an award-winning music industry weasel who has worked with artists like Big Star, David Bowie, Elvis Costello, Devo, Galaxie 500, Bill Hicks, Ministry, Misfits, Mission of Burma, Morphine, Yoko Ono, The Raspberries, The Replacements, Sugar/Bob Mould, They Might Be Giants, The Undertones and more. He's currently writing a history of Rykodisc and setting up the next GUNNING FOR HITS arc.

Moritat (artist) is best known for his work on The Spirit, Elephantmen, Jonah Hex, Harley Quinn and Hellblazer.

Casey Silver (colors and letters) learned to read on black and white TMNT comics and never looked back. He is one half of the Seattle based comic company, 80% Studios.

WITH INVALUABLE ASSISTANCE FROM: Hilary Diloreto (production), Heather Doornink (production), Kelli McCarthy (design), Deanna Phelps (production), Melissa Gifford (proofreading), Noelle Raemer (inks assist), and Kristi Valenti (edits).

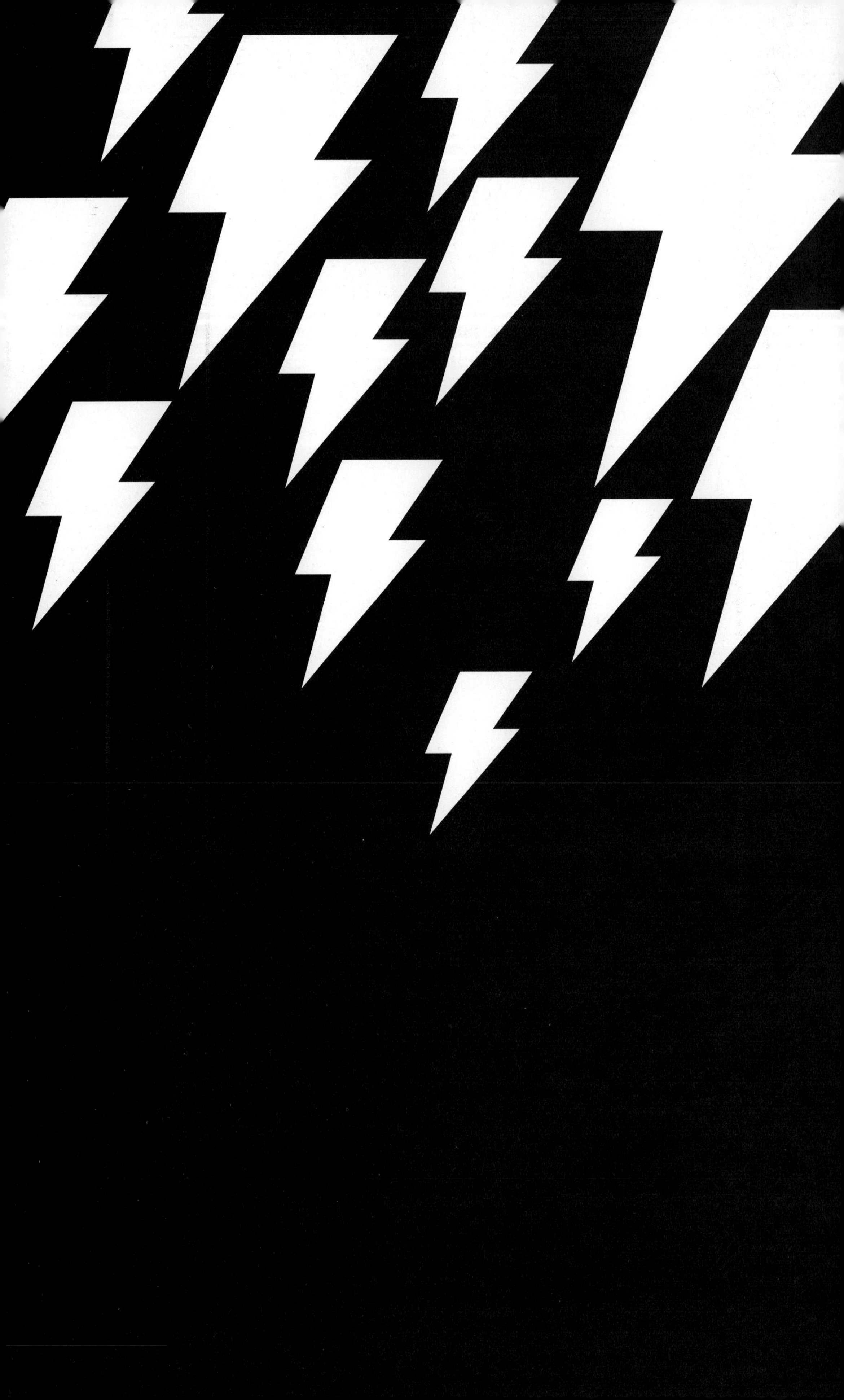